IRON AND MAGIC

ILONA ANDREWS

COPYRIGHT

NYLA Publishing
121 W 27th St., Suite 1201, New York, NY 10001
http://www.nyliterary.com

ACKNOWLEDGMENTS

This was such a fun book to write. As usual, we had a lot of help bringing it to you. We'd like to thank Nancy Yost, our agent, who worked tirelessly on our behalf, for her guidance, help, and friendship. We're grateful to Sandra Harding, our fantastic editor for her insights and suggestions as she helped us shape a manuscript into a book. We'd like to thank Natanya Wheeler for cover design and keeping us on track; Sarah Younger for arranging the print edition and moral support, lots and lots of moral support; and Amy Rosenbaum for tackling the gargantuan task of the audio edition.

Big thanks to Joanne Suh for coming up with a series name, Iron Covenant, for Hugh's and Elara's books.

We are further grateful to Stephanie Mowery for the copyedit and our beta readers, including Hasna Saadani, Mi Young Jin, Robin Snyder, Jessica Haluska, Julia Wheatley, Kristen Carter, the Carwrights, and M. C. Dy. Special thanks to Brandi Boldden.

All errors of fact are ours alone.

Finally, we would like to thank you, our reader, for taking a chance on us again. We hope the book will be fun.

QUESTIONS ABOUT IRON AND MAGIC

Technically this book is a spin-off from our Kate Daniels series; however, it can be read as a standalone work.

For Kate Daniels fans: although this story is the first in the Iron Covenant trilogy, and the entire trilogy takes place before the events of Magic Triumphs, it is actually written to be read in the following order:

- Iron Covenant 1: Iron and Magic
- Magic Triumphs
- Iron Covenant 2
- Iron Covenant 3

You don't need to wait for Hugh's entire story to be out. If you do, it won't be as fun, because there are some revelations in Iron Covenant 2 that are best discovered after Magic Triumphs.

INTRODUCTION TO THE SERIES

The world has suffered a magic apocalypse. We pushed techno-logical progress too far, and now magic has returned with a vengeance. It comes in waves, without warning, and vanishes as suddenly as it appears. When magic is up, planes drop out of the sky, cars stall, and electricity dies. When magic is down, guns work and spells fail.

It's a volatile, screwed-up world. Magic feeds on technology, gnawing on skyscrapers until most of them topple and fall, leaving only skeletal husks behind. Monsters prowl the ruined streets, werebears and werehyenas stalk their prey; and the Masters of the Dead, necromancers driven by their thirst for knowledge and wealth, pilot blood-crazed vampires with their minds.

In this new age, ancient beings awaken, brought out of their slumber by magic. One of them is Nimrod, the Builder of Towers, the man whose name terrified the ancient kingdoms of the Persian Gulf thousands of years ago. Possessing unimaginable power, Nimrod takes a new name, Roland, and sets about bringing his vision of the future to life. To build a new kingdom, one must first destroy the old. Roland requires a Warlord, a leader who will forge and lead his army, someone of great power and even greater cruelty, someone whose loyalty Roland will ensure by searing every shred of doubt with his own blood and ancient magic.

When shaping a human into a weapon, it's best to start young...

PROLOGUE

"**W**ake up!"

He sensed the kick coming through his sleep and curled into a ball. It didn't hurt as much this time. Émile wasn't really trying.

"You have a client."

He rolled up, blinking. He should've hidden deeper in the drum that was his nest. The drum lay on its side and was long enough that Émile couldn't land a good kick. But it was so nice and sunny, and he'd fallen asleep on the rags in front of it.

He looked at Émile and the man next to him. The man had dark eyes. He'd learned to watch the eyes. Faces lied, mouths lied, but the eyes always told you if the man would hit and how hard. This man was large. Big hands. Powerful shoulders. Next to him Émile looked skinny and weak, and he knew it too, because he forgot to sneer. All the street people called Émile Weasel, because of the sneer, but only when he couldn't hear. Émile was mean. He ran the street and when someone tried to stand up to him, he'd fly into a rage and beat them with a rock or a metal stick until they stopped moving.

Émile jabbed his finger in the direction of the man. "Fix him."

The man held out his left arm and pulled back the sleeve of his leather jacket. A cut snaked from his wrist all the way to the elbow. Shallow, only through the top layer of the skin. Easy to fix. He eyed Émile. Usually Émile made him say nonsense words and drag it out, so it would look mysterious, but the man was watching him, and it was making him uneasy.

He reached out and touched the man's arm, letting the magic flow. The cut sealed itself.

The man squeezed his forearm, checking the spot where the wound used to be.

"See? I told you." Émile bared his teeth.

"How much?" the man asked. His voice had an accent.

"How much what?"

"How much for the boy?"

His heart sank. He scooted deep into the drum, where he'd kept a knife hidden under his rags. He knew what happened to boys who were sold. He knew what men did to them. Rene was sold. Rene had been his only friend. Rene was fast and when he stole from the market stalls, nobody could catch him. He'd healed a boil on Rene's back, and since then Rene shared. They'd hide in his drum and eat the bread or pirogi Rene had nicked and pretend they were somewhere else.

Two weeks ago, a man took Rene away. Émile had sold him. Three days later, after dark, he saw the same man leading Rene on a chain like a dog as they walked into a house. Rene was wearing a pink dress and he had a black eye.

Émile had promised not to sell him. That was the deal. He healed clients and Émile gave him food and protected him.

"Not for sale," Émile said.

The man reached into his leather jacket. An envelope came out. A stack of money hit the dirt in front of Émile. A thick stack. More money than he had ever seen. Émile's eyes got big.

Another stack.

He was trapped in the drum. There was nowhere to run.

Another.

Émile licked his lips.

"You promised!" he yelled.

"Shut up." Émile squinted at the man. "He's a magic boy."

Another stack.

"Take him," Émile said.

The man reached for him. He shrank back, his hand clutching the knife hidden under his filthy blanket. He wouldn't be walking on a chain.

The man stepped toward him, his back to Émile.

"Drop the knife," the man said.

Behind him Émile's face turned ugly. He lunged, a dagger pointed at the man's back. The man turned fast. His hand fastened on Émile's wrist. Émile screamed and dropped the dagger. The man pulled him over.

"Take him!" Émile squealed. "Take him!"

"Too late."

The man locked his left hand on Émile's throat and squeezed. Émile clawed at the man's arm with his free hand, flailing, trying to get away. The man continued squeezing.

Magic told him the little bone in Émile's throat broke. It nagged at him, like an annoying itch. He would have to mend the bone to make it go away, but the man kept squeezing, harder and harder.

Émile's eyes rolled back in his skull. The annoying buzz of magic disappeared. You can't fix the dead.

The man let go and Émile fell, limp.

He gathered himself into a ball, trying to make himself smaller. The man crouched by the drum. "I won't hurt you."

He slashed with his knife. The man caught his hand, and then he was yanked out into the sunlight and set on his feet.

The man looked at his knife. "A sharp blade." He held it out to him. "Here. Hold the knife. It will make you feel better."

He snatched the knife from the man's hand, but he already

3

knew the truth. The knife wouldn't help. The man could kill him any time. He would have to bide his time and run.

The man picked up the stacks of money, took his hand, and together they walked out of the alley into the market. The man stopped at a stall, bought a hot pirogi, and handed it to him. "Eat."

Free food. He grabbed it and bit into it, the sweet apple filling hot enough to burn his mouth. He swallowed his half-chewed bite and took another. He could always try to get away later. Eventually the man would look away and then he would run. Until then, if the man bought him food, he would take it. Only an idiot gave up free food. You ate it, and you ate it quick before someone punched you and took it out of your hands.

They walked through the marketplace past the ruins of tall buildings killed by magic. Magic came in waves. One moment it was here, and then it wasn't. Sometimes he would go to Sainte-Chapelle on the day of the service to beg by the doorway. Everyone coming out of the church said the world was ending and that only God would save them. He always thought that if God came, he would come during magic.

They kept walking, all the way to the park, to a man sitting on a bench reading a book.

"I found him," the man with dark eyes said.

The man on the bench raised his head and looked at him.

He forgot about the food. The half-eaten pirogi fell from his fingers.

The man was golden and burning with magic, so much magic, he almost glowed. This magic, it reached out and touched him, so warm and welcoming, so kind. It wrapped around him, and he froze, afraid to move because it might disappear.

"Where are your parents?" the man asked.

Somehow he answered. "Dead."

The man leaned toward him. "You don't have any family?"

He shook his head.

"How old are you?"

4

"I don't know."

"Hard to tell because of starvation," the man with dark eyes said. "Maybe six or seven."

"You're very special," the man said. "Look at all those people out there."

He didn't want to look away from the man, but he didn't want to disappoint him even more, so he turned his head and looked at the people in the market.

"Of all the people out there, you shine the brightest. They are firebugs, but you are a star. You have a gift."

He raised his hand and studied his fingers, trying to see the light the man was talking about, but he saw nothing.

"If you come with me, I promise you that I will help your light grow. You will live in a nice house. You will eat plenty of good food. You will train hard and you will grow up to be strong and powerful. Nobody will be able to stand in your way. Would you like that?"

He didn't even have to think. "Yes."

"What's your name?" the man asked.

"I don't have one."

"Well, that's not good," the man said. "You need a name. A strong name, the kind that people will know and respect. Do you know where we are?"

He shook his head again.

"We're in France. Do you know who that man is?" He pointed to a statue of a man on a horse. The man had a sword and wore a crown.

"No."

"That's Hugh Capet. He was the founder of the Capet dynasty. The kingdom of France began with his reign. The descendants of his bloodline sat on the throne of France for almost nine hundred years. He was a great man and you too will be a great man, Hugh. Would you like to be a great man?"

"Yes."

The man smiled. "Good. All things exist in balance, Hugh. Technology and Magic. This world was born to have both. The civilization your parents built strengthened and fed Technology until the imbalance became too great, and now Magic has returned to even the scales. It floods the world in great waves, crushing the technological marvels and spawning wondrous creatures. It ushers in a new age from the birth pangs of the apocalypse. Our age, Hugh, mine and yours. In this age, you will call me Roland."

"Yes," Hugh agreed. He knew the truth now. God had found him. God had saved him.

"The world is in chaos now," Roland said. "But I will bring order to it. One day I will rule this world, and you will be my Warlord, leading armies in my name to restore peace and prosperity. Today is a special day because we met. Is there anything I can do for you on this special day? Anything at all? Ask me any favor."

Hugh swallowed. "My friend. His name is Rene. He has dark hair and brown eyes. He was sold to a man."

"Would you like him found?"

Hugh nodded.

Roland glanced over his head at the man with the dark eyes. "Find this Rene and bring him to me."

The man with dark eyes bowed his head. "Yes, Sharrum."

He walked away.

Roland smiled at Hugh. "Come, sit by me."

Hugh sat by the man's feet. The magic wrapped around him and he knew that from this moment on, everything would go right. Nothing would ever hurt him again.

1

God was dead.

No, that wasn't quite it. Hugh was dead.

No, that wasn't it either.

Voices tugged on him, refusing to let him sink back into the numbing darkness.

"Hugh?"

He was laying on something hard and wet. The stench of sour, alcohol-saturated vomit hit his nose.

He was drunk. Yes, that was it. He was drunk and getting more sober by the moment, which meant he had to find something to drink or pass out again before the void where God used to be swallowed him whole.

Cold liquid drenched him.

"Get up." The male voice was familiar, but to identify the speaker, he would have to reach deep into his memory. Thinking brought the void closer.

"This is pointless." Another voice he knew and decided to not remember. "Look at him."

"Get up," the first voice insisted, calm, deliberate. "Nez is winning. He's killing us one by one."

Something stirred in him. Something resembling loyalty and obligation and hate. He tried to sink deeper into the stupor. God didn't want him anymore, but the darkness was happy to take him in.

"He doesn't care," the second voice said. "Don't you get it? He's lost. He might as well be dead and rotting for all the good he would do us."

"O ye of little faith," a third, deeper voice said.

"Get the fuck off this floor!"

Sharp pain punched his skull. Someone had kicked him. He briefly considered doing something about it, but staying on the floor seemed the better option.

"Hit him again, and I'll split you sideways." Fourth voice. Cold. He knew this one too. That one rarely spoke.

"Think." The third voice. Collected, reasonable, dripping with contempt. "Right now, he's drunk. Eventually he'll be sober. Drunk we can fix. But if you kick him in the head, you'll injure his brain. What good is he then? We already have one brain-damaged imbecile. We don't need another."

One... two... three... The count surfaced from the muddled depths of his mind. He used to count just like this to see how long the insult would take to burrow through the hard shell that was Bale's brain.

Four...

"I'll fucking kill you, Lamar!" Bale snarled.

"Shut up," the first voice said.

Yes. All of them needed to shut up and leave him the hell alone. He was reasonably sure he hadn't finished the jug of moonshine. It had to be somewhere within his reach.

"Get up, Preceptor," the first voice insisted.

Stoyan, his memory supplied. Figured. Stoyan was always a persistent sonovabitch.

"We need you," Stoyan said, his voice quiet and close. "The Dogs need you. Landon Nez is killing us. We're being purged."

8

Eventually they would go away.

"He doesn't give a fuck," Bale said.

"Pass me the bag," Stoyan said.

Someone knelt next to him.

"It's not gonna matter," Bale growled. "He's all fucked up. He's laying here in his own piss and vomit. You heard that dickhead at the door. He's been in this shithole for weeks."

Hugh heard a zipper being pulled open. Something was put in front of him. He smelled the stench of rotting blood and decomposition.

Bale kept going. "Even if he sobers up, he'll crawl right back into the bottle and get shit-faced."

Hugh opened his eyes. A severed head stared back at him, the brown irises dulled by a milky patina.

Rene.

"He can't even stand anymore. What are we going to do, tie him to a stick and prop him up?"

The world turned red.

"To hell with this." Bale leaned back, readying for a kick.

Rage drove him up before Bale's foot connected with the severed head. He locked his hand around Bale's throat, jerked him off his feet, and slammed him down onto the nearest table. Bale's back hit the wood with a loud thud.

"Hallelujah," Lamar said.

Bale clawed at his arm, the muscles on his thick biceps bulging. Hugh squeezed.

Felix loomed on his right, reaching for him. Hugh hammered a cross punch into the big man's nose with his left hand. Cartilage crunched. Felix stumbled back.

Bale's face turned purple, his eyes glistening. His feet drummed the air.

Stoyan locked his arms on Hugh's right bicep and went limp, adding his deadweight to the arm. Felix lunged from the left and locked himself onto Hugh's left arm, trying to force an armbar.

The world was still red, and he kept squeezing.

Water drenched him in a cold cascade, washing away the red haze. He shook himself, growling, and saw Lamar holding a bucket.

"Welcome back," Lamar said. "Let go of the man, Preceptor. If you kill him, there will be nobody to lead your vanguard."

———+..

THE VOID GNAWED AT HIM, the big raw hole where Roland's presence used to be. Hugh gritted his teeth and forced himself to concentrate on the head on the table in front of him.

"When?" he asked.

"Six days ago," Stoyan said.

"What did he do?"

"Nothing," Stoyan said. "He did nothing."

"Rene was out," Lamar said. "He and Camilla walked off after you were forced out. Went civilian. Rene took a teaching job in Chattanooga, high school French."

"He wasn't a threat to anyone," Stoyan said. "They killed him anyway. I came to convince him to meet with you and found his body. They left him on the floor of his kitchen."

His throbbing head made it hard to think. "Camilla?"

Stoyan shook his head.

Rene's wife didn't make it. Pain stabbed at Hugh, fueling his rage. Rene hadn't been a great soldier. His heart was never in it, but he'd tried. He'd always talked of something better. Of living life after he was done.

"He and Camilla aren't the only ones," Stoyan said.

"Caroline?"

"Dead," Bale said.

"Purdue, Rockfort, Ivanova, all dead," Stoyan added. "We're it."

Hugh surveyed the four men. Stoyan, dark-haired, gray-eyed, in his mid-thirties, looked haggard, like a worn-out sword. Felix, a hulking mountain of a Dominican, leaned back, trying to stop a nosebleed. The bridge of his nose skewed right. Broken. Bale sulked in the corner. About five-eight, five-nine, with dark red hair, Bale was almost as broad as he was tall, all his bulk made up of bone and slabs of thick, heavy muscle. Lamar perched on the edge of the table to the far right. Tall, black, with a body that looked twisted together from steel cables, Lamar was closing on fifty and the age only made him harder to kill. His hair was trimmed short. A neat beard traced his jaw. He'd been an intelligence officer once and never lost the bearing. A pair of thin, wire-rimmed glasses rode his nose.

The second-in-command, the silent killer, the berserker, and the strategist. All that remained of his cohort leadership.

"This is the way things are now," Stoyan said.

"Nez is going down the roster of the Iron Dogs and crossing out the names," Lamar said. "Nobody is safe. We're all tarred with the same brush."

The Iron Dogs. *His* Iron Dogs, the elite private army he'd built for Roland. The name made him wince inside. The void gaped wider, scraping at his bones.

He'd led the Iron Dogs, and Landon Nez led the Golden Legion, the necromancers who possessed mindless vampires, piloting them like remote-controlled cars. The Iron Dogs and the Golden Legion, the right and left hands of Roland. He'd hated Nez, and Nez hated him, and that was the way Roland liked it.

Hugh would've found a way to kill Nez eventually, but he'd run out of time. Roland had purged him.

The memory punched him, hot and furious. Roland standing before him, devoid of all life and warmth. At that moment Hugh would've settled for rage, fury, sadness, anything. But there was nothing. Roland stood before him, cold.

The words scalded him. **"You've failed me, Hugh. I have no further use for you."**

He remembered every sound. He remembered taking a breath

and then the lifeline of magic that anchored him to the man who'd pulled him off the streets vanished. The void had opened, and all became pain. It bit at him now, its fangs shredding his soul.

His purpose, his teacher, his surrogate father, everything that was right and true in this fucked up world was gone. Life had no meaning. And he didn't even fully understand why.

The four men were looking at him.

"How bad is it?" Hugh asked.

"We're down to three hundred men now, with us," Stoyan said.

A few months ago, Hugh had left five cohorts of the Iron Dogs, four hundred and eighty soldiers each. He'd hammered them into an elite, disciplined, trained force, the kind of soldiers any head of state would cut off his arm to have.

"There are more out there," Stoyan said. "Some are in hiding, some are wandering about without any direction. Nez has blood-sucker patrols out. They are hunting us down."

What the hell had happened since he was banished? "Why?"

"Because of you!" Bale snarled from the corner.

Hugh looked at Lamar.

"Roland discovered an unpleasant fact," Lamar said. "We do not follow him. We follow you. You are our Preceptor. We're viewed as untrustworthy."

Idiots. He stared at them. "You swore an oath."

"Oaths go both ways. Show him your arms," Lamar said.

Stoyan yanked his sleeves up. Jagged scars marked his forearms.

"It's the same old story," Lamar said. "Roland wanted some land that was occupied. He offered the town money, but they refused to sell."

"He told me to raze the town," Stoyan said. "And hang the civilians on trees to send a message. I told him I was a soldier, not a butcher. He crucified the lot and hung me on the crosses with them. Thirty-two people. I watched them die for three days. I would've died there."

"What saved you?" Hugh asked.

"Daniels saved me. She pulled me off the cross and let me go."

The name cut like a knife. It must've shown on his face because Stoyan took a step back.

Kate Daniels, Roland's long-lost and newly-found daughter. The reason for his banishment.

Hugh shoved the name out of his mind and concentrated on the problem at hand. Roland would've known Stoyan would refuse the order to butcher civilians. That wasn't what the regular cohorts did. The dark arm of the Iron Dogs, which would've wiped the village off the face of the planet without question, no longer existed. Roland was painfully aware of that. The order had been a test of loyalty, and Stoyan had failed. Roland didn't just require loyalty; he demanded unquestioning devotion. When he failed to receive it, he must've decided to destroy the entire force.

A waste, Hugh realized. Hugh had sunk years into building the Iron Dogs, and Roland tossed them away like garbage.

Much like Roland had thrown him away. No, not thrown away. *I was his right hand. He's cut me off. What kind of man cuts off his own hand before going into a fight?*

This new heretical thought sat in his brain, burning and refusing to fade.

He groped for the tether of magic to banish the uncertainty and found only the void. It sank its fangs into his soul. The invisible tie had connected him and Roland even when the magic waves waned and technology held the upper hand. It was always there. It had linked them since the moment Roland had shared his blood with him. Now it was gone.

The void scraped the inside of his skull, the new sharp thoughts seared Hugh's mind, and he had no way to steady himself. An urge to scream and smash something gripped him. He needed liquor, and a lot of it.

The four men watched him. He'd known each one for years. He'd hand-selected them, trained them, fought with them, and now they wanted something from him. They weren't going to let him alone.

"Unless we do something, none of us will be alive this time next year," Felix said.

"What is it you want to do?" Hugh already knew, but he asked anyway.

"We want you to lead us," Stoyan said. "The Dogs know you. They trust you. If they know you're alive, they will find you. We can pull in the stragglers and hold against Nez."

"You don't know what you're asking." To stay awake and anchored to reality, with the void chewing on him. He would go mad.

"I'm not asking." Stoyan stepped in front of him. "I trusted *you*. I followed *you*. Not Roland. Roland didn't make me promises. You did. You sold me this idea of belonging to something better. The Iron Dogs are more than a job. A brotherhood, you said."

"A family, where each of us stands for something greater," Lamar said.

"If you fall, the rest will shield you," Bale said.

"Well, by God, we're falling," Stoyan said.

Fucking shit.

Rene's head stared at Hugh from the table. He'd saved Rene back then, many years ago, in Paris. He'd saved him again and again, in battle. In the sea of shit and blood that Hugh made, that was the one good thing he had done. Nez had killed Rene for one reason only – to stab at him. No matter what he did from now on, Hugh would always have Rene's death. He would carry it.

He's dead now. Because of me. Because I wasn't there. Because he was here instead, wallowing in self-pity and trying to drown the red-hot vise that clamped his skull.

Hugh studied the head, committing every detail to memory, and hurled the image into the void. The old days were gone. He would fill the bottomless hole with rage or it would drive him insane. Either way it made no difference.

"Do you know why you're still alive?" Lamar asked. "Every day, every week, there are less of us, but you're still breathing. If we found you, Nez can, too. I bet he knows exactly where you are."

"I'm alive because he wants me to be the last," Hugh said. "He wants me to know."

Nez wanted him to watch as his necromancers tore apart everything Hugh had built, and when nothing was left, he would come calling to squeeze the last bit of blood out of the stone. Nez wanted him awake and sober. No fun chasing a dog who didn't run. Fine. He'd be awake.

Lamar smiled.

"What do we have?" Hugh asked.

"Three hundred and two men, including us," Stoyan said.

"Weapons?"

"Whatever each one of us carries," Bale said.

"Supplies?"

"None," Lamar said. "We're close to starving."

"Base?"

Felix shook his head.

Hugh's mind cycled through the possibilities. Rock bottom wasn't the worst place to start from, and the Dogs who'd managed to stay alive were probably the smartest or strongest. He had three hundred trained killers. A man could do worse.

"We have the barrels," Stoyan said.

"How many?"

"All of them."

Life kicked him, then blew him a kiss. "Good."

Hugh strode to the door and flung it open. Fresh air greeted him. A small, ugly town sat in front of him, little more than a street with a few buildings and a rural road, leading into the distance and disappearing between some fields. A sunset splashed over the horizon, dying slowly, and the three street lamps had come on already, spilling watery electric light onto the stretch of road in front of him. He remembered the oppressive heat, but the air was cooler now.

"Fall or spring?" he asked.

"September," Lamar told him.

"What is this town?"

"Connerville, Tennessee," Stoyan said.

The last thing he remembered was Beaufort, South Carolina.

"Where is Nez?"

"In Charlotte," Lamar told him. "He's set up a permanent base there."

Far enough to keep out of Atlanta and the surrounding lands. They belonged to Daniels now. But not so far that Nez couldn't bring the Legion down if Roland became displeased with his precious daughter.

Stabilize three hundred Iron Dogs, arm them, and find a base to keep them alive. Simple to visualize, complicated to execute. Most of all, he had to convince Nez that attacking them now wasn't in his best interests. If he kept the Dogs alive through the winter, by spring he would have enough people trained.

The bottle of moonshine called to him. He didn't have to turn around to know exactly where it was, tempting him to do what severed limbs did - wither and rot. And while he rotted, his people would die one by one.

No. No, he owed Nez a debt. He was Hugh d'Ambray, Preceptor of the Iron Dogs. The Dogs paid their debts.

Magic rolled over the land. Hugh couldn't see it, but he felt an exhilarating rush that tore through him, washing away the headache that pounded at the base of his skull. The electric lamps winked out, and twisted glass tubes of fey lanterns flared into life with an eerie indigo light.

He raised his hand and let his magic flow out. A pale blue glow bathed his fingers. Felix grunted as his nose knitted back together.

Hugh picked up Rene's head. They would bury him tonight.

"Find me some clothes. And call Nez. Tell him I want to talk."

2

Black Fire Stables spread across twenty acres about a two-hour horse ride east of Charlotte. The large, solid house sat in the middle of the lawn, on a rolling hillside, with stables to one side and a covered riding arena to the other. The tech was up, and the inside of the house glowed with warm electric light. Sweet green grass stretched into the distance, to the wall of the forest, shaded here and there by copses of pines, their needles carpeting the soil in a brown blanket. Red and pink roses bloomed at the gate. A rooster perched on the fence. As Hugh rode up, it cocked its head and gave him and the men behind him the evil eye.

He'd brought Stoyan, Lamar, and Bale with him. He needed Lamar's take on Nez's strength, and Bale's axe would help to cut them out if things went sideways. He'd sent Felix to gather what was left of the Iron Dogs, and by all rights, he should've sent Stoyan with him too, but that would've meant listening to Bale and Lamar bickering the entire way with nobody to shut them up except him. There was only so much he could take.

Hugh halted his horse before the gate. The borrowed mare Stoyan had found somewhere wouldn't cut it, especially not with

Nez. They had to appear strong. He needed a horse, a war stallion. Problem was, he had no money.

Until a few months ago, money had been an abstract concept. He understood prices, he haggled on occasion, but he never worried where it came from. It was something he traded for goods and services, and when he needed more, he simply asked for it, and in a few days, it was there, in the appropriate account or in his hand. Now all of his accounts had been cut off. He didn't have a dime to his name. He must've earned money somehow to keep himself drunk, and he vaguely remembered fighting, but most of the months between his banishment and Rene's head had vanished into the darkness of an alcoholic haze.

The door of the farmhouse swung open. Matthew Ryan hurried out, stocky, balding, a big smile on his broad face, as if nothing had changed. The past stabbed at Hugh. *You were something. Now you're nothing.*

"Come in, come in." Ryan pulled the gate open. "Maria just got the table set. Come in!"

They rode up to the house, dismounted, and went inside.

The dinner was a blur, superimposed on the composite of his memories. He'd come to this ranch three times before. Each time he'd been treated to dinner and left with a horse. He sat there, watching his people attack mashed potatoes like starving wolves and tried to get a grip on reality. It kept slipping through his fingers.

After dinner, he and Ryan sat on the back porch of the house, beers in hand, watching the Friesians run through the pasture. The Friesians were his breed: jet black, built like light draft horses, but fast, nimble, and lively. He'd gotten his last three stallions from these stables. He'd paid at a premium for them, too. They were his mark - vicious black horses with flowing manes.

On the far right a stallion ran a lazy circle around his pasture, black mane flowing, his coat shiny like polished silk, high-stepping gait... Black fire in motion. Yeah, that one would do.

"I need a horse," Hugh said.

Ryan nodded.

Here came the part he detested. "I can't pay you now." The words tasted foul in his mouth. "But you know I'm good for it."

"We heard. Terrible business, that," Ryan said. "Work for the man for years and have nothing to show for it. Shame, that's what that is. A damn shame." He let it hang.

Hugh drank his beer. He wouldn't beg, and Ryan knew better than to push him.

Silence stretched.

"I've got no stallions right now. Nothing but the breeding stock. The market's been slow."

Bullshit. Ryan bred war horses, big and mean. In the post-Shift world, where tech and magic switched, a good horse was worth more than a car. It always worked. People who came to Ryan for a horse didn't want a gelding and demand was always good.

Ryan glanced at him and shrank away before he caught himself. A small drop of sweat formed on his temple.

That's right. Remember who you're talking to.

"I want to show you something." Ryan turned and yelled into the house. "Charlie, bring Bucky out. And tell Sam to come here."

Hugh took another sip of his beer.

Ryan's oldest son, stocky, with the same blunt features carved out of wet mud with a shovel, trotted over to the barn to the left.

A kid walked out onto the porch. Lean, blond. Young, eighteen or so. There was some of Ryan there, in the broad cast of his shoulders, but not much. Must've gone into the mother's side of the family.

The doors of the barn swung open, and a stallion strolled out into the small pasture.

"What the hell is this?" Hugh set his beer down.

"That's Bucky. Bucephalus."

Bucky turned, the afternoon sun catching his coat. He was

gray gone to pure white. He practically glowed. Like a damn unicorn.

"He isn't a Friesian," Hugh ground out.

"Spanish Norman horse," Ryan said. "A Percheron and Andalusian cross. Picked him up at auction. He's big the way you like them. Seventeen hands."

Hugh turned and looked at him.

Ryan squirmed in his seat.

"You're trying to give me a cold-blooded horse?" Hugh asked, his voice quiet and casual.

"He's warm-blooded." Ryan raised his hands. "Look at the gait. Look at the lines. That's Andalusian lines right there. The neck is long and the legs..."

Oh, he saw the Andalusian, all right, but he saw the Percheron, too, in the size and the big chest. Percherons ran too cold blooded for fighting under the saddle; all that bulky slow-twitch muscle dragged down their reaction time. They were difficult to anger, slow to charge, and heavy on their feet. Everything he didn't want.

Hugh looked at Ryan.

Ryan swallowed. "He's comfortable under the saddle. Trust me on this. After a Friesian, your backside will thank you. No feathers, so less grooming. He jumps like a Thoroughbred. Look at the lines of the head. That's a beautiful head."

"He is *white*."

"Nobody is perfect," Ryan said.

In his mind, Hugh reached out and squeezed Ryan's neck until the rancher's face turned red and his head popped.

Maria, Ryan's wife, came up to the doorway and froze. The young kid held completely still, waiting and watching Hugh's face.

"I bought him to breed. I thought I would diversify, you know?" Ryan was babbling now. "Had a particular mare in mind, but that deal fell through. He's a good stallion. Powerful and fast. Bad-tempered. Bit the shit out of me and the stable hands."

Hugh stared at him.

Sweat broke out on Ryan's forehead. His hands shook, his words tumbling out too fast.

"You two will get along. He's like you."

"How's that?"

"A big, mean sonovabitch that nobody wants." Ryan realized what he'd blurted out. His face went white.

A stunned silence claimed the porch.

"I didn't mean it…" Ryan said.

A cold realization rolled over Hugh, smothering all anger. He would take this horse. He had no choice.

He had no choice.

It felt like he'd fallen off of somewhere high and smashed face-first into the stone ground. A year ago, Ryan would've paraded every one of his stallions in front of him and he'd have had his pick.

Hugh rose slowly, walked down the steps into the grass, approached the pasture, and vaulted over the fence. Bucky spun in place and stared at Hugh. A scar crossed the horse's white head. Someone had taken a blade of some sort to him.

Bucky blew the air out of his nostrils, his amber eyes fixed on Hugh. A dominant stance. Fine.

Hugh stared back.

The stallion bared his teeth.

Hugh showed his own teeth and bit the air.

Bucky hesitated, unsure.

Once a horse decided to bite, there was no stopping it. Sooner or later you would get bitten, especially if the horse was a habitual biter. Some bit because they were jealous; others to show displeasure or get attention. Horses, like dogs and children, followed the principle that any attention, even negative, was still attention and therefore worth the effort.

A war stallion would bite to dominate.

He had to demonstrate that he wouldn't be dominated. Once the biting started, it was difficult to stop. Yelling, hitting the horse, or biting it back, as one guy he remembered used to do, had no effect. The point was to not get bitten in the first place. You treated a war stallion with respect, and you approached it like you were first among equals.

Bucky stared at him.

"Come on," Hugh said, his voice calm, reassuring. Words didn't matter, but the sound of his voice did. When it came to humans, horses relied on their hearing more than their vision.

Bucky pawed the ground.

"You're just wasting time now. Come on."

The stallion eyed him again. In his years Hugh had seen all sorts of horses. The Arabians who would rather die than step on a human foot; the strict, mean horses from the Russian steppes that gave all of themselves, but forgave nothing; the German Hanoverians that would just as soon walk through a man as around... With a cross like this he couldn't tell what the hell he was going to get, but he'd ridden horses since he was ten years old, all those long decades ago.

Their gazes locked. There was a fire inside that horse, and it shone through his eyes. A mean sonovabitch nobody wanted. *You will do. You belong with me.*

"Come here. I don't have all day."

Bucky sighed, raised his ears, and walked over. Hugh patted the warm neck, feeling the tight cords of muscle underneath, dug the sugar cube he'd stolen from Ryan's kitchen out of his pocket, and let warm lips swipe it off his palm. Bucky crunched the sugar.

"I knew it," Ryan said from behind the fence. The kid behind him rolled his eyes.

Bucky turned his head and showed Ryan his teeth.

Hugh stroked the stallion's neck. "How much do you want for him?"

"A favor," Ryan said.

The man really didn't know when to stop pushing. "What do you want?"

Ryan nodded at his youngest son. "Take Sam with you."

What the bloody hell? "I just told you I couldn't pay you for the horse, and you want me to take your son with me. You know who I am. You know what I do. He'll be dead in a month."

"I can't keep him." Pain twisted Ryan's face. "He isn't right in the head."

Hugh squeezed his eyes shut for a moment. It was that or he really would strangle the man. He opened his eyes and looked at the kid.

"How old are you?"

"Seventeen," the kid said, his face flat. His eyes were dull. A liability at best, a pain in the ass at worst.

"What's your name?"

"Sam."

"Are you slow?"

"No."

"I didn't mean like that." Ryan grimaced. "He can't act like normal people. He doesn't know when to stop. He caught a horse thief last month. Now, you catch a horse thief, you beat the shit out of him. Everyone understands that. That's how things are done. You don't get a rope and try to hang the man. If I had found him, that would be one thing. The sheriff saw him getting ready to string the thief up."

Hugh raised his eyebrows at the boy.

"He stole from us," Sam said, his voice flat.

"He had the rope over the tree ready to go right there by the damn road. Why hang him by the road, I ask you?"

"A warning is only good if people see it," Hugh said.

Sam looked up, surprise flashing in his eyes, and looked back down. The kid wasn't as dim as he pretended.

"He was always like this. He fights and don't know when to stop. The sheriff told me he would let that one go, but this idiot doesn't think he did anything wrong."

"He stole from us." A harsh note crept into Sam's voice. "If one person steals and we don't do anything, they will keep stealing."

"See?" Ryan reached over and smacked the kid upside the head. Sam's head jerked from the blow. He righted himself.

"Sheriff says he tries it again, he'll end up in a cage for the rest of his life, or they'll string him up instead and save everyone the trouble. He just isn't made for ranch life. It's not in him. At least this way he's got a chance. You take him and Bucky, we're even."

Hugh looked at the kid. "You want to die fast?"

Sam shrugged. "Everyone dies."

The void scoured Hugh's soul with sharp teeth.

"Get your shit," Hugh said. "We're leaving."

———◆———

THE MAGIC WAS STILL DOWN.

The tall, gleaming office towers that once proudly marked Charlotte's downtown had fallen long ago, reduced to heaps of rubble by magic. The waves would keep worrying at the refuse, grinding it to dust until nothing was left. Magic fought all technology, but it hated large structures the most, bringing them down one by one, as if trying to erase the footprint of the technological civilization off the face of the planet.

With construction equipment functioning barely half of the time and gasoline supplies limited and pricey, clearing thousands of tons of rubble proved an impossible task, and Charlotte did what most cities decided to do in the same situation: it settled. It carved a road roughly following the old Tryon street, with hills of concrete and twisted steel beams bordering it like the walls of a canyon, and called it a day. Stalls had sprung up here and there, clustered where the road widened, selling all the fine luxuries the post-Shift world had to offer: "beef" that smelled like rat meat, old guns that jammed on the first shot, and magical potions, which followed the tried-and-true ancient recipe of ninety-nine parts

24

tap water to one part food coloring. This early in the morning, only half an hour past sunrise, most of the vendors were still setting up. In another half hour, they would start squawking and lunging at the travelers, trying to hawk their wares, but for now, the road was blissfully quiet.

It didn't matter, because for once Hugh didn't have a hangover. Yesterday, after they'd left Black Fire behind, they'd spent the night in the open, at an old campground. He'd wanted to drink himself into a stupor, but then he would be no good the next day, so he stayed sober. His mood had soured overnight, and in the morning, when he found Sam waiting with the rest, the irritation heated up to a simmering hate.

He hated Charlotte. He hated the way it looked, the way it smelled, the rubble, the tortured skyline of the city, the white stallion under him, and the void waiting just beyond the border of awareness, ready to swallow him. He thought of getting off this damned horse, finding a hole within the rubble, laying down, and just letting it eat at his soul until there was nothing left. But he had a feeling the four men riding behind him would pull him out, set him back on the horse, and force him to keep going. There was nothing left but to stew in his own hate.

"Friends." Bale grinned and patted his axe.

Hugh glanced up. An emaciated figure crouched on top of the wall of the rubble canyon on the far left. Thin, a skeleton corded with muscle, the creature hunkered down on all fours as if it had never walked upright, its hairless hide turned to a sickly bluish gray by undeath. It was too far to see much of its face, but Hugh saw the eyes, red and glowing with all-consuming hunger. No thoughts, no awareness, nothing except bloodlust, wrapped in magic that turned his stomach. A vampire.

Not a loose one. Loose bloodsuckers slaughtered everything with a pulse, feeding until nothing alive remained. No, this one was piloted by a navigator. Somewhere, within the secure rooms of Landon Nez's base, a necromancer sat, probably sipping his morning coffee, telepathically gripping the blank slate that was the undead's mind. When the vampire moved, it was because the navigator willed it. When it spoke, the navigator's voice would come out of its mouth. He never liked the breed, the undead and the navigators both.

"A welcoming committee," Stoyan said.

"Nice to be recognized," Lamar quipped.

"Have you found a base?" Hugh asked.

"I found several," Lamar said. "None that would have us."

"What's the problem?" Bale demanded.

"We are the problem," Lamar said. "We have baggage in addition to a rich and varied history."

"What are you on about?" Bale asked.

"He means we've double-crossed people before," Stoyan told him. "Nobody wants Nez as an enemy, and nobody wants to take a chance on us stabbing them in the back."

"We need to find someone desperate and willing to overlook our past sins," Lamar said. "That takes time."

Hugh wished for something to happen. Some release. Someone to kill.

Bucky raised his tail and shit on the road.

"You gonna clean that up?" a male voice challenged.

Thank you. Thank you so much for volunteering.

Hugh touched the reins. Bucky turned.

A tall, dark-haired man stood on the side of the road. In shape. Clothes loose enough to move, but not to grab, light stance, plain sword, no frills. Flat eyes. There was emotion in the voice, but none in the eyes. He wasn't angry or riled up.

Behind him another man and a woman waited, the man shorter and stockier, holding a light mace, the woman armed with another plain sword. Long blond hair.

Professionals.

This was a test. Nez wanted to see if the months of drinking had taken their toll. Disappointment slashed through Hugh. He couldn't take his time. He would have to do this fast.

Hugh dismounted and held out his hand. Stoyan pulled his sword out and put it in Hugh's palm. Hugh started toward the three fighters.

"Should we--" Sam started.

"Shut it," Bale told him.

The leading fighter stepped forward. The man moved well, light on his feet despite his size. Hugh swung the sword in a lazy circle, warming up his wrist.

The shorter man stalked to his right; the woman moved to his left with catlike grace.

He waited until they positioned themselves. "All set?"

The leader attacked, his sword striking so fast, it was a blur. Hugh moved, letting the blade slice through the air half an inch from his cheek, and slashed, turning into the blow. The blade of Stoyan's sword met the mercenary's neck and sliced clean through in a diagonal cut. The man's head rolled off his shoulders, but Hugh was already turning. He batted the woman's sword aside, dodged the mace, and brought the sword down in a devastating cut. The blade caught her shoulder and carved through one breast. She stumbled back, her arms hanging by her side. Hugh stabbed, sliding the sword between her 5th and 6th ribs on the left side, withdrew, and spun. The mace wielder had already started his swing. Hugh leaned out of the way, caught the mace's handle on the upswing, throwing his strength and weight against the man and driving his blade up through the attacker's liver into his heart. The mace wielder was the only one to realize what was coming. His eyes widened as the sword pierced his gut. The lights went out. Hugh shoved him back, freeing the blade with a sharp tug, and turned.

The woman was still alive, but barely. She would bleed out in another thirty seconds or so. Death from blood loss was relatively painless. She'd close her eyes and go to sleep.

Hugh crouched by her. Her breath was coming in shallow rapid gulps. He wiped the sword with her pretty blond hair, got up, and handed the blade back to Stoyan. Sam stared at him, his face slack.

Hugh mounted.

"I think you didn't look hard enough for a base," Bale said.

"I wouldn't do so much of that if I were you," Lamar said.

Hugh nudged Bucky, and the white stallion started down the road.

"Do what?"

"Thinking. It's not your strong suit."

"One day, Lamar," Bale growled.

The void ate at Hugh. He closed his eyes for a long moment, trying to shut it out. When he opened them, he was still in Charlotte, still riding, and the air around him smelled like blood.

———

THE CANYON OF DEBRIS WIDENED. Shops and eateries popped up here and there, evidence of the city fighting back against the rubble. All were post-Shift, new construction: thick walls, simple shapes, and bars on the windows.

"Was that vampire from the People?" Sam asked.

"The Golden Legion," Stoyan said.

"Is that like the People?"

"The necromancers who work for Roland call themselves the People," Stoyan explained.

"They call themselves that because they feel they are the only people. The rest of us are lesser mortals," Lamar said.

"The People have ranks," Stoyan said. "They start as apprentices, then become journeymen, then finally they get to be Masters of the Dead. The best one hundred Masters make up the Golden Legion. The Legion is led by the Legatus, the prick we're riding to meet. Each Master of the Dead in the Legion can pilot more than one vampire. A Master of the Dead can wipe out a US Army platoon with one undead."

"Depending on how big the platoon is," Lamar said. "Regulation size for a platoon is between sixteen and forty soldiers. Forty would be pushing it for one bloodsucker. The Legion would need at least two, maybe three if the platoon is well trained."

"The point is," Bale said, "when we meet the Legatus, you'll be deaf and dumb, Sam, you get me? If I hear one squeak out of you, you'll wish you were back on the ranch getting strung up by that sheriff your daddy is so afraid of."

"How will I know if he's the Legatus?" Sam asked.

Hugh thought about turning around and knocking him off his horse to shut him up, but it would take too much effort.

"Because he'll look like the rest of the People," Stoyan said. "Like a dickhead in an investment banker's suit."

"That's redundant," Lamar pointed out.

"Who's Roland?" Sam asked.

"Someone you need to steer clear of," Stoyan said.

"An immortal wizard with a megalomaniac complex who wants to rule the world," Lamar said.

"Why does he want us dead?" Sam asked.

"All you need to know is that he does," Bale growled. "Now shut the fuck up, or I'll count your teeth with my fist and then you'll be busy picking them up out of the dirt."

The path turned. Ahead, on the left, a Viking mead hall stood on the corner. Built with thick timber, with a roof of wooden shingles, the mead hall resembled an upside-down longboat. A sign on the side proclaimed, "Welcome to Valhalla."

On the side, a low deck offered several wooden tables, flanked by short benches. Landon Nez sat at the corner table, in plain view of the street.

There you are.

Nez hadn't changed in the past few months. Still lean, like he was twisted together from steel wire. Same sharp eyes. His dark hair fell loose around his face. He wore a tailored charcoal suit. Good fabric, no padding on the shoulders, fitted through the waist, the English cut. About three grand, Hugh decided.

The Legatus of the Golden Legion. The most powerful Master of the Dead Roland could find besides himself or his daughter.

Nez nodded to him. Hugh nodded back. They'd been trying to kill each other for most of the last decade. The urge to borrow Stoyan's sword and ride Landon down was almost too much.

"Is he Native?" Sam asked quietly.

"Navajo," Stoyan said under his breath. "They kicked him out for piloting vampires."

Hugh altered course, aiming for Landon. Bucky obliged.

"Join me?" Nez raised a cup of coffee.

"Why not?" Hugh swung from his saddle, tossed the reins on the hook in the rail, walked up the two short steps, and landed on a bench opposite Nez.

Out of the corner of his eye he saw Stoyan and the rest of his people turn and park themselves across the street at a breakfast taco hole-in-the-wall.

"Coffee?" Nez asked.

"Nah. Trying to quit."

"What are you doing in my neck of the woods?"

"Have I told you you're lousy at sounding folksy?"

Folksy didn't come naturally to Nez, and he did it in a trained bear fashion, like a circus animal forced to perform against his will. If you decided to go that route, you had to mean it and sound genuine. Landon Nez had walked out of the Navajo Nation with nothing and climbed his way to a Harvard Ph.D. and the top of the People's food chain. The man would stab himself in the eye rather than be confused with common rabble.

Nez raised his eyebrows.

"It's just us." Hugh hit him with a broad grin. "Just go ahead and be the snobby prick you are."

"Why are you here, d'Ambray?"

"Came to see a man about a horse."

Nez glanced at Bucky. "Your horses do seem to be getting bigger and bigger. But white? Don't you think it's a bit on the nose?"

"Felt like it was time for a change. How's life been treating you?"

Nez gave a one-shouldered shrug. "Same as always. Research. Management. Undeath is a demanding mistress."

It would only take a second. Reach across, snap his neck. End all his earthly burdens.

Hugh wouldn't make it. Nez would never come here unprotected.

"What about you?" Landon asked. "Planning new campaigns?"

Here it was, probing for weaknesses. "Settling down," Hugh said.

"You?"

"There is a time and place for everything." Hugh leaned back. "I've got a nice place picked out. Good supply, good defenses. Trees."

"Trees?" Nez blinked.

HUGH NODDED. "Eventually a man's got to put down roots. Looking forward to sitting on my porch, drinking a cold beer."

Nez stared at him a second too long. *Got you.*

The Legatus drank his coffee. "Have you heard any odd news from the North?"

Odd. "There is always odd news from the North."

A shadow of alarm flickered through Nez's eyes. The Legatus grimaced and nodded. "That's the truth."

They stared at each other in silence.

"Do you miss *him*?" Nez asked quietly.

The void yawned in his face. Missed? The memories alone tore

Hugh apart. The clarity of purpose, the warm glow of approval, the flow of magic between them... The certainty.

"There's more to life than being a dog on a leash." Hugh rose. "Got to leave you now. Places to be, people to kill."

"Always a pleasure, Preceptor."

Hugh grabbed the reins, hopped over the wooden rail, mounted his horse, and started down the street. A few moments later his people caught up with him. They rode in silence for another ten minutes.

"How did it go?" Lamar asked.

"He'll attack us the first chance he gets," Hugh said. "He would've done it already, but something in the North has him worried. He's a careful asshole, who likes to know every card his opponent is holding. I put a doubt in his head. Right now, he isn't sure if we have a permanent position or not, so he figures we can wait. We're easy to find and we're not going anywhere."

He would have to tell Felix to send some scouts north when they got back, to look for anything strange that would give Nez pause.

The headache was returning, threatening to split his skull. A reminder of too many weeks spent drinking. Hugh gritted his teeth. "Find me a base, Lamar. Someone somewhere needs something protected or something killed."

"It all depends on the price we'd be willing to pay," Lamar said.

"I don't care about the price. Do whatever you have to do. We secure a base, or the Legion slaughters us like pigs come winter."

———+·—

THE MUTTER CAME from the center of the column. "I'm fucking done running."

Hugh stopped and turned.

"Century, halt!" Lamar roared.

Beside Hugh the long column of the Iron Dogs came to a stop, huffing and puffing, eighty soldiers arranged in two lines. When he'd arrived to Split Rock, where Felix had pulled together the remaining Iron Dogs, he found three hundred and thirty-three people who used to be soldiers. They were ragged, tired, hungry, and their morale was shit.

All military was tribal, his included. For the individual Iron Dog, the cohort was their tribe, the century within the cohort was their village, and the squad within the century was their family. In a fight, the Iron Dogs stood as one. It went back to the basic primal cornerstone of human nature: he who attacks my family must die.

There used to be good-natured competition between the squads, the centuries, and the cohorts, which Hugh encouraged, because it bound the soldiers closer together. But now, with the fragments of cohorts on his hands, he had to reform them into a new unit. Teach a man to fight and you made him into a warrior. He didn't need warriors. He needed soldiers. To make a soldier, you had to put her with other prospective soldiers and make them go through hell and back together, relying on each other.

They all had memories of walking through blood and fire with their old squad mates. He had to replace those memories with new ones, and so he did the only thing he could do to purge them. He'd sectioned off Felix's scout team and formed the rest of his force, three hundred and nineteen soldiers, into a single cohort, which he split into four centuries, eighty people for the first three and seventy-nine in the last. Stoyan, Lamar, Bale, and Felix each took a century. And then he ran them, tired and starving, into exhaustion. He smoked them until their arms could no longer hold their weight. He kept them from sleeping. He did it all with them, picking a different century every day. Respect had to be earned.

The weather had conspired with him. It was hot as hell again. The tents Felix's people managed to "acquire" – he didn't ask for details – did the bare minimum to keep out the bugs.

They were in their third week of training. Looking at the rage-filled eyes of the second century now, Hugh was reasonably sure that they hated his guts, which meant things were proceeding right on schedule.

"What was that, Barkowsky?" Lamar snapped, closing in on a tall, beefy Dog with a freshly-sheared head.

"I said, I'm fucking done running." Barkowsky had about an inch of height on Lamar and he made the most of it, but Lamar was harder and they both knew it.

"What did you say to me?" Lamar started.

"You're done?" Hugh asked.

"Yeah." Barkowsky jutted his chin in the air. The man had been spoiling for a fight for the last three days.

"Then go." Hugh turned his back.

"What?" Barkowsky asked, his voice faltering.

"Do you see a wall, Dog?" Lamar roared.

The old habit got the best of Barkowsky and he snapped to attention. "No, Centurion!"

"Do you see guards posted?"

"No, Centurion!"

"Any time you decide to leave, you can, isn't that right, Dog?"

"Yes, Centurion!"

"This isn't the SEALs. There is no bell to ring to announce you washing out," Hugh said. "When it gets too hard and you want to give up, just quit. Get your gear and walk away. I need soldiers, not quitters."

"Forwaard," Lamar drawled in the time-proven cadence of drill sergeants everywhere. "Double-time, march!"

Hugh started running again. The two lines of the second century moved with him. At least they were in step, he told himself. Out of the corner of his eye, he saw Barkowsky fall in to his place and keep pace.

In a perfect world, he would do this for another three weeks. He wasn't working with raw recruits, but seasoned soldiers. Six weeks, eight max, and he would have some semblance of a unified fighting force. He didn't have another three weeks. The game Felix's scouts brought and what little they managed to purchase with the remainder of their money were their only sources of food. He couldn't put his people through the crucible without feeding them. The Dogs were burning through the food supply like wildfire through dry brush. Once the grain and potatoes ran out, they would have nothing except venison and rabbit. They needed more than that to keep going.

The woods ended. They ran into the field, heading toward the tall, wooden walls of the palisade in the middle of it. Above the simple fortification, the sunset was beginning, painting the sky with red and yellow.

Three minutes later, they ran through the gates.

"Century, halt," Lamar snapped.

The twin lines of the second century halted.

"About face."

The sweaty, exhausted Dogs turned to face Hugh. Lamar looked no worse for wear.

"Tell your Preceptor 'Thank you' for the lovely stroll through the beautiful countryside."

"Thank you, Preceptor," the second century roared.

A magic wave rolled over them. Hugh reached for the familiar power and concentrated.

"Century, dismissed."

The twin lines broke as the Dogs shuffled their way past him, toward their tents. A faint blue glow emanated from him, clamping each soldier in turn. He healed their blisters, cuts, and bruises in a split second. They moved past him, murmuring their thanks.

"Thank you, Preceptor."

"Thank you, Preceptor."

"Thank you, Preceptor."

The last Dog headed to her tent.

Hugh's stomach wailed. He healed them every day, and the rations he took were barely enough to keep him alive. Soon he would cross the line where his body ran out of reserves to compensate.

Lamar halted before him. His gaze strayed past Hugh.

"What?" Hugh asked.

"He's doing it again."

Hugh turned. In the small corral before his tent, Bucky glowed. A silver light shone from the stallion's flanks, as if each hair in his coat was sheathed in liquid moonlight.

Hugh gritted his teeth. The next time he saw Ryan, he would kill him.

Bucky pranced in the corral.

"Everything but the horn," Lamar said, his voice filled with pretended awe.

"Do you have something to report, or did you come to jerk my chain?"

"Good news or bad news?"

"Bad news," Hugh said.

"We have food for five days."

In five days, they were done. The soldiers would need more than just meat; they burned too much energy for that. They required starches. Corn, grain, rice. There were none to be had. They were out of money, and unless they resorted to robbery, which would bring law enforcement on their heads, they were finished.

Stoyan emerged from the first century's tent and pretended to loiter. Bale joined him. From the other side, Felix came up and decided to be very interested in Bucky, who was still glowing up a storm. They were up to something.

"Good news?" Hugh asked.

"I found a base."

"Where?"

"Berry Hill, Kentucky, in the Knobs, right by Bluegrass."

Berry Hill. Sounded like something out of a child's cartoon. Hugh racked his brain, trying to remember what he knew about Kentucky. The eastern part of the state, the Eastern Coal Fields, was mostly forested hills bisected by narrow valleys. It flowed into the Bluegrass region in the north and central part of the state, where gently rolling hills offered the perfect horse country. South of Bluegrass spread Pennyroyal, a massive limestone plain full of sinkholes and caves. On the edge of Bluegrass, stretched in a rough semicircle from Pennyroyal to the Eastern Coal Fields, lay the Knobs, hundreds of steep isolated hills, like cones set to mark the border. Post-Shift, they were drowning in forests.

"East or West side?"

"West," Lamar said. "Closest city is Sanderville, population about ten thousand, give or take. Berry Hill is a nice settlement, about four thousand people, mostly families with children. Excellent farmland, rich in supplies. The village is built by a lake."

"Mhm." Why did he have a feeling there was a 'but' coming. "Any militia?"

"Not enough to protect them. They are mostly nature magic types. Some witches, a few stray druids."

The feeling grew stronger. "Why do they need protection?"

"Landon Nez is after their land. There is some sort of magically saturated spot on it Roland wants. Landon can't go after them directly, because he's been warned by the Feds that land grabbing won't be tolerated, so he recruited some asshole politician from Sanderville to harass them into selling their land to the town. Sanderville is escalating the pressure, and they don't want an all-out conflict."

Bucky trotted over. Hugh reached out and patted the stallion's cheek.

"Why not?"

"Because their leader does the kind of magic that panics good old regular folk," Lamar said. "They are trying to put down roots.

They don't want people coming for them with pitchforks and torches. They're desperate."

"And they think adding three hundred trained soldiers to their settlement will be enough of a deterrent."

"In a nutshell."

It sounded perfect. The settlement already had an issue with Nez. They had no militia to speak of, which meant there would be very little conflict. They had supplies that would keep his people fed.

Stoyan and Bale had drifted close enough to hear the conversation and were eyeing him.

"What's the catch?" Hugh asked.

"They don't trust us," Lamar said. "We walked away from Patterson. And Willis. Both when they needed us most. They expect us to betray them."

"We followed orders," Hugh said.

"It was still a betrayal."

He puzzled over it. Roland had wanted them out of those conflicts, so he took his people out. He tried to remember if he had argued against it. He wanted to think he did, but his recall was cloudy. The precise memory of the events slipped through his fingers as if he were trying to pick up water in his fist. He pulled his troops out, and their former allies died. An echo of guilt rose from the depths of his memories, and he pushed it away.

Did I even argue against it?

Yes. He did. There was a phone call when Roland told him to abandon Willis. Hugh was sure of it.

Things had been much simpler then. He didn't have to wonder if it was right. Roland wanted it; therefore, it was right. He longed for that simplicity, and at the same time, a hot, angry thought surfaced in his brain. He went back on his word. His word wasn't worth shit. He should've been able to say "I'll do it," and that should've been enough assurance to guarantee an alliance.

"Their track record isn't much better," Lamar said. "They had an agreement with a town in West Virginia and ended up bailing on them three years ago. Before that, they bounced from town to town, either leaving because they didn't like it or getting run off by the locals. The information is conflicting."

"Why do they keep running?"

"There are some nasty rumors about the kind of magic they practice." Lamar hesitated.

"Spit it out."

"The story is, our peaceful nature magic users had some disagreements with a few covens in Louisiana. The covens decided to wipe them out and banded together during the flare. Not the last one or the one before that. Two flares back."

A flare was a magic wave on steroids. It came once every seven years. During a flare, magic reigned for several days. Weird shit crawled out of their hiding places, gods walked the earth, and impossible things became possible.

During that flare, Roland had destroyed Omaha.

"The Louisiana covens called themselves the Arcane Covenant. When the flare came, they summoned something, a horde of dire wolves or demons, nobody quite knows," Lamar continued. "They should've wiped our nature guys off the face of the planet, but here they are alive and thriving, while the Arcane Covenant is dead as a doorknob. Rumor says human sacrifice was involved."

"Terrific." Of all the fucked-up magic, human sacrifice was the one threshold even Roland wouldn't cross. It opened the door to old primal powers nobody wanted to resurrect.

"Nobody has proof that any of it happened," Lamar said. "But it makes any alliance appear shaky. We're both desperate, and Nez will expect us to cut and run the moment things get hairy."

Hugh leaned on the corral's fence. That was a problem. The only way to hold off Nez was to project a show of strength. The alliance had to appear unbreakable, otherwise Nez would expect them to fracture and attack anyway. Lamar was right. They had to overcome that burden. They had to appear completely united.

"There is a tried-and-true method of making an alliance appear secure," Lamar said carefully.

Hugh glanced at him.

"A union," Lamar said, as if worried the word would cut his mouth.

"What union?"

"A civil union, Preceptor."

"What the hell are you on about?"

Lamar took a deep breath.

"Marriage!" Bale yelled out.

Hugh stared at Lamar. "Marriage?"

"Yes."

They had to be out of their minds. "Who would be getting married?"

"You."

The realization hit him like a ton of bricks, and he said the first thing that popped into his head. "Who would marry me?"

"You're handsome, a big, imposing figure of a man, and um..." Lamar scrounged for some words. "And they're desperate."

"What the hell have you been smoking? I'm penniless, I'm exiled, I own nothing..." He left out broken.

"And a recovering alcoholic." Lamar nodded. "Yes, but again, they're desperate. And we're running out of food."

Hugh shut his eyes for a long moment. The world was sliding sideways, and he really needed to get a grip.

"Who would I be marrying?"

"The White Warlock."

Hugh's eyes snapped open. "You want me to marry a man?"

"No!" Lamar shook his head vigorously. "It's a woman. A woman. Not a man."

Thank God for small favors. He couldn't keep the sarcasm out of his voice. "Well, I'm relieved it hasn't quite come to that."

"It's a business arrangement before anything else," Lamar said quickly. "But if you're married, that will cement the alliance. You said yourself, you told Nez you were ready to settle down. He will believe the marriage."

"They have a castle," Stoyan said. "Apparently, some rich guy bought an old castle in England before the Shift, had it disassembled and brought to Kentucky."

"You like castles," Bale said.

"It's a good defensible position," Felix said.

"At least meet the woman," Lamar said.

"Shut up," Hugh said.

They fell silent.

"Did you come up with this idiotic idea?" Hugh demanded.

"It was a joint effort between me and my equivalent on the other side," Lamar said. "If it helps, your prospective bride has to be talked into the marriage as well."

"Perfect. Just perfect."

He reviewed his options. He had none. He could marry some woman and feed his troops, or he could let them get slaughtered. What the hell, he'd done worse in his life.

"I'll see her," he said.

"That's all we ask," Lamar said.

3

The wind died. The tree line was still, the wide leaves of sycamores and the frilly foliage of oaks hanging motionless in the fading heat of the early evening. Nothing moved.

Elara leaned on the heavy gray stones of the parapet and sent her magic forward. A sick feeling flowed back to her, a greasy nasty smear on the soothing face of the forest, like an oil spill on the surface of a crystal-clear lake. *There you are.*

Rook reached for his small notebook, wrote a message, and passed it to her.

Do you see it?

"Yes. It's alone."

The blond spy nodded, an impassive look on his tan scarred face. Logic said he must've felt emotions, but if so, they were buried so deep that no hint ever rose to the surface.

"Thank you," Elara said.

The notebook disappeared into some hidden pocket of his soft leather jacket. He crossed the rampart to the inner edge of the battlements, hopped onto the parapet with the easy grace of an acrobat, jumped down, and vanished out of sight.

The vampire remained where it was, in the shadow of a

sycamore, invisible from the wall. But now she knew it was there. There would be no escape.

An undead here, only a few dozen yards from the castle and the settlement on the other side. A creature piloted by a Master of the Dead, capable of carving its way through their settlement.

Next to her Dugas stirred, brushing a persistent insect away from his gray hair. The older man was very tall and lean to the point of being almost wiry. A scar crossed his face, carving its way through his forehead, his dead milky left eye, and across his cheek until it disappeared into his short beard. Both his beard and hair had gone white long ago, but his eyebrows kept a few black hairs, stubbornly refusing to age. He was wearing his white robe today. It suited him much better than his usual getup of Bermuda shorts and a T-shirt.

The druid stroked his beard. "They're getting bolder by the day."

"It would seem that way." An undead so close to the castle meant a long-range navigator. Likely one of Nez's Golden Legion Masters of the Dead.

"I'll get the hunters," Dugas offered.

"No. I'll take care of it."

"They're due to arrive any minute."

"All the more reason to handle it myself." She smiled at him. "I'm faster than the hunters. We wouldn't want the undead to frighten our delicate guests."

The druid smiled into his beard. "I have a feeling this guest won't scare easily."

"I hope you're right. Don't worry. I'll be back in time."

She released her magic. It struck out like an invisible whip and splashed against the trunk of a white oak. She inhaled, took a single step toward that anchor, and let the air out.

The world *moved*.

She stood in the forest now. The wall of the castle lay fifty yards behind her. Massive trees spread their branches above her head. Magic waves destroyed technology, but they nourished the wilderness. The forest around her looked half-a-millennium old. A few yards to the left, and she would come across the remains of ruined houses, completely buried in the greenery.

The vampire ran.

She still didn't see it, but she felt it scuttle through the underbrush, sprinting away.

Oh no you don't.

Elara hurried after it, anchoring and moving, each of her steps swallowing fifteen yards. She could've moved faster, but expending magic came at a price. She would have to replace it. Thinking about it turned her stomach.

Thinking about their "guests" turned her stomach also. She should've let the hunters handle the vampire, but tension simmered in her, too close to the surface. She had to let some steam out of the pressure cooker, or she wouldn't be able to sit through the meeting.

The undead ran for its life, bouncing off the tree trunks. The hunger inside her woke. Elara chased it, losing herself to the speed. The vampire vaulted over a huge fallen tree, and she finally caught a flash of its back, once human skin and now a thick pallid hide.

Prey.

Ahead bright red ribbons tied to the tree trunks announced the end of their land. She'd run four miles.

The undead bolted for the safety of the ribbons, aiming for the gap between two trees.

She released her magic in a cold rush, stepped in front of the vampire, and caught the abomination by its shoulders. Her power clutched it. The hunger clawed at her from the inside. She bared her teeth.

The undead's red eyes sparked with a new, brighter fire – the navigator controlling the vampire had bailed. The sudden death of an undead could turn the navigator into a human vegetable. Those who reached the rank of Master knew when to let go.

The undead flailed, but it was too late. Elara found the small hot spark of magic within it and swallowed it. She could almost imagine tasting it on her tongue, as if it were a delicious morsel, and for a long moment she savored it.

The vampire went limp. Elara opened her arms, and the sack of dried flesh and bone that once used to be a human body, then an undead, and now was neither, collapsed to the forest floor.

Too little, the hunger howled inside her. *More. More!*

She chained it again with a brutal effort of will and forced it back into the dark place she kept it.

Horses.

Elara turned. She was only a few feet away from the narrow ribbon of the road that ran through the woods. Run or sneak a peek? Was there even a choice?

She stepped back a dozen yards, behind a wide old oak, climbed the low hanging branches, and settled above the ground, melting into the shadows among the foliage, as if she were one with them.

Riders approached.

The leading man was tall and dark-haired. That matched Dugas' description.

Her magic splayed out, masking her.

Do not see me.

The man halted his big white horse and turned toward her.

She couldn't see his face from this distance. She couldn't feel his magic either, but he had some, she was sure of it.

Do not see me.

Elara couldn't see his eyes, but all her senses told her he was staring straight at her. An excited shiver ran down her spine.

She was a complete and utter idiot, she decided. Sitting here, hiding like a child afraid to get caught. *Well, at least it's good to be self-aware.*

He gave the forest another long look and rode on.

Elara slipped from the tree and dashed back to the castle.

A few minutes later she stepped past the gates, straightened her long green dress, and checked her hair. Something skittered under her fingers. Elara plucked it from the long braid coiled at her neck. A spider. She walked out the gates and gently set it on the grass.

The spider escaped. She wished she could too. Anxiety flooded her. It's just nerves, she told herself.

Elara walked up the steps to the wall and touched the druid's shoulder. He turned, his brown eyes somber.

"I told you I would make it."

He shook his head. "I know you don't want to do this..."

"I don't. But I'll do it for my people."

Her people. She knew every single one of them. She was the reason they bounced back and forth across the country, desperately trying to find a place to call home only to be run off again and again. They deserved a home. This was their land, and she had to do everything in her power to protect it. Perhaps d'Ambray wouldn't prove too much of a problem.

"We could..."

"Pick up and leave again? No." She shook her head. "You said it yourself, we've been here too long. This is home now. I'm not going to uproot us again. Not for this."

They were done running. She wouldn't let Nez win.

A group of riders broke free of the canopy and rode up the road toward the gates at a canter. She clenched her hands together. This was ridiculous. She had nothing to be nervous about. She could pull the plug at any time.

The riders grew closer.

Elara nodded at the leader on the white horse. "Is that him?"

"Yes."

Hugh d'Ambray was huge. The stallion underneath him was massive, but the man matched the horse. He had to be well over

46

six feet tall. Wide shoulders. Long limbs. Very lean. Almost as if he should've been thirty pounds or so heavier. Dugas did say they were starving.

Starved or not, he looked like he could hold the drawbridge of a castle by himself.

It was suddenly very real. *I don't want to do this.*

"You want me to marry Conan the Barbarian?" A drop of acid slid into her tone.

"An attractive barbarian," Dugas pointed out.

"I suppose so, if you're looking at it from a purely animalistic point of view."

Dugas chuckled.

"Is his horse glowing?" She squinted at the stallion. If you looked just right, there was a hint of something protruding from its forehead, like a shimmer of hot air.

"It appears so."

They made a striking image, she admitted. The horse that was glowing with silver and the rider, all in black, his dark hair falling to his shoulders. But she wasn't interested in striking images.

"He's been here two minutes, and already he's riding like he owns everything he sees."

"He very likely always rides that way. Men like him project confidence. It's what makes others follow them into battle."

"Violent others."

"We agreed that we needed skilled violent soldiers with broad backs," Dugas said. "His back is broad enough."

The breadth of d'Ambray's back wasn't the problem.

She spared a few moments for his people. Two men rode directly behind him, one tall and black, with glasses perching on his nose, and the other athletic and white, with short brown hair and an attractive, smart face. The rider behind them was just a boy, blond and tan. Why bring a boy?

Wolves coming to her door.

The riders reached the gates. D'Ambray raised his head and looked up.

His eyes were a deep dark blue, and they stared through her. She held his stare.

Most women would find him handsome. He had a strong face, overwhelmingly masculine without a hint of the brutish thickness she'd expected. His jaw was square and strong, the lines of his face defined but not sharp or fragile, and his eyes under a sweep of thick black eyebrows were too shrewd and too cold for comfort. His eyes evaluated her with icy calculation.

She was about to share the power over her people with this man. Alarm squirmed through her. This was a bad idea. A terrible idea.

D'Ambray passed through the gate and out of her view.

"I shouldn't do this," Elara whispered to herself.

"Do you want me to send them off?" Dugas asked quietly.

If she said yes, he would.

She had to get a grip. She had to teach d'Ambray who she was. The White Warlock. Unclean. Cursed. An abomination. They would come to this meeting table as equals, and if they chose an alliance, she had to make sure they left as equals.

The magic escaped the world without so much as a whisper, stealing her power. That was fine. She didn't need magic to make Hugh d'Ambray understand where they stood.

"Let's wait to throw him out until he balks at our terms."

"Do you want them in the great hall?" the druid asked.

"No." She narrowed her eyes. "Put them in the green room. Next to the kitchens."

———+——

THE AIR SMELLED like fresh bread, just out of the oven, with a crisp golden crust. Hugh's mouth watered, while his stomach begged. Clever girl.

He once starved a woman to the brink of death, trying to break her. Poetic justice, he reflected.

"The castle is in good shape," Stoyan said softly behind him.

The castle was in excellent shape. It was built with pale grayish-brown stone. The forty-foot-high curtain wall and the massive barbican, the gatehouse protecting the entrance, were both solid, as were the two bastion towers at the corners and the two flanking towers. The bailey, the open space inside the walls, was clean and well maintained. He didn't see a well, but they must have one. The inner structure consisted of a constellation of buildings hugging the main keep, a hundred-foot-tall square tower. He caught a glimpse of the stables and the motor pool, attached to the east wall. The electric lamps suggested they had a working generator.

The place was massive. It needed a moat. Something he would have to remedy.

A large molosser dog trotted in through the open door, wagging its shaggy white tail. He'd seen three so far as they rode up and walked through the bailey, each dog over a hundred and twenty pounds. They reminded him of Karakachan hounds he'd come across in the Balkans. The dog wandered over to him and Hugh patted its shaggy head. Karakachans were wolf killers. If Lamar was right about the size of their livestock herds, the dogs made sense. The castle and the town attached to the shore of the lake were wrapped in dense forest. There would be wolves there.

The inside of the castle was as well taken care of as the outside. The room where he now sat at a big rustic table was simple, the stone walls without any decoration, but it was clean, his chair was comfortable, and the temperature inside was at least ten degrees cooler. Nice thick walls.

All Hugh had to do now was convince the owner of the castle to let him share it. He'd gotten a glimpse of her as he rode in. Her hair was completely white. Not pale blond or bleached platinum, white. Her hazel eyes were sharp, and she looked at him like she saw a wolf at her door. He wasn't a wolf. He was something much worse, but he needed her defendable castle and her delicious bread.

Hugh had tried to pin down her age, but the white hair threw him off. Her face looked young, but he'd barely seen anything beyond a glimpse.

Hugh leaned back. She was making him wait. That was fine. He could be patient.

Behind him someone's stomach growled.

He'd felt something in the forest, on the way here. Something that raised the hair on the back of his neck. He'd tangled with powers across three continents, and whatever had been in the woods had tripped all of his alarms. Then it had moved toward the castle and he'd nudged Bucky into a canter, trying to follow it.

His gaze stopped on a large hand-painted map above the side door, showing Berry Hill in the center, by the edge of the Silver River Lake, with the castle on the neighboring hill. On the right and slightly above, to the northeast, lay Aberdine, another small post-Shift settlement, next to a ley point. Higher still, past the woods, directly north, spread Sanderville. Above it in the distance on the far left was Lexington.

Hugh looked at Aberdine. Post-Shift, magic streamed through the world in currents, ley lines, offering a fast way of travel and shipping. Walking into the current would get your legs cut off, so you had to put some barrier between the magic and yourself, a car, a wooden pallet, anything would do. Once in, the ley line would drag its rider off until it reached a ley point, where the magic blinked, interrupted, and the current would jettison its riders out into the real world. There was only one road connecting the castle and that ley point and it ran through Aberdine. They would have to play nice with that settlement.

The heavy wooden door opened, and she walked in, followed by a one-eyed older man in a white robe, a black woman in her late forties in a pantsuit, and a petite blonde.

Hugh tilted his head and took in his future bride.

Somewhere between twenty-five and thirty. A loose green dress fell almost to the floor, hiding most of her. Nice full breasts. Long legs. Pretty features, big eyes, small mouth, eyebrows darker than her hair, pale brown – probably drawn in or dyed. Tan skin, almost golden. Interesting face. Not exactly beautiful, but feminine and pretty.

A cold expression stamped her face, a hint of arrogance, some pride, and a lot of confidence. There was something regal about her. Queen of the castle.

She would be a massive pain in the ass.

Just get through it.

Hugh rose to his feet. She held out her hand.

"Elara Harper." Her voice matched her, cold and precise.

He grasped her fingers in his and shook her hand. "Hugh d'Ambray."

"Nice to meet you." She sat in the chair opposite him.

Her advisors arranged themselves behind her.

"You already know Dugas," she said.

He didn't, but Lamar told him the druid was his counterpart, "a voice of reason." Someone had sliced up the older man's face. Hugh met his gaze. Dugas held his stare and smiled. A tough nut to crack.

"This is Savannah LeBlanc."

The black woman nodded to him. Expensive clothes, professional, well put together, her dark natural hair pulled back from her face and twisted into an elegant bun. She looked like a lawyer. Hugh met her gaze. A witch, a powerful one. He couldn't feel her magic with tech up, but he'd interacted with enough of them to recognize the bearing. Bad news.

"She is the head witch of our covens," Elara continued.

Covens. Plural. Interesting.

"This is Johanna Kerry."

The blond smiled at him. She had to be in her twenties, but to him she looked too young, almost a teenager. Barely five feet tall, slender, glasses. Petite smart blonds were Stoyan's kryptonite.

Her hand flew up to her forehead, thumb pressed against her palm in a kind of a salute. *"Hello."*

She was deaf or mute. Possibly both. His knowledge of American Sign Language was rusty. ASL had its own rules and grammar, but he remembered the basics.

He raised his hands and signed. *"Lovely day."*

Johanna's eyebrows rose. *"Interesting."*

Interesting was the right word. He would have to work on his gestures.

Hugh introduced his people. "Stoyan, Centurion of the First Century. Lamar, Centurion of the Second Century. And Sam. He's here to assess the horses."

Savannah moved to the side, so Johanna could keep them both in her view, and signed as he spoke. Her hands moved fast. She clearly didn't need any practice.

Another blond woman in jeans and a T-shirt slipped into the room through the side door. She was young and pretty, and she looked at him a moment too long.

"Can I get you anything?"

"Iced tea, please, Caitlyn," Elara said.

"Yes, ma'am."

The woman ducked into the doorway.

"You need an army," Hugh said. "We need a base."

She nodded. "You have an army, and I have a base."

So far they were in agreement.

"Shall we talk terms?" she asked. "What do you need from us?"

"My people will need barracks, rations, and equipment," he said.

"That's reasonable," she said.

"They aren't farmers. They won't be tending the fields or milking your cows. They won't assist your people in daily tasks unless it's an emergency."

She raised her eyebrows. "So what will they be doing all day?"

"They will patrol the grounds. They will drill, perform PT, repair and fortify the castle, and take care of any external threats we will face."

He slipped that 'we' in there. The sooner she saw them as allies, the sooner he would get his people fed.

"PT?" she asked.

"Physical training. You are hiring us as employees with specific jobs. We must be free to do those jobs."

"I'm picturing three hundred people lying about, eating my food, and drinking my beer all day," Elara said.

"Only when they are off duty. They will patrol the castle and the outer perimeter in shifts, and if they do choose to drink beer in their off hours, they will pay for it. Which brings me to another point. They will need to be paid."

Elara leaned back. "You expect me to feed them, clothe them, equip them, *and* pay them?"

"Yes. I expect them to put themselves between you and danger."

"If we paid each of your people $500 per month, the bill would come to $150,000 per month. If we had that kind of money, I would hire mercenaries. I wouldn't have to stoop to this farce of a marriage."

Stoop? Oh really. "When Nez slaughters your people like cattle, and you walk among their corpses, inhaling their blood, you should tell them that."

Elara drew back. "I've taken care of my people until now. I'll take care of Nez without you."

"I can take this castle with twenty people," Hugh said. "I can burn it to the ground, or I can kill all of you and take it."

She leaned forward, her eyes fixed on him, icy with rage. "Try it."

He leaned toward her. "I can do this, because my people are professional soldiers. You will treat them like soldiers."

"We don't need you."

"Yes, you do. I saw Nez a month ago. He's coming."

The blond Caitlyn appeared in the doorway. Savannah took the pitcher from her hands, waved her off, and set the tea on the table.

Elara's eyes narrowed. "And I should take your word for it?"

"Yes."

"The word of a man who betrays his friends?"

"The word of a man who is willing to marry you with all of your baggage. I don't see a line of suitors outside this door, do you?"

She recoiled. "How do I know you're not working for Nez?"

"He is the Preceptor of the Iron Dogs!" Stoyan snarled behind him.

Hugh raised his hand. Stoyan snapped his mouth shut.

"Nez wouldn't bother with subterfuge," Hugh said. "You're not worth the trouble. You're easy pickings."

She opened her mouth.

"How many of your people can kill a vampire one-on-one?"

She didn't answer.

"Each one of mine can. They've been trained to kill them, because Nez and I spent a decade trying to murder each other. He sent me the head of my childhood friend, and then he and I had coffee in Charlotte a week later. That's the kind of man Nez is. So snarl all you want, princess. But you will marry me, because you have no choice. You won't win this fight with farmers. You need a cold ruthless bastard like me, and I'm the only one here."

They stared at each other in silence.

"It has to be food, equipment, and board for now," she said. "Take it or leave it."

"I'll take it. In return, you'll let me make modifications and repairs to this place as I see fit. You will finance it, if needed."

"We will discuss each modification individually," she said.

"No."

"I may not have the money."

"Fine. We will discuss the budget for each modification with the understanding that my requests for materials and labor are to be given first priority."

"Fine," she ground out. "We do not tolerate crimes here. While your people are here, they will obey the laws. If one of them murders or rapes one of my people, you will kill that soldier. If you don't, I will, and believe me, they will wish you had done it."

She'd caved on the upgrades. Hugh had to give her something. "Agreed. I will need fifteen horses." They were seventeen mounts short, and horses were damn expensive.

"Done."

Shit. Should've asked for twenty.

"And just to be crystal clear," Elara said. "This marriage is in name only."

"Sweetheart, you couldn't pay me enough."

Pink touched her tan cheeks. "If you betray us, I'll make you suffer."

"We haven't even married yet, and I'm suffering already."

"We have that in common," she snapped.

They both leaned back at the same time. He was marrying an ice harpy. Fantastic. Just fantastic.

Dugas stepped forward, leaned, and spoke into Elara's ear.

"I'll need to inspect your troops," Elara said, her voice precise. "We need to know exactly what we are buying with our food."

"Fine." He gave her a lazy smile. "My men will need to inspect your horses and our quarters in the castle."

"Make your troops available to us first."

Hugh poured himself a glass of tea and nodded at the doorway. "Look outside your walls."

———+——

SHE WOULD STRANGLE THAT MAN. No, she would do worse.

55

Elara strode outside of the gate onto the top of the hill where the castle sat. Soldiers filed out of the forest, running three to a row. They wore black uniforms, some in armor, some without. Each carried a large backpack, a bedroll, and weapons. They moved in unison, their feet striking the ground at the same time.

She hadn't detected them in the forest, which meant they had to have been far behind.

The soldiers began to form a block, eight soldiers in a line. All of that equipment had to weigh at least twenty pounds. Probably a lot more.

"How long have they been running?" she asked and wished she hadn't. Any show of interest was an opening, and d'Ambray would wedge his big dumb shoulder through it and hold it open.

D'Ambray shrugged, looming next to her, a darkness shaped like a huge man. "From Aberdine."

"Ten miles?"

"Yes." He turned to her, his dark blue eyes calm. "Would you like them to run back and here again?"

He was completely serious, she realized.

"No."

He turned to face the soldiers. They formed four separate blocks, each eight soldiers wide, ten lines deep and froze, like dark statues against the green grass of the lawn.

"Do you want them to rest?" she asked.

"Are you tired?" d'Ambray roared next to her, his voice carrying across the field. She almost jumped.

The three hundred and twenty people roared back in a single voice. "No, Preceptor!"

"They're ready for your inspection," Hugh said.

Elara had to admit, they looked impressive. Guilt pinched at her. This wasn't about d'Ambray's people, she reminded herself. This was about keeping her people safe. If d'Ambray put his troops in jeopardy, it was on him.

The creaking of a wagon came from behind them. Slowly,

carefully, George, Saladin, and Cornwall came into view, leading Dakota, a massive Clydesdale, as he pulled the wagon forward. A brown tarp hid the contents. She knew exactly what was in the cart.

Elara stepped aside to let the wagon pass. D'Ambray didn't appear concerned.

The three men guided the wagon down the hill, slowly, as if it were made of glass. Dugas walked behind them, silent. Each of the men carried a shotgun.

The wagon came to a stop. Saladin unhitched Dakota and the three men walked away, back toward the castle.

Elara raised her head. "You said each of your people could take a vampire."

Dugas pulled the tarp off the wagon. An undead sat in a metal cage. The moment the tarp came off, it lunged at the metal bars, its eyes glowing with insane bloodlust.

"Prove it," Elara said.

D'Ambray nodded at his soldiers. "Pick."

Elara stared at the rows of soldiers. She was about to sentence one of them to death. A human, even a skilled human, had very little chance against an undead.

She had to do her job. He would put his strongest people in front and in the rear, so she had to pick from the middle. "Fourth row on my left," she said. "Third soldier."

"Arend Garcia," d'Ambray ordered, his voice rolling. "Step forward."

The third man in the fourth row took a step back, turned, and marched to the edge of the line, turned, marched toward them, turned again... Dead man walking. He was in his late twenties, dark hair cut short, light eyes. Like all of them, he was lean, almost underfed. A scar crossed his face on the right side of his nose, slanting to the side and barely missing his mouth.

He was about to die. If she showed any care at all, d'Ambray would use it to get out of this test.

Arend Garcia came to a stop.

She checked d'Ambray's face. It might as well have been cut from a rock.

"Kill the undead," d'Ambray ordered, his voice calm.

Garcia dropped his bedroll and backpack, stepped forward, facing the cage, reached behind his back, and pulled a brutal-looking knife free. It looked like a slimmer version of a machete, its blade black.

Dugas picked up the chain attached to a heavy metal bar securing the trap door release on the cage and backed away. Garcia watched, impassive. The undead hammered itself against the bars.

Damn it. "You're going to let your man face an undead with a knife?"

D'Ambray glanced at her. "Did you want him to kill it with his bare hands?"

"No." She barely knew the man, and she already hated him. "At least give him a sword."

"He doesn't need a sword."

Dugas yanked the chain. The bolt slid free.

The undead tore out of the cage, lightning fast, and charged Garcia.

At the last moment, the slender man stepped aside, graceful like a matador, and brought the machete down. The blade cleaved through the undead's neck. Its head rolled onto the grass. The body ran another ten feet and toppled forward, the stump of the neck digging into the grass.

Elara realized she was holding her breath and let it out.

Garcia pulled a cloth from the pocket of his leathers, wiped the blade, slid it back into its sheath, and stood at parade rest.

"Are you satisfied?" d'Ambray asked.

"Yes." The word tasted bitter in her mouth. She should've been happy. She wanted crack troops and she got them. Elara forced a calm expression over her face like a mask. "Thank you, Preceptor."

He smiled. He was clearly enjoying every second of this. "Anything for my betrothed."

She almost punched him.

D'Ambray nodded to Garcia. The man pulled a small knife out of the sheath on his belt. A woman broke ranks and ran up to him. Together they knelt by the fallen undead.

"What are they doing?"

"Harvesting the blood. It stays viable for quite a while when properly stored. I'll see those barracks now."

"This way." Elara turned and led him inside the castle.

"About this marriage," he said.

"I meant what I said."

"Good, because I liked the blond that brought us tea."

The nerve. "My people aren't slaves, Preceptor. If Caitlyn wants to let you climb on top of her, that's her business."

"Excellent. Am I going to get a bedroom, or should we come up with a rotation schedule?"

He was baiting her. He had to be.

"You're getting your own bedroom, Preceptor."

"Splendid."

She couldn't kill him. She needed his troops. But she really wanted to.

"One last thing. Does the castle have a name?"

"Baile." She pronounced it the right way, in Irish Gaelic, Balyeh.

Hugh smiled. "*Home.* I think I'm going to like it here."

"We'll do our best to make you feel welcome, Preceptor."

4

The void had finally caught him. Hugh stood at the window while it pierced him with needle teeth and shredded him, skinning one thin layer at a time. He'd known pain before. He'd been shot, cut, burned, broken, tortured, but this was different. This was the same pain he felt when Roland had sent him into exile.

He was on the fifth floor of the keep. It was midafternoon, three or four, he wasn't sure. The sky was blue, without a shred of a cloud. The wind cooled his skin. The sunshine played on the stone walls. Below him a sheer drop promised a speedy trip to the stone bailey. If he jumped now, even if he lived for a few seconds and reached for his magic in desperation, it wouldn't save him. Besides, the tech was up. His ability to heal was barely there.

It would solve all his problems. A brief flash of pain, almost an afterthought compared to what he felt now, and everything would be over.

If Hugh turned, opened the reinforced wood and steel door and strode down the long hallway, he would arrive at his bride's bedroom. She was in there, getting ready. They were going to be married today. Neither of them had wanted to delay. They'd been at each other's throats for the past week, but one thing they both agreed on: they had to marry fast and it had to be a real wedding, with a cake, flowers, gowns, and a reception afterward. They hired a wedding photographer and a videographer, because they planned to plaster the pictures everywhere they could. Which was why the wedding had to take place today, while tech held. The marriage had to appear real, because without it their alliance wasn't worth the forty some pieces of paper they had signed once their advisers finished bargaining with each other over the exact terms of it.

Hugh leaned on the windowsill. He never expected to get married. The thought hadn't occurred to him. The need for marriage came when a man realized he was getting older and wanted to start a family or when he wanted to prove a commitment to a woman or get one from her. During his decades as a Warlord, Roland's magic had sustained him. He didn't age. Back then, Hugh had centuries ahead of him. Hugh would stay at his peak, and if he wanted a woman, he got one. There had been a few that had resisted at first, but he had patience and experience, he knew how to listen and what to say, when he chose to do it, and power was one hell of an aphrodisiac. He was Roland's Warlord, the Preceptor of the Iron Dogs. Eventually, he won them over and they ended up in his bed.

He'd thought sex would get old, but it never did. A new day, a new interesting woman. Eventually, he ran out of new things to try and realized that the difference between good sex and great sex was passion. Great sex was less frequent, but he had no problem settling for good sex.

Marriage wasn't even in his vocabulary.

Still, if Hugh ever got married, he would've expected the woman to be eager. Excited even.

The harpy at the other end of the hallway acted as if he were some revolting creature that crawled out from under a damp rock. The woman drove him nuts. Hugh alternated between wanting to strangle her and trying not to laugh as she fought off his verbal jabs. Making her snarl in frustration was the only thing that made the situation tolerable.

He was mortal now. Eventually he would age. He would die. The thought turned Hugh's blood to ice. He couldn't even remember how old he was. He would die, and soon. His magic would keep him alive for a while, but he wouldn't last much more than another eighty years. Maybe a hundred.

Voron's ghost congealed from his memories. When Hugh was a child, Voron was larger than life. Tall, powerful, unstoppable. A different man looked at him now, old, gray, somehow less, as if age leached the color from his hair and skin. The ghost raised his sword.

Go away, old man.

Hugh pushed the memory aside. This hay ride had a definite end. He no longer had forever.

The stones of the bailey turned even more inviting. Instead of thinking about what do to with his meager lifespan, he could just stop both, his life and his thinking.

"Mmm," came a low feminine noise from the bed.

He turned. Caitlyn from the kitchen was too worried about what "the White Lady" would think, so he'd moved on to Vanessa. A brunette, with big boobs, long legs, a small butt, and lots of enthusiasm, she worked in the castle as a paralegal. She was also low maintenance.

Vanessa turned on her side and rested her head on her bent elbow, popping her chest to offer him a better view. He'd set the ground rules from the start, although he doubted she would stick to them. She was an opportunist.

She measured him with her gaze, pausing on his bare crotch. "Are we gonna keep doing this after you're married?"

"Scared of Elara?"

She shook her head. "If the Lady didn't want me here, she

would tell me. The Lady knows everything. She knows what I'm saying right now."

Interesting. Hugh leaned against the windowsill, studying her. "How?"

Vanessa waved her fingers at him. "Magic."

"The tech is up."

"It doesn't matter. She knows."

"Why do you call her the Lady?"

Vanessa shrugged one shoulder. "That's just what she is. She isn't like the rest of us."

"What makes her special?"

"If you wait long enough, she'll show you."

"That's not an answer."

"She protects us," Vanessa said.

"From whom?"

"From everyone. The undead. The Remaining."

He leaned forward. "Who are the Remaining?"

"We started out together, then we split," Vanessa said. "We call those who stayed behind the Remaining. They call us the Departed."

"Why did you split?"

Vanessa yawned. "It's long and complicated."

"You *are* afraid of Elara."

"No, I'm just not stupid."

Hugh moved toward the bed, leaned over her, and fixed her with his stare. She shrank back. Alarm flared in her eyes.

He glanced at the door, then back at her. She slid off the bed, grabbed her clothes, yanked her dress on, and hurried out, almost at a run, her underwear in her hands.

She would be back. He had her.

Vanessa was a born flunky. She feared Elara but she also felt some contempt for his future bride, or she wouldn't have climbed into his bed to test her leash. Elara must've been kind to her. That was a mistake.

He'd seen Vanessa's type enough over the years to recognize it instantly. Her kind of people understood strength and overt shows of power. They loudly proclaimed their support for the overzealous cops, local tyrants, and anyone willing to show brute strength. Vanessa respected authority that made her fear. As long as he terrified her, she would obey him and try to please, but she could never be trusted. If Elara scared her enough, Vanessa would spill his secrets. If she ever got a taste of real power, she would be petty and cruel.

Hugh turned to the window. The day was peaceful and quiet. He supposed he should shower and get dressed. He was getting married, after all. And he would buy food and safety for the Dogs with his marriage. And get a castle as a dowry. Once the moat was done...

The moat. The tech was up, it was midafternoon, and he'd ordered the construction to start this morning. Where were the fucking bulldozers?

———

"IT'S A BEAUTIFUL DRESS," Nadia said.

"Very beautiful," Beth agreed, brushing her hair.

Elara hid a sigh. They were doing their best to make her feel better. This wasn't the way she imagined the day of her wedding. This was some hellish caricature of it.

She was doing it for the right reasons. She promised to protect her people and d'Ambray's troops would protect them. The Iron Dogs seemed barely human, but they'd been inside the walls for a week and she couldn't fault them. They'd taken over patrols. They ran and did endless amounts of push-ups. They were unerringly polite to her people. The castle had come with the barracks, but there weren't enough spaces for all of them in the building, so she had to relegate them to tents in the bailey while the left wing was renovated. There wasn't a whisper of complaint.

They had almost no supplies, except for what they could carry and a covered wagon. They brought the wagon in and unloaded two dozen sealed plastic drums, which they dragged inside and locked in a room in the barracks. None of the spying and scrying her people had done had managed to shed any light on what was in the barrels. It wasn't money. D'Ambray was broke, so broke, that the contract they'd signed specified a week's worth of clothes for every Iron Dog. They didn't even have spare underwear.

Tonight she would have to marry that insufferable ass.

Some girls dreamed about getting married and planned their wedding. Elara never had. But when she thought about it occasionally, she always imagined getting married to someone who loved her.

"Have you decided what to do about the hair, my lady?" Eve asked from the back.

She'd given up on trying to get them to stop calling her that. At least when she was in earshot, they'd stopped referring to her as the White Lady. Having people pretend she was some medieval queen was better than the actual worship, Elara reminded herself. Worship had to be avoided at all costs.

"I don't know."

Her hair, the mark of her curse, fell around her face in soft waves after being twisted at the nape of her neck for the whole day. If she straightened it, the long white strands would reach past her butt. The hair was a pain. Elara had wanted to cut it for years, but it became a symbol of her magic, and she'd learned long ago that symbols were important.

"We could do a full updo," Beth offered. "Something with flowers. We could do a very loose braid."

"Or a waterfall braid," Nadia said.

Elara bit down on another sigh. She almost told them she didn't care, but it would hurt their feelings.

"We could leave it down," Eve suggested. "You almost never wear it down."

She didn't wear it down, because she hated it. She still remembered her real hair, the dark, chocolate-brown curls. Three years ago, just after they left West Virginia, she got two bottles of hair dye and soaked the white strands in it. She kept it on until her scalp began to itch. When she walked out of the shower, her hair was still pristine white. Not a single strand took the dye.

"Let me think about it."

"There are only two hours left," Eve murmured.

"It's not like they can have a wedding without me."

A soft knock echoed through the room. Rook.

Eve opened the door. "She is busy."

"Let him in."

Elara drew her thin white robe around herself, hiding the translucent white camisole she wore underneath.

The door swung open. The spy stepped inside, his hair hidden by the hoodie he always wore. She waited for a report, but he just stood there. He'd brought her something private.

"Give us a minute," she said. "I'll call you when I'm ready."

The three women left the room, with Beth closing the door behind her. Rook approached and held out a piece of paper.

Vanessa and Hugh:

V: Are we gonna keep doing this after you're married?

H: Scared of Elara?

V: If the Lady didn't want me here, she would tell me.

Elara read the rest of the conversation. Hardly surprising. That was the one thing that always set her teeth on edge about Vanessa. The woman didn't have an ounce of loyalty in her. Still, she was one of her people.

"Where is he now?"

He pulled on his pants and ran outside to the construction crew.

That meant he would be at her door in a minute.

"Thank you."

Rook nodded and slipped outside the door. Elara barred it and sat at her vanity. She had to do something about her hair. She couldn't care less about what it looked like, but the wedding had to appear genuine. She had to keep up appearances. She would manufacture the glow for the sake of her people.

Someone pounded on her door.

"Go away." Elara dipped her fingers into a small tub of lotion.

"Open the door."

There was something about his voice that made people want to obey. Some imperceptible quality. It was probably very handy in the middle of battle.

"Go away. I'm not dressed, and you can't see me before the wedding."

"Open the door."

"No." She dabbed the lotion on her face and in the hollow of her neck and worked it into her skin.

The door took a hit with a hard thud. It was a heavy wooden door, reinforced with steel, but the few days she'd spent with d'Ambray convinced her that he could be extremely single-minded.

"If you break it, the money for the replacement will come out of your discretionary budget."

Elara raised her hair up in a semblance of an updo. Ugh.

"Do you really want to do this through the door?"

"I don't want to do it at all."

"You cut the gas for my bulldozers."

"Yes, I did."

"Why?"

"Because it's expensive."

A furious silence fell. She imagined him on the other side of the door steaming and smiled.

"I need it. I need the gas."

"We all need things."

"Elara! We need to stay alive. The moat will keep us alive."

Moat, moat, moat... Moat? Moat. Moat! Ugh.

"You want to dig a trench that is ten feet deep and seventy-five feet wide. That's ridiculously large."

"It has to be that large to function."

Elara sighed and picked up the eyeshadow. Maybe rose gold?

"How are you planning to fill it up?"

"With water from the lake."

"Are you planning to make the water flow up the hill?"

"No, I'll pump it in."

She put down her eyeshadow. "You want to pump the water into that massive trench? Do you have any idea how much fuel that will take? So we'll be paying for the gas for that too?"

"It's necessary."

"Won't the water just seep into the ground?"

"We'll line the bottom with concrete."

"So magic can crack it."

"No, the magic won't crack it, because we'll use Roman concrete mixed by hand."

Rose gold was working out nicely. "Don't you need volcanic ash for Roman concrete?"

Another silence. She'd had a detailed discussion with the Dog he assigned as foreman before she took away their gasoline. It wasn't her first construction project.

"Where are you going to get volcanic ash?" she asked.

"I'll have it shipped from Asheville."

"I wasn't aware Asheville had suddenly sprouted volcanoes." She blended a darker shade of the eyeshadow into the crease of her eyes.

"Asheville had a Cherufe manifestation five years ago. They have an entire mountain of volcanic ash and we can buy it dirt cheap."

"More money."

"Elara," he growled.

"You're building a money pit, except it's not a pit, it's a moat. Why not just line it with money and set that on fire when the vampires come?"

"It wouldn't burn long enough. You will give me this moat. I'm trying to keep you and everyone in this place alive. Can you put a price on the safety of your people?"

"Yes, I can. The total operating cost of a single bulldozer is two hundred and thirty-seven dollars per hour. We have to factor in heavy use in soil that has been undisturbed for at least ten years; gasoline; lubricant; undercarriage adjustment for impact, abrasiveness and so on; repair reserve, parts and labor; and operator cost, since people do not work for free. Now we have to calculate the number of cubic yards of soil we must remove and transport somewhere else. Based on the dimensions of your trench—"

"Give me the moat or the wedding is off."

For a moment, she literally saw red. Elara jumped to her feet and jerked the door open. He stood on the other side, wearing nothing except jeans and boots.

"I can't believe you! You would endanger this wedding for your stupid moat?"

Hugh towered over her, his blue eyes dark. "Here is some math for you. Your settlement holds four thousand and forty-seven people, of which five hundred and three are children under the age of eighteen. When Nez comes, and he will, you will have three choices. You can evacuate, which means Nez will chase us down and slaughter everyone. You can hole up in the castle with the adults and send the children off, serving Nez a herd of hostages on a silver platter. Or you can hide everyone in the castle, which is the only real option you have."

He leaned closer, his face vicious. "This place was designed for a staff of three hundred. It can comfortably hold five hundred in a pinch. You'll have to pack four thousand terrified people, half of them parents with children, in here like sardines. Sanitation will go first. Sewage will start backing up. Water will be next. Your well will run dry. You'll try to conserve it, while Nez lobs chunks of corpses his plague spreaders have seeded with diseases over your wall, but it won't matter. The well will run dry anyway within a few weeks. Your people will start dying. Children and the infirm will be at the front of the line. You will watch them go one by one."

She blinked.

"We can't withstand a siege. We have to hit Nez so hard and so fast on his first charge, that he'll decide besieging us is too expensive. To do that, we need defenses that work against undead. The moat is such a defense. Without it, this place is a death trap. I realize you don't understand it, but you're not in charge of our defenses. I am."

White ice exploded inside Elara. "You have some nerve," she snarled. "Your moat will cut my budget by a third!"

"*Our* budget."

"Not yet, it's not! I have to fund the school for this year. I have to feed three hundred extra people who earn no money. It doesn't grow on trees. Did Roland not explain to you the concept of money when he doled out your allowance?"

Hugh's eyes narrowed. "I don't know if you're too thick to see it or if you're on a power trip, so I'll make it real simple for you: give me the moat or I'll take my people and leave. I'm not dying here because you're an idiot."

"Arrogant dickhead!"

"Screeching harpy."

"Asshole."

"Bitch."

The hunger clawed at her from the inside. It took every drop of her will to keep it from ripping out. She actually trembled with rage.

"You want to leave? Do it."

"Be careful what you wish for," he warned.

"Take your people and leave."

A stomp made them turn toward the hallway.

Johanna handshaped the letter E and moved it down her hair, indicating length. *"Elara."*

Johanna didn't use the name sign she invented for her often, and normally that would've stopped Elara in her tracks, but she was too irritated.

"What?" she snarled.

"Important fighting moment," Johanna said. *"But heads of the Lexington Red Guard and Louisville Mage College are downstairs."* She pointed to the floor.

Hugh turned to her. "Why?"

Johanna brushed back her blond hair. *"We invited them for the wedding to build good relations and to have witnesses. Don't be dumb."*

She moved her fingers, her gestures brisk.

"We need witnesses. Many, many witnesses. Wrap it up. Slap each other if you need to. Get dressed. Don't mind me." She took a step back. *"I will wait. Five minutes."*

Hugh was looking at her. Elara realized her robe was hanging open, showing off the thin white camisole that left most of her breasts bare and barely covered half of her butt. Suddenly she was sharply aware that he was half-naked and standing too close. Elara pulled the robe closed and glared back at him.

He no longer exhaled rage. Clearly, he'd changed his strategy.

"Compromise," he said. "What is your biggest need as a settlement?"

"Metal," she said. "We need iron and steel."

"There are several smaller towns around here that were lost to the forest. There is metal there. Used cars, a factory in Brownsville, and so on."

"That's not a friendly forest. A lot of those places are infested with magic creatures. It's too dangerous."

"Not for my people. I'll start making salvage runs. You will authorize the gas for the moat."

Elara shut her eyes. "Fine. You'll get enough gas for three days. More when you bring in your first load of salvage, and our smiths sign off on it."

"There may be hope for you yet."

"Rot in hell, d'Ambray."

"I love you too, darling."

Elara turned to Johanna and signed. *"We are fine."*

Johanna gave them both a bright smile. *"Good job."*

She turned and went down the stairwell.

Elara didn't slam the door. She closed it very carefully, walked to her vanity, sat down, and shut her eyes, trying to control her fury. And there he was, coming out of the darkness. She knew exactly why Vanessa had climbed into his bed. Up close, Hugh was overwhelming. The size, the breadth of his shoulders, the muscle, the hard stomach. Power. So much male, brutal power and strength. And she hated every inch of him. If she could've pushed him out of the hallway window, she would've. He'd splatter on the stones below, and she would smile when he did.

That was the wrong thought. She checked herself.

A hesitant knock came.

"Come in," she said without turning. "I decided what to do with my hair."

"Yes, my lady?" Beth asked.

"We'll leave it down," Elara said.

———+..

HUGH STOOD at the altar under an arched trellis dripping with white clematis flowers. A gentle fragrance spiced the air. The castle rose behind him and slightly to the left. The hill leveled here before rolling down, and beautiful Kentucky countryside spread in front of him: the blue-green hills and pastures, with dense forests encroaching on them like waves from a rising tide, and in the distance, more hills, each lighter than the next, fading into the beginnings of what promised to be a hell of a sunset.

He turned slightly. Benches had been set up in front of the altar, with a path between them, and they were filled. On Elara's side were women in pastels and men in suits or jeans, whatever qualified as their best. His side was black. The Dogs wore their uniforms, just as he wore the black of the Preceptor. It was the only formal clothes they had. They'd stowed their weapons under their seats, grim faced and quiet. He wasn't taking any chances on Nez crashing the wedding.

Hugh surveyed the Iron Dog ranks. All the family he would ever need.

"Where is he?" Bale growled next to him.

"He'll be here," Lamar said quietly.

"He better," Bale said.

The townspeople ran out of seats and formed a loose group, standing to one side of the benches. They waited, murmuring and shifting. Children chased each other. There were flowers everywhere. Looking down the center aisle, he could see the large white tent to the right where Elara hid, probably surrounded by her women, fussing over every inch of her hair and dress. Past the tent, tables had been set up with a three-tier black-and-white cake towering in the center.

Stoyan shouldered his way through the crowd. A fresh narrow scar crossed his neck.

"Speak of the devil," Lamar murmured.

Stoyan ran down the aisle to them, reached into his pocket, and offered a small black box to Hugh.

"Any trouble?" Lamar asked.

"Nothing I couldn't handle."

Hugh opened the box. A white gold ring lay inside, a half-eternity band of glittering pale-blue aquamarines between two rows of small diamonds. That was more or less what he'd described to Stoyan. A jeweler in Lexington had owed him a favor for over twenty years. He'd remembered it three days ago during one of his moments of clarity between trying to get his people settled, fighting with Elara, and fucking Vanessa to keep the void at bay.

A year ago, if he'd chosen a wedding ring, it would've been a work of art shining with diamonds, steeped in magic, and costing a fortune. This one couldn't be worth more than three grand, but the metal was white like her hair and something about the pure fire of aquamarines and diamonds reminded him of her. It showed some thought, which women valued. An olive branch.

They hated each other's guts, but there was no reason they couldn't coexist, at least until the threat passed. Hugh had no desire to battle to the death with her over every little thing. And Elara would fight to the bitter end. Although if she insisted on fighting with him half-dressed again, he was reasonably sure he could tolerate it for a couple of minutes. She wasn't the worst-looking woman in the castle, and, for a brief moment, he'd enjoyed the show.

She'd also confirmed something he'd suspected when she discussed the arrangements for the wedding. Elara didn't want him to see her in the wedding dress. It was a stupid tradition, but she clung to it. It was her first wedding, Hugh was sure, and like most women, she likely planned it since childhood, complete with sappy music and the release of doves.

The void bit at him. He blocked it off.

The castle harpy wanted a special moment. The ring would demonstrate that he took it seriously. For all he knew, she'd throw it in his face. His gaze snagged on the videographer filming the crowd. Maybe not in front of the cameras.

Stoyan took his place on his right. Bale handed him Hugh's sword, and Stoyan held it in front of him, point down. A long-standing tradition among the Iron Dogs, established by Voron, Roland's previous Warlord, who'd begun the order. Another void bite. Voron who had raised him.

The ghost stared at him from his memories.

I killed you because Roland willed it.

Hugh forced the memories down, concentrating on the weapon to keep them at bay. He missed his old sword, but the one Stoyan was holding for him now wasn't bad. Thirty-three and three quarters of an inch-long blade with a simple cross guard and a four-and-a-half-inch grip wrapped with cord. At two and a half pounds, it was meant to be used from horseback, but it was lively enough for him until he found something better.

He glanced over at Elara's side. Johanna stood in the Maid of Honor spot in a pastel-pink gown, holding a bouquet of pretty white flowers. She smiled at him and gave him a little wave with her free hand.

He shrugged.

Johanna tucked the bouquet under her arm. Her fingers moved. *"Scared?"*

He mimicked laughing.

The flaps of the tent opened. Music came from the speakers. It sounded vaguely familiar, but it wasn't the wedding march he'd expected. Hugh frowned. He'd heard it before...

Walking in My Shoes by Depeche Mode.

Lamar smiled.

"Your idea?" Hugh asked.

"It was a joint effort between me and Dugas. You said to pick something appropriate."

Elara stepped out.

She wore a simple white gown that hugged her waist and cradled her breasts before flaring down into a wide skirt. Her white hair fell on her shoulders in loose waves. A silver circlet studded with shiny stones rode on her head.

He saw her face.

Wow.

Elara glided down the aisle, feminine and graceful. Regal. She walked alone, and he realized the significance of it. She was giving herself away of her own free will. There was no father. Nobody had the right to walk her down the aisle.

Every gaze followed her. As she moved between his people and hers, the unease vanished from the Dogs. They watched her the way they would watch a clear sunrise after a night storm. Elara smiled at them, and they smiled back.

That's why her people followed her, Hugh realized. This was it, right here.

She walked up to the altar, beautiful like a vision. He was marrying a queen from a fairy tale.

Hugh held his hand out to her. She put her fingers into his and together they walked up three steps to the altar. She smiled at him, and something in his chest moved.

He had to break the illusion, so he made his mouth work. "Nobody to walk you down the aisle?"

Elara didn't look at him, her eyes fixed on the pastor. "I don't need anyone to give me away."

He needed more. She was still too beautiful, too regal, too much.

"Aren't you supposed to have some little kids running around throwing flowers? Or did you sacrifice them on the way?"

Her face jerked. "Yes, I did. And I devoured their souls."

There she was. "Good to know. The photographer is snapping pictures. Say cheese, love."

Elara gave him a brilliant happy smile. "Cheese, dickhead."

He did his best to look the way a groom might if he was actually marrying this creature and imagining getting her out of that gown tonight. "Rabid harpy."

"Bastard."

The pastor, a man in his thirties with dark hair and glasses, stared at them, his mouth slack.

"Start the ceremony," Hugh told him, putting some menace into his voice.

"Before we kill each other," Elara said.

The pastor cleared his throat. "Dearly beloved…"

Elara turned to Hugh, her face glowing with happiness. If he didn't know better, he would've thought it was real.

"…in matrimony commended to be honorable…"

Hugh reached deep, looked back at her with the same affection and saw a flicker of doubt in her eyes. Ha.

"...these two people decided to live their lives as one."

Perish the thought, he mouthed.

Shut up, she mouthed back with that same dazzling smile.

"If any person knows of a just reason why these two should not be joined together, speak now or forever hold your peace."

Silence. Good. Perhaps he would get through this without killing anyone.

"Hugh d'Ambray, do you, with your friends and family as witnesses, present yourself willingly and of your own accord to be joined in marriage?"

"I do."

"Elara Harper, do you, with your friends and family as witnesses, present yourself willingly and of your own accord to be joined in marriage?"

There was the tiniest pause, then she said, "I do."

"Hugh, repeat after me. I, Hugh d'Ambray, take you, Elara, to be my lawfully wedded wife. I promise to stay by your side in sickness and in health, in joy and in sorrow. I promise to love you, comfort you, and cherish you above all others."

He repeated the words, infusing them with the same sincerity that let him convince people again and again to trust him despite their best judgement.

"With this ring, I give you my heart. From this day forward you will no longer walk alone. I will be your shelter in the storm of life."

She held out her hand, and he slipped the ring on her finger. Her eyes widened. *That's right.* Surprise was good. She was off balance now.

"Elara, repeat after me..."

He heard her swear to love him. Then he held his hand out and she slid a ring on his finger, a white band with a braid of black and silver running along its length. It suited him. She'd thought about him too. For some odd reason, he liked that.

"I now pronounce you husband and wife. You may kiss."

Hugh stepped toward her. "Try to make this look good."

"I'll do my best not to vomit in your mouth."

Is that so? Okay. He wrapped his hand around the back of her head, feeling the silky strands of her hair slip through his fingers, leaned forward, and kissed her. She gasped a little into his mouth, and he kissed her the way he would kiss a woman he was trying to seduce, enticing, promising, claiming her. She tasted fresh and sweet. What do you know? He had expected poison and ash.

People cheered. Elara dug her fingernails into his arm. He nipped her lip on the way out and let her go.

She looked like she would claw him bloody.

He turned toward the crowd, his hand in hers, grinned and waved. She turned with him, smiling like today was the happiest day of her life, and waved. He had to give it to her. The woman could control herself.

Magic flooded them as a magic wave hit. His breath caught in his throat, then power came pouring in.

A woman caught his eye. She stood completely still in the middle of the reception area, away from the crowd. Middle-aged, dishwater blond hair.

He heard the sharp intake of Elara's breath.

The woman raised a knife with both hands and buried it in her own stomach, twisting the blade. Magic exploded in the middle of the reception area. Hugh couldn't see it, but he felt the blast. He grabbed his sword out of Stoyan's hand. By the time the blast of magic flared into a churning knot of darkness, Hugh was already moving.

The crowd surged in the opposite direction. Elara's people grabbed the children and fled to the back, to the altar. He didn't need to look to know that behind him the Dogs were breaking into a charge.

The darkness split. A beast spilled out. It towered above the reception, thirty feet tall, a hairy thing of long matted fur, hide, and bone. It hunched over on all fours, its limbs disproportionate and long, almost level with its head as it squatted. Its long skull ended in horse-like jaws holding a forest of crooked fangs. Above the teeth, two small black eyes stared at the world, and above them the fur flared into a dark mane between two wildebeest horns. The stench washed over Hugh, the sour acidic reek of rotting manure. A *tikbalang*. Not the modern shapeshifter version but the primordial ancient creature from Philippine nightmares.

The *tikbalang*'s magic drenched Hugh. It wasn't his own brand of power, or Roland's orderly manipulation. This was foul and wild, a sucker punch to the lizard brain. Witch magic gone corrupt.

The *tikbalang* screamed. Eight smaller versions of the beast popped into existence around it, each the size of a small sedan. They saw the fleeing crowd and gave chase.

The first leaped over the table toward Hugh. The wedding cake exploded, and the dark body hurtled toward him. He side-stepped and swung, putting the entire power of his momentum and weight into the swing. The sword cleaved through the *tikbalang*'s neck. The beast's head rolled off. Thick red blood gushed from the stump in a torrent, as if the creature were a canteen filled with it. The stench turned his stomach.

Hugh vaulted over the table. Another beast sprinted at him from the side. He sidestepped and carved a gash across the creature's shoulder as it tore past.

The Dogs charged past him, aiming at the bigger beast.

His smaller *tikbalang* whipped around and bore down on him. Hugh dodged and sliced a gash across its right legs, severing the tendons.

The massive beast screeched again and slapped a body in black. A woman flew past Hugh. Gina. He snapped his magic, healing her broken ribs before she landed, dodged again, spinning, and buried his blade between the beast's ribs. He felt the brief resistance as the sword slid into the tough muscle of the creature's heart, then the muscle released, and he jerked his sword free. Blood splashed him. The tikbalang fell at his feet with a moan.

All around Hugh battle raged. The training kicked in, the way it always did, and the battlefield turned crystal clear. He saw them all, his mind cataloging where every one of his people was on the field.

The Dogs had broken into teams, covering the six remaining beasts. At the far right, Bale was beating one to a pulp with his mace, while his team stabbed it. On the left, Barkowsky clapped his hands together and shot lightning at another creature, while Beth, one of Elara's women, circled it, a bloody katana in her hand. On the edge, Savannah stood, her hands raised, chanting something under her breath. Thick vines had sprung from the ground under her feet and wound around the nearest beast, keeping it still as his Dogs hacked at it. Stoyan and about thirty Iron Dogs were attacking the largest creature. It bled, drenching the grass, but it didn't slow down. It was too big and not easily panicked. They couldn't take it down with one blow, so they would cut it to pieces, methodically and carefully, until it bled out.

Hugh ran at the giant, snapping magic around the field to spot-heal those nearest to him.

The Dogs sliced and ducked, darting close to the beast to land cuts to the legs and arms, and running away. The tikbalang raked the ground with its claws, trying to grab them.

Hugh got there just as the massive monster went in for another pass. The Dogs scattered out of the way. To his left, Sam slipped on the blood. Clawed fingers closed over him. This required precision. Hugh lunged at the hand and sliced at the rough flesh of the furry forearm. The hand fell open, clawed fingers limp. He'd severed the flexors.

The tikbalang screeched.

Sam landed on the ground. Hugh grabbed him by the shoulder and shoved him backward, out of the way.

The tikbalang backhanded him. Hugh flew, tucking himself into a ball, and hit the grass. The impact rattled his ribs. Blood from the puddle on the grass splashed on his face. Hugh rolled to his feet.

Four of the remaining six creatures were dead. The reception lawn was a hellish mess of blood and corpses, and when he saw the figure in the white dress, it almost didn't register. Elara was walking toward the tikbalang. Blood, bright, alarming crimson, drenched the hem of her bridal gown, climbing up the white fabric as it soaked through.

Hugh sprinted to her.

She walked between his people and stopped in front of the massive beast.

The tikbalang dove at her, jaws open.

Magic snapped out of Elara, lashing Hugh's senses, a focused torrent unlike anything he'd felt before.

The beast tried to abort its attack, but it was too late. Her power touched it. The colossal creature reared, as if hit, swayed, and collapsed on its side, motionless. The two remaining tikbalang dropped dead.

Hugh halted in front of her. Elara turned, her face unreadable, picked up her blood-soaked skirt with her right hand, and waded through the gore out of the battlefield to her tent.

Silence reigned.

Elara ducked into her tent. All around them Elara's people were staring at the carnage. He saw pain on some of the faces, fear, sadness. He didn't see surprise.

"Start the cleanup," Hugh ordered. "Keep whatever we can scavenge from the beast, take blood and tissue samples, burn the solid remains, salt the blood, and hose this mess down. And get us another damn cake. We'll have the reception at the castle."

His voice snapped them out of their inaction, and by the time he reached the tent, everyone was moving.

Hugh walked inside. The tent stood empty. A red-stained

gown lay on the ground. He caught a hint of movement behind a screen to his right and crossed over to it.

"Were your people hurt?" Elara asked from behind the screen.

"Nothing that can't be fixed. Want to tell me about this?"

"What do you want to know?" She sounded tired.

"Who did this, why, and will it happen again."

"The Remaining. They think it's a real marriage."

"And?"

"They're afraid I might have a child." She gave a short, bitter laugh. "They will do everything they can to stop it. So, yes, it will happen again, and when it does, I'll handle it. We both have baggage. You have Nez and I have them."

Elara fell silent. Hugh stood by the screen, feeling something he couldn't quite identify. A new troublesome feeling that pulled on him. He felt an urge to fix things somehow, and it irritated him that he couldn't. He looked at her bloody dress and that irritated him even more.

A few years ago, he would've enjoyed the fight. Something fun to break up a boring ceremony. Right now, he would be celebrating a win, halfway into his first drink with a girl on his lap. Instead he was standing here, feeling whatever the hell he was feeling.

The void carved a path through his bones.

"It was a nice wedding."

"Was it?" she asked quietly.

"It was."

He walked out of the tent. She was a fucking harpy, but she just married a man she hated and had to walk through blood and kill instead of cutting the cake at her reception. She needed a few moments of privacy, and he would give them to her. Even he wasn't that much of a bastard.

5

Something was wrong with the forest, Hugh decided. Magic sped up the tree growth. That was an accepted fact. Five-year-old growth looked like twenty-year-old trees. The woods swallowed any abandoned property, and people in the forest towns spent a fair amount of their time trying to keep the wilderness from encroaching. But this place was something else.

An ancient wood spread on both sides of the path. Massive white oaks with trunks that would take three people to encircle. Hemlocks towering a hundred and thirty feet above the forest floor. Rhododendron and mountain laurel so thick, he would need to chop it down to get through. This forest felt old and rugged, soaked in the deep currents of magic.

Life thrived between the branches. Squirrels dashed through the canopy, birds sang, and quick feral cats slithered through the brush. Here and there a pair of glowing eyes blinked at them from the shadows as their party rode through what once was a two-lane rural road and now was little more than a few feet of asphalt, just wide enough for the horses and the truck to pass through.

The dual engine truck burned gasoline during tech and enchanted water during magic. Like all enchanted engines, it made enough noise to wake the dead and their top speed would be about forty-five miles per hour, but faced with dragging the salvage back by hand, Hugh had decided not to look a gift truck in the mouth. The sluggish vehicle lagged about two hundred yards behind them with the main body of his party, but its distant roar didn't travel far. The forest smothered it, as if offended by the noise.

Bucky loved the woods. The stallion kept trying to bounce and prance, his tail straight up in the air. Hugh held him in check. He didn't feel like prancing.

Yesterday, after the wedding, instead of getting drunk and celebrating, he'd walked through the second reception site, which Elara's people quickly set up inside the castle walls, reassuring, healing those who needed it, and expecting another attack. Elara had made an appearance, in a clean dress and her hair still perfect as if nothing had happened, and did the same, moving through the reception area, smiling and asking people about their children. They passed each other like two ships in the night, uniting briefly to cut the second cake, a carbon copy of the first one, which confirmed what he had already suspected. The Departed had expected trouble.

The void crept closer with the evening, and by the time the subdued celebration finally died down and Bale found him wanting to get drunk and celebrate, it was gnawing on him with sharp icy teeth. Hugh knew that the moment booze touched his lips and he felt fire and night roll down his throat, he wouldn't stop. The lure of a numb stupor, where the void was a distant memory, was too strong. But Hugh had to stay sharp, so he told Bale no. He went to bed alone. Vanessa was still sulking, and he didn't care enough to look for her. Seven hours later, at sunrise, he was on horseback and out the gates. There would be no moat without the salvage.

Ahead, the two guides Elara sent with him halted their horses. Hugh rode up, Sam at his heels. He would've preferred just one guide, Darin, the one barely in his twenties and obviously starstruck at being invited to lead twenty Dogs into the wilderness. It wouldn't have taken much convincing to get Darin to spill Elara's secrets, which was probably why his lovely wife saddled him with Conrad, who was in his fifties and had that unflappable quality farmers and older tradesmen got with age. He would be a tougher nut to crack.

"See him?" Conrad asked quietly.

Hugh scanned the forest. A few yards away, from the side of a fallen chestnut, a big shaggy wolf stared back at him. It was the size of a pony, gray, with golden eyes that caught the light, glowing softly with magic. A dire wolf.

The wolf turned and stalked off into the woods, melting into the green shadows.

"Pretty boy," Conrad murmured.

"Do they come close to the castle?" Hugh asked.

Darin nodded his dark head. "The woods are full of them. We've got three packs by the last count."

Three packs of dire wolves meant there was plenty of prey for them to hunt. "Any other predators or game?"

"There are all sorts in the woods," Conrad said. "Bears, cougars. Things."

"We've got stags," Darin jumped in. "Seven feet tall, with really big horns. Looks like there is a whole tree on their heads. And hippogriffs. We've got hippogriffs."

Better and better. Hippogriffs only hunted in old-growth woods.

"We should be going," Conrad said. "It's not far now."

Hugh shifted his weight, and Bucky danced forward. Hugh let him prance for a few steps and then reined him in.

"Tell me about this place we're going to," he said.

"Old Market," Conrad answered. "About five hundred people lived there before the Shift. Not much there: a grocery store, a post office, a gas station. Your typical one-street-light, one-church town. It was a bit of a hub for the country people in the area, so they did have a decent hardware and county store, which is where we're going. Should be some good salvage there."

"When did it go dark?" Hugh asked.

"About fifteen years ago." Conrad grimaced. "The flare came and the woods just blew up. Things came out of them that nobody ever saw before. That's when a lot of small towns around here died. People left for the cities. Safety in numbers and all that."

"What about the castle?" Sam asked. "When was that built?"

"That was pre-Shift. A guy called Mitch Bradford built it for Becky Bradford, his wife. His second wife." Conrad paused for dramatic effect. "Bradford made his fortune in bourbon and then branched out to international trade. He called Becky his princess, and Becky liked castles, so he went and got one for her from the Old Country somewhere. After the Shift, his company didn't do so well. Then there were some natural disasters. Fire in the left wing, bad plumbing, that type of thing. By the time we got here three years ago, his son practically begged everyone he knew to take the castle off his hands. It needed a lot of repairs, but we fixed the drafty old thing. It's home."

"Where was home before this?"

"Oh, we lived in all sorts of places," Darin said.

"Why did you leave to come here?" Hugh asked, glancing at Darin.

"Because of the Remaining," Darin said. "They—"

"Darin, why don't you go on and scout ahead," Conrad said. "Make sure we don't run into anything."

Darin clicked his mouth shut and rode on.

Conrad turned to Hugh. "I know what you're doing. If the Lady wanted you to know, she'd tell you. Leave the boy alone."

Hugh considered stringing Conrad up by his ankles. An hour or so with the blood pooling to his head, and the older scout would sing a beautiful song filled with all his secrets. Hugh was still deciding if he was going to do it, when Darin came riding back around the bend.

"A fort!" he reported. "Looks empty."

Hugh looked at Sam and nodded at the column behind them. "Get Sharif."

The kid turned his horse and rode back. Half a minute later, Sharif came riding up from the back. The lean dark-haired scout had been covering the rear. Sam followed him.

Hugh touched the reins, and they rode on. The path turned. A wooden palisade rose to one side of the road, a ring of sharpened tree trunks ten feet high. A crude guard tower stood on the right, just inside the palisade walls, overlooking the road. A bell hung from its ceiling. The gate of the palisade stood wide open. The road curved to the left, widening into what used to be Main Street. An old pre-Shift two-story house crouched on one side, a trailer on the other, both mostly eaten by the forest. He could just make out the sharp point of a church steeple in the distance between the new trees.

The palisade lay silent. No sentries. No movement.

Hugh glanced at Conrad.

"This is new," the older scout said. "Wasn't here nine months ago."

Sharif dismounted. Light rolled over his dark irises and flashed green. He inhaled deeply, crouched and sniffed the road.

"Nobody's home," he said quietly.

Hugh dismounted and fixed Conrad with his stare. "Stay here with the boy."

If something happened to those two idiots, Elara would screech at him for days.

Hugh walked inside the gates. Three large log houses waited inside, two to the left and one to the right. In the back, an animal pen stood empty. The wind brought a hint of carrion.

"The road smells odd," Sharif said quietly.

"Human, animal?"

"Odd. Nothing I've smelled before." He held out his arm. The hairs on it stood straight up. "I don't like it."

Shapeshifters had a freakishly strong scent memory, and among all of the shapeshifters, werewolves were the best. They had no problem taking a whiff of blood and sorting through a couple of thousand scent signatures to identify a guy they'd shared a drink with once two years ago. Sharif had been with him for five years. If he hadn't smelled it before, it had to be one hell of a rare creature or something new.

New. Hugh smiled. "Well, that's interesting, isn't it?"

Sharif rolled his eyes for half a second before schooling his features into a perfectly neutral expression.

Hugh turned to the nearest house, walked up the wooden stairs onto the porch and touched the door. It swung open under the pressure of his fingertips. A simple open floor plan with the kitchen and dining area to the far left and the living room space to his right. Dinner was laid out on the table. He moved across the floor on silent feet to the table. The reek of rotten food made him grimace. Fuzzy blue mold blossomed on the abandoned food. Looked like pulled meat of some sort with mashed potatoes on the side and a serving of formerly green vegetables. A fork lay by the nearest plate, its tines covered with mold.

He crouched and looked under the table. A broken plate.

Sam was hovering nearby. Hugh pointed at the plate. "Thoughts?"

"It happened in the middle of dinner?"

Hugh nodded. "There is a walkway built along the palisade and a tower. What was under it?"

Sam blinked.

"Go look."

The kid took off.

Sharif crossed his arms. "I don't like it."

"I heard you the first time."

Sam came back. "A broken plate."

88

"What does that tell you?"

"There was a guard on duty. They brought him dinner."

"And?"

"Something killed him so fast, he couldn't raise the alarm." Sam paused. "Was he shot?"

"No blood spatter," Sharif said. "But there is this." He slid his finger down the wooden frame. Four long bloody scratches gouged the wood.

"And this." He crouched and pointed to the floor.

A bloody human nail.

Sam's face turned pale. "Something dragged them out of here."

Hugh pivoted to his right. A row of guns and swords on the wall, just by the door. It would take him less than a second to cover the distance from the table to the wall. "Something smart and fast."

"Vampires?" Sam asked.

"It's possible."

"I don't smell the undead," Sharif said.

"But you do smell something. If Nez has resorted to snatching people from isolated communities, he wouldn't use the regular bloodsuckers to do it." Hugh straightened.

"But why?" Sharif asked.

"That's a good question."

Vampirism came about as the result of infection by the *Vampirus Immortuus* Pathogen. The pathogen killed its human host and reanimated it after death. Because every loose vampire would slaughter anything it could get its claws on, to an average human, the idea of vampires was terrifying. But to Roland, the undead were an effective tool. He'd made his first one accidentally, thousands of years ago, and he found them exceedingly useful. He wanted to seed his Masters of the Dead into every major city. They were his spies and his secret arsenal.

To accomplish this goal, Roland had to position the People as an operation with a flawless record, beneficial to the community.

They presented themselves as a research institution with a focus in undeath, financed by casinos and other similar venues, and they offered a valuable service. They removed and neutralized any undead reported to them free of charge, and they offered the dying a chance to guarantee a payout to their families. If you were terminally ill and chose to donate your body for voluntary infection by the *Vampirus Immortuus* pathogen, the People would deposit a substantial sum into the account of your choice. The People acted like academics, dressed like high-priced lawyers, and treated the general public with utmost courtesy, and it worked. The general public happily forgot that each Master of the Dead, armed with just one vampire, could wipe out ten city blocks in less than an hour.

It was one of Roland's greatest cons. He would go to any lengths to preserve it. If said general public suspected that the Masters of the Dead had begun grabbing warm bodies to turn into vampires, people would panic, and the entire carefully constructed network of the People's offices would collapse. Roland would be livid, and the guilty would be dead before they had a chance to repent their sins.

But the pattern did fit the navigators. A fast, stealthy surgical strike.

What are you planning, Nez? Is this you? Is this someone else?

Hugh needed more data. He headed for the door.

"Are there irregular bloodsuckers?" Sam asked behind him.

"You have no idea," Sharif told him.

The other two houses showed the same pattern. In the animal pen bones and chunks of rotting hide and fur told the story of a goat massacre.

"A cougar," Sharif said. "Came back more than once. Scaled the wall here and here."

The invaders hadn't been interested in livestock. Only in people.

Hugh walked out of the palisade. His convoy had arrived and waited on the road.

"Williams and Cordova, go through the houses. Do not touch the guns or any valuables. IDs only. Copy them and put them back."

The two Dogs who were his best artists peeled off and ran into the palisade.

"We get our salvage and we haul ass out of here. The less time we spend here, the better."

The Dogs moved. Hugh turned to Conrad. "From now on, nobody goes out alone, and nobody goes more than a mile into the woods without an escort. Pass it on."

Conrad swallowed and nodded.

Hugh glanced at the palisade one last time and followed the convoy into the Old Market. This was, indeed, proving interesting.

———⊹——

SOMETIMES KILLING a man wasn't an act of anger or punishment. It was a public service. One she would be glad to perform, Elara reflected as State Senator Victor Skolnik marched through the gates of Baile. Lean, about an inch or two above six feet, Victor Skolnik endeavored to personify his job: dark hair in that neither-too-long-nor-too-short, I'm-running-for-office cut, clean jaw, slightly droopy gray eyes, and a forced too-wide smile.

She knew entirely too much about the man. He was forty-eight years old, married, with two children. He made his money in real estate, prided himself on running marathons, and wore his piety on his sleeve. He'd also made a deal with Landon Nez. She didn't know the particulars of the deal, but it involved running them off their land, so Nez could have it.

Skolnik had spent the last six months whipping up the congregations of Sanderville's and Aberdine's largest churches and lathering up spit, trying to turn the tide of public opinion against them and sever their trade agreements. He didn't make much headway. Both Sanderville and Aberdine came to rely on their milk, cheese and beer, and especially on their medicines. Oh, they didn't like her or her people, but they weren't quite ready to storm the castle with pitchforks.

Thwarted, Skolnik went after the sale of Baile itself, trying to challenge its legality. The previous owner of the castle had left the state a long time ago and refused to come back from California to participate in Skolnik's scheme.

Now the senator resorted to open harassment and had been getting more and more bold, trying to provoke her. The moment Elara used her magic, he would run back to the churches with horror stories, and then public opinion would turn against them.

She'd just come out of the side tower when he showed up. Normally she would've come down the ten stone steps to greet a visitor, but right now she was a good eight feet higher than he was and that was how she liked it.

"Good afternoon, Senator," Elara said.

He saw her and turned toward her, plastering his fake smile on his lips. From her vantage point, she could see the entire yard. As he walked toward her, Hugh's people fanned out around him. Stoyan, Hugh's second-in-command, casually wandered on a course that would put him in Skolnik's way just as he reached the stairs.

Everyone in the yard stopped what they were doing and came closer, instinctively uniting against the common enemy.

Stoyan got to the stairs first and stopped two feet away, a pleasant smile on his boyish face. Skolnik eyed him and halted.

"Good afternoon," Skolnik said.

"What can I do for you, Senator?"

"I heard you got married. Congratulations."

"Thank you."

Skolnik glanced around. "So, is your husband around? I'd like to meet the man."

"He's out," Elara said. "Can I help you with anything?"

"You can reconsider my proposal." Skolnik raised his chin.

"Thank you, Senator, but the castle isn't for sale."

"I guess I'll have to talk to your man about that then. I'm sure he will see reason."

Yeah, let me tell you about his moat... "As I said, he's out."

Skolnik looked around, raising his voice in a practiced pitch as if giving a speech before an adoring crowd. "You do realize that if the castle is sold, all of you stand to make a great deal of money."

This was the same speech he gave the last time he came here. Alarm pinched her. He was up to something.

"Enough to make sure you are all set for life."

Yes, the exact same speech.

"You can set up a settlement anywhere..."

"The castle isn't for sale," Elara said, sinking ice into her words.

"If your leaders are too short-sighted to understand, you have to use your head and think for yourself."

The alarm blossomed into full-blown dread. Something bad was about to happen. Elara took a step down the stairs. She needed to get him out of the castle now.

D'Ambray rode through the gates on his enormous horse, a spot of darkness in his black uniform. One of the Dogs ran up to him and said something quietly.

D'Ambray turned Bucky toward her and grinned, a huge infectious smile. She almost smiled back, raising her hand to wave.

What the hell am I doing?

Elara snatched her hand back. How did he do that? How was it that this vicious sonovabitch of a man could smile like that and look as if he were the world's best hope? Hugh grinned and everyone around him wanted to be the one to make him happy.

D'Ambray took a lungful of air and roared. "Honey, I'm home!"

Skolnik turned to look. The stallion bore down at him and the senator took an involuntary step back. D'Ambray dismounted, ran up the steps, and pulled her to him, clamping her against his hard chest. "Give us a kiss."

She would murder him. He showed no signs of letting her go, so Elara brushed his lips with hers as quickly as she could.

D'Ambray was gazing at her adoringly. "Did you miss me?"

"Counted the moments since you were gone." In joy. She counted them in joy, hoping they would last forever.

D'Ambray finally released her and turned to Skolnik. "Who's our guest?"

"State Senator Victor Skolnik," Elara said.

D'Ambray smiled at Skolnik. His face practically radiated a good-natured "aw shucks" attitude. He looked impressed. "State Senator? Well. How about that? We're moving up in the world. Honey, couldn't you have brought Senator a glass of tea or something?"

What?

Skolnik's eyes lit up. "I do apologize for imposing on your hospitality."

"Don't mention it." D'Ambray walked down the steps. Elara followed him, trying to keep her rage from her face.

"State Senator," Hugh said, clearly impressed. "How many of you guys are in the Senate, what like a hundred from the whole state?"

Skolnik visibly relaxed, the tension seeping from him with every word. "Thirty-eight."

"Wow. Thirty-eight. Say, have you ever met Governor Willis?"

"As a matter of fact, I have." Skolnik nodded. "We had dinner together during the last session."

"Well, how about that, dear?" D'Ambray turned to her.

"Amazing," she said.

"Say, I heard he has a honey of a wife," d'Ambray remarked.

Skolnik grinned at him and leaned closer. "It wouldn't be

proper of me to comment, but yeah, she's a good-looking woman, if you know what I mean."

Hugh laughed and Skolnik smiled.

D'Ambray was pretending to be an idiot and was making her look like an idiot too, in the process. Elara strained to keep from grinding her teeth. Her magic coiled and uncoiled within her, an icy restless fire.

Stoyan had drifted away from them, moving all the way to the opposite castle wall.

"So, what brings you to our neck of the woods?" d'Ambray asked.

"Business."

"A man after my own heart." D'Ambray clamped his hand on Skolnik's shoulder. "There are only two important conversations in this world. The first is the kind that gets you money and the second we won't mention in mixed company."

A big horse grin again. She had an irrational urge to punch him.

"So, what sort of business are we talking about?"

Skolnik opened his mouth.

"On second thought," d'Ambray held up his hand. "I hate to be rude, but there is one small matter I have to take care of before we start, if you don't mind. I'd like to give you my full attention."

"Of course, of course." Skolnik gave him a magnanimous wave.

"Excellent." D'Ambray glanced at Stoyan. The Iron Dog raised his hand and made a come-here motion.

Four Iron Dogs came around the keep, dragging two men between them.

Skolnik froze for a moment. His expression shifted back to affable again, but she saw it, and the brief taste of his alarm was delicious.

The Dogs dragged the two men forward. The left one was taller, with a shaved head and hard eyes, his face pissed off. The one on the right, wiry and blond, wore a blasé expression as if this was just another day and he wasn't being half-carried by two hard cases.

Professionals, she realized. Mercenaries of some sort or private security.

"Caught these two trying to climb over the wall." Stoyan closed in and handed d'Ambray something.

D'Ambray held it up to the sun. A long, thin glass tube sealed with plastic with three pieces of cloth inside dipped in sand-like powder.

D'Ambray squinted at the tube. "Nasty bugger." He held the tube out to her.

She took it and concentrated. Traces of her magic wrapped around the tube. The powder on the cloth shifted in response, crawling across the fabric to pool against the glass. Whatever was inside was alive and hungry.

Her magic touched it.

A living disease, boosted by magic, a disease that would spread like fire and kill within hours. The tiny hairs on the back of her neck rose. She spat the word out. "Cholera."

"Mhm," d'Ambray said. "Our new friends planned to drop a present into our well. What would you say, honey, six hours and everyone in the castle would be dead and the disease vector would jump to the settlement, then to the lake? Or do you think it would be more like eight?"

She was too focused to answer, wrapping her magic around the vial, containing it.

The two mercenaries stared at him, the first still angry, the second still bored.

She finished the cocoon of magic and called, "Emily! Get Malcom and Gloria!"

Emily took off at a run.

Elara held the vial gently. They would have to dispose of this thing properly, with a lot of acid and fire.

Her gaze fell on Skolnik. It had to be him. He knew that once he walked in, everyone in the castle would gather around him, because he was a threat. While they were watching him, the two mercenaries would scale the wall and infect the well.

The fingers of her free hand curled like claws.

D'Ambray faced the two men, still smiling.

"Just get on with it," the shorter of the men said.

"Good attitude." D'Ambray pulled a knife out. It was a wicked blade, razor-sharp and thirteen inches long, with a tapered, slightly curved tip. The metal caught the sun and shone in Hugh's hand. "Let him go and give the man a knife, for goodness sake."

The two Dogs released the mercenary and took a big step back in unison. One of them pulled a black, foot-long blade and threw it. The knife bit into the ground by the mercenary's feet. He grabbed it and grinned, dropping into a fighting stance.

D'Ambray stood motionless, seeming to ponder the shorter man.

Elara clenched her fist. D'Ambray was strong, but he was also large, and in a knife fight strength didn't count and size was a detriment. Knife fighters were quick and small, and the mercenary looked like he'd been born with a blade in his hand. If d'Ambray lost...

If he lost, she would take matters into her own hands, Skolnik or no.

D'Ambray glided forward with predatory grace. His knife flashed, almost too fast to see. The front of the man's dark shirt turned darker. He blinked. The gap widened, and she glimpsed the rosy clumps of intestines through the cut. It was so shocking, it didn't seem real.

D'Ambray slashed again. The mercenary tried to counter, but the knife slid past his defenses, and he howled. Blood poured from where his left ear used to be. D'Ambray paused, frowning, like a painter examining a canvas, holding the knife like a brush. The mercenary charged. D'Ambray sidestepped and sliced off the man's other ear. The mercenary spun away and somehow d'Am-

97

bray was there. A man of that size shouldn't have moved that fast, but he did. The knife flashed again, slicing a gash across the man's cheeks, widening his mouth.

"What the fuck?" the other mercenary cried out.

D'Ambray stepped forward, his movements beautifully liquid. His left hand caught the mercenary's wrist. D'Ambray yanked the man's arm straight, and stabbed into the inside of the elbow, twisting the blade. The man's arm came off in d'Ambray's hand. Blood poured.

He deboned him like a chicken. This isn't happening, this can't possibly be real, it's too horrible to be real...

D'Ambray tossed the forearm aside.

The mercenary fell to his knees, his eyes wide, and toppled over. His intestines fell out in a clump.

The world had turned into a nightmare and she skidded through it, stunned and petrified.

"Look at that," d'Ambray said. His voice froze the blood in her veins. "He's going into shock. This won't do. Not at all."

D'Ambray held his hand out. A current of pale blue magic poured out of him, bathing the man.

The mercenary coughed.

"That's right," d'Ambray said. "Come on back. We're not done yet."

The blood over the stump clotted, sealing it. The mercenary tried to rise.

"Come on. Almost there. Let's get your guts back in."

The intestines slid back into the man's stomach. He stood up, shuddering and gripping his knife with his remaining hand.

"Very nice," d'Ambray said.

The current died.

The mercenary charged, trying to take a swipe at d'Ambray. He sidestepped and slashed across the man's back, stopping just short of the spine. The mercenary turned, ripping his stomach wound open. The innards slipped out again. They were hanging from him like some sort of grotesque garlands. The air reeked of blood and acid.

Elara finally saw the crowd around them, dead silent, her people horrified, the Iron Dogs impassive. Skolnik stared, his face completely bloodless. The other mercenary shook like a leaf, clamped tight by d'Ambray's people.

"Let's do the nose next," d'Ambray said.

"Hugh," she called.

He halted. "Yes, darling?"

"Please stop."

Hugh glanced at the disfigured stump that used to be a man. "My wife wants me to stop. We'll have to cut this short."

The mercenary stumbled toward him. Hugh stepped forward, clasping the man as if in an embrace, and slid the knife between the mercenary's ribs in a smooth precise thrust. The mercenary shuddered, held upright by Hugh's strength. His eyes dulled.

Hugh stepped back, freeing his knife, wiped it on the man's shirt, and let the corpse fall.

Someone in the crowd retched. Nobody moved.

Hugh turned to the other mercenary. The man went limp. A wet stain spread on the front of his pants.

"Bring me a pair of handcuffs and a big plastic bag," Hugh said.

A Dog ran off.

"Hugh," she asked again, hating the begging note in her voice.

"My wife is softhearted," Hugh said. "That's why I love her. You came here to murder my beautiful kind wife and our people. Families. Children."

The mercenary made a small strangled noise.

The Dog returned with handcuffs and a plastic bag.

"Let him go," Hugh ordered.

The Dogs released the mercenary. He fell to his knees. Hugh dropped the bag in front of him. "Pick up your friend."

The man gulped, grabbed pieces of bloody flesh and dropped them into the bag one by one.

"Don't forget the ear over there."

The mercenary crawled on his hands and feet.

Hugh caught her gaze and winked at her. She couldn't even move.

The man picked up the bag and straightened. Only the body remained. "He won't fit," he mumbled with shaking lips.

"That's okay. What you've gathered is good enough. Cuff him."

Two Dogs grabbed the mercenary's arms, forcing his wrists together. A third slapped the cuffs on. Hugh took the bag from the mercenary's hand and hung it around the man's neck.

Hugh took a few steps, circling the mercenary slowly. The man turned in response. Skolnik was directly behind him now. Hugh faced the mercenary, looking past him at the senator.

"You're going to go back to the man who hired you. You're going to give him this bag. You will tell him that if I see him or any of his people around here again, I will ride into his town. I will kill every man who gets in my way. We'll kill his wife, his two beautiful children, his pets, and we'll set his house on fire. We'll hang him from the nearest tree by his arms and then we'll leave. He'll hang there staring at the ashes of his house and begging for help, and the people of his town will pass by him as if he were invisible because they'll know that if anyone helps him, we'll return. Did you get all that?"

The mercenary nodded.

"Good man. Off with you."

The mercenary didn't move.

"Go on." Hugh waved him on. "You're losing daylight."

The mercenary spun and ran for the gates.

"Bury the garbage off somewhere," Hugh said, nodding at the corpse. "And clean the lawn. Fire, salt, the usual." He turned to Skolnik. "Senator? You had a bit of business?"

Skolnik opened his mouth. "Go."

"Sorry?" Hugh tilted his head.

"I have to go. Now." Skolnik started through the crowd. People parted to let him pass. He strode to the gates at a near run.

Hugh watched him until he disappeared. His face turned hard. "I don't believe Senator Skolnik will be visiting us in the future. Alright, show's over. We've got a truck full of metal to unload. Let's go, people. Every hour we don't work is another hour without a moat."

———+——

HUGH LIKED HIGH PLACES, but the price of height was measured in stairs, and today of all days he didn't feel like climbing them. There was no help for it, so he did. By the time all of the metal was unloaded and appraised by the smiths, fatigue had settled into his bones. He needed a shower and quiet.

At least most of the haul had been good. The smiths took everything except for the karaoke machine, which he had the Iron Dogs stash in the barracks. When tech hit, they would find out if it worked.

Hugh conquered the long hallway to his bedroom, pushed the door open, and walked in. He never locked it. There wasn't anything of value in the room. The most expensive item he owned was his sword, and he usually carried it on him.

How the mighty had fallen.

He needed to wash the forest and blood off. He pulled off his boots and tossed them in the corner. His socks followed. The floor felt nice and cool under his feet. Better already.

His jacket followed, then his T-shirt, and his belt. He was about to take off his pants, when the door behind him swung open. He didn't need to turn to look. He recognized the sound of the footsteps. High heels were rare among Elara's crowd.

"Not tonight," he said.

Vanessa slunk into the room. The spectacle in the bailey

must've proved too much for her. She was hot and bothered. He wasn't.

"I said, not tonight."

Vanessa leaned against the wall. She wore a skintight white dress and red shoes. She licked her lips.

"We haven't done it since you got married. Did you give Elara your balls at the wedding?"

He caught the slight tremor in her voice, fear and excitement wrapped in lust. Trying to goad him. He knew exactly what she wanted. She wanted him to grab her by the hair, slam her against the wall, and fuck her. She wanted proof that the man down in the bailey and the man in the bedroom were the same. He was too damn tired, and he had no interest in it.

Hugh turned and looked at her.

She squirmed, then threw her arms out to the side. "What? What?"

Someone knocked on the door. It wasn't an "emergency had occurred" knock. It was brisk and pissed off, which meant Elara.

Well, that didn't take long. From how green she looked after he started on the merc's ears, he thought she'd take the evening off. The hopes of mice and men...

"Not tonight," he called out.

The door flew open. Elara marched in, her jaw set, brimming with rage and magic.

Elara didn't bother looking at Vanessa. "Leave."

Vanessa opened her mouth. Something snapped in her eyes. "No."

Elara swung toward her. The storm within her was straining to break out, and Vanessa had just designated herself as a lightning rod. This ought to be good. Hugh landed in a chair and leaned back, his head resting on the interlocked fingers of his hands. He wished he had a beer.

"I'm not leaving," Vanessa said. "You leave. You're interrupting."

"I don't have time for this," Elara said. "After I'm done, you can come back and entertain the Preceptor all you want. But right now, I need you to go."

Vanessa swung to him. "Tell her I can stay."

"I already told you to leave," he said.

Vanessa pushed from the wall. "I'm staying."

Playing for keeps.

"You're pissed off, because he doesn't want you," Vanessa said.

And now she decided to dig a hole.

"He wants a woman," Vanessa said. "Not an iceberg."

Doubling down.

"I understand why that's upsetting, but I don't really care. He likes me, this is his room, and you're intruding. Go. You're not wanted or needed here."

Hahaha.

Elara regarded Vanessa for a long moment. She reminded him of the black-footed cat he had seen in southern Africa on a long trip to retrieve one of Roland's artifacts. They'd had to search a wide area, and every night, once they came back to camp, he would take the midwatch, and the little black-footed cat would leave her burrow to hunt for food for her two kittens. She would sneak up on the birds and rodents, line her jump, wait, motionless, calculating distance and wind, and spring just at the right moment to break her prey's neck. She was relentless, and she killed with a precision he had never seen in great cats. Now he saw the same calculation in Elara's eyes. She was about to leap into a kill.

"I was going to give you time to correct yourself, but you leave me no choice," Elara said. "First, the Preceptor isn't going to help you. He's here because he's responsible for the welfare of his people, just as I'm responsible for the well-being of mine. We rose to our positions of power, because we have learned how to lead and compromise. We hate each other, but we are both cognizant of the fact that we have to work together for our mutual survival and we both sacrificed a great deal for the sake of this partnership. There is much more at stake here than sexual gratification. In an argument between you and me, the Preceptor will always side with me. I'm the bigger threat. All you can do is withhold sex, while I can divorce him and throw his soldiers out of the castle."

Vanessa narrowed her eyes.

"Before you speak, remember that you are also one of my people. Your welfare is important to me," Elara said. "It's critical to your safety that you understand this: he isn't besotted with you. He is a cold, calculating bastard. Love isn't in his vocabulary. You don't hold any power over him and if you annoy him enough, he will replace you with a different warm body. You must never gamble your safety on his attachment to you. There isn't one."

Vanessa turned to him.

"She's right," Hugh said. "I told you this when we started."

Vanessa opened her mouth.

"I'm not done," Elara said, her voice cold. "According to your performance evaluation and the testimony of your coworkers, you are laboring under the mistaken impression that having sex with the Preceptor excuses you from your duties. As of last night, you have a nine-day backlog. You speak down to your colleagues, you imply that you are better than them, and you argue with your supervisor. One of your colleagues described your behavior as toxic."

"I do my work!"

"Should I ask Melissa to come up here and give you a detailed breakdown of the assignments you failed to complete?" Elara asked.

"She's lying."

Elara grimaced. "Please. Don't waste time, Vanessa. You've decided that you are better than your current position and you've made everyone around you aware of it. In this community, your position is based on merit, not your choice of bed partners.

Having a relationship with the Preceptor doesn't entitle you to any additional benefits. You don't get hazard pay."

Hazard pay?

"You have one week to catch up on your assignments. You won't be paid until your backlog is cleared."

Vanessa opened her mouth.

"You will apologize to your colleagues and to Melissa for your conduct," Elara continued.

"I won't," Vanessa snarled.

Elara's face was merciless. "If you no longer want to be employed as a paralegal, you are free to look for a different job. You know our rule: if you don't contribute to the best of your ability, you receive no support. If you don't like it, you know where the gates are."

An angry red flush heated Vanessa's face. For a moment he thought Vanessa would charge her. Instead, she spun on her heels and tore out of the room. The door slammed closed behind her.

Elara glanced at him. "Any idea what brought this on?"

"She thinks the balance of power shifted in my favor," he said. "Now, what the hell was so bloody important?"

"You found an abandoned palisade."

He got up, poured a glass of water from the pitcher on the table, and drank. He missed the wine, not the alcohol, but the taste.

He realized she was waiting for him to answer. "Yes."

"Were you planning on telling me?"

"No."

"What do you mean, no?"

Something peeked out from inside her. Something cold and lethal, a power coursing through her. Her hair was down again, and it floated about her like a silver curtain. Her blue dress was cut wide, leaving her delicate neck exposed.

"It doesn't concern you."

"It does concern me."

"It's a matter of safety. There is no immediate threat. If there was one, I would tell you about it."

"We have to report it."

He frowned. "Report it to who?"

"The sheriffs. The county."

"No." The harpy was insane.

She turned, pacing back and forth. "You're not listening to me. Something weird happened in the woods on the border of our land. If we don't report it, we will be blamed."

He crossed his arms. "Who will blame us?"

"The authorities."

She was really wound up tight. It was kind of amusing. He decided to stab and see what happened.

"Is this paranoia recent or is this something you've had for a while?"

Elara stopped in midstep and spun toward him, the long skirt of her dress flaring.

"We are always blamed. I'm speaking from experience. Whenever anything weird happens, they come after us."

"'They' won't find out."

Elara missed the sarcasm in his emphasis. "They will. They always do. We have to report it. You should've sent someone to report it the moment you found it."

"Do you trust your people?"

"What?" She tilted her head, giving him a look at the fine line of her jaw all the way to her neck. He wondered what she looked like under the dress.

"Do your people report to the authorities on a regular basis, because I have to tell you, I wouldn't tolerate that if I were you."

"Hugh! You can't possibly be this dense. No, my people don't talk to outsiders."

She'd used his name. Well, well. "Mine don't either. So, who's going to tell?"

"It will get out. It always does. Someone will come to check on them—"

"To check on three families of separatists living alone in the middle of the forest?"

Elara halted. "Separatists still trade, Hugh. They still need supplies."

"Try to get it through your thick skull: they abandoned society, built a palisade in the middle of a dangerous forest, and got killed. It happens all the damn time and nobody ever makes any effort to investigate."

"According to your own people, this time is different. You don't even know what killed them."

Hugh felt irritation rise. "I would know if I had access to a forensic mage. How is it that in all of your settlement there is not a single mage?"

Elara crossed her arms on her chest. "We have no need for mages. We have plenty of magic users who can do everything a mage can do but better."

"So why don't you take some of those fabled magic users and analyze the scene?"

"So when the forensic team does arrive from the sheriff's office, they'll find an empty settlement and our magic signature all over it? Brilliant. Why didn't I think of that?"

"Leave this alone. If you stir that pot, your pal Skolnik will run back here with torches and pitchforks. Is that what you want?"

Elara narrowed her eyes. "You know what, never mind. I'll take care of this."

Hugh's irritation boiled over into full-blown fury. His voice turned to ice. "You won't."

"Yes, I will."

"I forbid it."

"Good that I don't need your permission."

"Yes, you do."

"Says who?"

"Says the contract we both signed. Or did you forget the part where I asked for autonomy on the safety-related decisions and you put in the provision that all of them have to be jointly approved by you and me? It cuts both ways, sweetheart."

Her magic boiled just under her skin. Her eyes blazed. *Didn't like that, did you?*

"Do it," he dared. "Breach the contract. Give me an excuse for free rein."

Elara's hands curled into fists. Her cheeks flushed. She was so mad.

God, sex right now would be amazing. He would throw her on the bed and she would scream and kick and lash him with her magic. It would be fucking hot.

"I hate you," she ground out.

"Right back at you, darling." Hugh kissed the air.

Her face jerked. An ethereal growl rolled through the room, an echo of a distant snarl. Elara spun and within her he almost saw something else, hidden within silvery translucent veils of magic. She swept out of the room. The door slammed behind her, shaking the heavy wooden doorway.

Twice in one night. He'd have to replace the door if this continued.

Hugh poured himself another cup of water. For a few seconds, while she'd been in the room screaming at him, he'd felt alive. He lost it again and he could already feel the void drawing closer, but he'd tasted freedom in those fleeting moments and he wanted more.

———✦———

ELARA PACED IN HER ROOM. Traces of her magic slipped out of her, trailing her body. The gentle glow of custom fey lanterns bathed the room in a soothing buttery-yellow glow, but her temper needed a hell of a lot more than some ambient light to soothe itself.

That asshole.

That fucking bastard.

When she'd insisted on the joint decision provision, she was thinking of limiting his reach. At the time, it seemed like a perfectly reasonable choice.

Elara closed her eyes and whispered, projecting her voice. **"Savannah."**

The echo of her power flew through the castle, finding its target. Savannah was on her way.

Elara wanted to march back into Hugh's bedroom and crush him with her power until he groveled. To wipe that smug grin off his face.

She stopped and took a deep breath. Her magic swirled out and Hugh stood in her room, exactly as she remembered him, a perfect copy of the man, just slightly transparent when she looked at a fey lantern through him.

She circled him, examining the broad powerful shoulders, the sculpted arms, the flat stomach, the tree trunk legs... Built to crush all opposition. The man emanated a predatory confidence. If he said he would kill something, it would die. She was sure of it now.

A trail of faint scars marked his chest, no more than light lines across his left pectoral, over the heart, ribs, and side. She'd felt him heal his people. He had to be able to heal himself, or he would have a lot more scars.

What sort of damage was severe enough to resist his healing?

Food for thought.

Shapeshifters sometimes radiated a predatory power too. Theirs came from the natural sleekness of their lines, from the way they held themselves, ready to burst into action, never one hundred percent comfortable in either of their skins, always expecting an attack. Hugh had a different flavor. The shapeshifters were born into their power; he achieved his. His body was trained and honed, and the arrogance came from experience.

She looked into his blue eyes. There was something else there, in the eyes. A bone-deep weariness as if something gnawed on him, and no matter what happened, life hadn't fully reached him. She'd seen that same look in him when he carved the mercenary apart. There was no anger, no satisfaction. Just methodical precision. He'd decided it had to be done, so he did it.

It would be so much easier if he was an idiot, but no. D'Ambray was sharp and manipulative. She couldn't trust a single word coming out of his mouth. He would pretend to be a man's best friend, then stab him in the back and keep moving. He said one thing, did another, and thought only he knew what. She had no idea where he actually stood on anything.

And yet they clashed against each other like fire and ice. He hadn't bothered to manipulate her. Why? Did he think she wasn't worth the effort?

No answers hid in his eyes. Elara took a step back and looked at him again.

"Nice specimen," Savannah said from the doorway.

"He is."

"Vanessa certainly thinks so."

"Vanessa likes attaching herself to dangerous men." Elara shrugged.

"Tell me you're watching them."

"I know every whisper that passes between them. What do you think of him?"

"Brutal. Efficient. Trouble. To be watched. Take your pick." The older woman swept into the room. The light of the fey lantern brought out the rich red undertone to her skin. Normally a green wrap hid her curly hair, but right now it was down, floating about her head like a storm cloud. Power emanated from Savannah, vibrant and strong. So strong.

"What do you need?" the head witch asked.

"The palisade," Elara said.

"Conrad told me."

"Do we still buy supplies from that trader, Austin Dillard?"

"He comes around."

"Next time he comes around, someone might mention that there is a palisade near the Old Market in need of supplies, except we haven't heard from them in a bit."

"Someone will mention it. Do you want a divination?"

Elara shook her head. "Conrad didn't get inside to take anything to anchor the vision, and I'm not sending anyone to retrieve anything. Whatever took those people could come back. Besides, they would leave the signatures of their magic and their scent at the scene, and I don't want to chance it. I just need d'Ambray to see reason."

She stared at Hugh some more.

"We can always poison him, you know," Savannah said.

"Hugh?"

"Mhm. Something quick and sweet. He'll fall asleep and never wake up. Won't even know what hit him."

Elara grimaced. "We can't. We need his army."

"Men."

"Yes. Can't live with them, can't kill them." Elara crossed her arms.

"What's upsetting you?" Savannah asked.

"He makes me angry, Savannah. Raging angry."

"Has it been calling to you?"

"It always calls to me." Elara sighed.

"Do you worry you'll manifest?"

"I worry he may push me too far."

"Have you thought about going the smarter route?" Savannah asked. "When you offer men opposition, they take it as a challenge. Sometimes a softer approach is better. A bit of flattery here and there, an appeal to his pride, a moment of helplessness. You know."

Of course Elara knew. She'd done it before when she'd had to and she was good at it. "This one is too... aware. Besides, if I could bring myself to do it, I would've already done it. He opens his mouth and I want to kill him. I've actually had fantasies of ripping his head off, Savannah."

The older witch looked at her for a long moment.

"What?"

"Don't do it in front of his Dogs."

"Hopefully, I won't do it at all. If things get too bad, I'll divorce him."

"Better sooner than later. People aren't marbles. You can't keep them separate by the color of the uniform they wear. The longer his people stay with us, the more ties we forge."

"The harder it will be to purge the Dogs from us. I know."

"What do you want done about Vanessa?" Savannah asked.

"Nothing. I've handled it. Her choices are her own."

"Betrayal should be punished, Elara."

"What would I punish her for, Savannah? Bad judgement? Trust me, he's punishment enough."

Savannah nodded and left the room.

Elara raised her hand and touched Hugh's chest, tracing the line of hard muscle under the skin with her fingers. The projection rippled as if liquid.

It was too bad... If it was anyone but him...

She laughed quietly at the absurdity of it and dismissed the construct with a wave of her fingers.

6

Hugh lowered his hands and took a deep breath. Sweat dripped from his forehead. He'd pushed himself for the better part of an hour, alternating the heavy bag and weights with weapon practice. His body finally realized that food was once again plentiful, and he was starting to rebuild the muscle he'd lost. He would need it.

Next to him Lamar propped himself against the stone wall of the keep. Hugh leaned next to him and began pulling at the wraps on his fists. In front of them the western end of the bailey stretched, filled to the brim with tents. It had been three weeks, and still more than half of his people were camping out in the open. He'd left the barracks renovation to Elara. She had insisted on it, and he gave it to her to avoid having another delay on the moat. His wife was dragging her feet on renovations. At this rate, they would still be in tents at first frost.

"What did you find out?" Hugh asked.

"Pretty much what we suspected." Lamar kept his voice quiet. "Elara is at the top of the food chain. Below her are the two advisers. Savannah oversees the covens, infrastructure, and internal administrative issues. She also heads their legal department.

Dugas deals with logistics, imports, exports, trade agreements and so on. Their powers overlap somewhat, so they have oversight over each other. Elara views them both as her parents. No clue what happened to her real family."

In a war against Elara, the witch and the druid would be priority targets.

"What about Johanna?"

"Research and development. There are other administrators. The head accountant, for example. But none of them hold the power those three do. Most major decisions are made by them and Elara. Elara has the power to overrule them, but she almost never does. There is a fifth person involved too."

"Who?"

"I don't know," Lamar said. "But some of our people have seen him. He moves very fast and seems to disappear into thin air. We don't know what or who he is. We're not getting anywhere with the locals. They're all nice and friendly until we start asking leading questions about Elara and the Remaining."

"Keep digging. There are thousands of Departed between the castle and the town. Someone will talk."

"They're really interested in our barrels."

"Of course they are."

A tent nearby collapsed. Iris crawled out of it, swore, and kicked it.

Lamar fell silent. Hugh glanced at him. "What?"

The centurion hesitated.

"Lamar?"

"None of the bulldozer operators showed up for work this morning."

Fury began to rise in him. "Why?"

"According to the foreman, they and their bulldozers have something more important to do. They are digging on the north side."

Hugh forced himself to sound calm. "Are we upside down on the salvage?"

"No. According to the smiths, we still have three days of work paid for."

"Did you tell that to the bulldozer foreman?"

"I did." Lamar nodded. "He said the orders came from Elara. He says he isn't allowed to talk to us about it."

Hugh tossed the hand wraps on the wall and marched to the keep.

———✦———

ELARA DID most of her business in the small room off her bedroom, where she kept a desk, a computer she could access during tech, and paper files. Today she sat behind that desk, her head down, looking at some papers. Hugh strode through the door. A heavy-set Latino man was standing next to her, pointing at a paper in front of her. They both looked up at him.

Hugh unhinged his jaws. "Leave."

The man grabbed his papers and took off. Hugh waited until he ran down the stairs and turned to Elara.

"Yes?" she asked.

"You pulled the bulldozers off the moat."

She leaned back. "Yes, I did."

His temper threatened to gallop off like a horse running for its life and Hugh made a valiant effort to hold on to it. "For what reason?"

"I felt like it."

He stared at her. Elara stared back.

Hugh bit off words, pronouncing them with icy exactness. "Our agreement was, I get the salvage and you let us have the bull-dozers. I have three days' worth of salvage credit left."

"Yes, but we didn't specify when the bulldozers will be available to you. There is nothing in that agreement about any kind of timeline. You will get your bulldozers back. Just not right now."

He couldn't kill her. If he killed her, he would have to kill everyone else in this damn settlement. His rage was boiling over and he distilled it to a single word. "When?"

"When I feel like it," she told him.

She was toying with him now.

Elara reached over, picked up a folder from the desk, and held it in front of her so only her eyes were visible.

"What are you doing?"

"Waiting for your head to explode. I don't want to miss it, but I don't want to be splattered with gore."

He reached over, plucked the folder from her fingers, and dropped it on the desk. "I've explained the reason for the moat. It's an urgent matter. We've been here for three weeks and my people are still in tents. They haven't been paid."

Elara crossed her arms on her chest. "Nothing you said indicates that I'm in breach of our contract. It specifies that quarters for your soldiers will be provided in a reasonable time. I can't help that my definition of reasonable is different from yours."

"Elara!"

"They are soldiers, Preceptor. They are used to sleeping on the ground. Now then, I have two stacks of paperwork to go through. Why don't you go and punch that heavy bag some more? Take the edge off."

That was it. He needed to take his people and go. "I'm done," he told her.

"Excellent. Please go. And while you are out there venting your rage, if you're so interested in what the bulldozer team is doing, why don't you ask them yourself and stop wasting my time?"

Hugh walked off. A haze of fury floated around him. He walked into the bailey. The sunlight burned his eyes. He strode to the gate, flicking his fingers at a group of the nearest Iron Dogs.

They fell in behind him. He marched outside the walls, turned, and headed north.

It was simple. He would remove the bulldozer crew, confiscate the bulldozers, and put his own people on them.

The heavy machinery sat unmoving on the north side of the hill. The crew, a woman and three men including Jay Lewis, the foreman, sat on the grassy slope, drinking from thermoses and eating sandwiches. At Hugh's approach Lewis scrambled to his feet. He was about fifty, a shade under six feet tall, with a ruddy face that came from having northern European genes and spending too much time outdoors in the hot sun.

Hugh nodded, and the Iron Dogs formed a line between the crew and the four bulldozers. He fixed Lewis with his stare.

The foreman swallowed.

"What are you doing here?"

"Um, the thing is, sir, I'm not supposed to tell you."

Hugh sank menace into his words. "Are you afraid of me, Lewis?"

The foreman nodded several times.

"Do you see my wife anywhere?"

"No, sir."

"That's right. She isn't here, but I am. Do we understand each other?"

Lewis nodded again.

"Tell me why you're here."

Lewis opened his mouth, hesitated, and gave up. "The septic."

"Explain."

"We've doubled the personnel for the castle and the septic was never meant to handle that much volume. We had a bit of a problem, but it's all fixed now, you see?" Lewis waved his hand at a patch of freshly turned over dirt. "It will be great. You'll love it."

The septic did take priority. They didn't want to drown in sewage. She could've told him that. But no, the harpy took a chance to stab. He would remember that.

"Finish your lunch," he told Lewis. "Once you're done, I expect you back in the moat."

"Yes, sir."

A walk back to the gates took another five minutes. The Iron Dogs trailing him walked in silence.

Hugh walked through the gates and halted. The sea of tents had collapsed. The Iron Dogs crowded by the doors of the left wing. His gaze snagged on the pale spot of blue in the mass of black. Elara waved at him. She was holding giant scissors.

There was a blue ribbon strung across the doors of the left wing. It had a giant bow on it.

He'd been had.

"Will you do the honors, Preceptor?" Elara held the scissors out to him.

He would kill that woman.

He marched over, took the scissors from her, and cut the ribbon. The door swung open under the pressure of his hand revealing a front hall with a desk to the side. To the left and right, hallways shot out, their walls peppered with doors. In the middle of each hallway signs marked the stairways. In front of him double doors stood open, showing rows and rows of tables. She'd made them a mess hall.

"Since you're here for the long haul," Elara said behind him, "we felt dormitory style would be better than a single room with cots. There are twenty-eight dormitory rooms on the second floor, each containing four beds. There are two large communal bathrooms on each end of the second floor. On the first floor, you have ten more four-bed rooms downstairs and four pairs of single bed suits for officers. Each pair of suits shares a bathroom. You also have two large rooms to be used as you see fit."

Above the mess hall doors, a black wrought iron crest hung, shaped like the head of a snarling dog.

The Iron Dogs streamed into the barracks.

Hugh stood still and stared at the crest. Elara halted next to him.

He didn't say anything.

She leaned forward to get a look at his face. A smug smile curved her lips. It touched off something inside him, something new he couldn't quite grapple with.

"What are you thinking about?" she asked.

"I'm picturing cutting your head off with these scissors."

Elara laughed and walked out of the barracks.

HUGH RAISED his head from the purchasing agreement for the volcanic ash.

A teenage girl hovered in the doorway of his bedroom. He'd seen her before. Where was it? The stables.

"Let me guess. Bucky's gotten out again."

She nodded wordlessly.

"Did you chain the stall the way I told you?"

She nodded again.

"What happened?"

"The chain was on the ground."

Hugh sighed. "Fine. Wait for me downstairs."

He put away the paperwork. He's spent most of yesterday getting everyone into the new barracks, then went back to the moat, and when he'd finally gotten to bed, it was past midnight. He'd woken up early and went straight back to the purchasing agreements. It was close to nine am now. His stomach growled. After he caught that damn horse, he would have to get something to eat.

No matter how hard they tried to restrain Bucky, the stallion took off during the night. If he was corralled, he jumped the fence. If he was locked up in the stables, in the morning, the stall would be open, and Bucky would be gone. He always went to the same place.

Hugh made it downstairs. The teenage girl had fetched a length of rope from the stables and was waiting by the wall.

"Let's go," he told her.

They walked out of the gates and curved to the left, down the path toward the nearest patch of woods. The sun shone bright. The sky was a painful blue. It would be another hot, sunny fall day. He noticed days now that he knew his were numbered. Immortality had its perks, but with Roland gone, it was out of his reach.

He cut off those thoughts before they led him into the void.

The path brought them to the edge of the woods and dove under the canopy of hemlocks. They followed it a few dozen yards to a glen. Here and there, the sun managed to punch through the leaves, dappling the forest floor in golden light. The air was clean and smelled like life.

Hugh whistled. The shrill sound cut the air. The stable girl jumped.

They waited.

A streak of blinding white appeared between the trees and accelerated toward them.

Idiot horse.

The stallion was running at a near gallop. Any normal horse would've broken its legs by now, but for some odd reason Bucky dashed through the woods with the agility of a deer 1 /10th his size. He never tripped, he never put his feet wrong, he never ran into the branches. And he galloped around the woods at night, in near pitch-black darkness.

The stallion tore through the woods towards them, slid to a dramatic halt in the glen, and reared, pawing the air.

"Did you have fun?" Hugh asked.

Bucky trotted over and nudged him with his big head. Hugh

slid a carrot into the stallion's mouth, took the rope, and looped it over Bucky's head.

"Let's go."

Bucky followed him, docile. The picture of obedience.

"There are dire wolves in the woods," the stable girl said.

"He doesn't care."

"You could get a different horse," she said. "The Lady would give you whatever horse you wanted."

"Is that so?"

The stable girl nodded. "Yes. Any horse. She told us to give you whatever you need because you're protecting us."

He filed that bit of information away for further reference.

"So, you could trade him for a different horse."

"No. He's my horse. That's that."

She sniffed and squinted at him. "Is it true that you can ride standing up in the saddle?"

"I don't need a saddle."

She squinted harder. "Prove it."

Hugh hopped onto Bucky's back and nudged him into a walk. The stable girl followed. He pulled his legs up and stood on Bucky's back.

She grinned. He dropped, swung his leg over, and rode Bucky with his back to the stallion's head, facing her.

"How did you learn to do that?"

"Practice. Lots and lots of practice. The man who raised me came from steppe country. A place with mean horses. He taught me to ride when I was little." Voron had taught him many other things, but horses had been the first lesson.

"Can you teach me?"

"Sure."

A piercing scream rolled through the orchard from the right. Hugh jumped off Bucky.

"Help! He's got the dogs!" A man screamed. "Help!"

A wolf howl rose from the woods, floating above the trees.

Hugh tossed the rope to the girl and lifted her onto Bucky's back. "Get to the castle," he ordered. "Tell any Dog you see to send Sharif and Karen to me."

The girl nodded.

"Don't throw her," Hugh warned.

Bucky snorted and took off toward the castle.

———+——

THE BODY of the dog sprawled under a bush. Blood stained the brown and white fur. Next to the dog, Sharif crouched, leaning close to the ground, staring unblinking at the crushed bushes and red-stained leaves. Karen, the other shapeshifter, dropped to all fours on the other side and took a long whiff.

Shapeshifters had their issues, but Hugh never agreed with Roland's disdain for them. He understood Roland's position well enough and recited it with passion when the occasion called for it, but when it came down to it, shapeshifters made damn good soldiers and that's all he cared about.

He braced for the uncomfortable flash of guilt that usually flared when he thought Roland was wrong. It never came. Instead the void scraped his bones with its teeth. Right.

"He got some bites in," Karen said softly, her voice tinted with sadness. "Good boy."

Sharif bared his teeth.

The dire wolf was big and old. One of the shepherds had snapped a polaroid of him two nights before when the beast prowled the tree line, studying the cows in the pasture. From the paw prints and the pictures, the old male stood more than three feet at the shoulder and had to weigh damn near two hundred pounds, if not more.

Wild wolves didn't follow the strict alpha-beta pecking order people assigned to them. That structure was mostly present in big shapeshifter packs, because hierarchy was a primate invention. Instead wild wolves lived in family groups, a parent couple and their young, who followed their parents until they grew up enough to start their own packs. But this beast was solitary. Something happened to his pack or they ran him out, and now he was a lone wolf with nothing to lose. A night ago, he tried to take a cow. The dogs and guns chased him off. Then the magic hit.

The old wolf was a smart bastard, smart enough to figure out that when the magic was up, guns didn't bark. Still, he stayed away from the pasture and went for the easier target instead, a ten-year-old girl picking pears from the ground in the orchard while her parents were on ladders harvesting the fruit.

A dog's job was to put itself between the threat and the human. The two dogs with the harvesters did their job.

Hugh and the shapeshifters had found the first dead hound at the edge of the woods. The second was here. Now it was up to human Dogs to settle the score.

"Heartbeat," Sharif whispered.

Hugh reached out with his magic. The dog was a mess, torn and bitten, but a faint, barely-there heartbeat shivered in his chest. Hugh concentrated. This would be complicated.

He knitted the organs together, repairing the tissue, sealing the blood vessels, mending the flesh like it was fabric, muscles, fascia, and skin. The two Dogs by his side waited quietly.

Finally, he finished. The dog raised his head, turned in the brush, and crawled toward them. Sharif scooped the hundred and twenty-pound hound up like he was a puppy. The dog licked his face.

"Blood loss," Hugh said. "He won't be walking for a bit."

"I'll carry him," Sharif said. His eyes shone, catching the light.

"We're only a mile in. Take him back and catch up," Hugh told him.

The werewolf turned smoothly and ran into the woods, silent like a shadow, the huge dog resting in his arms.

Karen took the lead and they followed the scent trail deeper into the woods.

If he never saw another rhododendron bush until his next life, it would be too soon, Hugh decided. The damn brush choked the spaces between trees and getting through it wasn't exactly a cakewalk.

They pushed their way through the latest patch. The endless rhododendron finally thinned out. Old woods stretched before them, the massive oaks and hemlocks rising like the thick columns of some ancient temple, cushioned in greenery.

A shadow flittered between the trees, trailing a smear of foul magic. An undead.

The day was looking up. Hugh grinned and pulled his sword out.

The undead dashed right and stopped.

Another smear appeared on the left. Two. If it was Nez's standard rapid reconnaissance party, there would be a third, each piloted by a separate navigator.

Karen waited next to him, her anticipation almost a physical thing hovering in front of her.

"Happy hunting," Hugh said.

She unbuckled her belt with the knife sheath on it, unzipped her boots, and gave a sharp tug to her shirt. It came open. She dropped it on the forest floor. Her pants followed. A brief flash of a nude human, then her body tore. New bones sprang up out of flesh, muscle spiraled up them, sheathing the new skeleton, skin clothed it, and dense gray fur burst from the new hair follicles. The female werewolf opened her monstrous jaws, her face neither wolf nor human, swiped her knife from her clothes, and sprinted into the woods to the left.

Hugh went in the opposite direction, toward the foul magic staining the leaves. The smear hovered still for a moment, then moved north. *Run, run, little vampire.*

Another vampire to the far right, closing in fast. The undead moved in silence. They didn't breathe, they didn't make any of the normal noises a living creature made, but they couldn't hide their magic. The foul patina of undeath stood out against the living wood like a dark blotch.

The front bloodsucker played bait, while the one on the right would close in from the flank and try to jump him. They didn't realize he could feel them. This wasn't the Golden Legion. The Masters of the Dead would've just met him two on one. These were likely journeymen, piloting younger vampires. The undead were damn expensive, and the older they were, the higher the price tag ran.

Didn't want to risk the budget, cheapskate? It will cost you.

Hugh ran through the forest as fast as the terrain would let him, jumping over the fallen branches. *Let's play.*

The ground evened out. Hugh sped up.

The bloodsucker in front of him darted in and out of the brush, flirting.

Hugh dashed forward, pretending not to feel the undead gaining from the right.

Trees flew past. The flanking vamp was almost on him.

The first bloodsucker jumped over the trunk of a fallen tree. Hugh tossed his sword into his left hand, planted his right on the rough bark, and vaulted over it.

The undead from the right leapt at him before he landed, as he knew it would. The vamp came flying out of the bushes. Hugh braced and rammed the reinforced gauntlet on his right hand into the bloodsucker's mouth, taking the full weight of the vamp. The fangs sank into leather and met the core of hard steel. The bloodsucker hung still for a precious half-second as the surprised navigator processed the aborted leap. A half-second was just long enough. Hugh sank his sword between the undead's ribs, slicing through the gristle and muscle to the heart. The oversized sack of muscle met the razor-sharp point of the blade and burst, as only undead hearts did, spilling blood inside the undead's body cavity.

Hugh jerked the sword free, shook the vamp off his hand like it was a feral cat, and swung. The blade cut in a broad powerful stroke. The undead's head rolled into the bushes. The whole thing took less than a couple of breaths.

Fun.

With any luck, the journeyman piloting the vamp didn't break connection. When a vampire died under a navigator's control, the pilot's brain insisted that it was the navigator himself who had died. Most became human vegetables. A few lucky ones survived but they were never the same.

Behind him, the undead magic swelled.

Hugh spun, ready to meet the attack.

The vamp charged, red eyes blazing.

A white blur cut between him and the undead and turned into Elara, her hand locked on the bloodsucker's throat.

What the hell was this?

The undead shuddered in her grip. It should've torn her in two by now.

Elara looked into its eyes and opened her mouth. "Let go."

The vamp's eyes flared with ruby light as the navigator bailed. Elara squeezed. He felt the faint flicker of power, a silvery veil snapping to the vamp's hide from her fingers. Old magic licked Hugh's senses, awakening some long-forgotten instinct buried under layers of civilization. The hair on the back of his neck rose.

The bloodsucker went limp. She released it, and it crumpled to the ground. She picked up the skirt of her green dress and stepped over it.

Exactly the same as the first time with the tikbalang. His pulse sped up. He had no idea how she did it, and he had to find out before she did it to him.

Elara tilted her head. She'd braided her hair and wrapped it into a complicated knot on the back of her head. Stray wisps escaped here and there, shining when they caught a ray of sun falling through the leaves.

Hugh straightened, resting the blade of his sword on his shoulder. "Wife."

"Husband."

It had been a week since their last fight. She'd been conveniently busy. Hugh had a feeling she was avoiding him. The fun question was, did she do it because she didn't want to fight or did she do it because she looked at him a half a second too long when he stood near naked in front of her that time in the bedroom?

"You came to help me. How charming," Hugh drawled.

"That's me. Delightfully charming."

A distant howl echoed through the forest. Karen had caught her prey.

"Is there something you needed?" he asked.

"We got a call from Aberdine."

Magic was a funny thing. Sometimes it killed the phone lines, other times they worked. It mattered who made the call.

"I'm aflutter with anticipation. What did the phone call say?"

"There are sheriffs riding here from the county. I told you this would happen, and it did."

For a second, Hugh saw red, then he wrenched himself under control with an effort of will. "What did you do?"

"I did nothing," Elara said, her voice bitter. "Now we look guilty. They will expect us to greet them together. Try to keep up."

She blurred and vanished. He whirled and saw her, a pale silhouette fifty yards away. A voice floated through the woods and whispered in his ear, cold and mocking. "Too slow, Preceptor."

He sheathed his sword and took off after her. She was lying through her teeth. When he caught up to her, he would strangle her with his bare hands.

———+——

ELARA WAITED at the edge of the forest. He should've been out of there by now. To the north, against the backdrop of the tall hill

127

and the severe lines of the castle, the Waterson, Garcia, and Lincoln families were picking pears from the orchard. The pears made good wine and the way the birds had been going at them, they had to be at the peak of ripeness. A few more days and they'd get pear mush instead of fruit.

"If I chop off your head, will it grow back?"

Elara spun around and almost ran into Hugh. He loomed over her, his eyes dark, his face cold. A man that large shouldn't have moved that quietly.

"I don't know," she said, keeping her voice iced over. "We could do an experiment. You try chopping off my head and I'll try to chop off yours. We'll see who's left standing."

A spark flashed in the depths of his blue irises. "Tempting."

"Isn't it? You just have to tell me which head you want chopped off, the top one or the one you usually think with."

"Take your pick."

Elara narrowed her eyes. "Maybe later. We're being watched."

He glanced at the two girls waving at them from the orchard. Elara waved back.

"Is that supposed to stop me?"

She hated that she had to look up to meet his gaze. "You would kill me in front of the children?"

"In a minute."

"But you healed the dog."

"How do you know?"

"I know everything."

"You saw Sharif running out of the woods."

Hugh leaned toward her half an inch. Elara fought the urge to step back. The man could project menace like a raging bull.

She forced herself to stand still and glare back at him. "The point is, a man who would save a dog wouldn't usually do something to scar small children."

"A completely arbitrary connection."

"Saving a dog implies a certain set of ethics."

"I don't care about the children."

Elara shrugged. "In that case, we should get on with killing each other or start walking back. The sheriffs will be here soon."

For a moment Hugh appeared to waver, then he indicated the path to the castle with an elegant sweep of his hand. She strode down the path and he walked next to her.

The girls at the orchard waved again.

"Wave back, Preceptor. Your arm won't break."

Hugh spun toward the orchard with a big friendly smile on his face and blew the girls a kiss. They dissolved into giggles and ran away. He turned to her and she almost shivered at his expression.

"We had an agreement. You broke it."

The man homed in on crucial details like a shark sensing blood in the water. "I didn't speak to the authorities. I didn't order anyone to inform the county. You've made it perfectly clear that we are wearing the same straitjacket."

"It got out, because you wanted it to get out."

Elara sighed. "What did you want me to do? Muzzle everyone around us?"

"I expected you to stay true to the spirit of our agreement. I know you didn't."

"Let's review. I came to you, because I wanted to go to the authorities. You demanded that I didn't. I told you it was stupid. I told you things always got out. You dug your heels in."

"I don't believe you."

"Wait." She held up her hand. "Let me check if I care."

Hugh glared at her.

"No," she said. "Apparently, I don't. It's good that we got that straightened out."

She strode up the path, climbing the hill toward the castle. He had no trouble keeping up.

"By the way, Vanessa left." She couldn't keep a hint of sadness out of her voice. "She packed her bags and took off last night."

"And this makes you sad why?"

"She was one of mine."

"I suppose you're blaming me for it?"

"No. Her decisions are her own."

An Iron Dog emerged from the trees, on a roan horse, a cowboy hat on her head. Irina, Elara recognized. One of Felix's scouts. That meant the sheriffs weren't far behind. *Here comes the county.*

"Take my arm," Hugh said.

"Ugh." She rested her hand on his forearm and slowed. They strolled toward the gates.

"Why did you heal the dog?"

"Because he did his job. Loyalty must be rewarded." There was a touch of an edge to Hugh's voice. "And there are practical considerations."

"Such as?"

"The other dog died in the forest. This dog didn't turn back. He chased the wolf down alone, tried to kill it, and did a decent enough job fighting. We'll need to breed him. He'll make good war dogs."

"War dogs? To fight people?"

"And undead."

Yes, but it wasn't about the war puppies. It was about loyalty. She knew the story as well as everyone else: Hugh d'Ambray had served as Roland's warlord; then they had a falling out, Roland exiled Hugh and now his pet necromancer hunted the Iron Dogs. And that's all anyone knew. Despite everything she tried, the details of what exactly happened and why eluded her.

The way he said loyalty signaled there had to be a lot more to the whole mess. Whatever had happened between them left deep scars. She'd have to work that sore spot. If she could dig deep enough, she would figure out what made him tick. *Know thy enemy. That's the ticket.*

The sheriffs emerged, a small party of four people and a pack horse. The first two riders carried rifles and bows. The third had a staff strapped to his horse. Another sheriff's deputy brought up the rear.

"Three deputies and a forensic mage," Hugh assessed. "Happy now?"

"I didn't invite them here. But they're here now. They're the law."

"They are the law back home. Here, we are the law."

"Is that so?"

"Sheriffs, state troopers, and cops are for normal people. I thought you would've learned this by now."

He threw that 'normal' in there casually, but Elara knew Hugh was watching for her reaction, looking for a soft spot in her armor. He wouldn't find one.

"Nobody wants you to be the law, Hugh. Least of all me."

"You went behind my back, wife."

"That's the second time you used the 'w' word in the space of an hour without us being in public. You're past your quota, Preceptor."

"I'll remember this. Your tab is getting longer and longer. The next time you need something from me, I'll remind you."

"Be still my heart."

"I wish. Ready?"

She plastered a welcoming smile on her face. "No time like the present."

"Happy couple in three... two..." Hugh grinned and waved at the party. She waved too, fighting the feeling of sudden dread climbing up her spine.

———◆———

ONE LOOK at Deputy Armstrong and it was clear he was some sort of law enforcement, Elara reflected. He was in his thirties, short, but stocky and hard, with short blond hair, a clean-shaven square jaw, and sharp eyes. He held himself in a relaxed way that was almost casual, but she had no doubt that if a threat appeared, he would act fast and probably without thinking.

The other deputy, about fifteen years older, gray haired and white, was beginning to get thick around her middle, but had the same kind of look to her: calm but alert. The forensic mage, a black man in his mid-twenties, looked slightly bored. Veterans. The only outlier in the group was the third deputy sheriff, a man who was barely twenty and clearly out of his depth.

And Hugh worked them like they were butter.

"No, we haven't heard from them," he said, his face suitably concerned. "I wasn't even aware there was a settlement that way, but I'm new to the area. Honey?"

"Sometimes people come to the woods to get away from the world," Elara said. "You said it was a small settlement?"

"That's what the trader said," Deputy Armstrong confirmed. "He didn't go in, but he could see some houses from the road. The gates stood wide open."

She turned to Hugh, concern on her face. "Couldn't be dire wolves. There would be bodies."

Hugh grimaced. "I don't like it. Those aren't your usual woods. There is strong magic there."

So he'd noticed. She wasn't sure why that surprised her. Someone with the kind of power he had would sense the arcane air within the forest.

"I tell you what, Deputy," Hugh said. "Let me reinforce you. I don't like you riding all the way there by yourself."

Armstrong thought about it for a whole three seconds. "If you're offering, I won't turn it down."

Nicely done. "I'll come as well," Elara said. "We have experienced healers and a couple of good seers. If we find survivors, we can administer first aid."

Hugh gave her a look so besotted, she almost pinched herself. "Excellent. Give us fifteen minutes, Deputy. We pack light."

"So you're newlyweds?" Dillard, the female deputy, asked.

"Yes." Elara nodded.

They'd been riding for two hours now. The Old Market wasn't far, but the terrain slowed horses to a walk. Hugh and Armstrong had pulled ahead a few yards and were talking about something. She strained to listen, but only caught random words. Something about the advantages of ballistae. Deputy Chambers, the youngest of the four, was following them and hanging on every word. Behind them twenty Iron Dogs and eight of her people rode in a column, two abreast. Sam, in his new Iron Dog uniform, rode directly behind her. He trailed Hugh like a lost puppy who finally found someone to love and she had no doubt everything he said would be related to her husband word for word.

"That's a good man you have there."

Elara almost choked on her own breath. "Yes, he is. A good man."

"He looks at you like you walk on air." Deputy Dillard smiled. "Sometimes you get lucky, and it lasts past the first year."

"Are you married?"

"I'm on my second one. My first husband died."

"I'm sorry to hear that."

"He was a good man. My second husband is a good man too. But he doesn't look at me like that."

Hugh shifted in his saddle. Bucky turned and pranced over to her. Hugh turned him again, matching her horse's stride. "Hey."

"Hey yourself."

"I missed you," he said.

Quick, say something sweet back... "I missed you too."

"Maybe I could steal you away from Deputy Dillard for a bit?"

"Oh, go on, you two lovebirds." Deputy Dillard waved at them.

Elara nudged Raksha, and the dark bay mare stepped out of the column and pulled ahead with an easy elegance only Arabian horses possessed. Bucky stomped the ground next to her, clearly trying to look impressive.

Hugh reached over and held out his hand. The entire column was behind them, watching. She gritted her teeth and put her hand into his.

"Oh look, my skin isn't smoking," Hugh murmured.

"You're overdoing it with the PDAs."

"We're newlyweds. If I threw you over my shoulder and dragged you into the woods, that would be overdoing it."

The image flashed before her. "Try it. They won't even find your bones."

"Oh, darling, I don't think you'll have any trouble finding my bone."

She tried to jerk her hand out of his, but he was holding her tight and she couldn't yank her fingers out without making a scene. "Sure thing. I think I packed a magnifying glass."

He lifted her hand and kissed her fingers.

"You'll pay for that," she ground out.

"Mmm, are you going to punish me? Kinky girl."

Insufferable ass. Elara let a tendril of her magic slither from her fingers and lick his skin. He didn't let go.

They caught up with Armstrong and Chambers. Chambers was looking at them wide-eyed.

"Don't worry, Deputy," Hugh winked at him. "I'm just trying my wife's patience with public displays of affection."

"Ignore him," she said, smiling. "He has no boundaries."

"I'm only human," Hugh said.

Yes, you are.

A dark shape rushed through the woods and Sharif emerged on the road, his eyes shining with the telltale shapeshifter glow. Deputy Chambers grabbed for the vial on his belt.

"The road is clear," Sharif reported. "Empty palisade. The scents are old."

Chambers let go of the vial, and she glimpsed the pale-yellow substance inside. The color was almost gone. Opportunity.

"Your wolfsbane has soured, my friend," Hugh said, letting go of her.

Ah! He saw it too.

Chambers startled.

"He's right," she said, holding out her hand. "Here."

Chambers unclipped the vial from his waist and handed it over. She unscrewed the top and smelled it. Barely any scent. "Sharif, would you mind?"

The werewolf took the vial and held it to his nose. "Tingly."

"Thank you," she said, taking the vial back.

"Potent wolfsbane should've sent him into a sneezing fit," Hugh said. "A strong wolfsbane has a deep orange color."

"It should be stored in a dark container in a cold place," Elara added. "Until you're ready to use it."

"Sadly, the stuff they issue us is barely yellow to begin with," Armstrong said.

"We're the biggest producer of wolfsbane in the region," Elara said.

"We can cut them a deal, can't we, honey?" Hugh asked.

"I'm sure we can." They would take a loss on it. It didn't matter. The contacts and good will at the county level was worth more than all their wolfsbane put together. "How much are you paying per gram now?"

"We pay five hundred per half-pound," Armstrong said.

She waved her hand. "We can do better than that. We will supply you with premium quality wolfsbane at six hundred per pound."

Armstrong blinked. "We don't want to take advantage."

"Call it law enforcement discount," Elara said.

"Look," Hugh said, his face somber. "One day things could happen, and I may not be here when they do. My wife might be in danger. My future children. My people. When that day comes, I'll count on you to ride out here just as you're doing now and uphold the law. You can't do that if you're dead. Let us fix this small thing for you. It's the least we can do to help."

Wow, he was good. If she didn't know better, she would've believed every word. *What a "good" man I've got there.* Elara almost rolled her eyes.

"I'll have to run it by the chain of command," Armstrong said.

"The wolfsbane will be ready to go when you are," Elara said.

The road turned. The empty palisade loomed ahead.

———

HUGH WATCHED the forensic mage read the magic scanner's printout. The m-scanners sensed the residual magic and printed them as colors: blue for humans, green for shapeshifters, purple for vampires. They were, at best, imprecise and clumsy; at worst, misleading. He'd seen printouts that made no sense, and from the faint lines on the paper, this one held very little value. The magic signatures were too old. Whatever took the people was long gone. Might as well get some druids to cut open a black chicken and study its liver.

Speaking of druids. He turned slightly to watch Elara's magic users waiting patiently outside of the palisade. They wore the typical neo-pagan garb; light hooded robes, just generic enough to make it difficult to pin them down. They could be witches, druids, or worshippers of some Greek god.

Eight people. Not really enough for a coven.

His gaze slid to the harpy. There was something witchy about Elara. When he goaded her into letting her magic out, it felt odd, a touch witchlike, a touch female, and a whole lot of something else, sharp and cold. Daniels had felt like that, a little witchy, but mostly her magic felt like boiling blood. Elara was ice.

The void yawned at him. Thinking of Daniels always put him

on the edge of the chasm. If he lingered too long on her or her father, the void would swallow him again.

The mage came out.

Here it comes, the magic signatures are too old, there is too much interference, blah blah blah.

"The magic signatures are too old and faint for a clear reading," the mage said to Armstrong.

The deputy sighed. "Is there anything you can tell me?"

"It wasn't an animal," the mage said. "Animals would've left more evidence. It wasn't an undead and the scene isn't indicative of a loup attack."

When shapeshifters failed to keep their inner beasts at bay, they turned loup. Loups weren't playing with a full deck. When they attacked a settlement, they tore humans apart, usually while fucking them, they boiled children alive, and generally had a great time indulging in every perversion they could think of until someone put them out of their misery. The only cure for loupism was a bullet to the brain or a blade to the neck.

Armstrong sighed again. "Any idea at all?"

"No."

"Something comes into this place, takes sixteen people out, and leaves no trace of itself."

"In a nutshell." The mage shrugged.

Armstrong looked at him for a long moment.

"What do you want, Will?" The mage spread his arms. "The scene is three weeks old. I don't work miracles."

"Perhaps we could try?" Elara asked, her tone gentle.

"Are you done with the scene?" Armstrong asked.

The mage nodded. "Can't hurt. We're not going to get anything more from it at this point."

Armstrong looked to Elara. "It's all yours."

"Thank you."

She walked toward the gates. When she wanted to, she moved like she was gliding. Mostly she stomped like a pissed off goat.

The eight people followed her and formed a rough semicircle.

"Come on," Hugh said to Armstrong. "We'll want a front row seat for this."

They walked through the gates. The mage followed them.

Elara's people pulled the hoods of their robes over their faces, so only their chins were visible. A low chant rose from them, insistent and suffused with power.

She stood with her back to them, seemingly oblivious to the magic gathering behind her.

The chant sped up. They poured out an awful lot of magic, but it felt inert.

Time to see what you really are. Hugh grounded himself, focusing through the prism of his own power. The world rushed at him, crystal clear, the magic a simmering lake submerging the eight chanters. Feeling magic was one of the first things he learned under Roland. *Show me what you've got, darling.*

Elara raised her arms to her sides and waited, her eyes closed.

The magic streamed toward her, as if a dam suddenly opened. It drenched her.

She didn't touch it. She didn't absorb it, didn't use it, didn't channel it. It just sat there around her.

Elara opened her eyes. Magic whipped inside her, and to his enhanced vision she almost glowed from within.

They were treated to a show, he realized. The chanters were there to make it look as if she channeled their power. She didn't need them. Whatever was about to happen was hers alone.

His lovely wife didn't want anyone to know how powerful she was. Smart girl.

Elara knelt, scooped a handful of dirt, and let it crumble from her fingers, each soil particle glowing gently.

The chant rose with a new intensity, rapid and sharp.

A pulse of magic burst from Elara, drowning the palisade. For half a second every blade of grass within stood perfectly straight and still. She'd poured a shitload of power into that pulse.

138

Silver mist rose from the ground in thin tendrils, thickening in the middle of the clearing, flowing together into a human shape, translucent, tattered, but visible. A man, six feet tall, broad shoulders. Big bastard. Long blond hair braided away from his face. Pale skin. A tattoo in a geometric design marked his right cheek, a tight spiral with a sharp blade on the end. He wore dark scale armor with a spark of gold on one shoulder. Hugh rifled through his mental catalogue of scale mail, everything from Roman *lorica squamata* to Japanese *gyorin kozane*.

He'd never seen anything like it.

The dark metal scales lay close to the man's body, not uniform, but varying in size, smaller on the waist where the body had to bend, wider on the chest. This wasn't made with the ease of manufacture in mind. It was created from life. Whoever made this was looking at a snake for inspiration.

The man's eyes flashed with gold fire. He thrust his left hand forward. Mist spiraled up in five different spots, melding into the outline of creatures, barely visible. They stood on two legs, hunched forward, big owl eyes unblinking, their mouths slashes across their faces.

He felt a small remnant of humanity buried deep within the brown bodies, a barely perceptible hint of the familiar. *They were once human.*

The beasts darted forward into the nearest house. A ghostly door swung open and the first beast dragged out a body, a woman, her head hanging down from her twisted neck.

Another beast carrying a man followed. The man was large, at least two hundred pounds. The creature had slung him over its shoulder like he was weightless.

A scuffle, then a beast emerged with an adolescent girl, her long hair sweeping the ground. Blood dripped down her hand. The owner of the torn nail.

Another beast followed, one carrying a boy of about five, another a baby. Both dead.

The beasts laid them in a row and darted into the next house. The man watched, impassive.

"Sonovabitch," Armstrong ground out.

The neat line of corpses grew. Sixteen people lay in a row, their ghostly bodies shimmering and fading into the mist.

Hugh studied the corpses. Quick and efficient. It only took a moment to snap a human neck. He'd done it enough times to recognize the practiced skill. That's why nobody raised the alarm. The beasts killed them almost instantly.

The man turned toward the open gates and walked out, vanishing at the edge of Elara's spell. The beasts grabbed the corpses and scuttled after him, darting back and forth until all were gone.

"Can you bring him back?" Hugh asked.

"I can hold him still for a bit." Elara concentrated. This time he felt the power sink into the ground in a controlled burst. The armored man returned, frozen in mid-move.

Hugh circled him. The scales of the armor lacked polished shine, and the metal wasn't black, but blue and brown with flecks of green, like tortoiseshell. Scuffs on the armor. That's what he'd thought.

The mage grabbed a sketchpad and frantically drew. Hugh glanced to make sure his own people were sketching. They were.

"Who is this guy?" Dillard growled, her face contorted. "Does he look familiar to anyone?"

Armstrong grunted. "The question is, is he some random nutjob, or is he a part of something larger?"

Hugh would have to explain it. They didn't see it on their own. Hugh pulled his sword out, stepped back, and swung. The blade lined up perfectly with a barely perceptible scratch across the scales.

Armstrong crouched next to him, so his face was inches from the sword and tilted his head. "He took a swing."

"And survived." Bad news. The cut didn't angle enough to be a glancing blow. No, someone had slashed across this asshole's middle straight on and probably dulled his sword.

"How do you know he survived?" Chambers asked. "Maybe he took the armor off a dead man."

"The armor isn't broken," Sam said quietly. "And it was custom made for him."

The kid was learning.

Hugh kept his voice low. "You see the gold on the shoulder?"

Armstrong studied the gold star etched into the armor, eight rays emanating from the center with a bright gold stripe underneath.

"Insignia?" he guessed.

"There is no other reason to put it on armor."

Armstrong glanced at him. "You think there are more of them."

"He's a soldier. Soldiers belong in an army." Hugh sheathed his sword. "The insignia is a rank, an identification. He's clean-shaven, his hair is put away, the armor isn't ornate. This is a uniform. Put him in the woods, and he'll be near invisible. He's part of a unit. If we're really lucky, it's just a unit and not an army."

Armstrong rose and surveyed the woods around them. "We're done here," he said. "Let's go back before something else shows up."

The mist dissolved. Elara stood on the other side. She looked … in pain. No, not pain. Worry.

That same annoying feeling that flooded him when he'd looked at her bloody wedding dress came over him. He wanted to fix it, just to make it go away.

He strode to her and said, barely above a whisper, "Do you recognize this?"

"No." She looked at him, and a small hopeful spark lit her eyes. "Do you?"

"No."

The spark died. Hugh felt a sudden rush of anger, as if he'd failed somehow.

If they got hit on the way back, she would jump into the fight. She had too much power to sit back. If he lost her, her nature-worshipping cabal would riot. Like it or not, everything in Baile and the town revolved around Elara.

"Stay near me on the way back."

Surprise slapped her face. She turned it into cold arrogance. "Worried about my survival?"

"Don't want to miss an opportunity to use you as a body shield."

"How sweet of you."

"Stay near me, Elara."

He walked away before she could come back at him with something clever.

7

E lara leaned against the table. They were upstairs in the room designated as her "study," which she never used. She preferred the small room off her bedroom. The study held a large wooden table, flanked by five chairs on each side, which nobody was using, except her and Johanna, who sat cross-legged on the table, mixing reagents in small glass beakers.

Past the table, an open area offered four plush chairs set around a small coffee table, with smaller chairs scattered here and there along the walls. Hugh had taken one of the soft chairs. Stoyan, Lamar, and Felix picked seats along the wall. The crazy one, Bale, wasn't invited to the meeting because he was standing watch. Just as well.

On her side of the room Savannah sat in a plush chair, while Dugas leaned against the wall.

Hugh was in a foul mood. They'd had three of these weekly meetings so far, with cooler heads on both sides present, because when they tried to work things out on their own, their discussions ended in a barrage of mutual insults. She'd seen him irritated before, even enraged, but this was new. His gaze was focused, his eyes dark. He sat in a large Lazyboy chair, flipping a knife in his hand, tip, handle, tip, handle. At first, she watched, waiting for him to cut himself, but after the first ten minutes she gave up. Some people paced, Hugh juggled a razor-sharp knife with his right hand. Aw, the man she married.

Ugh.

Elara tried to sink some sarcasm into that inner 'ugh' but couldn't even fool herself. Hugh was worried. She never seen him worried before. Hugh always had things in hand and the grim look in his eyes was setting her on edge. He was wearing jeans and a T-shirt, but he looked like a king whose kingdom was on the brink of an invasion. And she was his queen.

Ugh.

What was even going on in his head? She had a feeling that if she cracked his skull open and somehow let his thoughts free, they would be echoes of her own. *What is that creature? Why did the warrior kill? What did he do with the bodies? How do we guard against him?* And the loudest thought of all, playing over and over. *What did I miss? What else can I do?* It was driving her crazy.

"Next item on the agenda," Dugas said. "Rufus--"

She pushed away from the table. "We should send people to the nearest settlements."

Savannah reached out, touched Johanna's shoulder, and signed.

Hugh gave her a dark look. "Why?"

"To warn them. And to set perimeter wards."

"What makes you think the wards would hold him?" Hugh asked.

Johanna put the beaker down. *"They would not. He would make noise breaking them. An early warning system."* She picked up the beaker, raised it, shook the dark green liquid in it, and put it down again. *"We have soil from the palisade where he stood. We can key the spell to him. It would not be expensive."*

Hugh stared at her for a long moment.

"Not very." Johanna gave him an apologetic shrug.

"I need your approval, Hugh," Elara said. "It's a safety measure."

"Your people will need escorts," he said.

"Yes."

"How many settlements do you want to warn?"

She glanced at Savannah.

"Seven," she said.

"Okay," Hugh said. "We'll do them one at a time."

"That will take a week."

"Congratulations, you can count."

She crossed her arms. "Hugh, this is important. Every day we delay, people may die."

"I will have to send at least twenty people with each party. Any less is inviting an assault."

"So what's the problem? Seven by twenty is one hundred and forty."

"Exactly. You want me to send almost half of my force out into the woods at the same time. That risks the lives of my soldiers and leaves us vulnerable, and I won't do it. One at a time."

She unclenched her teeth.

He beat her to the punch. "What makes you think that sending a party of twenty armed soldiers and some witches would predispose these settlements to trust us? A lot of these people are paranoid separatists. They'll see us as a threat."

"We have to try," she said. "They killed the children, Hugh."

"Fine," he said, his face still dark. "But one at a time."

That was all she would get. She could argue more, but he was putting the welfare of their people first. Elara couldn't really blame him for being cautious. "Thank you," she made herself say.

"You're welcome."

Silence fell. She relaxed a little. The rest of the items on the agenda were routine.

Dugas cleared his throat. "As I started to say, Rufus Fortner is coming here this Friday."

"The head of the Lexington Red Guard," Elara said.

"I remember," Hugh said. "He was at our wedding."

"He's looking for a supplier of RMD. The remedy," Savannah said.

The remedy was an all-purpose anti-magic contamination salve the same way Neosporin was an all-purpose antibiotic ointment. It was particularly useful in sterilizing wounds inflicted by vampires. The *Vampirus Immortuus* pathogen was weak at the start of infection and could be killed with rubbing alcohol, if it came to it, but the remedy was the established and proven sterilizing agent.

"How big is the order?" Hugh asked.

"We stand to make over a hundred grand in the first year," Dugas said. "Likely two, three times more, if they like the product and place additional orders."

"What do we know about this guy?" Hugh asked.

"He's a good old boy," Lamar said. "Neo-Viking. 'Work hard, play hard, beer me wench, if it breathes I can kill it' type."

"He's coming to hang out with you," Elara told him. "He was terribly impressed with the fight at the reception and he's starstruck, because you have a reputation. He wants to get drunk with the Preceptor of the Iron Dogs and swap war stories."

Hugh shrugged. "Okay, we'll ham it up for him. We'll need a feast and a barrel of beer."

She blinked. "A barrel? We don't really brew beer in barrels. We do it in big drums."

"That's fine, we'll pour it in a big wooden barrel. I saw it in an old movie once," Hugh said. "Trust me, it never fails."

She waved at him. "However you want to do it. We need this guy. We've been wooing him and the Mercenary Guild in Lexington and Louisville for over a year and they wouldn't give us the time of day until you showed up. It's not just his order."

Hugh nodded. "He's a foot in the door. If we can get him, we'll get the rest."

She smiled. That was one thing she never had to worry about.

Hugh was a massive pain, but when he saw an opportunity, he grabbed it.

Dugas checked his notes. "Last thing. The first escort from the Pack arrives tomorrow to pick up the two shapeshifter families. We don't anticipate any problems, but just in case…"

The knife stopped in Hugh's hand. "What pack?"

"The Pack," she said. "Atlanta's Pack. The Free People of the Code."

His people sat up straighter. Stoyan's face turned unreadable like a wall.

"Run that by me again," Hugh said, his voice deceptively calm.

What the hell was wrong with him? "Kentucky passed a law banning the formation of packs in its municipalities," Elara said. "We have a standing agreement with the Atlanta Pack. Any shapeshifter who wants to relocate to Pack territory can come here. We house them and feed them, until the Pack sends an escort to pick them up. They reimburse us for expenses and pay a nice fee on top of it."

"No," he said.

"Why not? It's a mutually beneficial arrangement. Is it because they are shapeshifters? Because you have shapeshifters in your ranks."

"I don't have a problem with shapeshifters. I have a problem with that particular Pack. I know Lennart. I know how he operates. We're not doing this."

"Curran Lennart is no longer in charge of the Atlanta Pack," Savannah said.

Hugh looked at her, then turned to Lamar. "You didn't think to mention it?"

"It didn't come up," Lamar said apologetically. "He retired to start a family."

Hugh stared at him for a second longer, then laughed, a bitter cold sound. "The moron left it all for her. You can't make this shit up. Who's in charge now?"

"James Shrapshire," Lamar said.

Elara had to grab this opening. "See? It's no longer Lennart's pack."

"Is Lennart dead?" Hugh asked.

"No," Dugas said.

"Then it's still his Pack." Hugh leaned forward. "Lennart is a First. His ancestors made a deal for their power with animal gods that roamed the planet when humans ran around in animal skins and hid from lightning in caves. It doesn't matter who's in charge of the Pack. When he roars, every shapeshifter will follow him, and we won't be doing business with him. This matter is closed."

That was just about enough. "No, it's not. The Pack is one of our biggest clients. They are churning panacea out, which—"

"I know what the damn panacea does," he snarled.

"—significantly reduces occurrences of spontaneous loupism in shapeshifter newborns and teenagers," she kept going. "It doesn't stay potent for long and they need large quantities of herbs, some of which only grow in the woods here. They pay excellent rates."

"I don't care."

"You should care, because Pack money is feeding and housing your Dogs."

"Do you not understand me? I won't work with Lennart. Elara, are you stupid or hard of hearing?"

"I must be stupid, because I married an idiot who stomps around and throws tantrums like a spoiled child! What the hell did this Curran do to you? Killed your master, stole your girl, burned down your castle? What?"

Hugh leaned back, his eyes blazing. Oooh, she touched a nerve. Direct hit.

She turned to Stoyan. "Let me guess, it was the girl."

"And the castle," Felix said quietly.

"Is this why you want the moat, Hugh? So Curran won't burn

this castle down?" She knew the moment she said it that she'd pushed him too far.

Hugh leaned back in the chair, a long-suffering look on his face. "You know what your problem is?" he asked, his voice bored.

"Please tell me."

"You should get laid."

Elara stared at him.

"It will keep you docile and reasonable. For the sake of all of us, find someone to fuck you, so you can resolve things like an adult, because I'm sick and tired of your hysterics."

Oh. Oh, wow.

Nobody moved. Nobody even breathed.

"Cute. This agreement predates our marriage," Elara said into the sudden silence, pronouncing each word clearly. "According to the contract you signed, it is exempt from your input. I don't need your permission. This exchange will go forward. And you will remember that you are a married adult responsible for the welfare of four thousand people. You'll reach deep down, find a pair of big-boy pants, and put them on. If I can pretend not to cringe every time you touch me in public, you can pretend to be civil. Bury that hatchet, and if you can't, hide in your room while they're here."

The rage in his eyes was almost too much.

"You signed on the dotted line," Elara told him. "Are you a man of your word or are you not, Preceptor?"

Hugh rose from his chair, turned, and left. His people filed out behind him.

She slumped against the table. "Well, that went well."

"We should poison him," Savannah said.

"Why do you always want to poison people?" Dugas asked her.

"I don't want to poison people. I want to poison d'Ambray."

"He'll come around," Elara said. "He's under a lot of pressure, because of that palisade. He's trying to figure out how to keep us safe from an enemy he doesn't understand and it's eating at him."

All three of them looked at her.

"It's eating at me too," she said. "Let's reinforce our wards."

"We already did."

"Let's do it again."

Savannah nodded, and she and Dugas left.

Elara turned to Johanna. "Any luck?"

"The warrior is human," the blond-headed witch signed.

"Are you sure?"

"Ninety percent. I have done everything I can, but the imprint was very weak. But human is the only thing that makes sense."

It would be so much easier if the armored man was a creature. One could key a ward to bar a creature. One could research and exploit its weaknesses. But a human... That was so much worse. The castle and the town were full of magically powerful humans. She couldn't ward everyone in.

Elara sighed. The irony of Hugh's lovely insult was that he was right. She needed to get laid. She could've used the release and the comfort.

"Give me some dirt," she signed.

Johanna put a small test tube into her hand.

"I will go play with it. Maybe I can see something."

When it came to research, Savannah was better educated than her, and Johanna was more talented. But Elara had to try.

Elara took her test tube and left the room.

Hugh was a stubborn asshole. The problem with stubborn assholes is that once they made up their mind, they followed through, logic and rational thinking be damned. She couldn't leave it as it was. She had to talk to him about it. If she didn't, he could snap and attack the Pack delegation tomorrow and ruin a carefully constructed deal that she spent months working on.

Elara conquered the first flight of stairs, when she heard light steps running down. A moment later Stoyan rounded the landing.

He saw her and halted. "Ma'am."

"Is he upstairs?" she asked.

"No."

"Where is he?"

Stoyan opened his mouth.

"Stoyan," she warned. "Where is he?"

"He stepped out."

"In which direction?"

"He needs... space," Stoyan said.

What he needed was a solid wallop on his head and a personality transplant.

Johanna emerged from the hallway and waved at them. *"Hello."*

Stoyan's gaze snagged on her for half a second too long. Well. That was interesting.

"Stoyan, where is he going? I'm going to find out anyway. Your Preceptor won't escape, but you would save me a couple of minutes."

"He's going to Radion's smithy," Stoyan said.

"Thank you."

She put the tube into the pocket of her dress and ran down the stairs.

———+——

ELARA STRODE out of the gates. The town sat behind Baile castle, hugging the lake shore in a ragged crescent. Radion's smithy was on the eastern edge of it. A path stretched before her. Hugh had two choices. He could turn right at the fork of the path, circle the castle, and take Sage Street down and east, which would put his course past the shops and houses. Or he could stay straight and walk through the Herbals, a carefully managed stretch of woods hugging the north side of the town and used for the cultivation of herbs.

Where would a violent man in a foul mood go? It was a no-brainer.

She blurred, stepping fast down the path through the woods. One, two, three, four…

Hugh walked on the cobbled path. He was out of uniform. His jeans were scuffed and worn, just like his black boots. His broad shoulders stretched the fabric of a white T-shirt, which hung loose around his waist. Cedric, the big dog he'd healed, ran along his side, tongue lolling. From this angle, Hugh almost looked like a normal guy out for a stroll with his adoring pooch.

It was so strange, Elara thought. By all rights, Hugh d'Ambray was a despicable human being, but for some reason dogs instantly liked him. Horses too. Bucky was practically overcome with joy every morning when Hugh came to brush him and pick his hooves.

She supposed some women liked him too.

Cedric looked at her over his shoulder. She hurried to catch up, making no effort to move quietly. Cedric trotted over to her. She petted him.

"You're insane if you think he will make good war dogs. His puppies will be just like him, goofballs."

Hugh ignored her.

Elara walked next to him. Tall trees spread their canopy above them, just far enough apart to let some isolated rays of sun through. The brush at their roots was gone. Instead carefully planted patches of herbs colored the ground on both sides of the path. The plants were both native and introduced: sage, mugwort, plantain, ginseng, goldenseal, black cohosh, and more. Being here soothed raw nerves, and she often walked this path. More often since Hugh arrived. She needed a lot of soothing these days.

"How can I get rid of you?" Hugh asked.

"Divorce me."

"As soon as I can," he swore.

Elara let him have a minute of silence. "Tell me."

He gave her a brooding look.

"Tell me about Lennart and why you hate him."

Exasperation stretched his face. He looked up, as if searching for the heavens.

"Our marriage is a sham. Our alliance isn't," she said. "We need each other. When people look at you, they see a murdering butcher who betrayed his allies. When they look at me, they see an abomination who leads a cult and feeds on human sacrifice. But now we're married and suddenly they see us as newlyweds. They assume that there must be something I see in you, some redeeming quality that made me love you and marry you. When they look at me, they see a wife. Surely, I couldn't be that abominable."

"Or I wouldn't have married you," he finished.

"Yes. Doors that were previously closed are beginning to open. The Red Guard guy is coming after ignoring us for months. The county sheriffs think that we are a lovely couple. Explain the problem with the Pack, so I'll understand."

"No."

"I'm not asking for your thoughts and secrets. Just for facts. I'll learn them anyway. Normally I'd pounce on a chance to explore your weaknesses, but right now I just want the Pack thing to go smoothly. I worked too damn hard for it. A three month-long bidding war, four trips to the Pack to woo them, almost ten thousand in extra herbs planted."

"Did you go yourself to woo the Pack?"

She laughed. "Because I am so sweet and charming?"

He gave her a dark look. "Your people are eating out of your hand."

"They are my people and I love them. They've proved their loyalty beyond anything I had a right to ask. There is no limit to how low I will sink to keep them safe."

"Interesting choice of words."

She faced him. "Accurate. I will do anything for them."

"Good." His smile was like the flash of a knife. "I'll use it against you later."

She rolled her eyes. "I'm so scared. I'll have to go and find someone to sex me up right away just to keep my composure. Tell me, how did all this start?"

He didn't answer. She strolled next to him.

"Roland found out he had a daughter," Hugh said.

"I know the story," she said. "The immortal wizard woke up after hibernating through the centuries of technology just before the Shift. He set about rebuilding his empire from the ruins of our modern world. He gathered necromancers and made them into the People. He hired an army and set a warlord to lead them. And he swore off having children, not sure why."

"They always turn on him," Hugh said.

Just like you? Maybe he had turned on Roland. Maybe not. There was something wistful in the way he said Roland's name.

"He fell in love in spite of himself," Elara continued. "And he had a daughter, but his wife ran away."

"He tried to kill the child in the womb," Hugh said.

She stopped and glanced at him. "What?"

"It didn't work. Daniels is hard to kill."

Elara recovered. "And then her mother took her and ran away with Roland's Warlord."

"He raised me," Hugh said.

"The Warlord?"

"Yes. His name was Voron. He'd trained me since they found me in France. Then Kalina, Daniels's mother, decided she needed his help, and it was all over. One day he was simply gone. That was her power. If she wanted to, she could make you love her."

So his surrogate father had abandoned him to be with his boss's wife and their child. That had to hurt.

"It didn't last," Hugh said. "Roland tracked them down eventually and killed Kalina. Voron escaped with the child. I thought Voron would come back, after her magic wore off, but he never did."

"After Voron left, what happened to you?"

"I became the Warlord. Later Roland found out that his daughter survived."

"How?"

Hugh shrugged. "She started using her magic. Daniels isn't a subtle type. I could've brought her to him, but he wanted her to come to him, voluntarily, which was a lot more complicated. By that point, she had decided that Curran Lennart was her one and only. As long as they were together, inside the Pack's Keep, I wouldn't have made any progress. I had to get them to turn on each other."

He was describing it matter-of-fact, in a detached voice.

"You lured them out of the Keep?" she guessed.

"Yes."

"How?"

"Panacea. I wanted a lot of distance, so I went to Europe, to the Black Sea. I had a castle there, a quiet base for Middle Eastern operations. There are a lot of potent old powers in Arabia. Best to stay out of their way, on the outskirts."

"Did Lennart and Daniels come?"

Hugh nodded.

"What was it like meeting her?" Elara asked. "What was Daniels like?"

"You wanted just the facts, remember?"

"Did she like your proposal?"

"No. We danced around for a while. Sparred once."

"Is she good?"

"Yes."

"Better than you?"

"Faster. Voron taught us both. It was like fighting myself. She's a killer. If you take away her sword, she'll pick up a rock. If you take away the rock, she'll kill you with her hands. She zeroes in and doesn't let go."

Suppressed admiration slipped into his words. Elara felt an uncomfortable pinch.

"Aside from fighting Voron, it was probably my best fight," he said.

"You fought Voron?"

"I killed him."

She stared at him. "Why?"

"Roland wanted him dead."

So his second surrogate father ordered him to kill his first surrogate father. And he obeyed. Either he was truly a monster or...

"Did it hurt when you killed him?"

"He wasn't exactly in his prime." Hugh smiled, but his eyes didn't. It hurt, she realized. It hurt, and it haunted him still.

"Voron was bound to Roland the same way I was bound," he said.

"How?"

"Roland pulled the blood out of my body, mixed it with his, and put it back."

She stared at him. "How is that possible?"

"Roland's magic is ancient. He is capable of wonders. The blood brings with it certain powers. Blood weapons. Blood wards. Long lifespan. Healing is mine alone. I was born with it. Some things I learned like any other mage can learn. But blood powers come from Roland. When Roland killed his wife, he expected Voron to come back. We all did. When he didn't Roland purged him the way he purged me."

"What does that mean?" she asked.

"When I found Voron, he was an old man. He had aged. He could no longer make a blood sword. He couldn't use magic. He still had his skills, but his body betrayed him. I had waited a long time to meet him. There was a conversation I wanted to have. But he wouldn't talk to me, and I killed him quickly, because it hurt to look at him."

Is that what would happen to Hugh? "You haven't aged."

He grinned at her. "Give it time."

They walked some more.

"I knew how that damn trip to the Black Sea would end from the start," Hugh said. "Violence, magic, and fire. An old power got involved and broke open the mountain under the castle to release the magic of a dormant volcano. It melted the castle from the inside out. Solid stone ran like a glowing river. Beautiful, in a way."

"What happened?"

"I knew I had to kill Lennart, or Daniels would never leave him. We fought. I broke his legs. He broke my back and threw me into the fire. The whole thing was idiotic."

Volcanic fire powered by magic that melted stone. He should've been instantly burned to a crisp. "How did you survive?"

"I teleported out. Had a water anchor in a vial around my neck. There wasn't much of me left. Roland put me inside a phoenix egg for three months. Took me another two to get my strength back."

He'd spent three months in excruciating pain. He'd said it so casually, as if it didn't matter.

"If it wasn't for Lennart, I might have convinced her. She wavered."

"I don't think she did."

—✛—

HUGH TURNED TO HER. He didn't want to speak about it in the first place, but somehow Elara was pulling it out of him and once he started, he couldn't stop. The void was ripping him apart, and still he talked.

"You said she was a killer," Elara said. "An orphan. Her real father was a mystery. Her adoptive father made her hide."

"Your point?" he asked.

Elara tilted her head to glance at his face. "Roland took care of your needs. He probably taught you, right? Provided you with money? You were his right hand."

"Everything I got, I earned," Hugh told her. "I worked and bled for it. Everything he asked, I did. No matter what it cost."

Daniels was Hugh's only major failure. He never knew he was only allowed one.

"But you got whatever you wanted, right?"

"Your point?"

"She was an orphan, living on the run, probably hungry, poor, always looking over her shoulder. You were exactly like her, but you had everything, and she had nothing. Hugh, you're an astute, experienced man. Put yourself into her shoes. You were both trained by Voron. You both lived your lives in Roland's shadow. You worshipped him, and she feared him. Of all the people on this planet, you are the ones who truly know what it's like to be Roland's child."

"Except I wasn't his child."

Daniels hated her father. She fought Roland on every turn, while he'd spent decades serving him. But Daniels was blood and that mattered more to Roland than anything Hugh had done. Like the prodigal child, when Daniels was found, she eclipsed the decades of his service without trying simply because she was Roland's daughter and he would never be his son.

"Try to think like her for a moment," Elara said. "You knew her father in a way she never did. You knew Voron and you likely had him longer than she did. You have so much in common. Then you killed Voron, whom she must've loved; tried to kill Lennart, whom she loves; and then tried to force her to go back to the father she hated, even though you, of all people, knew exactly what waited for her there. The betrayal was catastrophic."

Hugh felt a vague unease. The void spun around him, making it harder to think. He pushed it aside and focused. A memory came to him, he and Daniels fighting in the castle at the Black Sea. She'd won that fight and trapped him with her sword. He'd had to submit. He'd said, "Uncle." But there was a hint of something there, when they fought. Rage poured out of her, powerful and seductive. That red-hot boiling rage. It turned him on. He wanted to keep fighting her. He wouldn't have stopped until one of them was dead, and she knew it.

Her face flashed before him. Daniels had looked horrified. And then she almost fled.

The recollection disturbed him. He groped for the connection to Roland, for the clean feeling of surety that clarified all his doubts, but it wasn't there. He was on his own.

Hugh locked his teeth, sorting through his memories, going through Daniels's facial expressions. He remembered the last one best, the time he had starved her, trying to force her to submit to her father. She had this look of resignation on her face as if she had given up on him ever getting it.

She never saw him as a man. He was never in the running; he had known that from the start. He was either an extension of Roland or…

It hit him like a ton of bricks. Daniels saw him as a sibling. She probably didn't even realize it.

On some level he had always understood it. It wasn't the woman he had wanted. It was what she represented. He wanted her acceptance. He wanted her to admit how good he was. He would've seduced her to get it and then rubbed Roland's face in it. One way or the other, the bastard would acknowledge him then.

Validation. So simple.

At the Black Sea, Lennart had played a ruse, pretending to be interested in another woman. It was a moronic tactic, one that always backfired, and it took a lot of work to cut off all possible escape routes until Hugh forced Lennart into that path. Hugh had quite enjoyed watching it play out at the time. It seemed odd, when Hugh thought about it now, as if it had happened to someone else. It had made Daniels desperate. It had made her vulnerable.

How the hell did he miscalculate so badly? It was painfully obvious now.

"I should've played the brother angle." He didn't realize he had spoken out loud until he heard his own voice.

"Come back to your true family?" Elara asked.

He nodded. "It would've been so easy too. 'Look at everything you sacrificed for Lennart, and here he is, sniffing after the first attractive shapeshifter girl that fluttered her eyelashes at him. You'll never belong with them, but you belong with us. We are your true family. He'll never understand you, but we will. I will. I know exactly what it's like. Come with me, and you will have a father and a brother who love you above all others.' Damn it! I could've had her."

She didn't say anything.

"Why the hell didn't I see it?"

"Because you wanted something from her, Hugh," Elara said, her voice gentle. "And it made you blind. What did you want?"

"Doesn't matter now."

He wanted acceptance. If not from Roland, then from her. He would never have it now, and when he thought about it, the ball of conflicting crap those thoughts dragged in their wake was too complicated to deal with.

"Should I worry about this Daniels coming here to kill you?" Elara asked. "If I were her, I'd hunt you to the ends of the Earth."

Hugh struggled for a moment with the paradox of someone worrying about him. "No. Her hands are tied. She claimed Atlanta as her domain the night Roland exiled me. If she leaves, he will attack."

"So she sacrificed revenge for her people."

"That's the way she's wired."

"Do you still want her?"

She'd asked the question so casually, so perfectly flat. Hugh glanced at her. She looked at the road ahead, her face relaxed, but it was too late. He'd caught that one tiny note of female jealousy in her voice.

The untouchable goddess of the castle. Would wonders never cease?

Elara turned to him. "Hugh? I need to know if you will take off looking for her if you get a chance."

Sure, you do. You shouldn't have shown your hand, love.

"It doesn't matter now. It's in the past."

"Is it? Is Roland in the past?"

The void opened its mouth and swallowed him whole. For a moment he couldn't even speak, then the thing that drove him into battle reared its head and he tore free.

She was waiting for an answer.

Perceptive and smart, his dangerous harpy. His lovely wife. Elara had thought about it, about him. There was a spark there. All he had to do was blow on it and feed it, and he would get her. If their fights were anything to go by, he was in for a hell of a time.

"Roland no longer matters," he lied.

"If Roland and Daniels don't matter, neither does the Pack."

The woods ended. They turned down the street to the smithy.

"So much effort to keep me from blowing up your deal. I have to give it to you, you really tried. Good show."

She bared her teeth at him. "If you pick a fight with the Pack tomorrow, I'll kill you and bury you in those herb beds back there."

"That's my sweet harpy. Come on, let me see those claws."

"I mean it, Hugh."

"Is it Hugh now? Not Preceptor?"

She eyed him. "I'll call you Preceptor when you're done with your immature tantrums."

He laughed.

Elara looked into his eyes, her gaze searching. "What is it you stand for, Hugh d'Ambray?" she asked.

He reached for the answer. It eluded him for the moment. "Good times and loose women."

Elara rolled her eyes and peered at the smithy. "What are we doing here anyway?"

He reached into his pocket and pulled out the sketch of the warrior. "We're going to ask your best smith how hard it is to make this scale mail."

He already knew the answer, but he wanted confirmation anyway.

She sighed.

"Come on, then, wife. Put on a happy face."

"Ugh." She reached over and slid her fingers into the crook of his elbow.

"Good God, control yourself, woman. We're in public. At least wait until we're in the bedroom."

"Your corpse will grow lovely goldenseal."

He laughed again and walked her down to the smithy.

———+——

HUGH STOOD in front of his bedroom window, leaning on the windowsill. Night breathed in his face, cool and soothing after the day's heat. Early October had been surprisingly hot. He'd left the door to his rooms open, and the night breeze swirled past him, sucked out the door, down the hallway and into the depths of the castle.

Things used to be simple. Too simple.

He was a man who killed one father, failed the other, and left a trail of destruction in his wake four continents wide. When he looked back now, he saw bodies. It never bothered him before. He'd felt vague pangs of guilt, but never this.

It wasn't natural. That was the only explanation. If he felt all this shit now, he would've felt it when he was doing it. He should've been bothered. That part of him had been suppressed and he wasn't the one doing that suppressing.

An absurd urge to find Nez gripped him. Did he feel this? Was his leash longer? Was he allowed guilt?

"What is it you stand for, Hugh?"

Fuck if I know.

He wanted the bottle tonight. More than anything. He wanted to get drunk and forget all of it.

He heard footsteps behind him. "You called?" Lamar asked.

"Come in."

The tall lanky man came over and leaned against the desk.

"Tell me what happened after my exile."

"I thought you didn't want to know."

"I do now."

Lamar pulled a cloth out of his pocket, took off his glasses, and cleaned the lenses. "The same night Roland exiled you, he went to Atlanta. There was a bargain. Lennart gave up the Pack. In return Roland agreed to a hundred-year peace with Daniels."

"He separated her from her power base."

"Yes. Once I was out of the picture, he began the systematic purge of the Iron Dogs. Anyone loyal to you became a target."

"What about Atlanta?"

"Roland began building on the edge of it."

"He was baiting her," Hugh said. "He can't help himself."

"For a while he played father of the year, but Daniels never trusted him. Eventually he kidnapped one of her people, a polymorph named Saiman. She came to visit Roland at the fort he was building and demanded Saiman back. He refused. They screamed at each other in the language of power. She called him a usurper. Stoyan was there on the cross. He didn't understand most of it, but he said the day was bright and sunny, and by the end of it, the sky turned black and lightning struck the ground. When they were done, she got Stoyan and got the hell out of there."

It sounded like something Daniels would do. Subtle like a runaway bulldozer.

"She defended you," Lamar said.

Hugh turned to him.

"You said you wanted to know. Stoyan memorized that part. He thought you would want to know one day." Lamar reached inside his pocket and pulled out a piece of paper.

"Read it to me."

"'You were everything to him. He committed all those atrocities for you and you stripped him of your love, the thing he cared about most.' 'Hugh outlived his usefulness. His life had been a series of uncomplicated tasks and eventually he became his work.'"

A simpleton. That's how he saw me. And she understood.

"'He was raised exactly like you wanted him to be.' 'He was like a fallen star. I melted it down and forged it into a sword. It's not truly his fault, but the world is becoming more complicated not less. Some swords are meant to be forged only once.'"

The void turned to fire around him.

I am a sword. A weapon. Okay. But you've made me into a really sharp sword and I know how to cut you.

Lamar took a step back and swallowed. "Are you alright?"

"What happened next?"

"Roland brought an army. Not his main force, the secondary divisions he had spaced out through the region. Daniels turned the Atlanta Chapter of the People."

"Of course she did. Ghastek is her Legatus?"

"Yes. How did you...?"

"Ghastek is terrified of death and Daniels can bestow immortality," Hugh said. "What happened with the battle?"

"They fought. Roland assaulted the Keep. It was the crudest assault known to mankind."

"Don't tell me he formed up his troops and marched them to their fort."

164

"He did exactly that."

Moron.

The word sliced across his nerves like a red-hot blade. He'd just called Roland a moron in his head. The pain echoed through him, but the world kept spinning.

"The combined forces of Atlanta massacred his army," Lamar said. "Daniels and Lennart tried to kill him. He fled."

His brain chopped through the words trying to make sense of them. "He fled?"

"He did." Lamar smiled. "Teleported out."

A chance. Daniels had a shot at the title.

His mind ached, reeling from the red-hot pain.

"Daniels is pregnant," Lamar said quietly.

"Is it Lennart's?" He already knew the answer.

"They're married, and she doesn't seem like the cheating type."

"Roland's worst fear," Hugh thought out loud.

"Why?" Lamar asked.

"Roland's magic is like a science. It's systematic, it's logical, and it has laws. It supports all of the cornerstones of the scientific method: the observation, measurement, experimentation, and formation and testing of theory. He views it as a civilizing force. Shapeshifter magic is ancient and wild. It relies on instinct. It predates Roland's systematic approach. He derides it as primitive, but he fears it and he's drawn to it because he doesn't understand it. He's fascinated by witches. His daughter is half a witch and now she's conceived a shapeshifter child."

Understanding shone in Lamar's eyes. "He's afraid his grandchild will surpass him."

Hugh nodded. "He'll do anything to get his hands on that kid. Except that he's thinking a generation too late. It's not the baby he needs to worry about. It's the mother."

"What does it mean for us..." Lamar frowned.

"My wife allied us with the Pack. The Pack is allied with Daniels. That moves us from Nez's Personal Amusement column to Weaken Roland's Enemy. We have two choices: we can sever all association with the Pack or we can openly declare ourselves their allies."

Lamar rubbed the back of his head. "Pick your enemy time."

"Betraying the Pack buys us time." And will make Elara nearly unmanageable. "Standing against Roland now complicates things. Tomorrow the Pack people are arriving. Nez will force the issue. That's the way he thinks."

"What do you want me to do?" Lamar asked.

"Your cohort is standing watch tomorrow."

"Yes."

"We're going to do a repeat of Fort Smith."

Lamar blinked. "Okay. How many do you want at the castle?"

"Give me twenty-five."

"Will do." Lamar grinned. "Bale's got the graveyard watch. It will kill him."

"He'll survive. That's all," Hugh said.

Lamar nodded, walked to the door, and turned. "Preceptor?"

"Yes?"

"If he wants you back, what will you do?"

To be back in the light of the magic again. Everything forgiven. All the doubts forgotten. To bask in Roland's approval was like walking into sunshine after an endless cold night. He craved it like a drug.

"I don't know," he said.

Lamar nodded and walked out.

8

The morning sun shone through the open arches of the breezeway. The short bridge between two towers had a roof, but no windows. Instead large arches were cut into its walls, open to the wind and the sunshine. Elara strolled through it. She liked it here, above the castle, away from work and obligations. And looking down through the arches gave her a slight chill of alarm. She did it now, standing still, looking for a few torturous seconds at the land far below.

Such a long way down.

Slowly, deliberately, Elara took a step back to the safety of the breezeway. Familiar relief came to her. She smiled. She needed that after last night. Six hours of research and divination and she had nothing to show for it.

She did have plenty of time to stew in her hate of all things Hugh d'Ambray. Yesterday at the smithy, he was insufferable. They did learn one useful thing: Radion couldn't duplicate the pattern of the scale mail and he didn't know of anyone who could.

Rook emerged from the other tower, moving quickly.

"Yes?"

He reached into a pocket and rolled a glass marble to her. With the magic up, he had no need for paper.

The marble stopped by her feet and Hugh tore out of it, swinging his sword.

She jumped back on pure instinct, but not fast enough. The sword passed through her, harmless, and kept going, because it was only Rook's memory. Hugh twisted like a feral tiger, and struck again and again, fast, sharp, sinking so much strength and speed into his swings, they would've cut anyone standing in his way in half. The raw power, tempered by skill, was mesmerizing. He wasn't wearing his uniform or armor. He wore a T-shirt, dark pants, and boots. He wasn't actually fighting. This was practice, but it definitely wasn't routine. Some inner demon saddled Hugh and drove him into a controlled devastating frenzy.

He was oddly beautiful, the way superior athletes sometimes were, as they pushed their bodies to the limit. Still a touch too lean from starvation, yet a pinnacle of what a human body could do. The way the sun caught the blade of his sword added an almost mystical touch to it, as if it weren't practice, but a sacrifice of sweat and skill to some vicious war god.

Sun. Practice? In open air?

You... you bastard. "Where is he?"

Rook pointed down. She leaned out of the nearest arch.

Hugh whirled below, striking and slicing invisible opponents. Beside him about twenty of his people were doing the same thing, some paired off into practice fights, some by themselves, going through the exercises. In the main bailey. Right in front of the gates.

Rook raised his hand. She looked in the direction of his fingers. Six riders coming up the road. The Pack delegation. They would ride right into the middle of Hugh's training spree.

Damn that man.

Elara turned and ran to the tower.

She made it out of the tower onto the landing just as the Pack delegates rode to the gates. Dugas was already there, watching.

Hugh showed no signs of slowing down. He had at least two dozen soldiers and he'd ordered the horses out too. They waited on the side, already saddled and tied to the rail at the wall, Bucky with his silver hair standing out like a sore thumb.

"What is he doing?" she ground out.

"Not staying in his room like you told him to," Dugas said. "I suppose he doesn't like being grounded."

The first rider entered through the gates. He was surprisingly young, maybe eighteen at most, dark-haired, dark-eyed, and shockingly beautiful. He saw Hugh. A red sheen rolled over his eyes.

She sighed. There was no way to stop it.

Behind him the second rider saw Hugh and stopped.

The leading rider said something and started toward Hugh, slowly.

Dugas turned to her.

"If I run down there now and dramatically thrust myself between him and Hugh, it will destroy Hugh's credibility and make me look like an idiot."

"Yes," Dugas said.

Elara plastered a smile on her face. "Then I will slowly walk. Here is hoping they don't kill each other." She crossed her fingers and walked down the steps.

The boy got there first.

Hugh finished his swing, wiped the sword with a cloth, thrust it into the weapon rack, and picked up a bucket.

"Fancy meeting you here," the boy said.

"Hello," Elara said. "I take it you're Ascanio Ferara. I see you know my husband."

"Yes, I do. The last time we met, he tortured me," Ascanio said.

He what? Could this get any worse?

"You're still alive," Hugh said. "Clearly my heart wasn't in it." He raised the bucket and poured water over his head.

"He tortured you?" she asked.

"He was trying to get a friend of mine to come out of a cage, so he could take her to her father," Ascanio said. "So he would heal me, then break me, then heal me again. I don't remember it, but I heard such wonderful stories about it. Your husband is a man of many accomplishments."

Oh, there was no doubt of that.

"Let's see, his people killed the alpha of my clan, he broke the Beast Lord's legs, he kidnapped the Beast Lord's mate, dumped her into a shaft filled with water inside her father's prison, and almost starved her to death. These are just the highlights." He laughed, an eerie crazy cackle.

A bouda, Elara realized. A werehyena. They were notoriously quick-tempered and crazy. And Hugh didn't mention kidnapping Daniels. He'd kept that to himself.

She couldn't believe it actually bothered her.

This had gone far enough, Elara reminded herself. Pulling his feelings out of him was about understanding your enemy, not fueling insecurities.

Hugh regarded the shapeshifter, his face slightly bored. "Do you want to do something about it?"

"Mmmm, let me think..." Ascanio leaned forward, his agile face taking on a pondering expression. "I attack you, you kill me, I start a war, shame the Bouda Clan, and my mother will never get to hear the end of it as long as she lives. Not to mention she would be sad. Tempting, but no. I'm here to retrieve the two families and that's exactly what I will do. The question is, are you going to do something about it?"

She caught her breath.

"No," Hugh said. "Are they ready to go, Elara?"

"Yes, they are."

Hugh looked back at Ascanio. "They were treated well. If more come, they will be treated the same. We'll keep them safe until you pick them up."

The bouda squinted at Hugh. "That's it?"

"That's it." Hugh turned his back to Ascanio.

She felt like sitting down. Instead she smiled at Ascanio. "Do you need any provisions for the road?"

———✠———

HUGH STRETCHED HIS SHOULDERS. The small shapeshifter group was about two-thirds of the way to the tree line. They were moving at a crawl, the possessions of the two families loaded into two large carts. They were planning to catch the leyline by Aberdine. At the ley point, they would transfer the furniture and clothes to the shipping platform, board, and let the magic drag them east. Once they got close enough to Atlanta, they'd likely load the possessions into trucks, but the carts were a prudent move for the road that snaked its way through the forest. Any truck that ran on enchanted water would've made enough noise to wake the dead, and Ferara clearly wanted to do this quietly. They had barely twelve miles to go, and on this occasion slow and quiet would win the race.

A woman from the town had come to get Elara fifteen minutes ago. Something about a child. His cantankerous wife finally decided that he wasn't going to do anything and left.

The wagons crept on, slower than molasses. The shapeshifters were sitting ducks out there.

Perfect.

Hugh swung into Bucky's saddle and rode up to the gates. The twenty-five Dogs on horseback formed up into a column behind him.

Dugas strode up to him. "Interesting kid."

"He'll be the next bouda alpha."

And they would all be worse for it. He remembered the files on

Raphael and Andrea Medrano, who ran the clan now. At Ferara's age and under similar circumstances, Raphael would've charged Hugh the moment he saw him. Boudas lost a lot of children to loupism, especially males. They spoiled the surviving boys beyond reason. That Ferara had the presence of mind to set aside pride and personal history to preserve the alliance was nothing short of a miracle. Shrewd.

It would be prudent to kill him now, before he matured.

Dugas stepped closer to him. "What do you think you're doing? Running him down now, after he thinks he's in the clear?"

Hugh turned and held the old man's stare. "Step back."

Dugas blinked and backed away.

"They're fifty yards from the trees," Liz called from the wall.

Far enough.

He pulled the magic to him and leaned forward in the saddle. "Charge."

Bucky shot through the gates. Behind them the Iron Dogs spilled out of Baile, breaking into a canter.

A horn bellowed from the castle walls, a harsh declaration of war.

Ascanio spun his horse around. Hugh couldn't hear the words from this distance, but it didn't take a genius to read the kid's expression. Ascanio shouted.

They'd either break for the trees on foot, scattering, every shapeshifter for themselves, or they'd make a stand. Either way Hugh would get what he wanted, but the stand would make them easier to contain.

Bucky sped up into a full gallop. Hugh had forgotten this, forgotten the rush of a full charge, but it was coming back. He used to live for this.

The shapeshifters threw the kids into the wagons. Lennart's tactics. Stand together and live or die together.

Hugh raised his hand. Behind him the column of riders fanned out into a line.

The shapeshifters turned as one, fur and claws and snarling mouths filled with fangs.

The horn screamed from the walls.

Hugh pulled magic to him. He hadn't tried to do this since he'd been exiled. This wasn't his native magic; he'd learned it as a child from Roland. He had no idea if the power was still there. He began whispering the incantation, paving the way for the release.

Ascanio raised two curved foot-long knives, his face a meld of hyena and human, eyes blazing. His people crowded around the wagons, shielding the four children inside.

Twenty-five yards to the wagons.

Twenty.

Fifteen.

He angled Bucky. His force split in half, flowing around the wagons like a river. Ferara's face flashed past him, fanged mouth hanging open in surprise. The trees loomed ahead.

Now. He reached for the smudges of foul magic.

"Ranar kair!"

Power poured out of Hugh, channeled through words of power so old, they shaped the very nature of the magic.

Come before me.

Agony tore through him, so sharp it felt like death, and for a moment Hugh felt a spark of hope that it would kill him. The world wavered and snapped back into focus instead.

The aftershock of the power words tore through the trees. The woods quaked and spat eight undead.

Predictable, Nez. So predictable.

The vampires spun, turning back to the trees, away from the cavalry charge.

Fifty Iron Dogs charged out of the trees, moving in a line, trapping the vampires between the two forces.

The first bloodsucker loomed in front of Hugh, still dazed from the impact of the power words. Hugh tore past, swinging his sword. The undead's head rolled off its shoulders. The two forces closed in on the vampires like scissors coming together. An eerie cackle rolled through the battlefield – the shapeshifters joining the fight.

Hugh brought Bucky in a wide circle and leapt off his back. Fighting the undead on horseback would only get the stallion killed.

"All teams!" a male voice snapped from among the undead line. "Engage the enemy. Pursue at will. I repeat, pursue at will. Alpha Two, Alpha Three, on me. Contain the Preceptor."

Three undead broke off and charged him.

Hugh let them come, gripping his sword with both hands in front of him, aiming to impale the front bloodsucker. The undead charged at him, eyes burning with red. The real fight wasn't here. It was with the man behind the vampire, and that man had drilled Nez's tactics until they became second nature.

So had Hugh.

At the last moment, the vamp twisted to the left, relying on its superior speed, counting on him to thrust. Had Hugh lunged, the blade of his sword would've missed the bloodsucker by an inch, leaving his own left flank completely exposed. Instead he stepped forward with his right foot and turned left, stepping back and driving the blade with all his weight. His sword caught the vamp just above the collar bone, severing the neck. Hugh turned into the spin, raising his blade, and brought his sword straight down, cleaving the second vamp's head like a ripe melon.

The third undead spun, twisting away from his sword, bounced off the ground, and leapt at him. Hugh dodged. Claws grazed his shoulder. Hugh took the hit and smashed the back of his sword into the base of the vampire's skull as it tore past him. The undead stumbled forward. Hugh kicked it in the back, stomping hard on the spine. The vamp sprawled on the ground, and Hugh drove his sword straight down, through the back into the heart. *Contain this.*

The whole thing took less than two seconds.

His heart beat faster. The world turned crystal clear. This –
this – was living.

Hugh freed the blade with a sharp tug. All around him battle
boiled. The Dogs struck at the vampires. Two boudas locked on
one bloodsucker from opposite sides and tore it apart like a
blood-filled ragdoll. He flicked the blood off his blade and dove
into the slaughter, looking for something to kill.

———

HUGH SURVEYED THE FIELD. No undead moved. The smears of
their magic had faded. Nine serious gashes, two broken limbs, no
casualties on their side. His people had the element of surprise
and magic on their side. Everything except dead could be fixed.

A blood-stained bouda strode toward him, seven feet tall and
corded with muscle under sparse fur. They really did look like
shit in warrior form. Part of the reason why Roland detested
them, Hugh suspected. The human and animal meld wasn't graceful. This one, at least, was more cohesive than most.

The bouda unhinged his jaws. "Motherrrrfuckrr," Ascanio
snarled.

Most shapeshifters couldn't speak in warrior form. Their jaws
didn't fit together correctly. Hugh was right before. It was better
to kill the kid now and avoid complications.

"You used us as bait!"

"Shut up," Hugh told him. "You're still breathing."

"How did you know?"

"I knew because I've been a warlord longer than you've been
alive." Hugh nodded at a fresh detachment of Dogs riding up to
them. "This is your escort to the ley line."

"You could've told us!"

"You wouldn't have believed me. Tell Shrapshire I have no
problem with him when you get home."

Ascanio towered over him.

"Are you going to stand here all day with your dick in your hand? You're losing the light."

The kid turned, snarling orders under his breath.

He watched the shapeshifter wagons roll past him, the shapeshifters in warrior forms running along the sides, their horses hitched to the back. A little girl, no more than two or three, stared at him from the second wagon, her big dark eyes round and terrified on her brown face.

She would get where she needed to go. They did that much.

For some odd reason, that thought brought Hugh satisfaction. He puzzled over it. It shouldn't have mattered. She was a random child. She didn't belong to any of his people. They had no connection to each other and he would never see her again.

"Preceptor," Lamar said next to him.

Hugh rested the sword on his shoulder and turned.

A figure in a green dress stood on the wall of the castle. He couldn't see her face, but she stood with her feet planted and her arms crossed.

He growled low in his throat.

"Do you require backup?" Lamar asked quietly.

"No." Elara was his wife. He would handle her himself. For now, he'd let her stew.

Hugh took his time supervising the loading of the undead bodies on the cart. By that point, a group of Elara's people had showed up with bags of salt, and jugs of water and gasoline, and set about purging the traces of undead blood. When Hugh truly had nothing left to do, he whistled for Bucky and rode him back to the castle, the Dogs and the wagon loaded with undead right behind him.

He got there just as Bale came running from within the castle, half-dressed, his hair sticking up.

"Vampires!" Bale bellowed and pointed behind them. "You fought vampires and I didn't get to go?"

The Dogs snickered. Hugh cracked a smile.

"It was a glorious battle," Lamar said. "You slept through it all."

Bale stared at him, incredulous. "You took Lamar? Lamar instead of me?"

"Don't worry," Lamar said. "I'll tell you all about it."

Bale shook his arms and howled at the sky. "There is no justice in the world!"

The Dogs laughed. Hugh chuckled, dismounted, and took Bucky to the stables. This was good. They all needed a victory after getting their assess handed to them for the last eight months and this one was theirs alone. The shapeshifters helped, but the victory belonged to the Dogs.

Hugh was settling Bucky into his stall when he heard light footsteps. She'd chased him down.

"A word in private, Preceptor."

"Not right now," he told her without bothering to look at her face.

"Yes, now. You put children in danger. You didn't tell me what you were going to do. I could've helped. We could've killed them without jeopardizing the shapeshifters."

He turned to her. Fury lit her eyes. Her mouth was a flat narrow line. She was clenching her teeth. She wasn't just mad; she was livid.

"First, I'm going to take care of my horse. Then, I'm going to change and wash the blood from my face. If I feel like talking then, you can come and discuss whatever it is. Or you can make a hysterical scene right here in the stables where everyone can hear us. Your choice."

He turned to Bucky. When he looked back, Elara was gone.

———•—

HUGH OPENED HIS EYES. A square room stood before him, the stone walls lit by the gentle glow of electric lamps. A square pool took up nearly the entire floor, with a three-foot walkway along the walls. Five steps led into the pool. The water lay placid, reflecting the light of the lamps. The soothing aroma of lavender and jasmine floated in the air.

How the hell did he get here? He looked over his shoulder. Another chamber, shrouded in gloom. The last thing he remembered was going upstairs to his room. He'd showered, had a steak sent up from the kitchen, ate it all, washed it down with some beer, and passed out on his bed.

A quiet feminine laughter floated to him. He turned back. Three girls soaked in the pool. One sat on his right, kicking her feet gently in the water, her long blond hair spilling over soft glowing skin. A brunette waited straight ahead, her plump breasts lifted slightly by the water. On the left a redhead sat, half-submerged on the steps, her long hair swirling in the water.

A dream. And a nice one. A welcome change from the usual shit he dreamt about. Whatever they brewed in that beer, he would need more of it.

The brunette raised her hands and stood up, her arms opened wide, exposing her breasts with pretty pink nipples. "Hugh!"

"Join us," the blond giggled.

His clothes were missing. He was already hard. Hugh walked into pool. The water was hot. The aroma of lavender grew stronger. The redhead wound herself around him, the blue eyes on her freckled face laughing at him. The blond jumped into the water and surfaced next to him. The brunette kneaded his shoulders. He pulled the blond closer, her skin slick against his own, her body pliant under his fingers. Oh yes. Yes, that would do.

"Enjoying yourself?" Elara said.

She stood at the steps. Her hair was down, a soft silky cascade. She wore a simple white dress. It left her shoulders bare. A slit climbed its way up the skirt, revealing a leg with a slender ankle and rounded thigh.

Even better. "Come into the pool," Hugh said.

She shook her head. "Greedy, greedy, greedy."

He had to get her into the water. "Come here, Elara."

She ignored him. Vapor rose from the water. There was something witchy about her, arcane and female. He would peel that dress from her.

"Tell me about the boy?"

"What boy?"

"The shapeshifter boy you tortured." Elara walked along the pool to the left.

"Come closer and I'll tell you."

"Tell me and I'll think about it."

Hugh rose and began striding through the water to her. The three women hung onto him and he dragged them forward.

Elara leaned forward, her hazel eyes bright. "Are you going to chase me?"

"Do you want me to?"

She dipped her foot into the water. "You used the kids as bait today."

"They weren't in danger."

"Tell me about Ascanio."

Hugh was walking through the water but not making any progress. "Fine. What do you want to know?"

"Did you really torture a child?"

"Yes. He was sixteen at the time. I was chasing Kate through the city and she didn't want to be caught."

He drew closer. As long as he kept talking, the distance between them shrank.

"I used a wendigo to herd her, because I knew she was smart enough to stay out of its way. The kid was with her and he tried to fight it. It tore him up."

If he could grab her ankle, he would yank her into the pool.

"What happened next?"

"Kate ran for the Order of Merciful Aid, and then knights stuck her into a loup cage. I killed them all."

"You killed off the knights of the Order of Merciful Aid?"

"Yes." Elara was almost within reach. "Kate was angry. The last one was her friend. She watched me kill him."

"Why would you do that in front of her?"

"He didn't give me a choice. It was a hard kill. Roland wanted his daughter. Nothing mattered except getting her to him. Nothing else existed."

Hugh struggled to explain the relentless pressure and the finality in Roland's eyes when he had given the order. He'd gone into it with a kind of grim determination that now seemed desperate. He couldn't find the words.

"I had to get her out of the cage, she was pissed, and they left Ascanio on the table. His stomach was in ribbons. The wendigo crushed his ribs and bones stuck out through the skin. The shapeshifter virus kept him alive up to that point, but he was dying. The knights didn't treat him, because he was a bouda."

Her ankle was within his reach. Two more steps and he was there. There were things he needed to do to her.

"So what did you do?"

"I healed him."

"What else?"

"The virus had fused some of the broken bones. I had to rebreak him to fix his chest. I made her think I was alternating between killing and healing. She promised to come out of the cage if I healed him, but someone interfered."

"Would you have killed the boy to get her?"

"Yes."

"But he was a child."

"Nothing mattered except getting Kate to Sharrum."

"What does that word mean, Sharrum?"

"King. God. Everything. Everything that I am is shaped by Sharrum. He is wisdom and purpose. He is life."

"Not everything."

Hugh lunged forward but her foot slipped out of his reach. She vanished. Hugh spun around and saw her on the stairs.

"No more talking," he told her. "Come here, Elara."

She laughed softly.

"I said come here." He sank steel into his voice.

"You have no power over me," she told him. "I don't obey your orders."

The water boiled in front of him. A blunt white head surfaced, eyeless and noseless, a wide monster mouth gaped open, studded with razor-sharp teeth, and bit down at his groin, ripping through his flesh.

Agony tore through Hugh. He jerked upright and saw darkness. Cold sweat drenched his face. He was sitting in his bed. His body shuddered in pain. He yanked the sheet aside and grabbed himself. Everything was still there. He was intact.

A ghostly voice whispered in his ear. *"The next time I want to talk to you, make the time."*

Damn that bitch. Hugh sprung out of his bed. His door flew open under the pressure of his hand, revealing the hallway lit with fey lanterns. He marched through it and hit her door and it banged open. He strode through her bedroom. The big wooden canopy bed stood empty, but a stone doorway in the wall opposite the entrance glowed with a buttery-yellow glow. Hugh tore through it and stopped.

A square room offered the square pool from his dream. She was in it, long white hair swirling, steam and water hiding all of her, except for her face. And she was smiling.

"Stay the fuck out of my dreams."

"Aww. You didn't like the girls? Should I have made them with Vanessa's face?" The water around her glowed with a pale light as if something much larger and glowing moved underneath.

"I mean it, Elara." Hugh didn't want to go into the water. The pain was still too real. Every instinct in him screamed when he caught glimpses of the glowing thing. He would do almost anything to avoid the pool.

"Have you ever killed a child, Hugh?" Her voice was completely serious.

He felt a powerful compulsion to answer. "Not directly."

Elara stared at him, her face worried.

"I've never run a child through with my sword. But I led an army. We fought. People died. You can't control war, Elara. Nobody leaves it with their hands clean."

She tilted her head, studying him.

The lights on the wall were electric. The illumination outside in the hallway came from fey lanterns, but here electric lamps glowed with golden light. He was still dreaming. She was still fucking with his head.

"You want to see inside my mind, Elara?" He strode into the water. Panic bit him, but he crushed it. Magic bathed his legs. "Go ahead and look."

He remembered it all for her. The razor-edge flash of ending a life, one after another, the endless chain of deaths he caused, the blood, the pain, watching friends fall, the screams, the clamor of metal on metal, the staccato of guns, failing, breaking, burning, getting up again and again, and killing... Everything that he used to shrug off and that now haunted his nightmares, he let it all out. He owned all of it. He was ordered to do it, he was praised when he succeeded, and it didn't matter, because every drop of blood, every last gasp, all of it was his fault.

Blood spread from him through the water, thick and red. She shrank from it, but it stained her skin and hair.

The pool vanished.

Hugh opened his eyes to the welcome darkness of his bedroom. He wished he weren't alone, but he was. He lay in darkness, listening to his heart beating too fast and waiting until the memories faded enough for sleep to come.

9

E lara paced back and forth. The scent of fresh bread and roasted meat filled the great hall in front of her. Long wooden tables covered with white cloths had been set out to form a horseshoe with breaks between them for the guests and staff to walk through. In the center of the horseshoe stood a massive wooden barrel into which the staff of Honeymead Brewery busily poured beer out of large metal casks.

Rufus Fortner, the head of the Lexington Red Guard, was due in less than an hour. The original plan was for him to bring a couple of his "fellahs" with him. As of the last phone call, a couple ballooned to fifteen, including Rufus. It didn't seem like much, but she had seen what Hugh could do with twenty Iron Dogs. The Red Guard was the best in private security. Five guardsmen felt like guests. Fifteen felt like a raid. It could be just that Fortner wanted to show off Roland's Warlord. It could be something else. Either way, when he got here, they had to offer him the kind of feast he would remember.

Hugh's Dogs were hanging weapons and banners on the walls. The place looked like some Viking hall or the chamber of some medieval king.

She turned to Hugh, who was standing next to her. "Is that a good idea?"

He glanced at her. His eyes were very blue and clear this evening. They hadn't spoken for the last three days after the dream. It wasn't that she made a conscious effort to avoid him. It was that she'd been busy with offering protection to the nearby towns and processing the harvested roots of Lady's Seal, while he was supervising deliveries of the volcanic ash for the mortar to line the moat's bottom. Both of them had limited success. Of the five settlements they reached so far, only one took them up on their offer of wards. They'd saved Aberdine for last, since it was the closest. The party they had sent was due back any minute.

On the flip side, Hugh's sample mortar refused to set, and nobody knew why. Elara'd been going over the budget requests and she'd seen him through the window down in the trench, mixing the mortar over and over. She'd had breakfast, then lunch, then dinner, and he was still there. Hugh had finally come in, chased indoors by darkness. He'd spent sixteen hours in that trench, then went out with the salvage party first thing in the morning. The Iron Dogs had been raiding the forest ruins, dragging in every scrap of valuable salvage they could find to offset the costs of the moat and the new siege engines they assembled on the towers.

They'd both had their hands full and had no reason to interact. Until now.

"The weapons and the beer," she explained. "Is that a good idea to have both available to Rufus's people?"

"The weapons are welded together," Hugh told her. "If they manage to pry them from the wall, it won't do them any good. I'm not about to arm drunken idiots."

Well, at least he was sensible.

Five women walked into the hall and lined up in front of them, all young and pretty, with flowers in their hair, and wearing floral print wrap dresses that hinted at cleavage and revealed just enough leg without suggesting anything. Kelly and Irene's tattoos were showing, a skull with arcane script above Kelly's left breast and a wolf ripping apart a human heart on Irene's right shoulder, but there was no help for that.

"What are these?" Hugh asked.

"Serving wenches. For your beer."

Hugh squinted. "Irene? Serana?"

The Iron Dogs snapped to attention. "Preceptor!"

"You stole my hand-to-hand experts," Hugh said.

"Borrowed."

He eyed the other women. "What do the rest of you do?"

Kelly pointed at herself then at the other two women in turn. "Witch, witch, pagan with a shichidan in judo. That's a ..."

"Seventh dan black belt," Hugh said. "Okay, you will do."

"Remember, we need their money," Elara said. "Don't maim anyone if you can help it."

The serving wenches took positions around the barrel.

"Where are you putting Fortner?" Hugh asked.

"You and I are going to sit in the middle of the head table, with me on your left. He will sit across from us with his people. I'm keeping Dugas and Johanna on my side. The rest is up to you."

He nodded. "I'll put the centurions on my right."

"Do you want Fortner's people all at our table so it would be easier for the marksmen to shoot them? I don't think we can fit all of them in."

He considered it. "No, let's split them between the three tables."

Elara surveyed the hall. It was almost done. The beer barrel was full, the places set, the food was nearly cooked. Everything had to go smoothly. If they lost Rufus, they'd lose the chance at business contacts in Lexington. They needed the contacts, the money and their influence.

"Food, decorations, beer," she rubbed her forehead. "What am I forgetting?"

"Herbal samples," he said.

"We have them ready in the Florida room. I don't think he'll be looking at them until tomorrow anyway. Did you double the patrols?"

"Yes. And I put extra marksmen on the balcony."

She glanced up to where a narrow balcony ran along one wall of the room. Nice. Fortner would be sitting with his back to them. If anything went wrong...

If anything went wrong, they were as ready as they were going to be.

A commotion broke out at the doors. Johanna walked in, flanked by three Iron Dogs and Sam. A line of blood stretched from Sam's scalp, running down his temple into his hair.

Hugh and Elara moved at the same time.

"What happened?" Elara asked.

"Aberdine does not want our help," Johanna reported.

"They met us on the road," an older female Iron Dog reported. "They made a road block."

"Cops?" Hugh asked.

"Civilians," Sam said. "They said Aberdine is a good Christian town and they didn't need any help from devil worshippers."

Of all the idiotic... "What happened to your head?" Elara demanded.

"Someone threw a rock." Sam shrugged.

"We withdrew," the female Iron Dog said. "It was that or kill the lot."

Hugh looked at Sam. "You'll live. Next time someone throws a rock, duck." He raised his hands and signed. *"Are you hurt?"*

"No. Sam took my rock. He moved in front of me, so it hit him instead," Johanna signed.

Anger boiled in Elara. "Marcus!"

Marcus turned to her. "Yes?"

"Stop all shipments to Aberdine."

"Okay," Marcus said.

She turned to Sam. "Don't you worry. Nobody does this to our people. They'll come crawling back to us in a week."

"I doubt they'll run out of cough tea in a week," Hugh said.

"They'll have plenty of tea," she told him. "But we supply all of their wine and most of their beer. As of today, Aberdine is a dry town. They'll be back with their hats in hand. Just wait."

Nicole ran into the hall. "The guests are coming!"

Hugh turned to her and grinned. "It's show time."

———⊁⊢———

"AND THEN!" Stoyan waved his cup, pretending to be drunker than he was. "Then the Preceptor says, 'To hell with it, we'll burn it.'"

The table broke into thunderous laughter.

Hugh cracked a smile. Elara smiled, too, watching Rufus Fortner. He was a big bear of a man, a couple of inches over six feet and at least two hundred and fifty pounds. He was in his fifties, but time didn't soften him, it just made him grizzled. His shoulders barely fit through the door. Caucasian, with skin tanned by sun and weather, Rufus had one of those masculine faces that looked overly exaggerated: square, jutting chin; massive jaw; short, broad nose; prominent eyebrows; narrow blue eyes. His mustache, which he kept trimmed, was still red, but his hair and beard had gone gray.

He was into his fifth beer and he appeared to be enjoying himself.

Rufus raised his mug. "Beer me!"

Make that sixth.

Irene dipped a pitcher into the barrel of beer, glided over, and refilled the mug.

"Thanks, sweetness."

Irene moved out of his way.

Elara glanced around the table. The six guardsmen Fortner

had sat at their table were a mixed lot. Five men and only one woman. They were drinking, and eating, relaxed.

"It's a nice place you've got here," Rufus said.

Something tugged at Elara's consciousness.

"Can't complain," Hugh said.

"We've worked a castle once. In Cincinnati," one of the guardsmen offered.

"Ah, yes, the Cus.. Ces... What the hell was that fellah's name?" Rufus wrinkled his forehead.

"Cousteau," the lone female guard supplied.

"That's right."

Here it was again, a faint tug.

"Excuse me." Elara rose from the table.

Hugh caught her hand. "Where are you going, pumpkin?"

To cast a death spell that will sear your eyes from their sockets. "Somewhere you can't come with me." She winked. "To the room down the hallway with the word LADIES on the door."

He let go. "Don't be too long."

"I won't."

Elara walked away. Behind her, Rufus said in what he probably thought was his confidential voice, "You're a lucky man, Preceptor. No offense."

"Oh I am," Hugh said. "I am."

She was one hundred percent sure he was watching her backside as she was walking away. Elara put an extra wiggle into it. *Eat your heart out.*

In the hallway, she turned left, walked through a door, and ran up the flight of stone stairs to the hidden balcony. Savannah stood in the shadows, watching the room. From the floor this area was practically invisible.

"What is it?" Savannah asked.

"I don't know. Something... I need a minute."

Below Hugh clapped Rufus's shoulder and laughed.

"D'Ambray plays his role well, doesn't he?" Savannah observed.

"Yes. He's a chameleon. He'll be whatever the circumstances require him to be." *It's finding the real man that was the problem.*

"The two of you have been avoiding each other."

Hiding things from Savannah was impossible. "I walked through his dreams. He caught me."

"Elara!"

"I know, I know."

Dreams were woven from emotions, from the most basic wants, the strongest desires, the sharpest fears. Logic and reason didn't exist there, except as twisted shadows of themselves. Walking through them was dangerous. She'd stepped into Hugh's inner world. Elara had trespassed, and he knew it. He would make her pay one way or another.

"Why?" Savannah shook her head. "Expending your power? Letting him see you?"

"You weren't on the wall when he fought the vampires. I was. He used a spell, Savannah. It wasn't like his normal magic. He pulled it to him and then he altered it, shaping it into something else. He said two words. He was clear across the field by the trees and I felt it all the way on the wall. It wasn't just powerful, it was precise. He pulled the undead out into the open, but he'd already had his people in the woods and they weren't affected."

"Power words," Savannah said. "They call Roland the Builder of Towers. Maybe there is a reason for that."

"You think this is the language of the Tower of Babylon?"

"That's what rumors say. It's supposed to command the magic itself."

"It did. I went into his dreams. I had no choice. I wanted to know what else he was capable of."

Elara fell silent. Below Hugh laughed, flashing white teeth.

"What did you find out?" Savannah asked.

"He's a monster. Like me."

"We've had this talk," the older witch said quietly.

"I am what I am. You, of all people, know that." Elara hugged her shoulders. "You should've heard him speak about Roland."

"What did he say?"

"That he was his king, his god, his life. He thinks that everything he is comes from Roland."

"And since there is no Roland now," Savannah said, "there is no Hugh."

"The exile should've broken him. I don't understand how he survived, but he did. He's extremely dangerous, Savannah. There are things I saw in his past..."

"Things?" Savannah asked.

"Killing is second nature to him. It's like breathing. Once Hugh decides someone has to die, he does it. There is no doubt."

"We've dealt with killers before," Savannah said.

"Not like this." She wasn't explaining it well, three fourths of her attention on trying to narrow down the feeling that brought her here. "Hugh has more magic than he lets on and he is very skilled. He's trained beyond anything I've seen."

Savannah raised one eyebrow at her.

"He threw me out of his dreams."

Elara had glimpsed something in those dreams. A twisted maelstrom inside Hugh, made of guilt, shame, and pain. He'd torn it open for her to show her his memories.

Savannah startled. "We shouldn't have made this alliance."

"We had no choice. It doesn't matter now. The die is cast. Now we just have to make sure he remains on our side. We—"

Elara, glorious one, shining one, have mercy on me in my hour of need.

An influx of power flowed into Elara. She jerked as if burned.

"What is it?" Savannah thrust herself into Elara's view.

I'm dying. Hear my plea. Hear my prayer.

"Elara?"

She jerked her hand up, silencing Savannah.

She'd forbade it, but here it was, a prayer, stretching to her like a barely existing lifeline.

Please save us. Please. I'll do anything.

She reached along that lifeline. It led her into the woods into the dark night, where a desperate man ran for his life.

I beg you, shining one. Please help. Please don't let them get us.

Alex. Alex Tong. He was running through the woods, from the north. She saw him, a gently glowing shape, so weak. He was bleeding. He didn't have long.

They killed all of us. Everyone is dead.

A vision hit her, hot and raging. Rows of bodies laid out in the street, nightmarish creatures scuttling, and soldiers in scale armor looking over it all. A hundred people slaughtered. The scent of blood and fear, stark blinding terror that twisted her insides. She jerked away from it before it dragged her under.

Please help me. I'm scared. They're coming, and I don't want to die.

Alex Tong lived in Redhill, one of the settlements that rejected their offer of wards. Her people had just come from it the day before yesterday.

Elara snapped back to reality, holding on to the fragile thread of magic with her mind.

"Redhill was attacked."

"When? Who?"

She shook her head and ran down the stairs. They had very little time. If she went after Alex, she would reach him, but he wouldn't survive. She had to get Hugh and she had to extract him out of that damn dinner without raising any alarms. They didn't know what was chasing Alex, although she could make a pretty good guess, and being attacked now would sever their relations with Rufus.

Elara took a deep breath and forced herself to walk slowly into the hall. The dinner was winding down. She wove her way around the table, came up behind Hugh, and draped herself over him, making sure to mash her breasts against his shoulder.

"Hi." Hugh glanced up at her and grinned. It was the kind of grin that would make a professional escort blush.

She leaned closer and brushed a kiss on his mouth. His lips were hot and dry. His hand reached into her hair. She pulled away slightly. "Do you think I can borrow you for a few minutes?"

He caught a strand of her hair between his fingers. "I think we can work something out."

She smiled at Rufus and the guardsmen. "Excuse us, gentlemen."

Hugh winked at Rufus and let her lead him out of the hall by hand. Behind them the Red Guard leader chuckled. "Newlyweds."

Elara drew him into the hallway. As soon as they were out of sight, he spun her around. "Who died?"

"Dying. Redhill was attacked."

Hugh's eyes turned dark. "The scale mail pricks?"

"Yes. They massacred it. One man escaped. A boy. He used to be Radion's apprentice, but he liked a girl in Redhill and left with her."

Hugh's eyes turned darker. "Where is he?"

"Running through the woods toward us. I can find him, but I can't heal him. He's barely hanging on. If we wait any longer, he won't make it."

Hugh was already moving to the exit.

———————

ELARA ANCHORED her magic and pulled herself forward, tracing the faint line of Alex's prayer. He was still whispering to her under his breath, begging, his voice fading. The tree trunks flew at her.

Behind her Bucky charged through the forest along a narrow trail. The giant horse shouldn't have been able to run in the woods in the dark, but Bucky pushed on like he was part deer. A weak radiance sheathed his flanks. He almost glowed silver.

She paused, waiting for them to catch up. Expending magic that quickly would cost her, but for now only Alex mattered.

Hugh caught up. She *stepped* again, then again, moving trunk to trunk.

The line of the prayer anchoring her to the man faded. She stepped again, fast and desperate, in the direction it had come from. Bushes, rhododendron, thick trunks, forest floor, all steeped in shadow.

Where was he? He had to be somewhere around here. Before he fell silent, she was almost on top of him.

"Alex," she whispered, sending her voice in a wide pulse. It flew through the woods. *"I'm here. I've heard you. Speak to me..."*

Nothing. Bucky burst out of the bushes next to her and Hugh brought him up short. The big horse turned in a circle, as Hugh surveyed the forest.

"Speak to me..."

. . .

"...shining one..."

He was right in front of her. She dove through the patch of rhododendron, forcing her way through the brush, and burst out on the other side. Oaks thrust from the forest floor, too thick to wrap her arms around. The moon shone above and the air between the trees glowed slightly with a bluish haze.

Alex lay slumped by the roots of the nearest tree. He was always thin, with a slight build, but now he seemed barely a boy, fourteen instead of his eighteen. He didn't move. His eyes were closed, his head drooped to the side. She dropped to her knees. Blood drenched his clothes, the fabric a solid mass of red.

Where was the wound? She could barely see him, let alone the injury.

Hugh knelt by her. A blue glow sheathed him. She'd seen glimpses of it before in the fight, but now it was obvious, a dense, rich blue, almost turquoise, the magic within it alive and strong, like a river. Hugh's eyes glowed with the same electric blue.

The glow stretched from Hugh's hand, sheathing Alex's body.

She felt movement and looked up. Shadows moved through the blue haze between the trees. Humanoid shadows.

They'd massacred Redhill. They'd killed everyone there, men, women, children. Now they were coming after one of hers.

No.

"You got it?" Hugh asked.

"Yeah," she said through clenched teeth. "I've got it."

She rose and walked through the forest toward the advancing shapes, making no effort to hide. Creatures slipped through the brush on both sides of her.

A warrior stepped out of the haze twenty-five yards away. As tall as Hugh, he wore scale armor and a helmet that left his face bare. Tattoos marked his cheek. His long red hair spilled in a horse tail through an opening in his helmet and fell down his back.

He was a distraction. Bait. Elara stared at him, waiting. If he had a bow and fired, she could avoid the arrows. But a crossbow bolt travelled a lot faster and would prove to be a problem.

A creature darted from the right, impossibly fast. She locked her hand on its throat. It hung in her hand, limp. It used to be human, but now the corruption suffused it, twisting its very essence. It wasn't the fetid stench of a vampire, reanimated after death. This was a living alteration and it left this beast with a shred of humanity hidden deep inside. Elara locked on the hot spark of magic within its body and swallowed it. It tasted delicious as only a human did. The lifeless sack of bone and muscle fell to the ground.

There were three warriors now. Same armor, same helmets, same swords in the scabbards on their hips. All three big men, the shortest only three inches or so under Hugh's height. They watched her, mute. No bows then. All the better.

Elara smiled, showing them her teeth.

The creatures burst from the bushes all at once, clawed hands out, ready to rip her apart. The forest came alive with shadows. She dropped the mask she wore and let her magic out. A brush of her fingers, and a creature collapsed. A claw on her shoulder, and its owner crashed to the ground. She ripped the magic from them and fed.

The ring of bodies around her grew and still they kept coming.

The final beast collapsed at her feet.

The three warriors still looked at her.

Apparently, they were just going to stand there. No worries. She would come to them. Elara picked up her dress, carefully stepped on the corpse of the creature in front of her and walked across two bodies toward the three.

The magic died. One moment it was there, and the next it vanished like the flame of a candle snuffed out by a breath. Her power vanished, a weak coal smoldering deep inside her instead of a raging fire.

The three armored men moved forward as one, unsheathing their swords.

She backed away, circling the bodies.

The first warrior bore down on her, his pale eyes locked on her with the unblinking focus of a predator.

A hand landed on her shoulder and jerked her back. Hugh thrust himself into the space she'd occupied half a second ago and drove his sword into the man. The blade sank into the warrior with a screech of metal against metal just under the breastbone.

The warrior gasped.

Hugh freed his sword with a brutal jerk, twisting the blade as it came out, and spun out of the way as another tall warrior closed in from the left.

The injured man dropped to one knee. Blood poured from his mouth.

The tall warrior charged Hugh, feigning left, but Hugh dodged, spinning, batted aside the third warrior's sword and backed up, facing her, drawing them away. The two warriors followed him, the taller on Hugh's right and the shorter on his left.

She needed a weapon.

The injured fighter in front of her drew a hoarse breath. Elara grabbed at the sword in his hand. She might as well have tried to pry it from solid stone. He clenched it tighter and swiped at her with his left hand. She jumped out of the way, almost tripping on a rock. Perfect. Elara crouched and wrenched the chunk of sandstone out of the forest floor.

Behind the injured warrior, Hugh backed away another step. The right fighter thrust with bewildering speed. High blocked the blade and hammered a punch into the man's face with his left hand. Cartilage crunched just as the other swordsman thrust at Hugh's ribs. The Preceptor twisted out of the way, but not fast enough. The blade sliced through the leather and came out bloody.

Hugh didn't seem surprised. He must've known the man would cut him. He'd calculated the whole thing and decided that taking a cut was worth it. She had to help him.

Elara clenched the rock and smashed it into the injured fighter's face. He cried out. Blood splattered. She struck his face again and a third time, turning his features into bloody mush. His helmet came off. He dropped the sword. She let go of the rock and swiped the blade from the ground. It was wet with hot human blood. Elara raised it and brought it down on the fighter's slumped back. The blade glanced off the metal collar of his armor and bit into his neck. It didn't cut all the way through, but he collapsed.

Elara gripped the sword and pulled it free.

Hugh was on her right, the two fighters on her left. The one closest to her bled from his nose, his eyes swelling into slits. Hugh charged the fighter with the broken nose. Broken Nose cut at him in a fast, wild slash. Hugh leaned back, and Broken Nose's sword sliced air. Before he could recover, Hugh cut at the fighter's extended arm. The man let out a short guttural howl. His sword fell to the ground. His right arm hung limp, useless. The warrior grabbed his wounded arm with his left hand and stumbled back. The other fighter slashed at Hugh's back. The blade connected. Hugh spun about, parrying the next strike, and attacked, driving the shorter man back.

Elara ran three steps forward and thrust the sword into Broken Nose's armored back.

It didn't penetrate.

The fighter turned around, swinging his blade. Elara rammed him, throwing all of her weight into him and his bleeding arm. He tripped and sprawled on the ground. She thrust her sword straight down into his chest and threw herself onto it.

The blade sank a couple of inches, screeching against the armor. The fighter screamed and clawed at the skirt of her dress with his remaining hand. Elara strained, digging her feet into the ground. She wished she still had the rock, so she could hammer the sword into his body.

The man screamed, staring straight at her. Blood poured from his mouth in a thick red gush. The metallic stench hit her. She had to finish it. Elara strained, summoning every last reserve she had. Something cracked in the man's chest and the blade slid in. He jerked one last time and lay still.

Elara straightened. Blood dripped from her hands.

Hugh and the other man danced between the trees, their swords a blur. Steel clanged. She could barely see the blades. How in the world was Hugh even parrying that?

The weapons clashed, the two men throwing all their strength and speed into their strikes. The magic was down, but Hugh moved with insane precision: fast, flexible, strong, anticipating his opponent's movements.

The warrior attacked him in an elaborate slash. Hugh parried and charged, raining blows on his opponent. The shorter warrior backed up. His blade danced, blocking, but his hand shook every time he countered a blow. Hugh was beating on him with methodical savagery. There was something almost business-like about it. Killing was a job, something that had to be done, and Hugh was an expert in it. He would get it done. The other man wouldn't last long.

The warrior must've realized it. He launched a counterattack, bringing his sword in a wide arc from the left, blindingly fast. Hugh parried before the sword could bite into his side. The warrior reversed the swing and cut at him from the right. Hugh stepped into it, blocking the swing, his sword pointing down. The warrior lunged at him, closing the distance. The two men struggled, locked, face to face, Hugh's sword on top of the warrior's, both pushing, blades immobile.

Hugh planted his feet and shoved.

The warrior stumbled back.

Hugh sliced his opponent's arm from left to right. The warrior jerked back and clamped his left hand over his shoulder. Blood seeped between his fingers. He passed the sword into his left hand and gave it a light swing, his eyes fixed on Hugh.

A furry shape tore out of the bushes. The warrior tried to turn toward it, but it was too late. One hundred and twenty pounds of hound hit him in the chest. Canine teeth flashed and bit down. The warrior toppled over, Cedric on top of him, snarling and biting.

"Damn it," Hugh swore.

Blood wet the dog's mouth. He bit the man again, ripping chunks of flesh from the ruined throat.

"Enough," Hugh ordered.

Cedric ignored him, tearing into the body like he was rabid.

"I said enough!" Hugh grabbed the hound by the collar and hauled him back. Cedric strained, snarling, bloody foam dripping from his jaws. She'd never seen the dog that upset.

Cedric gave up on snarling and howled.

Hugh jerked him upright, stared into his eyes, and said calmly, "Shut up."

The massive dog struggled a moment longer, then closed his mouth and sat back.

The three corpses lay on the forest floor in their identical armor.

"You were right," she said. "There is an army out there."

And they had just killed three of their soldiers. Someone would come looking.

They moved at the same time. Hugh ducked behind the tree where they'd left Alex and picked him up like he weighed nothing and whistled. Bucky pushed through the brush.

Elara grabbed the fallen man's sword. The man's neck looked like raw hamburger. Acid shot into her throat. She swallowed it back down and stepped over to the first corpse. Elara brought the sword down in a sharp chop. The blade severed the thin shred of muscle and skin that attached the head to the body. It fell with a thump. She picked it up, helmet and all. If the army came to retrieve the bodies, at least they would have something. You could do a lot with flesh and a little magic.

Hugh threw Alex over the saddle.

A stray thought came to her. Elara froze.

"What?" Hugh asked.

"Us. When he…" Prayed to me. "He said save *us*."

Hugh turned, studying the woods. Bushes trembled to the right. He snapped toward it. She put her hand onto his forearm and stepped forward.

"It's alright," she said softly. "We'll protect you. We'll keep you safe. You don't want to stay here in the dark all alone."

The bushes lay still.

"It's okay," she said. "It will all be okay."

Something moved within the bushes.

Elara stepped forward and gently parted the branches. A child. Seven or eight, covered in mud and blood. She reached in and scooped the child up. He or she, it was too hard to say, hung limp in her arms. Wide eyes stared at her, unblinking. Like a baby rabbit shocked into playing dead.

Hugh took the child from her arms. The girl – she guessed it was a girl – clung to him on pure instinct. He was huge and scary and covered with blood, and she needed a protector. Hugh held her for a long moment and slid her into Bucky's saddle. "Hold on to Alex."

The child just stared.

"Hold him," Hugh said, his voice calm and reassuring. "So he doesn't fall."

The girl reached out and clenched Alex's shirt.

They hurried from the clearing, Cedric in the lead.

"Will he live?" she asked under her breath.

"Yes."

"Will you?"

"Yes."

"Don't die on me, Preceptor."

"I'm touched you care."

"I don't," she told him. "I'm worried your Dogs will riot if you don't come home."

"Then you better take good care of me. We're going to run now. You got it?"

"Yeah. I got it."

"Good. You get tired, tell me."

They broke into a run.

———◦——

ELARA STUMBLED out of the woods into grass. Baile rose before them, backlit by moonlight, its main tower tall and reassuring. She bent over. Fire drenched her lungs, red-hot spikes of pain shot through her right side, and her stomach was trying to empty itself, convinced she'd been poisoned. A dozen small cuts covered her legs. If she never saw the inside of the woods again, it would be too soon.

A warm hand rested on her back. "Almost there," Hugh said. "One more push and we're there. You have it in you."

She straightened and bit a groan in half.

The child was still holding on to Alex, her knuckles white even under the layer of blood and grime. If she could hold it together, Elara had to do the same.

They ran through the grassy field to the road and up the hill. She never realized before just how far it was from the castle walls to the first tree trunks.

The castle gates opened in front of them and a dozen Iron Dogs poured out, Stoyan and Felix in the lead, followed by, Savannah, Dugas, Beth, and half a dozen of her people. Relief rolled through Elara in a cooling rush. They made it.

Savannah ran up and took the child out of the saddle. "Micah, Rodney, take the boy from the horse. Beth, get Malcom." The witch turned to her. "Are you hurt?"

"No."

Savannah's eyes blazed. "I'll deal with you later." She turned and hurried toward the keep. Micah followed her, carrying Alex over his shoulder.

"What happened?" Stoyan asked under his breath.

Hugh jerked the saddlebag off Bucky's saddle and marched across the yard. She struggled to keep up. Everyone followed, looking at them, waiting for answers.

"Redhill has fallen," Hugh said. "We may be next."

Stoyan nodded, as if Hugh had told him they were having bologna sandwiches for lunch.

"How are our guests?" Elara asked.

"Sleeping in the left wing," Dugas said. "We put several guards around it. They're not doing anything without us knowing."

"Good," Hugh said.

They reached the kennel. He pushed the door open. A long

hallway stretched before them with dog stalls on each side. The hounds looked back at him. He tossed the bag onto the floor. The warrior's head rolled out.

The dogs bared their teeth in unison. Vicious snarls rose. The hounds lunged at the stalls, biting the air.

"Double the patrols," Hugh ordered to Stoyan. "Here and in town. Bring the dogs."

Stoyan took off at a run.

"Felix, take a small force and get the bodies," Hugh said. "Bring wolfsbane and whatever else you've got that would throw off the scent. Stay safe. If you spot a force coming back, draw them back to the castle. We'll deal with them here. Corpses aren't worth dying over."

Felix nodded.

"It's just north of Squirrel Hollow," Elara told Dugas. "Go with them, please."

He nodded, and he and Felix left. Hugh scooped up the head, tossed it into the bag, and offered it to her. She thrust it at Johanna. The blond witch nodded and ran out.

Hugh turned.

"Where do you think you're going?" Elara asked him. "You're bleeding."

"I have things to do."

"No. There is nothing more you can do right now. You asked me to run, I ran. Now you will come with me and get patched up."

For once Hugh didn't argue.

———

THE WATER RAN from Elara's body, first red, then pale pink, then finally clear. Elara turned off the shower, stepped out, and wrapped herself in a white towel. She'd scrubbed the blood and forest off her skin. Her legs had been cut in a dozen places, nothing more than scratches, the pain more annoying than sharp, and now they burned. Her whole body ached, sore. Every time she closed her eyes in the shower, she saw the three men stalking through the woods to her. In her memories, their eyes glowed with blue light, unblinking.

They would've killed her tonight. Elara wasn't sure how she knew, but she felt it with absolute surety. Thinking about it raised the hair on the back of her neck. She had training both with guns and with bladed weapons. She had brought neither.

Elara reached for the underwear she'd laid out, put it on, and slipped into a dark-blue gown. She ran a brush through her hair on autopilot.

They'd almost killed her.

That's how fragile it all was. One moment she brimmed with power. The next the tech crashed into her and all her powers were gone. She had grown too complacent. There was a time when she never would've left the safety of her people without a gun.

It was the call. It had muddled her thinking.

Elara opened the door and walked into her bedroom.

Hugh sat on a chair, naked to the waist. A four-inch gash ran down his side, curving toward his spine. Another cut, about three inches long, carved its way down his back, over his shoulder blade. Nadia and Beth had already washed his wounds. Now Beth sat next to him. She saw Elara, picked up the needle holder, and plucked the surgical needle from the plastic holder.

Beth's hands shook. She was a gentle person. She would run at a monster and kill it with her sword, but when it came to humans, Beth could barely defend herself and D'Ambray scared her. Elara never witnessed him being mean to Beth, but there was something about him that deeply unsettled the young woman.

"Thank you, Beth." Elara stepped out, wiped her hands on a towel, and took the needle holder from her. "Please check on the child and Alex for me."

Beth retreated into the hallway and took off.

Hugh's cuts weren't too bad. She'd had a lot of practice in suturing wounds. This time wasn't any different.

Nadia slipped through the door, carrying a platter with a glass of greenish liquid on it. She offered the glass to Hugh.

"Drink," Elara said.

Hugh studied the glass. "What's in it?"

"All-purpose antidote."

"There is no such thing."

"You've been stabbed, and we have no idea what was on that sword. This will help fight off several common poisons."

He squinted at the glass.

"I realize that you can cure all your ills when the magic hits, but we don't know when that will be, so drink. I have to keep you alive until the magic wave comes."

He tasted the liquid. "It's foul."

Her voice was cold and detached. "Don't be a baby, Preceptor."

Hugh drained the glass.

"Any news on Alex?" Elara asked.

"He's still sleeping. Malcom says he's stable."

Nadia took the empty glass and left the room. They were alone.

"Arms," Elara said. They had already tried to get him to lay down on the table and he refused. The look in his eyes told her there was no intelligent life there.

Hugh raised his arms, locking them on the back of his head. His big biceps flexed. The carved, defined muscle on his chest stood out under tan skin. His dark blue eyes grew warm and inviting. He was thinking about sex and watched her like she was naked. It was distracting as hell and he knew it, which was exactly why he was doing it.

Elara sat on a low footstool, gently lifted the edge of the wound with sterilized forceps, punctured the edge with the needle, and rotated her hand to neatly slide the needle through the skin and muscle.

He didn't move. No grunting, no indication at all that something painful was happening. She concentrated on making even knots.

"Had a hard time stabbing that guy through the armor?" Hugh asked.

Elara didn't answer.

"Happens to the best of us."

She was almost done.

"The next time aim for the back of the neck or the inside of the thighs."

"I managed."

"Yes," he said, a smile waiting on his lips. "Yes, you did."

"What?"

Hugh just looked at her.

"What's so funny?"

"You and your murderous spree. Do your people know that you're bloodthirsty?"

Elara snipped the last bit of thread. "Don't you think we have more pressing things to discuss? Like who are they? What do they want? Why are they killing people?"

"Those are good questions. In fact, I was going to get answers to those questions, except you killed the people who had them."

Elara stopped. "I was trying to help you stay alive, you ungrateful ass."

"Did I look like I needed help?"

She glared at him and moved onto his shoulder.

"What did you think they were going to do to me?"

Dickhead. "Remind me, which one of us is cut up?"

"Okay," Hugh said, "I'll give you the guy with the broken nose, his eyes swollen shut, and his right hand hanging by a thread. He still had one hand left. He might have pounded his remaining fist on my chest as I dragged him off. But why the guy with the cracked liver? He was on his knees hacking his blood out."

The light dawned in her head.

"I set these guys up, so we could question them, and every time I left one breathing, you killed them."

She did kill them. That was dumb. Wow, that was dumb. Not one of her brightest moments.

Hugh cocked an eyebrow at her. "What happened to my calculating ice bitch? Were you actually so worried about me, you couldn't think straight?"

He was openly mocking her.

Elara stood up and leaned in close. With him sitting and her standing, she was slightly taller. "Yes. I was worried about you. I killed fourteen creatures. You only had to take care of three men, and I had to finish two of them for you and poor Cedric had to help you with the third. That fight didn't go well for you, did it?"

"Really? This is what you're going with?"

"If you died while you and I were alone in the woods, your people would assume I killed you. They don't know that I don't need a crude chunk of metal to take your life. If I wanted you dead, I would eat your soul. It would taste bitter and rotten, but sacrifices must be made."

Hugh bared his teeth in a feral grin. "How about now? Take a little bite of my soul, just for fun."

She squeezed her eyes shut for a second and looked down, to the source of all life below. "Please give me strength to not kill this man. Please."

"Why don't you try?" Hugh offered. An inviting heat lit his eyes. "It might be fun."

Oh, it would be *fun*. He looked so good in the light, every line of his torso strong, every muscle defined. She liked it all, his crazy blue eyes, the stubble on his square jaw, his broad shoulders, his chest, his flat stomach... She liked his size, the arrogant way he sprawled in her chair, the power in his body, but even more, the power in his eyes. Everything about him said strength and she needed strength tonight. She craved it, craved him, being wrapped in him.

Elara remembered the way he looked at her in the dream, with an almost feral need.

No. Not this man. Anybody but him. Not only was he too dangerous, but she could barely stand being in the room with him.

And she still felt stupid. That was okay. In a minute they would both feel stupid.

"Fine," Elara ground out, finishing the last stitch. "I did kill them. But what about you? Did you forget how to talk?"

Quick steps approached, and Felix appeared in the doorway. Cedric slunk in behind him and sat in the doorway.

"In all of that dazzling display of swordsmanship, couldn't you have found two seconds to manfully growl, 'We need them alive?' or 'Don't kill him?' You're supposed to lead your soldiers. Don't you issue orders, or do you just telepathically broadcast your battle strategy?"

Hugh glared at her.

"Let's ask Felix," she said.

The big man startled.

"Felix, how do you know when Hugh wants you to do something?"

"He tells me," Felix said.

"Ah!" She clapped her hands together. "He tells you. Imagine that. So you *are* able to communicate with actual words rather than grunts and snarls. What happened? Why didn't you tell me you wanted them alive after I killed the first one? It took me like three minutes to slide the sword into that second guy. I had to lay on it."

Hugh made a low noise in his throat. If humans could growl, it would sound just like that.

She gave him a sweet smile. Any sweeter and you could spread it on toast. "Use your words."

"I didn't tell you because it didn't occur to me that you would be that dense."

"So you expected me to think clearly after having killed fourteen mysterious monsters and have three men run at me with swords? Did it ever occur to you that I might have been too focused on killing them?"

"And," Hugh continued, "because I still had the third guy."

"That wasn't me. That was your dog. I'm not responsible for the actions of your loyal hound."

"He isn't my dog."

She pointed at Cedric. "Tell him that."

Hugh turned his head. Cedric took it as a sign that it was okay to run into the room and stick his head into Hugh's lap. Hugh looked like he wanted to kill something. Or someone. Preferably her.

"See, even Cedric decided you needed help."

Hugh raised his hand and patted the dog. "Did you want something?" he asked Felix.

"We retrieved the bodies," Felix said.

Hugh got up. "Would love to stay and play doctor, love, but duty calls." He headed for the door.

Play doctor? "Jackass."

"Harpy."

"Thank you for saving me in the woods," she said to his back. "And for healing Alex."

"You're welcome. I'll see you downstairs in ten minutes.

He left.

A moment later Rook slipped into her room and held out his writing pad.

Hugh needed help?

"No," Elara said. "He was terrifying."

10

The beast stretched about five feet ten inches on the shiny metal surface of the autopsy table. Fine brown hair, more like the coat of a horse than the fur of a dog, sheathed it. It thickened on the backs of its arms and at its crotch. Hard, ropy muscle wrapped its skeleton. It was likely incredibly strong, Hugh decided. Elongated digits, both toes and fingers, were sturdy and tipped with triangular, hook-like claws. No tail. Big ears with tufts of fur on the ends.

The face was a nightmarish mess. The eyes, human enough in shape, were unnaturally large, almost owl-like, surrounded by deep wrinkles, as if they pushed aside the flesh around them to make room. A short snout replaced the nose. Its upper lip split like that of a cat or a dog. The mouth slashed across its face, too wide to be human. Surgical clamps pulled the lips open on the right side, displaying long, conical fangs.

Next to Hugh, Felix grimaced. Hugh glanced at him. Felix waved his hand in front of his face. The stench. Right. The bitter harsh scent had to be hell on the shapeshifter nose. Bale, on the other hand, appeared to be completely unbothered. He had taken these two with him. Stoyan and Lamar manned the wall.

Elara had brought Savannah, Dugas, and Johanna. They stood on the other side of the table. The head witch wrinkled her face in disgust. Dugas appeared thoughtful.

They were in a large laboratory in the basement of the main tower. Three groups of people clustered around three tables. The first table, where he stood, supported the autopsied body of a beast, the second offered a similarly cut open warrior, and the third, where the smiths quietly argued with each other, held pieces of the warrior's armor.

Hugh had to give it to Elara. Her people were efficient and well-trained, and their work spaces were always in good order, no matter if it was a pottery shop or an infirmary room.

The coroner, an older man with brown skin and sharp dark eyes, folded his hands together.

"It used to be human," the coroner said.

Elara raised her hands and signed for Johanna.

Hugh examined the internal organs. Heart, liver, lungs. All the usual suspects. Some of the organs were deformed, but still appeared functional.

"How to explain this," the coroner began, clearly trying to come up with a dumbed-down version. "Umm. Well, to simplify..."

"The orthograde spine," Hugh told him. "None of the other bipedal vertebrates show the same adaptation. Penguins stand erect, but their biomechanics are completely different. The other upright vertebrates, ostriches, kangaroos, and so on, do not exhibit an orthograde spine during locomotion. The S curve of the spine with lumbar lordosis is unique to humans. Other primates show a C curve."

He moved his hand to indicate the hip. "The examination of the femur head will likely indicate large femur size and valgus angle typical to humans." He moved his hand further to the foot. "Evidence of longitudinal arches. Even though there is hallux opposability, the structure of the foot indicates adaptation to bipedal locomotion. There is no reason for a predatory simian animal to exhibit these characteristics."

Silence fell.

"He's a healer, Saladin," Elara said quietly, then signed it.

"Well, this simplifies things," Saladin said.

"Hallux whatchamacall it?" Bale asked.

"Opposable big toe," Saladin translated. "Like in an ape."

"They're good climbers," Dugas said.

Felix leaned forward, examining the feet. "And good runners. Calluses."

"So they're like cave people," Bale said.

Everyone looked at him.

"Hairy, strong, stupid. Troglodytes." Bale looked around. "What? We have to call them something."

He was right.

Johanna finger-spelled something he didn't catch. Hugh turned to Elara. "What did she say?"

Johanna stomped her foot and moved her fingers slowly.

"Mrogs?" he asked.

Elara grimaced. "Yes."

"What's a mrog?" Stoyan asked.

"A scary magic monster who lives in darkness," Dugas said. "It's a story we tell children to warn them away from dangerous magic they don't understand. Most children have an instinct when it comes to magic. They know when things don't feel right. Those who don't listen to that instinct know that mrogs are waiting in the darkness for those who cross the line."

"It fits," Hugh said. "Mrogs it is."

"What about those armored assholes?" Bale asked.

"Mrog masters?" Dugas suggested.

"Mrog soldiers," Elara said.

"Whatever was done to this... um... mrog was done in child-hood," Saladin said. "There is no evidence of undeath or atrophy typical of vampires. But the abnormalities in the organs are severe enough that a normal human wouldn't survive the transformation unless it was a gradual process that took place when the body's healing was still at its highest. Unless we're dealing with some sort of regenerative virus like Lyc-V."

The Lycos Virus was responsible for existence of shapeshifters and came with fun side effects. It also left irrefutable evidence of its presence in a human body.

"Is there any evidence of past regeneration?" Elara asked. "Bands of new tissue on the bones? New teeth?"

"Not in the three we opened up so far. I'll let you know if we find it."

"Do you have protocol for handling vampires?" Hugh asked.

Saladin looked offended. "Yes."

"Keep to that protocol for them until we know they're not going to regenerate and rise."

"We're not amateurs," Saladin said.

"If I thought you were, I'd put my people here to stand guard."

Felix walked over and stared at the mrog's face.

"Yes?" Hugh asked.

"Bigger eyes, longer nose, bigger ears," Felix said.

"Every sense pushed into overdrive," Elara murmured.

"Predators," Savannah said.

Tame predators, like dogs. Trained to do what their masters told them.

"Anything else?" Hugh asked.

Saladin shook his head. "When the magic is up, maybe we can learn more."

"Let's see the human," Elara said.

They moved to the second table. A large man lay on the steel surface, butterflied, his insides exposed for everyone to view. Geometric tattoos covered his skin, but only on the left side. An Indian woman in her late thirties stood next to him, holding up gloved hands. He'd met her before, Hugh remembered. Her name was Preethika Manohari and she ran the pediatric clinic in the settlement.

"He's human," she said. "His heart is about 25% larger than average. The lungs are larger as well. Nothing outside of the realm of human norm, but with those hearts they can pump much larger volumes of blood and their VO2 max, the maximum amount of oxygen the lungs can intake, is much greater. The other two are the same."

"So they're stronger?" Bale asked.

"They have high endurance," Preethika told him. "Some of this is genetic, some of it is training. Look here." She picked up the man's right hand and held it up. "Calluses from sword use. Scars here and here." She traced the thin lines of old scars. "All done by a bladed weapon. Except here, looks like an acid burn. The scars are of different ages."

"A veteran," Hugh said.

She nodded. "Same story with the other two. These men fought for years. But there is something I don't see."

"Bullet wounds," Dugas said.

"Yes. All three of them are in their thirties and professional soldiers. Most men of that age who are professional soldiers have been shot at. It's possible that these three were lucky. Some other interesting things." Preethika used forceps to lift the man's upper lip. "No evidence of dental work in any of them. Their wisdom teeth are still there. No surgical scars. No inoculation scars. No piercings. Then there are their tattoos. Most people with tattoos tend to choose at least one or two for cultural reference. A tattoo must mean something to the owner. There are no modern cultural reference tattoos on these men."

She stepped aside, and a man in his forties stepped forward. He was white, with a head full of reddish curly hair, a sparse beard, and light-blue eyes behind silver-rimmed glasses. He looked out of place in here, as if an English professor had wandered into the autopsy by accident.

"This is Leonard," Elara said. "Our head druid scholar. I asked him to look at the tattoos because they look vaguely Celtic to me."

Leonard nodded. "Most of these are unfamiliar to me, but there is something interesting here."

He pointed at a tattoo on the man's thigh, where an ornate crescent marked the skin, points down. A thin V-shaped line crossed the crescent, the point of the V under it, as if someone had shot an arrow just under the inverted moon, and the arrow snapped in a half.

Well, now that was interesting.

"V-rod and Crescent," Leonard said.

"They're a long way from home," Hugh said.

"It appears to be so," Leonard said.

"Is it Celtic?" Elara asked.

"No. It's Pictish." Leonard pushed his glasses up his nose. "We don't know too much about the Picts, and what we do know depends on who you talk to. Some people say that the Picts were the original inhabitants of Scotland, predating British Celts and distinct from other groups like Celtic Scots and Britons and Germanic Angles. Other people say that they were ethnolinguistically Celtic to begin with. There was a DNA study done before the Shift and apparently, they were similar to Spanish Basques. None of which helps us, and I do realize I'm rambling. They left behind carved stones and the V-rod and Crescent is a reoccurring motif. But I've never seen one this elaborate. The detail on this tattoo is remarkable. I only had a few minutes with him, so I may be able to tell you more once I go over all three bodies with a magnifying glass. So give me time and more to come."

All of that was good, but they needed to figure out how the bond between the mrogs and humans worked.

"We need to know how they're controlling the mrogs," Elara said. "We need to preserve the bodies until magic."

That's my harpy.

"We'll put them on ice," Preethika promised.

"One more thing," Leonard said. "We all agree on this: whatever was done to these people and creatures is permanent and foreign. It has a different flavor."

"What are you trying to say?" Elara asked.

"We are positive they can only survive in our world during magic. Tech will kill them."

"They seemed to have survived tech just fine," Hugh said.

"It probably takes some time," Preethika said. "An hour, maybe two. Eventually they will die, though."

"How sure are you?" Elara asked.

"I'd bet my life on it," Leonard said.

They moved on to the third table, where three people waited: Radion, a short, muscular black man who seemed almost as wide as he was tall; Edmund, a white man in his late fifties who looked like life ran him over and that just pissed him off; and Gwendolyn, a tall redhead with hair like honey and the kind of eyes that warned men to stay the hell out of her way. The three best smiths in the place. A chain mail helmet, two boots, and two gauntlets lay in front of them.

"You do it," Radion told Gwendolyn.

She raised her chin. "We can't replicate it, we don't know how they made it, or what the hell it is made of."

Great. "Is it steel?"

"Possibly," Radion said.

"There's no evidence of rust and it hasn't been oiled, so it may be some form of stainless," Edmund said. "It's non-magnetic, but that doesn't mean anything."

"Stainless steel comes in two types, austenitic and ferritic," Gwendolyn said. "It has to do with atomic structure. They both form a cube on the molecular level, but austenitic steel is face-centered. It's a cube with an atom in each corner and in the center of each cube's faces. Ferritic steel is body-centered, with an atom in each corner and one atom in the center of the cube."

"Austenitic steel doesn't respond to magnets," Radion explained.

"We weighed it," Edmund added. "It's running too light for stainless steel."

"But then we ground it," Gwendolyn said. "And it sparks like steel does."

"We also filed it," Radion said. "It's almost as hard as steel but it's flexible."

"And we dropped 45% phosphoric acid on it, and it didn't bubble, so it's definitely not a low-chromium steel," Edmund finished.

Hugh fought an urge to put his hand on his face. "So it may or may not be steel?"

"Yes," they said in unison.

"Is it metal? Can you tell me that?"

"Yes," Radion said.

"It's a metal alloy of some kind," Gwendolyn said.

Fantastic. *Good that we cleared that up.*

"How can we know for sure?" Elara asked.

"We have to send it off to a lab in Lexington," Edmund said. "For photoelectric flame photometry or atomic absorption spectroscopy."

"Both," Radion said. "We should do both."

"I agree," Gwendolyn said.

Here it comes. Three, two, one...

"How much will it cost?" Elara asked.

Right on cue.

The three smiths shrugged.

"Find out," she said. "When you do, take it to the Preceptor. He will approve or deny the expense and arrange for the security for the transfer to Lexington."

Wow. That was new. Apparently, the key to Elara's bank account was saving children from monsters in the dark woods.

"We could bird it," Radion said. "They'd need a very small sample. A carrier pigeon should be able to handle it."

"We may do that," Elara said. "Talk to the Preceptor when you have something concrete." She turned to him.

"You have tonight with it," he told them. "Tomorrow, as soon as our guests leave, the armor is going up on targets and we're going to cut it and shoot it."

The three smiths drew a collective breath. Gwendolyn paled. Radion gave him a horrified look.

"We don't need to know how it was made," Hugh said. "We need to know how to break it."

"But it's like painting over the Mona Lisa," Gwendolyn said.

Right. Pissing off all three smiths at the same time wasn't a good idea.

"You can keep one," he told them. "When we figure out how to crack it, I promise you all the armor you can stand."

"Can we have the beat-up armor after you're done?" Gwendolyn asked.

Hugh almost sighed. "Yes."

"Okay," Radion said. "We can live with that."

———◆———

ELARA STRODE DOWN THE HALLWAY. The after-battle jitters had morphed into unease, then outright dread. Exhaustion set in, as if a massive weight rested on her shoulders and kept getting heavier and heavier.

Quick footsteps echoed behind her.

Just what she needed. Elara caught a sigh before it gave her away. She didn't have the energy for verbal sparring right this second.

Hugh caught up with her.

"How much do you want to spend on tests?" he asked, falling in step with her. "Give me a ceiling."

She almost pinched herself. "How badly do we need them?"

"We don't need them at all," he said. "We don't have to know what the armor is made of. We need to know how to break it and we'll find that out tomorrow. Basically, how much money do you want to spend to keep the smiths happy?"

Thinking was too difficult, and making a decision was even harder. "A thousand. Fifteen hundred at most."

They started up the staircase.

"More than I would've given them," Hugh said.

"Since when are you fiscally responsible?"

"I spend money to keep us alive."

She almost groaned. "Please don't start about the moat, Hugh, I can't take it right now."

"Begging? Not like you. What's bothering you?" he asked.

She missed her magic. It was her shield and her weapon; she felt naked without it. She wanted it so badly, it was almost a physical pain. This was wrong, Elara reminded herself. She tried to push the need out of her mind, but it refused to leave. The stakes were too high to give in to magic cravings. If she did, it would undo her in the end.

"Fourteen," she said, grasping at a distraction.

"Yes?"

"There were three men and fourteen mrogs. If they all had the same number of creatures, where is the fifteenth mrog?"

"Perhaps one of them only had four."

"The man at the Old Market had five too," she said.

Hugh's face showed nothing, but his eyes said he wasn't happy. She wasn't happy with that thought either.

They came to the third floor and she turned into the hallway.

"Where are you going?"

"To check on Deidre," she told him. "The little girl."

"Is she alone?"

"No. Lisa is with her, and she is good with guns. Savannah got Deidre to talk. She has an aunt in Sanderville. We called her, and the family will be coming to pick her up in the next few days."

"I'll send an escort," he told her.

"Thank you."

"It's one o'clock in the morning," he said. "The kid is probably asleep."

"I know. I just want to make sure she's okay."

He followed her. They walked together through the shadowy hallway.

It was comforting, walking like this next to him. It was like walking next to a monster, but if something jumped out at them from the shadows, he would kill it, both because it was his job and because he would enjoy it. He wasn't carrying a sword, but it didn't matter. At the core, Hugh d'Ambray was a predator. She understood that all too well. There were two monsters in this hallway, he was one and she was the other, both of them horrible in their own ways. The vision of blood spreading through the clear water came to her. She shivered.

"Cold?" he asked.

"No. Hugh, do you think Redhill is like the Old Market?"

"Yes."

"Where do they take them?" She glanced at him. "They kill these people, so they have pounds and pounds of dead weight. They have to transport them out, but the shapeshifters lost their scent at the palisade. You would need vehicles or wagons to transport the people. It wouldn't just leave a scent trail, it would leave a regular trail a mile wide."

"Yes."

"There is no trail. There is nothing. The people and the warriors vanished into thin air."

"Yes."

"Are we dealing with an elder being?"

His face was grim. "Probably."

She almost hugged herself. Certain creatures required too

much magic to survive the seesaw of magic and technology. Djinn, divine beasts, gods… They only manifested during a flare, a magical tsunami that drenched the world every seven years. The rest of the time they existed outside of reality, in the mists, in the secret caves, in the primordial darkness. A dark swell of memories rose inside her, and she crushed them before they had a chance to drag her under.

An elder being could open a portal to its realm. She had seen it firsthand during a flare. An elder being brave enough to risk appearing during a magic wave would be infinitely more dangerous. Nobody could predict tech shifts, and if the magic wave suddenly ended, the elder creature would likely die.

"We need to figure out the nature of the bond between the beasts and the handlers," she murmured.

"Could be telepathic navigation," Hugh said. "Would explain why the humans stood still."

It took concentration to navigate. "But five? Most Masters of the Dead can hold what, two vampires? Three?"

"Depends on the navigator. Daniels can hold a couple hundred."

Elara stopped and pivoted toward him. "A couple hundred?"

"She can't do much with them, but she can hold them. There is a lot of power there, which she doesn't use most of the time. Like you. Why do you hold back, Elara?"

Excellent time to make her escape. She pointed at the door ahead. "This is my stop."

"Not in the talking mood?"

"Good night, Preceptor."

He nodded, turned without a word, and strode down the hallway. He'd walked her to the door. That was almost… sweet.

The only way the Preceptor of the Iron Dogs would ever be sweet is if he were walking her into a trap. Elara turned around, peering at the shadows, half-expecting something to leap out at her.

Nothing. The soft gloom of the hallway was empty. The man had her paranoid in her own castle. This marriage was a gift that kept on giving and just when she thought she had him figured out, he changed his stride.

Outside the walls a dog yowled, its howl breaking into hysterical furious snarling. Alarm shot through her.

The door swung open under the pressure of her fingertips. The window stood wide open, the white curtains billowing in the night breeze. Deidre sat on the bed, still like a statue, her eyes wide and unblinking. Lisa's body slumped on the floor by the window, her shotgun on the rug, next to the bed. A creature squatted over Lisa, its clawed hands hooked into her flesh, biting into her neck. It had nearly chewed through it and Lisa's head dangled, her brown eyes dark and glassy.

The creature looked up, big owl eyes empty, flat, like the eyes of a fish. Blood stained its nightmarish fangs.

She had to save the child.

The only weapon in the room was Lisa's shotgun. Knowing Lisa, it would be loaded. The other door in the room led to the bathroom; it would be too flimsy to hold against the beast and once they got inside, they would be trapped. The only way out was through the doorway where Elara stood. If the little girl ran to her, the beast would catch her before she could.

"Deidre," Elara said, her voice calm. "Crawl toward me. Do it very slowly."

The girl swallowed. Slowly, ever so slowly, she shifted onto her hands and knees. Elara took a slow gliding step sideways toward the bed and the gun.

The beast watched her, Lisa's blood dripping from its mouth. It licked its fangs, running its tongue on the shreds of human flesh stuck between its teeth. Outside the dogs snarled in a frenzy.

Deidre crawled to her. An inch. Another inch.

Another.

Elara took another step.

Ten feet between them.

Nine. Deidre was almost at the edge of the bed.

Eight.

The creature leaned forward, lowering Lisa to the floor, its gaze locked on them. Elara held her hand up, palm toward Deidre.

They froze.

The monster stared at them.

Elara took short shallow breaths.

A moment passed, long and slow like cold molasses.

Another...

The creature dipped its head and bit Lisa's neck.

"Deidre, when I say run, I want you to jump off the bed, run outside, and scream as loud as you can. Scream and keep running. Don't stop. Do you understand?"

The child nodded.

Elara shifted her weight onto her toes.

The beast tore another shred of flesh from Lisa's throat, exposing more of the broken vertebrae. She'd make it pay. Yes, she would.

Deidre perched at the very edge of the bed.

Now. "Run!"

Deidre jumped off the bed and dashed to the door. Elara lunged forward and grabbed the shotgun.

A piercing, desperate scream tore through the castle. "Hugh! Hugh!"

The beast sprang at her. There was no time to aim, so she drove the butt of the gun into its face. The creature reeled. She pumped the shotgun and squeezed the trigger. The shotgun barked. Pellets tore into the beast's face, knocking it back.

Elara sprinted to the hallway, slammed the door shut, and threw herself against it, back to the wood. She had to buy time.

The beast let out a screech behind her. It lashed her senses, whipping her into a frenzy.

"Hugh!" The terror-soaked shriek sounded further away. *Run, Deidre. Run.*

The beast slammed into the door from the other side. The impact shook it like the blow of a giant hammer. Elara's feet slid. She dug her heels in.

The door shuddered again, nearly throwing her. It would break through on its third try.

She leaped aside and pumped the shotgun.

The door flew open, the creature tumbling out all the way to the other wall of the hallway. Elara jerked the shotgun up and fired.

Boom!

The blast tore through the beast. Blood spatter landed on her face. The monster surged upright, its face a mess of bloody tissues, its left eye leaking onto its cheek.

Pump. Boom!

The creature jerked back, then lunged at her.

Pump. Nothing.

Elara flipped the shotgun, brandishing it like a club.

Hugh came around the corner, running at full speed and plowed into the beast, knocking it off balance. As the monster came back up, Hugh grabbed it, twisting it around to face her, muscling it, his face savage, and caught its throat in the bend of his elbow. His forearm pressed against the beast's neck. It kicked, jerking and flailing, claws ripping the air only a foot from her face as it struggled to break free, and for a second, she didn't know if Hugh could hold it.

Hugh caught the creature's head with his left hand. The powerful muscles of his arms flexed, crushing. Bones crunched. The beast's head lolled. It went limp.

Relief flooded her. She lowered the shotgun.

Hugh dropped the beast like a piece of trash and turned to her. "Hurt?"

"No."

"Others?"

She made her mouth move. "I only saw one."

Deidre ran to them and wrapped herself around her, trembling uncontrollably.

"It's okay," Elara cooed. "It's okay. Safe now. It will all be okay."

"What if it comes back?" the little girl whispered.

"If it comes back, Hugh will kill it. That's what he does. He protects us. It will be okay."

Hugh gave her an odd look, but she was too tired to care. Exhaustion mugged her like a wet blanket, smothering her thoughts. The danger had passed. Hugh's sentries had failed, and he would take it personally, which meant not even a fly would make it into the castle for the rest of the night. And, knowing Hugh, probably for the rest of all nights.

Lisa was dead. Lovely, kind Lisa.

She was so tired.

Iron Dogs, hounds, and a couple of her people charged up the stairs, pounding into the hallway. The dogs tore at the corpse.

Hugh grinned at her, showing even white teeth. "You were right. There were fifteen."

She didn't have any witty comebacks. She put her arm around Deidre and walked toward the stairway, heading for her room.

———•——

THE DOOR to Elara's bedroom stood wide open. Serana stood on the side, guarding. She snapped to attention as he passed.

Hugh stalked through the doorway. Elara lay on the bed, fully clothed, her eyes closed. Her breathing was even.

Asleep.

An assault rifle lay on the night table, within her reach. She'd washed the blood from her face, but small red drops peppered her dress. The child curled next to her, asleep.

He moved closer and sat on the edge of the bed. She didn't stir.

The adrenaline still coursed through him. He came to tell her that the beast had come over the wall and scaled the tower. The grate on the window had been loose and it ripped it out. His people checked the creature's hands and found no sign of injury. The silver in the metal of the grate would've burned most magical beings, but not that one.

The creature was fast and sly. It must've watched the patrols and waited for the best time. There was less than thirty seconds between the walking sentries. It timed the assault perfectly and by the time the dogs picked up the scent, it was already scurrying up the tower.

The creature could've caught them in the forest. It was fast enough. But it must've weighed the odds and realized that it was outmatched. That likely meant it wasn't telepathically controlled by its master. A telepathic bond required a blank mind, and the moment the warrior controlling it died, the beast would've taken off into the woods, to freedom. That's why loose bloodsuckers slaughtered everything in sight. Without navigators to direct them, they acted on pure instinct.

This creature followed them, waited for the right moment, then got inside hoping to kill Deidre. Still, it wasn't too bright, otherwise Lisa's presence wouldn't have distracted it. It likely killed Lisa to get to the child, but once it started chewing on her, it didn't want to stop. He'd seen similar behavior in feral dogs.

He came to tell Elara that this would never happen again. She didn't wait for his assurances. She trusted him enough to fall asleep.

If it comes back, Hugh will kill it. That's what he does. He protects us.

The world had sat askew, until he'd come to the castle. All the cornerstones of his life had fallen: Roland gone, his position as Warlord eliminated, his immortality over. But now he had a place, here in the castle, and a purpose.

If it comes back, Hugh will kill it. That's what he does. He protects us. It will be okay.

When he'd heard the child scream, he had imagined the worst. If someone had asked him this morning what was the worst that could happen, he would've had to think about it. Now he knew. The worst would be Elara dying.

The fights, the compromises, the maneuvering, pissing her off until she turned purple in the face and forgot to keep a hold on her magic, so it leaked from her eyes, all of it took up so much of his time. It was fun. If she was no longer here, he wouldn't know what to do with himself. Would he leave? Would he stay?

This new life, it was just his. Hugh didn't owe it to anyone. He was building it himself, brick by brick, one shovel of cement at a time, the same way he had built that damn moat. He was building his own castle, and for better or worse, the harpy wormed her way into his world and became its tower.

When he'd thought she might be dead, fear had scraped him raw. For a moment he felt the piercing icy pain of what must've been panic.

But she'd survived.

Hugh reached out carefully and rested his hand on her chest, just under her breasts, to reassure himself that he wasn't imagining it. She felt warm. Her chest rose and fell with her breath.

She'd survived.

All was good. Tomorrow it would return to normal. The crisis had passed.

He raised his hand and walked out the door.

———•——

ELARA'S EYES SNAPPED OPEN. She saw Hugh's wide back disappear through the doorway.

He had reached out and touched her. It was such a light touch, hesitant, almost tender, as if he'd been reassuring himself she was alright.

Hugh d'Ambray cared if she lived or died.

He'd given himself away. It was a fatal mistake. There was so much she could do with it. Now she just had to decide how to use it.

What did she want from Hugh d'Ambray? Now there was a question.

If she wanted Hugh – and she wasn't ready to say she did – but if she did decide that she wanted him, she would have to approach it very carefully. By tomorrow the man who'd gently touched her would disappear and the old Hugh d'Ambray would take his place. That man wouldn't respond to overtures of peace. If she came to him, looking for relief or reassurance, or offering him either, he would either view it as a weakness or try to use it to his advantage. Nothing that went on between the two of them was either tender or loving. She would have to back him into a corner or let him think he backed her into one. And if she ever let him into her bed, she would fight him in there too.

Was it worth it? She still wasn't sure.

Elara closed her eyes and went to sleep.

11

Elara strolled through the sunroom. At some point it had been a rampart, one of many extending from the main tower. When they first took over the castle, the battlements here were badly damaged, so instead of repairing them, she chose to extend the roof and install floor-to-ceiling glass panels. As with every available space in the castle, soon the sunroom acquired plants, some grown in large floor containers, others dripping from hanging pots. Tall hibiscus plants offered bright red and cream-colored blossoms next to the delicate orange blooms of flowering maple. White jasmine rose above purple oxalis leaves, sending a sweet perfume into the air. The pottery came from the village shop and the children had painted them in bright vivid hues. There was even enough sun for some herbs, although they found herbs grew best outside. Johanna had added long constellations of colored glass hanging from wires. When the sun hit them just right, the entire room glowed with turquoise, indigo, peach, and red. Dugas had delivered a huge wooden table, enough to seat sixteen people, and the sunroom was complete.

Today the table held an assortment of their herbal offerings. She supposed to some the sight of jars, bottles, and dried bundles would've seemed ominous. Most of their concoctions wouldn't be touched unless someone's health was in question. But to her, it brought a deep, quiet sense of joy. She'd needed comfort after last night, and so she came here.

A whisper of movement made her turn. Rufus Fortner knocked on the doorframe. Behind him Rook waited, impassive, next to Johanna.

"Good morning," Elara said.

"Good morning," Rufus answered. "May I come in?"

"Of course."

The big man walked into the sunroom. Behind him Rook slipped in and parked himself by the wall, a silent shadow. Johanna glanced at her, a question in her eyes. Elara barely shook her head. She could handle the Commander of the Red Guard on her own. Rook was more than enough backup. The blond witch retreated into the hallway.

"Nice selection," Rufus said, looking at the collections of jars and bottles on the table. "It's like a pharmacy in here."

"Not like. We are a pharmacy, one of the best in the area."

"Herbal pharmacy. Natural cures."

"Do you know what they call natural cures that work, Commander?" Elara's lips curled into a soft smile. "They call it medicine. For two and a half thousand years people extracted salicin from the leaves of white willow trees and used it to soothe headaches and inflammation. A French chemist, Henri Leroux, extracted salicin in a crystalline form in 1829. An Italian, Piria, produced salicylic acid from it. Then in 1853 another Frenchman synthesized acetylsalicylic acid. Finally, in 1899 Bayer packaged it into pills and put it on the store shelves. They called it aspirin."

"How about that?" Rufus said. He picked up a jar of wolfsbane and looked at it. "Good color on the wolfsbane." He set the jar down and picked up a small green bottle. "What is this one?"

"An all-purpose antibiotic," she said. "Excellent against urinary tract infections."

Rufus rocked his head side to side, nodding in appreciation, set the bottle down, and pointed to a red heart-shaped jar filled with chick pea-sized pills. "Love potion?"

"Hardly. The heart symbol comes from the seed of a once extinct plant, silphium, used by the Romans and Greeks as a cure all for many ills. Also, as a contraceptive for women, just like the contents of that jar." She reached over and picked out a tall vial of pale green liquid with a dropper at the end. "But we do offer a love potion of sorts. They don't make Viagra anymore. This is the next best thing."

Rufus's eyebrows crept up.

"Three drops in a glass of water half an hour before the date. Don't mix with alcohol. It tastes vile, and the drops are hard to get out, and that's on purpose."

"Why?"

"Because there hasn't been a man alive who doesn't subscribe to the philosophy that six drops surely must be better than three. Three does the job. Six will leave you in an uncomfortable situation and possibly warrant a trip to the hospital."

Rufus pondered the bottle. "There was a commotion last night."

She met his gaze. "We live in the middle of a magical wood, Commander. Once in a while something scales the wall in the deep of night and tries to eat the children. The Iron Dogs took care of it. And then Hugh insisted they bring the hounds on patrols. I'm sorry the barking was distracting."

Rufus nodded, his face thoughtful, and set the jar back on the table.

"Is something bothering you, Commander?" Elara asked.

The big man leaned back. Last night at dinner – which felt like a month ago – he'd played the brawler so well. Just a good old boy, not too bright, easily pacified with good food and beer. Today his eyes were shrewd. Rufus Fortner was a lot sharper than he wanted people to believe.

"I get him," he said. "This is a great place. Defensible, well-supplied, and isolated. No law enforcement to get in the way. No troublesome politics. Nobody tells him what to do. His men are fed and housed. He's got everything a man could want: a castle, of which he's lord and master, an army, and a beautiful wife. But what do you get out of it?"

There it was. *Loving spouse,* she reminded herself. *I don't want to kill Hugh on a daily basis. He is my favorite. I adore him, and he makes my toes curl.* "He's my husband," she said.

Rufus grimaced. "You've got to know the man is a butcher. People call me a rough man. I've got a rough reputation, and I've earned it. I've done things that keep good folks up at night. Hugh d'Ambray scares me. He is the monster rough men like me fear. I've got blood on my hands. Hugh is up to his neck in it."

The memory of thick blood spreading on the surface of the water came to her and she glimpsed Hugh again, standing with his feet in her pool, a twisting fiery maelstrom of raw pain and guilt burning behind him.

"He's not that anymore," Elara said.

"A tiger doesn't change its stripes," Rufus said.

"You misunderstand. I don't want him to change his stripes. You said it yourself, he is the monster rough men fear." She smiled at him, sharp, pinning him with her gaze. "He puts himself between evil creatures and small children. He protects us. He is *my* monster, Commander. Should any rough men come here and try to take what is ours, he will remind them of that."

Rufus studied her. "I see you are well matched."

"We are."

"What happens when he takes his army and marches out to conquer?"

Elara almost laughed. If he'd only seen Hugh's troops a month ago, when they had gotten their first helping of fresh bread in weeks. The Iron Dogs had been strays for too long. They knew where their food came from. They were in no hurry to leave and neither was their Preceptor.

"This castle is my home, Commander. I'm not going anywhere. I can't leave my people and Hugh won't leave me."

"Are you sure about that?"

Elara motioned to him. "Come."

Rufus walked over to where she stood at the window. She pointed to the empty moat far below, past the curtain wall. "You see that man testing the concrete pad over there? That's him."

"How can you tell from this distance?"

"I know him. I know the way he holds himself. The engineer came and got him at dawn." Rook had dutifully reported it to her. "They finally got their Roman concrete to set. Does this look to you like a man set on conquering or does it look like a man obsessed with fortifying the castle for his people?"

Rufus didn't answer. Below Hugh straightened and spoke to his engineer. Next to him a much smaller figure crawled onto the concrete, straightened, and hopped up and down. Cedric jumped next to her and flopped on his side.

"Who is that?" Rufus asked.

"Deidre. He rescued her, and now she follows him." She'd run to find him the first chance she got.

Hugh picked Deidre up, carried her to the wall of the moat, and lifted her above his head. A woman in the Iron Dog uniform leaned in from above, grabbed the little girl's hands, and pulled her up out of the moat. Hugh followed. He headed to the castle gates, and Deidre followed, Cedric trailing them.

"You're right," Elara said, "he is up to his neck in death. He's had all the conquering a man could want and then some. All he wants now is to stay here, live in peace, and wash some of that blood off."

"I hope you're right. For all of our sakes."

"I do too," she told him and meant it. "So, will you place any orders, Commander?"

He spread his arms and the 'oh shucks good old boy' was back. "You've convinced me. Let's haggle?"

Elara glanced one last time at Hugh, as a woman who loved him would, and turned to the table. "I do so love haggling."

———+·—

GETTING the Red Guards out of the castle proved to be a longer affair than Hugh hoped. At first light, he'd sent Stoyan out with thirty Red Guards to Redhill. They'd made the three-hour round trip and come back. The report was short. Same as the palisade in the woods, except this time seventy people were taken. He'd called to the sheriff's office himself. Will Armstrong didn't sound thrilled. A palisade with a few families was one thing. A small settlement like Redhill was a different thing entirely.

They'd spent the rest of the phone call dancing around the fact that Armstrong didn't have the manpower to handle this and they both knew it. He promised to send a man down to investigate and interview Alex Tong. Hugh thanked him. They made some polite noises and hung up. They were *on their own*.

They needed to get the moat done. Hugh was chomping at the bit to get back down there, but he had to have lunch and exchange pleasantries. It was almost noon, and still the Red Guards dragged their feet. Finally, Rufus climbed onto his eighteen-hand Belgian draft and prepared to take off.

"It was lovely meeting you folks." Rufus favored them with a huge grin.

"The pleasure is all ours, Commander," Elara told him and smiled as if Rufus and she were bosom buddies.

Hugh briefly considered pulling Rufus off his horse and dumping him on the ground on his ass. It was an odd urge. He pondered where it came from.

"Visit any time," he said and held his hand out.

Rufus gripped it. "We came for the beer, stayed for the company. Love to do it again."

They shook.

"You two make a lovely couple," Rufus told them. "Have fun without me, newlyweds!"

"Oh, we will," Hugh promised him.

"Well, we're off." Rufus swung his horse toward the gates. The Red Guards rode out. Hugh caught Elara's arm and strolled with her to the gates.

The Red Guardsmen rode down the path. The female Guard glanced back at them over her shoulder.

Elara smiled and waved. Hugh slid his arm around her and squeezed her to him. Her smile sharpened.

The moment the woman turned back, Elara tried to stomp on his foot. He was ready, and she missed. Her sandal hit the stone, but she was out of his hands.

"If you're going to do that, love, you should wear heels."

She shot him a look of pure venom. "Eat dirt and die."

Oh good. He leaned closer to her and murmured, "Careful. Your new best friend isn't quite out of earshot yet."

"He won't hear." She gave him the stink eye, then her eyes brightened. "I rather like him. He came to me very concerned this morning."

"Why?" More importantly, why didn't anyone tell him about that?

"He wanted to warn me that you were a butcher."

"Oh that."

"I reassured him that I was aware of that."

"I bet you did."

"You know," Elara murmured thoughtfully. "He is kind of handsome. In that older grizzled veteran way."

"Rufus the Ashes? Sorry to disappoint you, but he's happily married."

"Really?"

"For about thirty years now. Marissa likes splitting people with her axe, so I would think twice if I were you."

"You're making this up," she said.

"Go ahead. Test the waters. Just don't come running to me when she shows up here looking to make you a head shorter."

She narrowed her eyes. "I wouldn't run to you if you were the last man on Earth."

He smiled at her, leaned closer, and murmured, "You did yesterday."

Elara actually growled. A real growl, under her breath, but still a growl. He almost laughed.

"I see your concrete finally set," she said.

"Mhm."

"In that case, you should consider being very nice to me during the next few days."

"Why?"

"You'll be needing gasoline for your cement mixer and you're over your limit. Again."

Bloody woman. "Are you telling me that with all that beer and all your eyelash fluttering, you couldn't con that old man out of some money?"

"I don't con! I conduct business by selling a quality product."

Johanna emerged from the tower and walked in their direction.

"How much?" he asked.

"We're going to make about eighty-seven grand after expenses on the Red Guard order," Elara said. "Another twenty in the next few months if he comes back for seconds. And he will. Oh, and five hundred dollars from him personally."

"Five hundred bucks? What the hell did he buy?"

Her eyes narrowed into slits. "Wouldn't you like to know."

"So we made sixty-seven thousand five hundred," he said. "Not bad."

"How do you figure that?"

"I bought two 50 Cal Gatling Guns from Rufus. Ten K each."

She stared at him, stunned.

He braced himself. "We need the guns, Elara."

"And you just made that decision without me?" Her voice was so sharp, he wanted to check himself for cuts.

"A 50 Cal GAU doesn't sound like a firecracker. It sounds like a jackhammer, because it fires up to 2,000 rounds per minute. It's belt-fed from the ammo box and it will turn a vampire into hamburger in less than two seconds."

"Damn it, Hugh."

"We're both stronger during magic. The Gatling guns will guarantee that Nez doesn't attack during tech."

Johanna reached them and waved. Elara turned to her. "Yes?"

"Boy is awake," Johanna signed.

Fear flickered across Elara's face. She blurred and then she was at the tower door, thin tendrils of white magic snaking through the space she had just occupied.

There was something the boy knew she didn't want Hugh to know. Hugh broke into a run. Ten seconds to the door, another twenty to clear the stairs. He burst into the hallway and sprinted to the room.

The door stood wide open. He heard Elara's voice, soft yet insistent.

"... never do it again. I understand why you did. I'm not upset with you. But you must promise me to never do it again."

"I promise," a young male voice answered.

He'd missed it. Damn it.

Hugh walked through the doorway. The kid lay in bed, still pale from the loss of blood. He let his magic slide over the boy's body. The vitals looked good, though, for how complicated the patch job was. Elara sat on the edge of his bed. She glanced up at Hugh's approach.

"You're making eyes at my wife?" Hugh asked.

The kid went a shade paler. "No, sir."

"Hugh!" Elara turned to the boy. "He's joking."

"Tell me about the village, Alex," Hugh said.

He heard quiet footsteps in the hallway. Deidre. The footsteps stopped.

Alex licked his lips. "Deidre likes the forest. She goes off sometimes and doesn't come back for a while. We heard dire wolves howling, so when it started getting dark and she wasn't back, Phillip, her dad, asked me to go look for her. I'm better with the woods than he is. I don't get lost."

"Does she usually stay out past sunset?" Elara asked.

"No. She always comes back before dinner, but this time she didn't, so everyone was worried. It took me awhile, but I found her. We were heading back, but..."

He fell silent.

"Take your time," Elara told him.

"Deidre didn't want to go back. She kept stopping. I just had a feeling that something wasn't quite right. Every step I took toward the village it was like a big hand I couldn't see was pushing me back. So, I told Deidre to wait and climbed a tree to try and see anything." He swallowed. "There were soldiers and monsters in the village. Killing everyone. They pulled them out of the houses, and killed them right there on the street, and laid them out like cordwood. Like they weren't even people. They killed kids. Little kids. They took Maureen's baby and slit her throat."

He stopped and looked at them.

It confirmed what they already had known.

"What happened next?" Elara asked.

His voice shook slightly. "I told Deidre to climb the tree and stay there, and then I circled to the north, because the wind was blowing from the south. I had my bow with me."

"What was the plan?" Hugh asked.

"I wanted to get Courtney out," he said. "She's my girlfriend. I was climbing over the wall when a monster saw me. I shot it and it died."

"Where did you shoot it?" Hugh asked.

"Through the eye," Alex said.

"He's a very good marksman," Elara told him softly.

"It was a lucky shot. As soon as it went down, one of the soldiers blew a horn. They couldn't see us, but somehow they knew it was dead. So I ran. I didn't try to go and get Courtney. I just ran. Deidre was waiting for me, and then we ran together. They shot at us through the woods. I got hit twice, and then I don't remember it that well. I just kept running."

His voice faded.

"You saved Deidre," Elara said. "You survived."

Alex looked at her. "I ran," he said. "I left Courtney to die."

"No," Elara said. "You did everything you could."

"I ran like a coward."

He had to fix this or they would lose a steady pair of hands with a bow. The kid didn't need forgiveness. He needed direction and purpose.

"You've got two days," Hugh said.

The kid's gaze snapped to him.

"In two days I need you up and moving. Once you're up, go to the barracks and find Yvonne Faure. She will evaluate your archery skills. If you do well enough, you'll be given a bow and assigned to the auxiliaries. For every bastard you shoot down, another Courtney will live."

He turned and walked out. Elara followed him.

Deidre sat on the stone floor in the hallway, her back to the wall, her arms locked around her knees. She looked up at him. "I want a bow."

Elara crouched by her. "What about your aunt and uncle?"

Deidre shook her head. "I don't want to go with them. I want to stay here."

"But they are your family."

"I don't know them. I want to stay here. It's safe here. Can you make them let me stay?"

"We will ask." Elara sighed. "But they are not here now, so let's worry about this later."

"Do I still get a bow?"

"Why do you want one?" Elara asked.

"So I can kill the monsters if they come here."

"A bow can be arranged," Hugh said.

"Have you ever shot a bow?" Elara asked.

"No."

"Don't worry. Hugh will teach you. But if you decide that the bow isn't for you, come and see me. I may teach you some things as well."

"Go downstairs and wait for me," Hugh said. "We'll see about getting you a bow."

The child jumped to her feet and dashed down the hallway. He watched her go. There was something disturbingly familiar about the look in her eyes, like a small feral animal backed into a corner. Rene used to look like that.

"We have no legal standing," Elara said. "We can't keep her."

"We can bargain," Hugh said.

She eyed him. "Do you actually care, Preceptor?"

"Don't know the meaning of the word," he said.

———·+·———

HUGH LEANED against the step leading from the upper bailey to the keep and watched Stoyan stab the armor on a wooden mannequin. Or rather he watched Stoyan try. The centurion executed another beautiful slash. The blade glanced off the breast-plate. The two Iron Dogs who were Stoyan's second and third watched him.

Lamar leaned next to Hugh.

"Have you gotten anywhere with the Remaining?" Hugh asked him quietly.

"Nope. Nobody is talking." Lamar shrugged his wide shoulders. "Everything is great, everyone is friendly and welcoming. The minute we try to ask any leading questions, they clam up." He shifted on his feet. "You ever get a feeling we stumbled into a cult? Because I do."

"As long as they keep us fed and clothed, I can deal with a cult."

Stoyan stabbed the armor, putting all of his weight behind it. The point of the sword penetrated. He leaned forward, examined the nick, and spat.

"What about Elara?" Hugh asked. "Anything on her?"

"No."

"There are thousands of people in that village. You're telling me none of them have anything to say about her?"

Lamar shook his head.

Stoyan attacked the armor's side, aiming at the armpit.

"Look on the bright side," Lamar said. "They aren't having much luck figuring out what's in our barrels either."

"Did they ask?"

"They did."

Hugh grinned. Clever girl.

Stoyan moved back, resting his sword on his shoulder, and critically examined the armor.

Bale turned the corner.

"Here comes trouble," Lamar murmured.

The berserker walked up to the weapons rack and pulled a mace out.

"Perhaps going from the bottom?" one of Stoyan's people suggested. "An up stroke?"

"Possibly," Stoyan said.

Bale charged.

The Iron Dogs jumped out of the way. The red-headed berserker smashed the breastplate with the mace, denting it.

"Damn it!" Stoyan barked.

Bale pounded the armor with his mace, denting it with every blow. Clang. Clang. Clang.

Stoyan threw his sword on the ground. "Fine. Just fucking smash it then. Smash everything."

"How many maces do we have?" Hugh asked.

"Not that many," Lamar said.

"Get more."

"Will do."

———

THE OLD TRUCK rolled through the gates of the castle, flanked by two Iron Dogs on horseback, the escort Hugh had sent for protection. The water engine spat noise and screeched. The driver got out without shutting it off. A bad sign.

"Go get Hugh," she told Beth. "Tell him Deidre's family is here."

Elara put a smile on her face and walked out to the vehicle. The driver, an average size man with dark blond hair and skin ruddy from the weather waited for the passenger. A woman climbed out of the vehicle, dark-haired, white, thin. The two of them walked toward her, away from the truck's noise. Both were closer to forty than to thirty. The man wore jeans, a denim shirt with the sleeves rolled up to the elbow, and a black-and-white baseball cap. The woman wore a blue T-shirt over a pair of washed-out jeans.

"Hello," Elara said.

"We're here for Deidre," the man said.

Right. No pleasantries, then. "And you are?" Elara asked.

"I'm her mother's brother," the man said.

"My name is Elara," she said and held her hand out.

Neither of the two shook it.

"I'm going to need some proof of identity before I release the child to you," she said.

The man looked like he was about to say something unpleasant, but the woman reached out and put her hand on his arm. He shut his mouth, pulled out a wallet, and held out his driver's license. Wayne Braiden Harmon. The name matched what Deidre told her. The woman produced her own driver's license. Jane Melissa Harmon.

"We are deeply sorry for your loss," Elara said.

"Thank you," Jane said.

"I'm not sure how much you were told," Elara said. "Redhill was attacked by monsters. They slaughtered everyone inside. Deidre happened to be outside of the walls when it happened, and she and a young man escaped. A monster chased them through the woods in the middle of the night. The young man almost died."

Jane bit her lip.

"The child is deeply traumatized. We were hoping you could allow her to stay with us for a couple of days, just to settle her down. We would be happy to put you up for the night."

"That's kind of you," Jane said. "But we would like to take Deidre home."

"She will get settled with us," Wayne said.

This wasn't going well. "Please reconsider," Elara said. "She just lost her father and mother."

Hugh came around the tower, leading Bucky. Deidre was riding on the huge stallion's back. She saw her aunt and uncle and went still like a baby rabbit caught in the open.

Elara's heart turned over in her chest.

Hugh walked over to them, reached for Deidre, gently took her off the horse and set her on her feet.

"Hi, honey," Elara threw him a smile. *Help me, Hugh.* "This is Wayne and Jane Harmon. This is my husband, Hugh. He is the one who saved your niece."

"Hey there." Hugh offered his charming grin and held his hand out. Wayne Harmon met Hugh's gaze and held it for a long moment. Hugh showed no signs of moving. Finally the sheer force of his presence won out and Wayne shook his hand. Hope fluttered in her.

"Your niece is very brave," Hugh said.

The brave niece looked like she was about to bolt at any second.

"I was just explaining that Deidre isn't in any shape to travel," Elara said.

Wayne ignored her and crouched. "Hi, Deidre. Remember me? It's uncle Wayne."

Deidre didn't move.

"It will be okay," Jane told her. "Everything will be okay now. You're coming home with us."

Deidre shook her head. "No. I want to stay here."

"You can't stay here," Wayne said. "You have to come with us. You remember Michelle, your cousin? She's waiting for you. We have a big yellow dog named Tyler. You'll like him. He's big and fluffy. Come on, sweetheart."

Deidre stayed completely still.

"Why don't we have lunch?" Hugh said. "You'll get to know us, and we'll talk about it."

Wayne straightened and drew himself to his full height. "We know you. We know who you are. We know what you've done."

He took a step toward Hugh. D'Ambray towered over him and Wayne had to look up.

"You're a killer and a villain. Your wife is a witch. This child comes from a good Christian family. If her father knew where she was now, he'd fight every single one of you to get her out of here."

Oh no.

"So, no, we won't be breaking bread with you. There isn't a godly man alive in fifty miles who would let his flesh and blood anywhere near you. We know you want her to stay here. Well, you're not getting her. What would you turn her into if I left her here?"

Hugh's face shut down. The charming veneer vanished and only the Preceptor of the Iron Dogs remained.

"What happens when the beasts come for her?" he asked, his voice pure ice.

"We'll fight them," Jane said. "And if she dies, she'll die as a Christian."

Wayne walked over and reached for Deidre.

The child screamed as if cut. "No!"

Hugh stepped between them. Wayne locked his teeth.

It wouldn't be a fair fight. Hugh would kill him with the first blow and then Deidre would see the rest of her family die.

An electric jolt of alarm dashed through Elara. *Do I grab the child first, do I stop Hugh, do I stop Wayne?*

Hugh looked at Deidre. "I know you want to stay here," he said. "But you have a family. Your uncle loves you. If I tried to keep you here, your uncle would fight for you. He has no chance against me. He knows that, but he would do it anyway. You're that important to him. I don't want to kill your uncle. He hasn't done anything wrong. You have to go with him."

Elara moved, letting her magic spill out of her. Wayne saw her and stumbled back, hands raised. She swept Deidre up and gently brushed her tears off with her fingers.

"And if he ever mistreats you," Elara said. "If he or your aunt ever hit you or hurt you, all you have to do is call to me. I will hear, and I will come." She kissed Deidre's forehead. Her magic touched the child's skin, leaving a hidden blessing.

Elara took three steps and placed Deidre into Jane's arms. "Take her now and leave. Quickly, before my husband and I change our minds."

The Harmons ran for the truck, carrying Deidre. She watched them turn around and roll out, aware of Hugh standing next to her like a thunderstorm ready to break.

The truck left the gates.

Hugh turned and walked away without a word.

12

E lara leaned forward, rocking on her hands and knees, and sniffed the soil under the patch of wilting jimsonweed. It smelled moist, green, and alive. She sat back on her feet and pondered the thorny plants. Only yesterday, the patch was in good health, the stems standing straight, spreading the toothed leaves, and cradling white and purple trumpet shaped flowers. Today, the stems had wrinkled and shrunk, curling down. It was as if all the water had been sucked out of the plant, and it was dying at the end of a long drought. But the soil was moist.

Next to her, James Cornwell twisted his hands. A white man in his forties, he was of average height, but his arms and legs seemed too long somehow, his shoulders too narrow, and his frame too lanky. He wore a straw hat and he often joked that from the back people mistook him for a scarecrow. He was the keeper of poisons. If it was poisonous and they grew it, James was in charge of it. Normally he was upbeat, but right now agitation took hold of him.

"Never seen anything like this," James said.

"Have you dug one up?" she asked.

He turned, plucked a plant from his wheelbarrow with his

gloved hand, and held it in front of her. The root, normally thick and fibrous, had shrunk down, so desiccated it looked like a rat's tail.

"What could do that?" James asked.

"I don't know," she said.

"The entire crop is a loss."

He was right. Jimsonweed, *Datura stramonium*, wasn't one of their most valuable plants. A powerful hallucinogenic, it belonged to the nightshade family, sharing ancestry with tomatoes, potatoes, and chili peppers, but also with belladonna and mandrake. Once it was used as a remedy against madness and seizures, but the toxicity of the plant proved to be too high and it was abandoned as soon as safer alternatives were found. Now it was mostly harvested to induce visions. They sold a small quantity of it every year to specialized shops and made sure it came with bright warning labels. It wasn't a significant earner, but the sudden wilting was worrisome.

Elara glanced to the left, where a patch of henbane bloomed with yellow flowers. *Hyoscyamus niger*, also poisonous and hallucinogenic, brought in a lot of money, mostly from German and Norse neo-pagans. The plant was sacred to Balder, son of Odin and Frigg. Balder was famous mostly for his resurrection myth, detailed in Prose Edda, but the medieval text glossed over one important detail: Balder wasn't a martyr. He was a warlord, proficient with every weapon known to ancient people. The neo-pagans prayed to him before every major obstacle, and henbane was a crucial part of those prayers. Henbane was too toxic to be grown and harvested by amateurs. It came with a big price tag.

If whatever killed the jimsonweed jumped to the henbane, they would take an expensive hit.

"What do you want to do?" she asked.

"I want it warded."

"The henbane?"

He nodded. "I'll put plastic up too, but I would feel better with a ward."

"Okay," she said. "I'll tell Savannah."

James twisted his hands some more.

"Would you like *me* to do it?" she guessed. "Now?"

"Yes?" he asked.

"Okay."

"Thank you!" He reached into the wheelbarrow and withdrew a bundle of elm sticks.

The rapid thudding of a galloping horse sounded through the trees. Elara frowned. A rider came around the bend, emerging from the trees. Sam, wearing his Iron Dog black.

He slowed the horse, bringing the mare to a stop in front of them. "Trouble."

She jumped to her feet.

"What?"

"People from the Pack are here. The guy who was here before and two others, a man and a woman. They said they were the alphas of Clan Bouda."

Just what they needed. "Where is the Preceptor?"

"In the moat, on the other side. We didn't tell him yet."

Clan Bouda, Clan Bouda... What was it the boy said before? *His people killed the alpha of my clan.*

Oh no. "Keep the Preceptor away from the bailey. Do whatever you have to do. Don't just sit there, go! Go!"

Sam turned the horse around and rode back the way he came. She focused on the trees in the distance.

"But the henbane," James moaned.

"I'll be back."

Elara stepped. The trees rushed to her. She stepped again, hurrying to the castle, burning magic too fast. Three days had passed since Deidre was taken from the castle and Hugh had gone inside himself. He didn't want to fight with her. When he spoke, it was short and brisk. He spent all his time finishing the moat.

She'd snuck into his dreams last night and found fire and death, ruins littered with corpses, and him, a terrifying monster prowling through it to the chorus of screams and killing, the fiery maelstrom behind him so big, it took up half of the sky. She couldn't tell if it was a nightmare or a distorted memory.

In that moment, before he'd turned away and left as Deidre's family drove out of the castle, she had seen his eyes. Hugh hadn't realized his legacy. He knew what it was, he knew himself to be a killer, he let it torment him, but inside the castle walls he was sheltered from its full impact. The Iron Dogs admired him; her people looked to him for protection. Whether he knew it or not, Hugh leaned on that human net to keep going. He saw himself as strong, violent, and ruthless, but also as someone who protected and led. He was feared but respected and even envied.

He had never stopped to think how people from the outside saw him. There was no respect in what Wayne Harmon had said. Only contempt and revulsion.

Hugh was a man who couldn't be trusted with children. A villain. A butcher without a single redeeming quality to him. And she was a witch, Satan's consort, an evil creature, a deceiver and defiler, fit only to be stoned to death. It didn't sting her. Elara was used to it. She had grown up with it.

She'd known both kindness and utter contempt. A Baptist church had sheltered her and her people once, knowing what they were, because they were hungry and had no place to go. In the next town, only ten miles down the road, the Christians had lined up along the road with loaded shotguns to make sure they kept moving.

Some people in the world only saw in black and white. They were driven by fear. They had learned how to survive in their little corner of the world and they saw any change as a threat to their survival. But they still liked to think of themselves as good people. Good people didn't hate without a reason, so they grasped at any pretext, no matter how small, that gave them permission to hate. A line in a holy book. The color of a person's skin. The brand of their magic. They were not in the habit of taking a second look or giving chances. Their fear was too great and their need to defend themselves too dire. They always lost at the end. Life was change. It would come to them, as inevitable as the sunrise, despite all their flailing.

She had years to armor herself against it. Hugh didn't. He was on top. On the winning team. No doubt was allowed.

And now the alphas of Clan Bouda were here. She had no idea how he would react to that.

Elara stepped onto the wall and forced herself to stop and catch a breath. The shapeshifters had dismounted in the bailey. A tall, dark-haired man wearing black, his movements fluid and quick. He looked like he was barely holding it together. And a woman, who was his polar opposite: short, blond, and calm. She was telling him something, and her movements seemed soothing. Ascanio Ferara hung behind them, a long-suffering look on his handsome face.

Elara realized that her blue dress was stained with dirt. There was dirt under her fingernails. No time. She descended the stairs. At the foot of it, Dugas waited.

"That man is about to do something violent," he murmured.

"I know."

She walked past him and put a smile on her face. "Hello."

Ascanio and the woman turned to her. The man was still scanning the bailey. The blond woman put her hand on his arm and gently pulled on him, until he turned to face Elara.

"Hello," the blond said. "So sorry to barge in on you unannounced. I'm Andrea Medrano. This is my husband Raphael. You've already met Ascanio, of course."

"I have," Elara said. "You must be tired. Would you like something to eat?"

Ascanio's eyes lit up.

If she could get them out of the bailey and safely settled inside before Hugh showed up, maybe they would dodge this bullet after all.

"We would love something to eat," Andrea said. "Wouldn't we, honey?"

Hugh d'Ambray walked through the gate, with Stoyan right behind him.

Raphael saw him. Their gazes locked.

Raphael pulled his leather jacket off with a single jerk of hishand.

"Raphael!" Andrea said. "You promised me you wouldn't do this. Raphael!"

Raphael yanked two daggers from the sheath on his belt and started toward Hugh.

"I told you," Ascanio said. "I said this would happen."

Hugh pulled a knife from the sheath on his waist and moved forward.

The two men reached each other. Raphael struck, so fast he was a blur. Somehow Hugh dodged.

"Go get him, honey!" Andrea called out.

What? Elara looked at her.

"I'm so sorry," Andrea said. "The Iron Dogs killed my mother-in-law."

"My condolences," Elara said. "What happens when my husband makes you a widow?"

"Raphael won't lose."

Hugh spun out of the way and kicked Raphael in the stomach. The shapeshifter rolled, sprung to his feet, his eyes growing blood red, and charged Hugh.

Don't lose, she willed silently. *Don't lose, Hugh.*

The two men clashed and broke apart. Hugh's left forearm bled. A blue glow clamped the wound. It knitted closed.

A cut snaked down Raphael's face. He wiped it off and flung the blood away. His skin sealed itself. Lyc-V, the virus responsible for shapeshifter existence, gifted them with unmatched regeneration.

They clashed again, slashing, carving, stabbing, so fast she could barely guess at the attacks. Raphael was a whirlwind, but Hugh was stronger. They tore across the bailey. If it wasn't for the knives, they could almost be dancing.

Hugh staggered back. Cold rushed through her. He must've taken a hit, but she couldn't see it. Raphael dove into the opening, slashing. The tip of his dagger grazed Hugh's throat, drawing a sharp red line.

Elara gasped.

Hugh grabbed Raphael's wrist with his left hand and twisted. Bone snapped with a crunch. The shapeshifter snarled and dropped the dagger. Andrea clicked her teeth.

Hugh kicked the dagger out of the way. They lunged at each other.

Seconds stretched into minutes, slow and viscous, like dripping honey. Hugh was covered in a blue glow now. Raphael was bleeding. The Lyc-V couldn't fix him fast enough. The stones under their feet were smeared with red.

Something was wrong. She'd watched Hugh fight before. This wasn't him. He was precise and deliberate. This was a frenzy, almost as if... as if he were letting Raphael vent his anger on him.

If he used magic, this fight would be over.

Hugh was punishing himself.

Raphael smashed his fist into Hugh's side. Hugh took the hit, clamped Raphael's arm, and stabbed Raphael in the kidneys. The shapeshifter tore free. The blue glow jumped from Hugh to Raphael's wound and lingered.

She watched it for a long moment, in disbelief. Her hands clenched. That was enough. Elara started forward.

"What are you doing?" Andrea asked.

"I'm going to stop it."

"Oh, I don't know," Andrea said. "They don't look like they need any help."

Elara let her magic spill out of her. It rolled off her, cold like the bottom of an iceberg in the deep dark ocean. The shapeshifter woman drew a sharp breath.

"Hugh is healing him."

Andrea squinted at the fighters. "No..."

The blue glow clung to Raphael's other side.

Shock slapped Andrea's face. "Yes. He is. Why?"

"Because he is punishing himself. The man your husband came here to kill doesn't exist anymore. The man here now is going to let himself be hurt because he thinks he needs to be punished. This has gone far enough. Nobody is dying today. I won't allow it."

"Raphael," Andrea called out. "Stop. Enough!"

Raphael drove his knife into Hugh's side in a vicious upward stab. Hugh punched him in the face. Raphael staggered back, his lips drawn back in a grimace. Hugh had gone pale. Fear pinched her. She'd let it go on for too long.

Raphael spun a kick. His back was to her. She grazed his shoulder with her fingertips, stealing just a tiny drop of his life.

The shapeshifter halted. His black dagger drooped. He took a halting step back and dropped to his knees.

She thrust herself in front of Hugh and slid her arms around his neck, her magic bathing them both. "It's over."

He took a step forward, carrying her dead weight on his neck.

"It's done," she murmured, wrapping her voice around them. "No more. I need you. We all need you. Please, Hugh. Let it be."

He stopped and looked at her. Awareness came back in his eyes. Elara exhaled.

Behind them Andrea knelt by Raphael and put her arms around him.

"So tired," Raphael whispered and slumped to the ground.

"You fought well," she told him. "You killed him at least four times. Aunt B would be proud."

Hugh was looking at her. He dipped his head. She didn't realize what he was doing until his lips found hers. It was a hungry desperate kiss. She tasted his pain on her tongue and stepped away. The entire front of her dress was soaked in blood. Hugh stumbled and toppled forward like a log. She barely caught him and her knees shook under the impact of his dead weight.

"Can we have lunch now?" Ascanio asked.

———

HUGH OPENED HIS EYES. The ceiling above him was shrouded in gloom. He was in his bedroom.

Everything hurt.

He blinked at the ceiling, trying to find some equilibrium between the pain in different parts of him, a magic spot where it hurt a little less. He failed.

What time was it? It had to be late. The last thing he remembered was fighting Medrano. He didn't really have a plan for that fight. He wasn't sure how it would have ended. He hadn't wanted to kill Medrano in front of the man's wife. He had some vague idea of letting the shapeshifter tire himself out, but then it became something else. He was pretty sure one of them wouldn't survive that fight.

He remembered Elara and the cooling touch of her magic. Like walking into a cloud of mist on a hot summer day.

Then he remembered nothing.

Did he kill Medrano?

No, she must've stopped him.

A smell floated down to him. He smelled orange, butter, and something else, some sort of dough. Suddenly he was ravenous.

Sitting up proved to be an effort. Someone had stripped him

down to his underwear. He didn't smell blood, so he'd been washed.

He staggered to the door. Across the hallway, Elara's door stood open. Soft light glowed inside. The aroma was coming from there.

He stumbled around, looking for something to wear, and settled on a pair of black pants and a white T-shirt. He managed to put both on without making noises and headed down the hallway.

The scent got stronger. The castle lay quiet around them. Outside the windows in the hallway, night spread across the sky, glittering with stars.

Hugh made it to the doorway. The front room of Elara's suite lay empty. He walked through, following the smell, turned and saw her. She stood in a small nook off her bedroom. A big stone oven occupied a large part of the far wall. In front of him was an island with a cooktop and a prep sink. Between the stove and the island stood Elara, with her back to him. Her blue dress clung to her, draping over her butt. Her hair was braided and pinned up, and he could see her slender neck.

Mmmm.

He leaned in the doorway.

Elara grabbed something out of the stove and turned toward him. She was holding a metal platter, her hands in kitchen mittens.

She was wearing an apron. A frilly little apron, white, with pink cherry blossoms on it and wide black ties, wrapped around her and knotted into a bow on the side.

He laughed.

"What's so funny?"

This couldn't possibly be real. It was another dream. "I wonder which part of my demented brain wanted to see the Ice Harpy in an apron. Baking cookies."

"These are not cookies."

He glanced into the pan. It was full of crepes, folded into quarters and drenched in melted butter. The heat had browned the crepe edges. She must've sprinkled them with sugar, because a thin layer of caramel dotted the edges. The last time he had a crepe Suzette was in France, ages ago. He couldn't recall why he was there or what he was doing, but he remembered the dessert and bright red flames licking the crepes as it was flambéed at the table.

Elara pulled off her oven mittens. "Is that what I am, an Ice Harpy?"

"Yes." And he was on fire. He couldn't even think straight.

"You're not going to get any of my crepes with that attitude."

He moved toward her, stalking. She crossed her arms on her chest but didn't move. He walked behind her, slowly, aware of every inch of space between them. She smelled of jasmine and green apples. Too subtle for a perfume. A hint of shampoo or a lotion, maybe. He wondered if he would taste it as he licked her skin.

"Be careful, Preceptor."

He reached down, caught the end of her apron tie, and tugged on it.

"Quit it," she told him.

Oh, he would enjoy this. "It's my dream," he told her.

"I don't care."

Of course she didn't. He laughed, his voice low, and tugged on the tie again.

"Will you stop it?"

"I told you to stay out of my dreams." He leaned in close, inhaling the scent of her skin and whispered into her ear. "You're trespassing."

Her eyes widened. He looked into them and caught the exact moment where a hint of white flame burst in their depths. On the battlefield of Elara's mind, banners of war unfurled, and soldiers broke into a charge. He'd learned to watch for this look when they argued. That's when it got really good.

"Perhaps you should ask yourself why you're letting me waltz in and out of your dreams, Preceptor. What is it you want?"

He was so hard, it hurt.

"Perhaps I'm hungry." He reached over her shoulder and stole a crepe from the platter. She tried to slap his hand, but he was too fast.

"They're not done yet."

"They look done to me." He held the crepe, out of her reach. "Do you want this back?"

"Yes."

He leaned closer. "What will you let me do to you to get it back?"

"Give me back the crepe, Hugh."

He held it in front of her. She snatched it out of his hand and turned her back to him to drop it back into the pan. He locked his hands on the island, caging her between his arms.

She stood completely still. He felt the tension vibrating in the angle of her spine and the set of her shoulders and it made him harder.

He leaned forward and kissed her on the right side, just below her ear. She gasped. Her skin felt warm and soft under his lips, like warm silk. He touched the sensitive spot with his tongue, painting heat over the nerve, and she leaned back slightly, looking for him in spite of herself. He wanted to crush her to him, to rip off her clothes, and lose himself in her soft body. It was a wild, uncontrollable need, simple and violent in its intensity. He wanted to pin her to the bed and run his tongue over the nipples of her breasts and then slide lower, over her stomach, down below. He wanted to hear her moan, to see her breathless, to watch her open her legs for him, and make her come like she never came before. He wanted to thrust into her and hear her scream his name, because she couldn't get enough. He wanted her to love it, because he was doing it to her.

"Stop, Hugh," she whispered.

He caught a tendril of her white hair into his fingers and kissed it. "Why?"

"What if this isn't a dream? What if you're awake?"

"And you're cooking crepes Suzette in the middle of the night in a pretty apron?"

"What if I am? If we wake up in the morning in the same bed, what then?"

"I don't know. Tell me." He kissed her neck again, on the other side. She took a sharp breath and swallowed.

"We finally learned to work together. If you don't stop..."

He bit her neck, pinching the skin between his teeth. Her voice broke. She shivered, and it almost pushed him over the edge.

"...if you don't stop, we'll go to war in the morning, because this isn't you. Your body was straining so hard to repair all the damage, you glowed for hours. You're exhausted and not in your right mind. You'll regret this moment of weakness. You'll make me pay for it."

His lips traveled down to the bend of her neck. Her breath was coming in ragged gasps. She wanted him. His whole body had gone hard, every muscle, every nerve screaming for her.

"I can't afford the price. Stop, Hugh. Stop."

The words finally penetrated. He could force her. It was a dream and he could do whatever he wanted to, but it wouldn't be enough. He wanted more, something his subconscious refused to let him have even in his dreams. This was another nightmare. He just hadn't realized it until now.

He rested his forehead against the back of her head. "Elara..."

"Please," she whispered. "Please don't say anything you'll regret in the morning."

His voice was a low snarl. "Sometimes when I lay awake in the middle of the night, I think of you."

"Don't..."

"Sometimes there is nothing left and all that's anchoring me here is knowing you'll pick a fight with me in the morning."

"Hugh..."

"What do you want more than anything? Tell me what it is, and I'll rip the world apart to bring it to you."

She turned in his arms slowly and raised her hands. Her fingers touched his hair, brushing it back from his face. He savored it.

She stood on her toes and brushed his lips with hers. "Ask me again in the morning."

"Now."

"You have to go now, Hugh."

The tightrope broke under him and he fell. "No."

"Yes. We'll talk about this again, in the morning. Please go to your bedroom."

She pushed him. He could've stayed where he was. She didn't have the strength to move him. But instead he moved for her. He walked to the doorway and stepped outside. She shut the door and he heard her sag against it on the other side.

There was nothing left but to go back to his room. That was the only way out of this twisted dream.

The void opened behind him. He stared into its burning depth, swore, and went to his bed.

———+—

HUGH OPENED HIS EYES. The morning light flooded his room. The windows stood open and a light breeze floated through his bedroom, bringing with it a hint of the first autumn chill.

His stomach growled. He sat up and saw Lamar in a Lazyboy chair, his glasses perched on his nose.

"Well, hello there, Sunshine," Lamar told him.

Hugh looked at him.

"We missed you," Lamar said.

"How long was I out?"

"Three days."

That explained the hunger and the fucked-up dreams. "The shapeshifters?"

"Still here. Medrano wants to talk to you. Your wife has been holding the fort. I think she's about to serve them breakfast."

Hugh stood up. His limbs ached, and his insides felt raw and tender. Too much healing too quickly. There was a book lying on the table by the chair. Hugh picked it up. "Harry Potter?"

"Bale read it out loud to you. It's his favorite."

They had sat with him for three days, making sure he didn't die. He would've done the same for them, but he never expected they would do it for him.

Hugh pulled on a pair of pants. "How's the moat?"

"We're done."

There was two weeks' worth of work left when he had gone under. "How?"

"Elara mobilized her people. They came out in droves to lay the concrete."

The harpy had helped him. Huh.

"Do you want the best news? They have a family of stonemasons that speed-cured it. They do their thing and instead of 28 days, we get cured concrete as soon as they walk on it." Lamar grinned. "There is one section left they didn't get to, because the magic's been down, but once it's done, we'll be ready to flood."

"Lamar?"

"Yes."

"Punch me."

Lamar unfolded his hard frame from the chair and sank a punch into his gut. The pain pulsed through Hugh, a welcome shock to the system.

"What was that about?" Lamar asked.

"Making sure I'm awake."

"You are," Lamar said. "But don't do that again. You let Medrano gut you like a fish. I watched you do it. You promised Stoyan, Bale, and Felix. You promised me. You can lie to those motherfuckers, but I'm going to hold you to your word. We need you. We're not safe yet."

"Get the hell out of my room," Hugh growled.

Lamar grinned and headed for the door.

A stray thought hit him. "How long did you say the magic's been down?" Hugh called.

"I didn't. It crashed the evening after you stabilized, about ten hours after your fight with Medrano."

Lamar kept moving.

If the magic had been down for most of the three days, Elara couldn't have walked through his dreams.

Did he imagine the whole thing? It felt sharp and real, the same way it felt when she had first let herself into his head.

He had never seen her in the kitchen. He'd been in her bedroom when she patched him up, but he couldn't see that side of the room from where he'd sat.

Ten minutes later, dressed and showered, he crossed the hallway and knocked on Elara's door. No answer. He tried the door handle. It turned in his hand. Hugh walked in. The bedroom stood empty. He picked his way along the familiar route to the far wall and turned left. A kitchen nook greeted him. The same island, the same stove, the same fridge. He pulled the refrigerator door open, knowing what he would find inside.

A plate rested on the middle shelf, holding a stack of crepes.

Hugh stared at it.

It was real. He'd gotten up in the middle of the night, walked here, and told her all that stupid shit. She'd warned him, but he spilled it all out, like an idiot, giving her all the ammunition she would ever need. He stood there, like some starving dog, whining to be let inside. She'd practically had to shove him out of her room.

Pathetic.

It happened.

Everything would change now. They had a back and forth and he fucked it up. If he walked down there and saw pity on her face, it would kill him.

For a long moment he stood there, numb, until finally some cold emotion took hold of him. He puzzled over it and recognized it. He felt cold, crystalline anger. He let it wash over him, freezing every inconvenient emotion he had.

He was the Preceptor of the Iron Dogs. His wife was serving breakfast to a man who tried to kill him. A man who was still a threat.

It was his job to neutralize threats.

He would attend.

———✦———

HE KNEW.

Elara gripped her fork tighter. One moment the doorway to the sunroom was empty, the next Hugh loomed in it, and instantly she realized he knew the conversation in her kitchen happened. His blue eyes were iced over. Cedric sat by his feet, wagging his tail.

He walked over to her.

She had no idea what he would do. At the table, Andrea and Raphael went still.

Hugh leaned over her. His lips brushed her cheek. It was about as dry and emotionless as rubbing chalk over her skin.

She conjured up a smile. "You're finally up."

"You know me, I need my beauty rest."

His voice was warm, the hint of a smile tugging on his lips was just right, but his eyes were hard.

She took his hand and held it in hers. "I was worried."

He freed his hand. He did it smoothly, and an observer

wouldn't have been able to tell, but she felt it. He didn't want her touching him.

"I'm sorry. I won't worry you again." He'd sunken some awful finality into those words.

Hugh picked a chair next to her and sat. The big dog sprawled at his feet.

Raphael and Andrea were looking at Hugh like both he and Cedric had gone rabid. She'd reached a comfortable balance with the shapeshifters over the last three days. Given time, she would win them over, but none of it mattered. It all hinged on what would come out of Hugh's mouth next.

The silence hung over the table, ominous and heavy.

Hugh frowned.

She tensed. The shapeshifters leaned forward slightly.

"Where is the bacon?"

She exhaled, got up, lifted the lid off a platter, and set the huge plate of cooked bacon and sausage in front of him.

Hugh filled his plate, took a gulp of coffee, and paused for a moment, savoring it. "Makes me feel almost human."

"Are we going to talk about it?" Raphael asked.

Hugh set the mug down and faced him. "I'm sorry my soldiers killed your mother."

There it is. Elara held her breath.

"I respected your mother," Hugh said. "She was a leader and she led from the front. She died because she wanted to buy you time. I didn't dislike her, and I didn't specifically want her to die. Daniels was the target. But your mother and I were on opposite sides, and anything that weakened the Pack was judged to be good for Roland's cause. She was dangerous, powerful, and popular and she exercised a great deal of influence over Lennart and Daniels and the Pack in general. Her death left a big gap in your power lineup. So I would be lying if I said that killing her wasn't a victory at the time. However, I no longer support Roland's causes.

I deeply regret her death and the pain I caused you and your family."

Andrea exhaled quietly.

"I understand why you attacked me," Hugh said, cutting a pancake with his fork. "I get it. It was fair. It's done now. Each of us has a wife and people we are responsible for and our business interests intersect. We can continue to work together, we can look for alternative business partners, or we can kill each other. Figure out what do you want to do."

Raphael leaned back, his face calm. "By my count, I killed you four times during that fight. How are you still alive?"

"I'm difficult to kill," Hugh said.

"Where do you stand on the Roland issue?" Andrea asked.

"He wants us dead," Hugh said. "We are not the highest priority target at the moment, so he likely told Nez to take care of us at his discretion."

"What happens if Roland attacks Atlanta?" Andrea asked. "Who will you help, d'Ambray? Elara told us you weren't the same person. Is it all lip service or not? Where do you stand?"

They pushed him too far and too fast. She had to step in. "My husband's first priority is the survival of our people."

Hugh chewed his bacon and took another gulp of coffee. "Right now, Daniels is the best chance of stopping Roland. If he takes Atlanta, he will roll over us. We can hold out for a while, but it won't be long. So if there is a coalition forming in Atlanta, we will aid it."

She almost fell off her chair.

Raphael leaned forward. "Do we have your word?"

"Yes. The more relevant question for you is where will the Pack stand?" Hugh chewed a bit more. "Shrapshire, your new Beast Lord, is a paranoid perfectionist driven by the fear of not living up to his responsibilities. He is naturally a loner and he can't believe he found a woman who loves him. Dali Harimau is his sole pillar of support."

"He has a family," Andrea said.

"Yes, all of whom are typical werejaguars: solitary. They come together for family occasions, but aside from that, they lead separate lives. Shrapshire cares about two things: his mate and doing the absolute best job he can in whatever position within the Pack he assumes. His father failed to put a child who went loup to death. It was his responsibility as the medic for the pack. He was tried and imprisoned for this failure of duty. Shrapshire's never gotten over that."

He was delivering all of this with clinical precision, while eating. No trace of Hugh from that night had lingered, Elara realized. Only the Preceptor of the Iron Dogs remained. It made her want to grab him and shake him until the ice broke.

"Right now Shrapshire is in a position of ultimate responsibility as the Beast Lord. If you knock him off his stride with the right catastrophe – like injuring Dali or killing some Pack children – he will respond with overwhelming force and, once that assault fails, become progressively more irrational as he retaliates."

The two shapeshifters were staring at him as if he had sprouted a second head.

"Back when I worked for Roland, he called on me to come up with a comprehensive plan to dismantle the Pack. He doesn't have me anymore, but if he works from my playbook, he will likely target Dali. It's easier and cleaner than other targets. Once Shrapshire is convinced he can't even keep his mate safe, he will spin out of control and there is no telling where he will land. He abandoned both Lennart and Daniels before. If you hit him the right way, he may pull everyone into the Keep and forbid anyone from leaving. Andrea, Daniels is your best friend. So what are the two of you going to do when she is out there, Roland is coming, and Shrapshire has you holed up in your fort?"

The two shapeshifters gaped at him. Elara felt a small twinge of satisfaction.

"This is the side of him he doesn't usually show to anyone," she said. "Sounds like your best bet is to keep the Beast Lord's family safe."

"I'll give you an answer." Andrea bared her teeth. "If Shrapshire tries to keep Clan Bouda from that fight, we will split from the Pack. Clan Heavy and Clan Wolf will as well. We stand with our friends."

Cedric raised his head and barked at her. Hugh held a piece of bacon out and the big dog wolfed it down. She'd have to talk to him about feeding the dog from the table.

"You're right," Raphael said. "We have intersecting business interests. We don't have to be friends, but it's mutually beneficial to cooperate. I miss my mother every day. I'd like nothing better than to put you in the ground, but that would benefit nobody at this point, least of all our clan. If my mother was alive, she would point it out to me. We're not in the habit of wasting resources. You're useful, d'Ambray. We're going to use you. You owe us that much."

"Fair enough. What do you need from us?" Hugh asked.

"Same thing you are doing now," Raphael said. "We need a safe harbor for the shapeshifters in Kentucky. In return, we will aggressively push the Pack to purchase your herbals over competition."

"Works for me," Hugh said.

"Thank you for the lovely breakfast." Andrea rose to her feet. "And your hospitality. We will be on our way now."

"You're always welcome," Elara said.

Raphael got up and the two shapeshifters walked out.

For a couple of minutes, they sat in silence.

"Where is Ascanio?" Hugh asked.

"Exploring the castle."

"You let him run around unsupervised?"

"Sam is with him," she answered.

Hugh sighed. "By now he likely knows the complete layout of our defenses. No matter. I'll handle it."

He got up and picked up his plate.

"Don't bother," she told him. "I'll clear it."

Hugh set his plate on the floor. Cedric nearly lost his mind with joy. Hugh set the plate on the table after Cedric was done and tilted his head to catch her gaze.

His voice was quiet. "The next time you interfere in one of my fights, I'll serve you with divorce papers. Are we clear?"

Right. The asshole was back. "The next time I have a chance to save your life, I'll give it a thought."

He walked out, his hound at his heels.

She wanted to pick up his plate and shatter it against the floor. But he would hear, and she refused to give him the satisfaction.

13

Hugh leaned on the parapet walk of the keep. Below, the concrete stretch of the moat rolled out, waiting for the water. Six pump rigs waited, ready to dump water from the lake into the moat through large pipes. The magic had flooded thirty minutes ago, setting them back, and now three teams chanted, moving from pump to pump, coaxing the water engines to life.

Every Iron Dog not on duty lined up along the shore of the moat. Most of the village was here as well, mingling. Kids ran back and forth, laughing. A pirogi seller showed up and was doing brisk business, carrying trays of pirogi through the crowd.

Like some damn festival.

Elara was down there too. If he concentrated, he could pick her out of the crowd. He chose to stare at the concrete and the pumps instead.

Stoyan leaned on the parapet next to him. "Do you want to go down there?"

"No."

The team at the furthest pump on the left waved a rag.

"Pull the trigger," Hugh said.

Stoyan raised a horn to his mouth and blew a loud angry note.

A spark of magic dashed through the pumps, dancing on the machinery like yellow lightning. The pumps roared.

Nothing happened.

The crowd mulled about, the noise of voices rising.

A minute passed. Another...

Another...

Water gushed out of the right-most pipe. The crowd cheered. The other pipes added their own stream one by one and a foaming current poured into the moat.

Finally.

He looked along the flow of the water and saw Elara in a white dress. Her face was tilted up. She was looking straight at him.

Hugh pushed from the parapet and turned to Stoyan. "Have them check the water level every thirty minutes once it's filled. We need twenty-four hours of stable water level."

"The engineers are on it," Stoyan said. "What do you want to do about the money?"

"How far overbudget are we?"

"Thirteen thousand."

"Anything left to salvage?"

"The scouts found ruins to the south, about thirty minutes into the woods. Looks like it was a serious distillery operation at some point. Stainless steel storage tanks, copper percolators, heating coils. We got quite a bit we can pull out of there..."

A high-pitched scream rang out below. Hugh spun to the parapet. On the grass by the moat a woman and two men convulsed in the grass. Elara's people formed a ring around them. He swore and took off at a run.

It took him three minutes to get down to the moat. Hugh shouldered his way into the ring. Elara knelt by the older of the men, holding his head in her lap, while two other cradled the younger man and the woman.

"Let it come," Elara intoned. "Almost there. Almost."

There was a rhythm to the convulsions. He studied the bodies, the timing. The tremors pulsed in a distinct pattern, closer and closer to becoming synchronized.

"Here it is," Elara murmured.

The three people jerked upright in unison, like vampires snapping out of coffins in some old movie. They stared into space, identical blank expressions on their faces, and spoke in a chorus.

"Tonight Aberdine will fall."

Well, fan-fucking-tastic.

He left the circle. Stoyan followed.

"Double the patrols," Hugh told him. "Keep the pumps going. I want to see everyone in my quarters in fifteen."

———+·—

ELARA CLIMBED THE STAIRCASE. Hugh'd taken one look at the seers and run away to his rooms. That was fine. There was no escape. She would track him down.

She reached the hallway. His door was open. His back was to her. He was looking at something on his desk. He wore his Iron Dog uniform, and from this angle, silhouetted against the light of the window, he looked like pure darkness, cut out in the shape of a man.

Memory conjured up his hands on her shoulders and the phantom touch of his lips on her skin. She shoved the thoughts aside. Not now.

She walked into his room. He didn't even turn. He had to have heard her.

"Hugh."

"Busy," he said.

Ugh. "A moment of your time."

He turned to her and leaned against the desk, his arms crossed. "Anything for my wife."

She almost snapped back but bit the words off before they had a chance to escape. She had to make him understand.

"Aberdine will fall tonight. The Heltons are never wrong when all three of them are synchronized."

He didn't say anything.

"It has to be a reference to the warriors and the mrogs. They will attack Aberdine tonight."

"Quite possibly."

"We have to help them."

He gave her a long look. "Let me get this straight. You want me to take my soldiers and ride out there to defend people who threw rocks at us because three creepy assholes foamed at the mouth, swooned, and had a vision?"

Ugh. Ugh! "They are not assholes. They are very nice people. They can't help it."

"I'm sure they are lovely when they are not announcing imminent doom."

"How is it that Raphael made more holes in you than in swiss cheese, but your assholeness survived?"

"Raphael doesn't have a knife big enough to kill my assholeness."

"There are children in Aberdine. Children didn't throw rocks at us. Almost twenty-five hundred people live in that settlement and they're about to be slaughtered. How can you just do nothing?"

"Very easily," he said.

She stared at him.

"If they are truly trying to take Aberdine, they will come in large numbers," Hugh said with methodical calm. "You want me to leave a fortified position and ride out against what will likely be a much larger force. There will be casualties. I'll have to watch my people die."

"Our people, Hugh. They are our people, and I'll be sending people from the village as well. You will have support. And if they die, it will be on my head."

His stare made her want to back away from him.

"No."

"We can't just do nothing."

"Yes, we can. Every Dog who dies on that field is one less soldier to protect this castle."

"Babies, Hugh. They will murder babies."

"There are babies here. Do you really want to orphan them for the sake of Aberdine?"

This was a pointless conversation. "I'll go myself."

"And do what? Lob herbs at them until allergies bring them down?"

She wanted to punch him in the face. "I want you to be the hero, Hugh. I want you to gather our people, and ride with me to Aberdine to save innocent people. What do I have to do to make this happen?"

He pushed from the desk and took the six steps separating them. Menace rolled off him in waves, so thick, it was almost choking her.

"Are we bargaining now?"

An electric shiver of alarm dashed down her spine. Elara raised her head. "If that's what it takes."

He reached out and caught a strand of her hair. "What will you give me if I save Aberdine?"

"What do you want, Hugh?"

"What I want you won't give me."

"Try me."

He leaned toward her, his lips only inches from hers. She felt too hot, as if her clothes had somehow grown too tight on her. Her instincts wailed in alarm.

"I want you..." his voice was intimate, each word precise. "... to stay here and guard my pumps."

She blinked at him.

"I want that water running and the castle standing when I come back. Do we understand each other?"

Oh, you epic, epic ass. "Yes," she said.

"Good."

She heard footsteps in the hallway and turned. Stoyan, Lamar, Bale, and Felix were approaching.

"Run along now," Hugh said.

She ignored him. "Why are all of you here?"

Nobody said a word.

"Answer her," Hugh said.

"We're here to plan the battle of Aberdine," Stoyan said, clearly wishing to be anywhere but here.

"We have to defend it," Lamar said. "If we lose Aberdine, we lose access to the ley line. They'll cut us off from the rest of the state."

She would kill him.

"Too bad it took you so long," Hugh said. "You missed a stirring performance, complete with emotional appeals to my better nature. Apparently, my wife wants me to save Aberdine for the babies."

She pictured him exploding into bloody mist. No. Too quick.

Stoyan looked at his feet. Lamar stared at the ceiling. Bale studied his nails. Felix turned back and checked the hallway behind them. Nobody was looking at her.

"Explaining doesn't quite do it justice." Hugh invited her with a sweep of his hand. "Honey, would you mind doing an encore for the guys?"

She spun on her feet and walked out.

Behind her Lamar murmured, "One day that woman will drown you in the moat and I won't blame her."

"Honey?" Hugh called.

She kept walking.

"Elara?"

She stopped and turned to look at him.

"Any plans on helping me with any of this? Or is it pouting time? You can walk away to beat your fists prettily on your pillow or you can tell us more about Aberdine."

The bastard got off on goading her. "Ask nicely," she said.

"Please join us, my lady." He bowed with exquisite grace, sweeping his arm to the side with a flourish, as if he were some medieval knight bowing before a queen.

Bastard.

She launched her magic into the room and *stepped*. The centurions jerked back. One moment she was in the hallway, the next she stood next to Hugh, wisps of her white magic melting into thin air.

He stared at her, his blue eyes amused.

"**Dugas,**" she called, sending her voice through the castle. "**I need you.**"

Bale shivered, his eyes wide, looking like a freaked cat. Felix crossed himself.

She walked to Hugh's chair and sat in it. His lips curved.

Elara rolled her eyes.

They waited.

"How many people are you leaving me?" she asked.

"Lamar and his entire century."

"That means you're only taking two hundred and forty people. Aberdine has almost two and a half thousand people in it. You said the mrog handlers would come in large numbers. Is that going to be enough?"

"It will have to be," Hugh said.

"How many people can we press in Aberdine?" Stoyan asked.

Elara frowned. "Not many. These same people threw rocks at us when we tried to ward them. It will take a lot to make them trust you. Unless you do something impressive enough to cut past the fact that they're scared of us, you won't get much help."

"Let's assume I'll do something impressive," Hugh said.

"There are two thousand two hundred and three people in Aberdine," she told him. "Forty-seven percent men, fifty-three percent women. About half are between the ages of twenty and sixty. They are used to fighting the forest every day, so they are armed, and they won't have a problem defending themselves, but they're not professional killers."

"That's fine," Bale said. "We are."

Dugas walked into the room, nodded to her, and parked himself to the side.

"Let's cut that in half," Lamar said. "Accounting for the infirm, parents who have to stay with children, and cowards. That gives us about four to five hundred people."

"I'll give you half of my archers," Elara said. "Forty people, all very good."

"Thank you," Hugh said.

He stepped to the desk. The centurions and Dugas clustered around him. She got up and walked over. Stoyan and Lamar made a space for her. A map of Aberdine lay on the desk.

It was a typical post-Shift settlement. Once a small town spread out in the shadow of Coller's Knob, Aberdine compacted under the onslaught of the magic waves. Coller Road ran through town, snaking its way ten miles to the southwest to touch Baile castle and stretching another three miles to the northeast to catch the ley line. Somewhere around the first few houses inside Aberdine's city limits, Coller Road turned into Main Street. The forest took no prisoners, especially during the magic waves, so to keep themselves safe, the villagers walled in Main Street and the few surrounding blocks, protecting the municipal buildings, the marketplace, grocery store, the gas station and a few other essential places with a concrete wall topped with razor wire. Two gates punctured the wall, where it crossed Main Street. Each gate had a guard tower. All of that was painstakingly marked on Hugh's map.

Most of the houses hugged the wall, with braver or stupider homeowners venturing further into the cleared land, their homesteads wrapped in fields guarded by deer fence and barbed wire. About a hundred yards or so of cleared land ringed the farms. The rest was dense forest. The woods tried to take back the land and Aberdine's residents spent a great deal of time holding it back. Elara knew the struggle very well. They had to do the same thing to keep the land around Baile cleared.

In times of crisis, bells would ring, and the residents would run for the safety of the wall.

"You'll have to evacuate them," Dugas said. "The ley line seems like a natural point, but moving fifteen hundred people to it will be a nightmare."

"I can take evacuees," she said.

Hugh looked at her.

"We have experience in caring for refugees," she told him. "We can keep them for a day or two."

"What if the mrog dickheads burn the town down?" Bale asked.

She looked at him. "Make sure they don't."

"We split the evacuees," Hugh said. "Anyone able to walk, ride, or drive ten miles will come here. Everyone else will go to the ley line. Stoyan, set up two squads to escort them."

The dark-haired centurion nodded.

Lamar leaned over the map. "For a settlement this size, we can expect several hundred enemy troops at a minimum. They rely on surprise, armor, and their mrogs. We know they are coming, so the element of surprise is on our side, but it takes three of us to kill one of them because of that damn armor."

"We draw them inside the walls," Hugh said. "It will negate the number advantage."

"If there was some way to confuse the mrogs," Lamar thought out loud.

"Correct me if I'm wrong, but the standing theory says they follow visual cues from their masters?"

Hugh nodded.

"Would fog help?" Dugas asked.

"What kind of fog?" Stoyan asked.

"Magic fog." Dugas wiggled his fingers at him.

"Can you control it?" Stoyan asked. "Will it stay inside the wall?"

"Yes," Dugas said.

"Fog is good." Hugh bared his teeth. A dangerous, sharp expression twisted his features, and Elara fought a shiver. No matter what kind of life Hugh d'Ambray lived, a part of him would always look for the most efficient way to kill.

He was going to Aberdine, she reminded herself. It was all that mattered.

———

ELARA HUGGED HERSELF. From the window in Hugh's room, she could see most of the bailey. Iron Dogs and their horses swarmed, filling the entire courtyard. A mass of men and women in black on dark horses. The day was overcast, the sky choked with gray bloated clouds, and the gray light only made everything look grimmer.

The centurions had left. Hugh sat in his chair, putting on a new pair of boots. He was dressed in black from head to toe. She should've left, but she had stayed, and she had no idea why.

She turned to the desk where Hugh's breastplate, solid black and reinforced with metal plates waited, and touched it. It felt hard like wood or plastic, not at all how she expected leather would feel.

"Cuir bouilli, reinforced with steel plates," Hugh said.

"Will it stop a sword?"

"Depends on who is holding it."

He got up, picked up the armor, and fitted it over himself, pushing his left arm through the opening between the chest and back piece.

"Since you're here..."

She grimaced at him and buckled the leather belts on his right side, pulling the armor together. "Good?"

"Tighter."

"Now?"

"Perfect."

He buckled a sheath on his hip and thrust his sword into the scabbard. Hugh grabbed a length of black fabric from the chair and shook it open with a quick jerk of his hand. A cape edged with fur. He'd worn it when he first came to the castle.

He wrapped it around his shoulders. She took the leather tie away from him, reached for the other side of the cape and pressed it on the two metal studs there. Hugh picked up a helmet from the desk. It was a Roman style helmet with cheek pieces and a crest of black hair. A stylized dog snarled at her from the wide piece of the helmet that would be positioned just above Hugh's brow. He put the helmet on his head. It didn't hide that much of his face, but somehow altered it. Two blue eyes stared at her with a focused intensity.

She took a step back. Hugh was a big man, but the cape, the helmet, the armor, it made him look giant.

"You look like a villain in some fantasy pre-Shift movie," she told him. "Some dread lord about to conquer."

"Dread lord," he said. "I like that."

He would.

"Won't the cape get in the way?"

"The cape and the helmet are for Aberdine. We don't have time to play politics. Once I've got the town, I'll take them off when the battle starts."

Something had been nagging her since the strategy meeting. "What you told me about the ley point made sense at first. But the mrog soldiers don't hold towns, Hugh. They wipe them out and disappear. Aberdine's massacre wouldn't affect our access to the ley point. Why are you really going there?"

"They broke into my castle. They attacked my wife. They attacked a child in our home. The point of having a castle isn't hiding inside its walls; it's being worthy of it. It's being able to control everything around it. They're growing bolder. They're taking larger settlements. They've got my attention now. They will wish they didn't."

In her head she saw him let Raphael's knife strike him again and again. He was riding into battle. Anything could happen in battle. All he would have to do is not try as hard. To not step out of the way of a sword. To let himself get shot.

She wanted him back.

"Preceptor?"

"Yes?"

Her voice was steady. The words rolled off her tongue. "You like making bargains. Here is one for you. Come back to me alive, and I will stay the night. The whole night."

Outside the horns screamed and she almost jumped. There was something dark and primitive about the sound. A steady beat rose, thumping like a giant's heart. The war drums grew louder and louder. She heard horses neighing, the clang of metal, the voices of fighters, all of it mixing with the drums into a terrifying marching hymn. Someone howled like a wolf, in tune with the horns.

She turned to Hugh. He had somehow grown darker, grimmer, scarier, as if he emanated some imperceptible magic. The darkness curled around him, like a willing pet with savage teeth.

"Done," the Preceptor of the Iron Dogs said.

———+—

HUGH WALKED the line of Aberdine defenders. Men, women, some almost children, others well into retirement. Four hundred and seven people, who volunteered to defend their home. Behind him a line of the Iron Dogs waited and behind them Dugas and his druids chanted in low voices, brewing herbs and powders in their cauldrons. The air smelled of old ways and half-forgotten magic.

He'd sent Felix in first, keeping the rest of the Dogs hidden in

278

the tree line. The scouts scaled the wall with no one the wiser, took the firehose, and rang the bell. The residents of Aberdine lived in a wood filled with magic. The firehouse bell meant running for the safety of the walls, which was exactly what they had done. Then, once they dropped everything and gathered on Main Street, Hugh had pushed the Iron Dogs into a canter.

The guard at the western gate was too focused on the bell. He didn't see them until it was too late, which didn't bode well for Aberdine's chances in a real fight. They thundered inside the wall at a near gallop. Bucky reared in the market square, before an old Dollar General, pawing the ground and screaming. Hugh dropped a power word and the entire town went silent while he pulled a mrog's head out of his bag and told them what was coming. He was there to defend their town. They had two options: leave or fight. The choice was theirs.

It took less than two hours to round up the die-hards holed up in their houses, but now finally everyone was on their way: two long caravans, one of horse-drawn wagons and enchanted water vehicles heading to the ley point and the other, mostly people on foot and horseback, to Baile Castle. They went armed.

Now he faced a ragged militia. A third of it was too old, a third too young and green, and the remaining third looked ready to bolt. He had to make them count, because Aberdine's defenses were shit. Of the two ballistae mounted on the walls, the first had rusted through and the second fell apart when they tried to test fire it. There was no time to set up defenses. Warm bodies were all he had.

"An army is coming," he said. "They're armored, organized, and trained. They have monsters who serve them like dogs. They don't want your money, your cows, or your homes. They don't want what's yours. They want you. Your bones. Your flesh. Your meat. And they will keep coming back until they get it."

They listened to him, watching him with haunted eyes.

"This isn't a fight for your town. This is a fight for survival.

Some of you have fought before. Some of you have killed creatures. Some of you have killed people. This will be nothing like you've seen before. This will be a slaughter. It will be hard, ugly, and long."

Directly across from Hugh, a kid about Sam's age licked his lips nervously.

"You're scared," Hugh said. "Fear is good. Use it. There are few things as dangerous as a vicious coward on his home turf. Kill and show your enemy no mercy. If you get an urge to spare one of those bastards, he will kill your friend next to you and run you through with his dying breath. Kill him before he kills you. This is your town. Make them pay for every foot of ground in it."

The line of shoulders rose slightly, as some of them straightened their backs.

"You will be broken into teams. Each of your teams will get an Iron Dog. These men and women are trained killers. They've fought battles like this before and they've survived. Obey your Iron Dog. Stay together. Don't run. Fight dirty, do as you're told, and you too might survive this."

He raised his hand and flicked his fingers. The first Iron Dog, Allyson Chambers, peeled from the line. Solid, broad-shouldered, with pale skin and blond hair pulled back from her face.

"You, you, you, you, you and you!" she barked. "With me."

The first six fighters peeled off and followed her down the street at a run.

Arend Garcia stepped into his place and pointed at a rough looking man twelve defenders down the line. "Everyone up to this man – with me."

Hugh turned and walked to Dugas. The druid looked up from the cauldron. Sweat sheathed his face. He'd taken his eye patch off, and his bad eye sat like a chunk of moonstone in his tan face.

"How long?" Hugh asked.

"We're ready now," the older man said.

"Good. How long will it take to saturate the village?"

"Thirty seconds."

"And it will stay inside the wall?"

"It will," Dugas promised. "You'll get about twenty minutes worth of cover."

Twenty minutes would have to do. "Be ready to flood us."

Dugas nodded.

Hugh walked past him to the ladder on the side of the firehouse, pulled off his helmet, and climbed the metal ladder up to the roof, where Stoyan crouched by a short bell tower next to Nick Bishop. Bishop, an athletic black man in his forties, adjusted his glasses. He was the town's chief of police, National Guard Sergeant, and Wildlife Response Officer, all of which put him in charge of the same six people. He was quiet and held himself like he knew what he was doing, which was more than Hugh had been hoping for.

From here Hugh could see the western gate and the fields. He'd bet on the western gate. Its eastern twin faced the mountain and was better defended and fortified. It was the approach he would have chosen if he came for Aberdine.

In the field, a group of Bale's berserkers, dressed in civilian clothes, enthusiastically poked the ground with farm tools.

"How's the bell?" Hugh asked.

Stoyan grinned at him. The bell hanging in the faux tower on the roof looked as decorative as the tower itself. "It works," Stoyan said. "I rang it."

Bale sank his hoe into the dirt. It must've gotten stuck, because he wrenched at it. The hoe came loose, snapping up, and flung a chunk of dirt into the air. Bale ducked.

"Has your man even held a hoe before?" Bishop asked.

Stoyan grimaced. "Not that kind."

An eerie glow appeared in the middle of the field, barely noticeable, a shimmer more than light. *Here we go.*

"Dugas," Hugh called down. "Now."

The druid raised his head to the sky. His good eye rolled back in his head, matching the dead milky one. Fog shot from the cauldron in spiraling geysers, expanding, flooding the streets, and turning around the corners to collide.

The glow snapped into a line of bright golden light.

Bale and his berserkers backed away, toward the gates.

The light flared, forming an arched gate, as if a small second sun was rising out of the dirt.

The inside of the wall was milk now, the thick fog hiding the contours of the buildings seven feet up. Across from them, on the roof of the Dollar General, archers took positions behind a wooden barricade nailed together from packing crates and plywood. By the west gate, the roof of a Wells Fargo bank had gained three feet of height from a makeshift wall built with chunks of concrete and rocks. A dark head popped up above the wall for a moment and ducked back down.

The glow snapped clear. Hugh saw sunshine through the hole in the fabric of existence, and then mrogs flooded out of the portal in a ragged horde.

Behind them a row of warriors stepped out in unison, twenty men to a line. The shoulder of the first man in the line shone with gold.

"One," Stoyan counted.

A second line followed the first. Another leader with a gold shoulder. Officers.

"Two."

With that many, there should be a commander.

"Three. Four."

The berserkers turned and ran for the gate. The mrogs gave chase, dashing across the field on two legs.

Bale hesitated.

"What is he doing?" Bishop muttered.

"Trying to get a better look at where they came from," Hugh told him.

Behind the fourth line a man rode out atop a white horse, his armor heavy and ornate, the shoulders gleaming with gold.

There you are, asshole.

The glow vanished.

Bale turned and sprinted like a bullet aiming for the gate. The mrogs were barely a hundred yards behind.

Seventy-six warriors, four officers, one commander, and at least three hundred mrogs. The armored ranks waited, unmoving, in a precise formation. Each armed with a sword and shield. A long rectangular shield.

Fifty yards between the mrogs and Bale.

Thirty.

Twenty.

Bale shot through the gate and spun to his right, vanishing into the fog.

The mrogs poured into the main street. The fog churned as the beasts searched it.

"Not enough people," Bishop said.

"Eight berserkers is plenty," Stoyan said. "Bale knows what he's doing."

Metal clanged, and the heavy gate dropped in place. The wall on top of Wells Fargo quaked like a rotten tooth about to come out and collapsed. Boulders and chunks of old concrete, some with rebar still sticking out, tumbled into the street onto the shifting fog and the crowds of mrogs beneath. Yowls and shrieks cut the silence.

The trails in the fog split, running from the falling rocks. The main mass sprinted deeper into the town, along the main street. Arrows whistled through the air as the archers on the rooftops fired blindly into the fog. The mass of mrogs broke and split as individual beasts took to the side streets trying to escape the barrage.

The remaining mrogs turned back to the western gate. They

hadn't gone far before a bright red glow burst through the fog, blocking their escape. The fog parted, blown away in a circle, revealing Bale and a mass of snarling mrogs in front of him. The berserker stood with his feet planted, a mace in one hand, a red aura sheathing him. He stood with his back to the gate, and the street narrowed here, funneling the mrogs at him four or five at a time.

The red aura sheathing Bale flared brighter. Muscles rose on his frame, monstrous, swelling, growing larger. His arms thickened, muscles building, turning him into a hulking human monstrosity.

The beasts hesitated. They were closer to animals than to humans, and their instincts told them here was a primal force not to be fucked with. They knew a better beast when they saw him.

"What the hell is that?" Bishop whispered.

"Battle warp," Hugh told him.

The berserker's eyes bulged, his face contorted by rage in a grotesque mask. Bale roared.

The first mrog lunged at the berserker. Bale brained it with one swing. Blood and brains sprayed. The second mrog charged in. The first swing broke its shoulder; the second crushed its skull like an eggshell. Blood sprayed.

Bale bellowed something that didn't belong to any language a human used.

The mrogs charged. The furry dark mass smashed into Bale and broke on his mace like a storm tide upon a wave breaker. The berserker howled, snarling like a rabid animal, and pounded them with his mace, cracking bones, crushing skulls, smashing flesh. Bodies flew and smashed against the buildings.

The fog flooded in, but Bale's red glow fought through it like a beacon of rage. The street in front of it churned with bodies. Shrieks and yowls rose in a din. Along the periphery, flashes of weapons cut at the fog – Bale's berserkers carving at the edges of the horde while they focused on Bale.

In the east two mrogs jumped out of the fog and climbed up

Dollar General's wall. The archers peppered them with arrows, but the mrogs kept climbing. They reached the roof. Four Iron Dogs stepped forward and drove their blades into the mrogs. Two furry bodies fell to the street. Three more jumped out of the fog, climbing up, then another two. Bishop raised his crossbow, sighted, and fired. A sorcerous bolt whined, slicing through the air, and bit into the back of the center mrog. The bolt flashed green and exploded, taking three other mrogs with it. The building quaked but stood.

Stoyan slid off the roof and down the ladder. The fog gulped him, and he vanished.

Fighting broke out here and there as individual teams saw their chance and stabbed at the passing mrogs in the fog. A human shriek sliced the fog from the left, then another, followed by eerie howling and yelps of pain. Another ragged scream, from the north this time, followed by more cries.

The four lines of fighters remained where they were.

"What are they waiting for?" Bishop asked.

"They're used to relying on mrogs to do most of the fighting," Hugh said. "We cut them off from their hounds, so they are waiting for them to bleed us. Once we're injured enough, they will move in for the kill."

The slaughter raged. Bishop kept firing, choosing his targets carefully, sometimes with sorcerous bolts, sometimes plain. Hugh smelled blood now, rising from the streets. It lashed at him, pushing him to fight, to act, to do something. Instead he waited.

———✛——

ELARA HUGGED HER SHOULDERS. She stood on the balcony in her quarters. In front of her the land stretched, the forest rolling into the distance, the isolated knobs silhouetted against the evening sky. By now the enemy would have attacked Aberdine.

By now Hugh would be fighting.

The worry gnawed on her. A part of her hated him for it. She wanted him back, alive, in one piece.

When she'd thought of her future husband, which she hadn't done often, she'd always defaulted to this vague idea of a nice man. He would be kind, and calm, and he would treat her with respect, and their relationship would be peaceful and without any sharp edges. Instead she got this asshole, who made her see red at least once a day. Hugh d'Ambray was as far from nice as you could get and still remain human.

And if she could, she would sprout wings and fly to damn Aberdine to make sure he didn't die some stupid death.

Ugh. UGH.

The familiar sound of light feet made her turn. Johanna walked into the room.

"What is it?"

"There is a problem with the pumps."

"There can't be a problem with the pumps." Elara marched out of the room.

———•••———

A GUST of wind pulled at Hugh's hair. The wind was rising. The fog below thinned. He could see faint outlines of the streets and Dugas and his druids below. Dugas had traded his staff for a spear. His apprentices, two men and two women, held blades, flanking him and the cauldron.

On the field the mrog troops split. Two front lines peeled off with the commander in the lead, moving east at a fast march. The remaining two lines swung toward the western gate, reforming as they moved.

A young brown-skinned girl came running out of the fog, her eyes wide. Three mrogs loped after her.

Stoyan stepped out of the fog and sliced at the mrogs. The beasts screeched, raking at him with their claws. The centurion carved at them with methodical precision, sinking his blade into flesh. Blood poured.

Hugh ignored the snarls, concentrating on the troop movement. The eastern force reformed into a rectangle, eight soldiers wide, five rows deep.

Stoyan climbed the ladder and landed next to him, splattered with blood.

The western formation swung north, closing in on the other gate. The eastern formation advanced. He didn't expect the split. No matter. He could adjust.

The archers fired from the rooftops at the eastern formation. As one, the soldiers snapped their shields up and to the front, covering themselves like a turtle. A testudo.

The arrows glanced off the shields. On the Wells Fargo rooftop, Renata Rover barked out a short command. "Stop firing. Save your arrows."

"A shield wall," Stoyan said softly. "You were right. East or West?"

"East," Hugh told him.

Stoyan nodded, slid down the ladder, and disappeared into the firehouse.

"They're planning to hit us from both gates," Bishop said. "Like pincers."

"Yes, they are."

The shield wall crawled forward.

In the west, the second testudo approached the gate.

The western gate exploded into flames. The wood went up instantly, as if it were tissue paper thrown into a bonfire. The metal holding the thick boards together melted. Their magic packed a hell of a wallop.

Bishop swore.

The eastern gate went up in a flash of crimson fire.

So that was the end game. Burn them from both ends, pushing the defenders toward the center of town, where they would be crushed between two walls of steel. One flaw in that plan. The mrog soldiers still thought they were facing farmers.

The remnants of the western gate collapsed onto the street, breaking apart. The testudo moved forward, through the fire, boots grinding the embers into the pavement. The shield wall crawled forward and stopped. Someone barked a guttural command and the rectangular formation split, revealing the commander and two officers flanking him. He towered over them by at least half a foot.

Big bastard.

The officers sucked in a lungful of air and spat torrents of fire at the Dollar General and the bank across the street.

They spat napalm-grade fire. Perfect. Just perfect.

"THERE HE IS," Oscar said.

Elara took a step forward. A gaunt shape crouched atop the pump station at the edge of the lake. A vampire. She felt no others in the area.

They hadn't warded the pump station. They should have. It was set up in a hurry, and now they paid the price for it. The undead could've killed Oscar. The older mechanic was supposed to keep an eye on the pump station. That was a death she could've prevented. She would kill the undead and correct the oversight before Hugh came back.

The undead watched her with glowing red eyes. In the twilight, its grotesque form looked even more eerie. It sat on top of the pump station, emanating magic that felt like a fetid smear, like someone had taken a rotting piece of greasy meat and rubbed it all over the station's roof.

"You have some nerve," she said.

The undead straightened. His mouth stretched open and a

clear male voice came through. "Ms. Harper. I've come to discuss business."

"You and I have no business to discuss. And it's Mrs. Mrs. d'Ambray."

"But I think we do. My name is Landon Nez. I have a proposition for you."

Oscar raised his crossbow. "Would you like me to shoot him?"

Even the best navigators only had a range of several miles. That meant Nez was close. Nez came "in person." There was no good reason for him to be here unless he was planning something. She had to find out what it was.

"Oscar," she said. "Give us some privacy."

Oscar backed away about fifty yards. That was as far as he would be willing to go.

"We both know that this marriage is a sham," Nez said. "I understand why you agreed to it. At the time it must've seemed like the right strategic move. But now you've had a chance to live with d'Ambray under the same roof. The man is violent and unstable."

Nez paused. She didn't say anything. If you kept quiet, the other person usually kept talking to fill the silence.

"I've known him a lot longer than you have. D'Ambray has one purpose and one purpose only: to destroy. When Roland wanted to take over a location, he would use Hugh as a bulldozer to level the existing power structure. By the time d'Ambray was done and Roland entered, the people hailed him as a savior."

"Does your employer know how you talk about him to outsiders?"

"I'm giving you the courtesy of frank exchange, Ms. Harper. D'Ambray cannot build; he can only wreck. He has been doing it longer than you've been alive."

Hugh had built the Iron Dogs. She had watched him work with them every day. But rushing to Hugh's defense wasn't in her best interests. Not if she wanted to keep Nez talking.

"The man isn't without guile," Nez continued. "He can be shrewd and hard to kill, but in the end, he always reverts to his true nature. Do you know what he was doing before he came to you with his marriage proposal? He was drinking himself to death. He bounced from one hellhole to the next, earning just enough to get drunk. I personally have seen him stagger out of a bar reeking of urine and vomit and fall asleep in a ditch. With nothing left to demolish, he dedicated his talents to destroying himself."

And yet, you fear him enough to personally keep an eye on him.

"D'Ambray is an animal. If you allow him to nest under your roof, he will eventually destroy everything you've built."

"Is there an offer on the table or are we just discussing my husband's finer points?"

The vampire shifted. "Abandon d'Ambray to his fate and I will leave Baile in peace."

She laughed. "Just like that? You've been trying to run us off this land for months and now suddenly you changed your mind?"

"Hugh d'Ambray is a higher priority target. I'm willing to let go of your castle if it means I get d'Ambray."

"Why do you want my castle?"

"That's not important. I'm offering you a way to keep your people safe from me at a price you not only can afford but would welcome. I suggest you take it."

"And I would trust you why?"

"Unlike d'Ambray, I'm a man of my word. Of course, I'm willing to formalize this arrangement via contract. A peace treaty of sorts, if you will."

"And how do I know this peace treaty is binding? Nothing prevents you from attacking us the moment you find it convenient."

"Fair point. In addition to the formal agreement, I'm offering an additional incentive. The town of Aberdine has overextended itself. They borrowed, quite heavily, to build their wall and clinic and they've put up their municipal land as collateral. I've bought their debt. In simple terms, I own Aberdine. I'm willing to sell it to you for a nominal sum. Let's say, a dollar."

What else did he buy? "What am I supposed to do with Aberdine?"

"Oh come on now, Ms. Harper. No need to demur. The town has been problematic for you and they control the only access to the ley line passable by truck. All of your shipping goes through them. You can hold the threat of bankruptcy over their heads and have the town council be your willing slaves. You can turn the town into a cash cow and collect the loan payments, which come with significant interest. You can move your people into Aberdine and expand. You can force them to move and turn the main street into a parking lot. It is entirely up to you. Whichever course you choose, Aberdine will no longer be a problem."

She would do none of it. "It's a tempting offer."

"It is."

"However, I married d'Ambray. You're asking me to go back on my word."

The vampire smiled. The sight was enough to give most people nightmares. "It would hardly be the first time for you."

Bastard. "Still, there are contracts. What happens if I say no?"

"I'll assault Baile directly and kill every living thing I find in its walls."

He said it so casually, as if it had already happened.

"In that case, why bargain with me at all?"

Nez sighed. "Vampires are expensive, Ms. Harper. Make no mistake, I will take Baile. Water and walls are not a barrier to the undead. However, the People would sustain a significant financial loss, and nothing inside your castle is valuable enough to offset it."

If she had nothing valuable, then why did he keep trying to force her out before Hugh showed up?

"Suppose I say yes. How exactly do you envision this happening? I can divorce d'Ambray, but there's the small matter of three hundred trained killers who won't like being put out on the street."

"Three hundred trained killers who depend on you for their rations, water, and shelter."

He wanted her to poison the Iron Dogs. Elara smiled. "I need to think about your proposal. Do you have anything in writing?"

A large envelope hit the ground next to her. She picked it up. How much time could she ask for? The more time she bought, the better prepared they would be, but asking for too much would show her hand. He would simply push the timeline forward.

"I'll need at least two weeks," she told him. "My legal council needs to review the documents and we'll have to make some inquiries in Aberdine. Until then, I don't want to see you anywhere near Baile. Do not interfere with the operation of the pumps. My husband is difficult when he's agitated."

"Two weeks from now," Nez said. "Same time, same place. You're a smart woman, Ms. Harper. Make the right choice for your people."

The undead leapt away and took off into the night. She walked back to Oscar. The mechanic looked at her.

"Have you ever noticed, Oscar, that when people say, 'You're a smart woman,' what they really mean to say is 'But I am smarter?'"

Oscar smiled at her.

"Weren't there some Iron Dogs guarding the station?"

"There were. Two of them fellahs. They're sleeping under that oak over there."

Elara sighed. "Oscar..."

"You know how I like the quiet. Evening, that's me time."

"They were supposed to be here for your protection."

"I know, I know. They looked tired anyway."

"You better wake them up. And don't magic them back to sleep either."

Oscar sighed. "What do I do if that undead shitweasel comes back?"

"Shoot him and let the 'fellahs' do the rest. These pumps must keep working, do you understand me, Oscar? Keep the water flowing."

"Yes, my lady."

Elara thought of fussing at him about the "my lady" bit, but she had bigger fish to fry. It was only her imagination, but the envelope in her hands was too heavy and she couldn't wait to put it down.

———•——

THE CONCRETE WALL of Dollar General began to sag. The archers on the roof shied back, trying to escape the heat.

The eastern gate collapsed.

"What do we do?" Bishop was looking at him, wild-eyed. "They're going to burn us alive."

The eastern shield wall crawled up Main Street. The archers from the rooftops fired a few arrows, but the missiles just glanced off the shields. As expected. Attacking them head on would do no good either.

The testudo kept moving, unstoppable behind its wall of steel. In the west, the two lieutenants spat more fire, hosing the buildings down.

"What do we do?" Bishop repeated.

"Ring the bell," Hugh told him.

Bishop stared at him.

"We have a fire," Hugh told him. "Ring the fire bell."

The police chief swore, turned to the roof tower, and rang the bell. It tolled, a surprisingly high note. The doors of the firehouse snapped open. The snarl of an enchanted engine pealed like thunder. A firetruck sped out of the firehouse with Stoyan at the wheel, turned left, and hurtled down the street, picking up speed. The eastern shield wall had no place to go. The truck rammed into them at fifty miles an hour, scattering armored men like pinballs. Stoyan punched through the center of the formation, reversed, and doubled back, mowing them down.

Welcome to the 21st century.

The Iron Dogs streamed from the side streets onto the broken formation. Fighting broke out, as they jumped the enemy three, four to one.

The western shield wall started forward.

Perfect. That's what he'd been waiting for. He had to check them now. It needed to be quick and brutal. Take the head, and the body should run.

Hugh slid down the ladder and walked into the street. The war drums rose, followed by howling horns. Behind him the street turned black as the Iron Dogs emerged from the streets and houses.

The two front lines of mrog soldiers dropped to their knees, revealing the commander and two officers.

The commander watched him approach from behind two lines of his troops, his face impassive. Thicker armor, long heavy sword, twenty-seven-inch blade, double edged. Simple but effective.

Cutting through that armor would be a bitch. He'd need an edge. A blood edge. Too bad he couldn't make one anymore. Blood swords and blood wards were behind him. Hugh unsheathed his sword and swung it, warming up his wrist.

The two officers turned to him, their faces emotionless. Their mouths gaped open. Two streams of fire shot at him.

His body reacted before his mind did. Hugh sliced the back of his left arm and threw the blood in an arc in front of him, sending his magic through it.

What the fuck am I doing?

The blood sparked. The blood ward flared in front of him in an arched screen, a wall of translucent red. The fire smashed into it and glanced off, shooting at an angle to the side. The torrents died.

How the hell...

Hugh groped for the connection to Roland but it was still gone.

He didn't have time to puzzle over it. He pulled the magic to him, building his reserve and kept moving. Darkness curled from him, pulsing from the ground with his every step. The arcane currents built within him, familiar, strong, obedient.

Without a blood edge, he would be fucked.

The blood ward worked. Why not the blood sword?

The pair of golden-shouldered assholes sucked in air. Round two. Fire tore toward him. He threw up another blood ward, let the inferno die trying to break it, and kept moving.

The magic vibrated inside him like a firehouse under the full pressure of a hydrant. Blue sparks pierced the darkness rising from him, lighting it from within.

He was only ten yards from the front line.

The commander opened his mouth. His eyes sparked with bright fiery amber. A torrent of fire shot out of his mouth, white-hot, and met the wall of Hugh's third blood ward. The spell took the full brunt of the impact. The fire raged, pounding on the translucent wall of red. Hairline cracks formed in the ward.

If it shattered, he would never know.

The fire torrent raged.

Now or never. Hugh drew the full length of his blade over the cut, soaking the flat of his sword in his blood. He reached for the power in his blood. For a terrifying half second, nothing was there, and then he found it, a bright spark of hot magic. He fed it and it burst into an inferno. Magic dashed down Hugh's blade, like fire along a detonation cord. A bright red edge overlaid the sword.

The fire died.

Hugh dismissed the ward with a wave of his hand.

"Is that all? My turn." His magic saturated him to the brim, threatening to boil over. All he had to do was aim it. *"Karsaran."*

Darkness shot out of him, exploding, streaked with blue lightning. It clutched at the two front lines, jerking the armored men off their feet into the air. They hung three feet above the pavement. He moved through the gap he made, as their skeletons snapped, contorting, the staccato of their breaking bones crunching like broken glass under his feet.

An officer spun into his way. Hugh sidestepped, letting the man's momentum carry him by, and sliced across the officer's neck. The blood sword cut through solid metal like it was butter. The officer's head rolled off his shoulders.

Ha. It still worked.

The second officer charged at Hugh. Hugh braced himself and met the charge, driving his shoulder into the man. The officer bounced off, knocked aside.

Hugh kept the momentum and swung. The commander parried, letting the blade slide off his sword, and came back with a devastating strike from the left and down.

Fast asshole. Not fast enough though. That armor had a price.

Hugh shied back, letting the point of the sword whistle by, and cut at the man's elbow. Sword coated in magic met metal and bit through it. Blood wet the blade. One arm down.

The bigger man reversed the blow, as if the wound never happened, slashing high from the right. Hugh dodged, surged into the opening, and buried his sword in his opponent's armpit. The blade screeched as it cut through metal and struck home.

The commander staggered back, blood pouring over his armor.

The second officer rammed into Hugh from the left, locking his sword against Hugh's. Hugh jerked his knife out and stabbed him in the left eye. The man fell as if cut. Behind him the commander opened his mouth. Shit.

Hugh dropped down, scooping up the fallen officer's shield, and raised it. Fire splashed over him. The shield turned too hot. Pain scoured his arm. His left hand blistered. He sank his magic into it, trying to keep the flesh on the bone, healing it as fast as the shield cooked it. Agony tore at him. Dark stars wavered in his vision. He could barely feel the hand, bathed in blue glow.

The fire ended. Hugh surged to his feet and hurled the shield at the enemy. The big man batted it aside and stomped forward, eyes bulging.

Die, you persistent sonovabitch.

The commander swung, blows coming fast and desperate.

Cut, dodge.

Cut, dodge.

Cut.

Hugh batted the sword aside and thrust. It was a precise, lightning-fast stab. The sword caught the commander in the throat, piercing it through just above the Adam's apple. The man's mouth gaped. He struggled on the blade, like an impaled fish. His sword crept up.

Sonovabitch.

"Arhari arsssan tuar."

Magic tore out of Hugh. The pain bit his gut with molten fangs, letting him know he'd overspent. The commander's body split, his ribs thrusting up and out, through the armor, like bony blades. Gore sprayed Hugh's face. The commander gurgled, still alive. *How the hell...*

Hugh reversed his grip, snarled, and drove the blade with all his weight behind it into the man's waist. Metal and flesh gave way and the top half of the man's body slid to the side, hanging by a narrow strip of muscle and gristle. Hugh kicked it, toppling the body, raised his sword like a hangman's axe, and chopped the commander's head off.

The three pieces that used to be a human body lay still.

Hugh dragged his hand across his face, trying to clear blood from his nose and mouth, spat, and turned. A dozen mrog warriors stared at him. As one, they raised their weapons.

He swung his blood sword and bared his teeth. "Next."

14

The woods looked different at night, the dark trunks and braided branches crowding the road. It was well past midnight and the forest was pitch-black. Things shifted in its depths, calling out with eerie voices. Glowing eyes tracked the long column stretching behind Hugh, filling the woods with human military noises: horses snorting, gears clanking, and muffled conversations coming from the back.

After he finished off the leader, he'd expected the warriors to run. They didn't. They simply stood. When approached with a weapon, they fought back to the bitter end. They screamed when cut, but they didn't speak. They didn't fear. They didn't speak even when overpowered, and when the Iron Dogs managed to restrain one long enough to tie him up, he burst into flames from the inside, burning the four people holding him. It cost him a good deal of his power to heal the burns.

They'd had to kill every last mrog fighter, and Hugh had walked that line, making sure the kills happened. It wasn't fighting. It was slow, methodic butchery. Some of his people couldn't do it. They would kill something that was fighting back if the odds were even, but hitting another person over the head with a mace until you were sure his skull was mush while four of five of your friends jumped them was beyond them.

He spared his people from it as much as he could.

It took forever. And when they were done, he worked with the wounded, while the rest of his troops fought the fires. By the time they put the flames out, it was well past midnight. Nobody wanted to sleep in Aberdine tonight. It took another half an hour to arrange the survivors into a column, load the injured onto carts, and move out to Baile. He was dragging almost half a thousand extra people with him. Elara would just love that.

He wanted to go home and wash away the blood. It clung to him, seeping into his pores and coating his tongue, and he had to fight the urge to spit every few seconds to clear it out. He'd been through hard battles before, but it never felt that raw. The void was so loud tonight, Hugh could almost see it hovering over him.

The woods parted, the trees falling back, and Bucky carried him into the clearing. A full moon shone in the sky, spilling silvery gauzy light onto the grassy slopes. On the left Baile rose. He had expected it to be quiet and dark. Bright fires burned on the side towers. Someone had set out fey lanterns along the path leading to the gates, and their pale bluish glow fought back the night. The place was lit up like a Christmas tree.

A lone figure stood on the battlements, her dress bright white against the darkness. She'd waited for him.

He jerked himself back from that thought before he read too much into it.

A horn sounded in the castle, triumphant. The gates swung open. Bucky raised his head and pranced.

"What are you doing, you fool?" Hugh growled.

The stallion doubled down. They pranced to the gate. A huge cistern was set by the gate, with a shower rigged to it. The air smelled of fresh bread and roasted meat.

"Oh my god," Stoyan groaned behind him.

They went through the gate. Long tables waited in the bailey, with a buffet line against the outer wall, the cooks waiting.

"I'm going to cry," Bale announced from somewhere down the line. "Does anybody have a hankie?"

People ran up to take their horses. Hugh turned in the saddle. Elara was still on the battlements. They looked at each other for a long moment. Then June came to take Bucky's reins and Hugh dismounted.

———•••

HUGH STEPPED out of the shower, toweled dry, pulled on a pair of pants, and dropped into the chair by his desk. He'd stayed in the bailey long enough to make sure everyone would be settled, but it was quickly clear he wasn't needed, so he'd climbed the stairs to his bedroom, took off his armor, cleaned it, then went into the shower.

He'd stood there for a good quarter of an hour, letting hot water run over his face. Alas, he couldn't stay in the shower forever. Tomorrow he would need to review their losses. Three of his Iron Dogs had died. Twenty-one of the villagers. Twenty-four was better than two thousand, but math didn't make the weight of the dead any lighter.

His whole body ached, but his brain was awake.

He'd made a blood ward and used a blood weapon. How? The purge hadn't failed. He couldn't feel Roland. He shouldn't have been able to do it, but he did. And he could do it again. He stared at the cut on his arm. He could feel the magic humming in his blood. That was one hell of a mystery.

He needed sleep, but he knew the moment he closed his eyes, he would see fire and blood and death. If he managed to fall asleep, he would dream tonight. It was inevitable. He would relive the battle. It would cycle through his head until the morning. The void gnawed at him, taking long bites with its sharp teeth, and the void was never satiated.

Tattered memories slid across his mind, death groans, blood spray, the screech of a sword forcing its way through metal into the flesh underneath... Right now Roland would be reaching through the distance for reassurance and absolution. The voice of reason, the parental voice of God, who would tell him he had done what was necessary and what he had done was just and right and would make everything better.

He had lost the soothing certainty of Roland's connection, but he'd traded it for a grim clarity. He had done what was necessary. It was bloody and it tore him up, but he had done it, not because Roland deemed it right, but because Hugh himself decided it was right.

The fight still simmered under his skin, a hot spattering mix of adrenaline, bloodlust, and sheer endurance.

Hugh glanced up and saw her through the open door of his bedroom. She wore white and she was walking toward him.

Elara stopped in the doorway. She was holding a thick envelope in her hands.

"What's that?" he asked.

"That's for later."

She walked into his bedroom, shut the door, and slid the latch, locking them in. He raised his eyebrows at her.

"We had a deal," she said.

"Ah." Wee lamb come to the slaughter.

A year ago, he would've stayed downstairs. He'd wash the blood off, eat, drink, and when a woman came his way, he'd fuck her until he couldn't think straight. But it was no longer simple. He didn't want to be her Aberdine.

"Leave."

She put the envelope on the chair by the door.

"Did you not hear me?"

"I heard," she said.

301

"Maybe I wasn't clear. I don't want your noble sacrifice."

She raised her hands to her hair. Her braid fell from her head. "Oh please. I gave you three gorgeous naked women, and you practically dislocated your knees chasing me around the pool instead."

She ran her hands through her braid and it fell apart, her long white hair spilling over her shoulders, soft and silky. It framed her face, bringing something new to it, some unspoken intimate promise. He almost never saw her with her hair down. He wanted to think it was for him alone.

Elara shook her head. He watched her, because he was a raging idiot, and he noticed everything: the bend of her neck as she leaned forward to take off her sandals, the way her hair fell, the way the dress hugged the curve of her ass...

He didn't want payment. He didn't want obligatory sex. He wanted her to want him. To scream for him. He wouldn't get what he wanted, and right now, he wanted her gone.

"Last chance, Elara. Leave."

Her light eyes laughed at him. "I'm staying."

They stared at each other across the room.

"Well?" she asked. "Or should I get an apron?"

The remnants of the fight drove him on. He would make her run from this room screaming and then he would rest.

———

THERE WAS something irritatingly erotic about the way he sat.

He sprawled in a chair, huge and golden, his muscular body draped over it. His shirt was nowhere to be found. Strong powerful muscle corded his shoulders. His carved chest was clean-shaven, his body slimming down to a narrow waist and flat, hard stomach. His dark hair, still wet from the shower, fell on his face. His blue eyes were cold and dark.

"Fine," Hugh said. "Rules are simple: while you're here, you do

as I say. Any time it gets too much for you, say 'stop,' and everything will stop, and you can walk out that door."

"Fine by me."

He tilted his head and looked her over. She could almost feel
his gaze sliding over her face, down, lingering over her breasts,
and moving down, to her hips. He looked at her as if he were
buying her and was trying to decide if she was worth his money.

Oh, it's like that now, is it?

Elara raised her arms to the sides and turned, rolling her hips
as she did. *There you go, get the whole picture.*

She completed her turn and winked at him. He didn't move.

"Take off your clothes."

She pushed the straps of her dress off her shoulders, and let it
fall off her chest. She wore a lacy white bra underneath. She had
picked it especially for today. It cradled her breasts, lifting them
up, the outline of darker nipples barely visible through the lace. It
wasn't the kind of bra a woman would wear for comfort, and
she'd been stuck in it for several hours, waiting for him to
come back.

He stared at her. He still hadn't moved.

The thin fabric of the dress snagged on her hips and Elara
pushed it down, revealing a pair of lacy panties, so small they
were barely there. The dress fell and pooled around her feet. She
stepped out of it and kicked it aside.

He looked almost bored. Arrogant prick.

Her hands went back, and she unhooked her bra. The pale
straps came loose, and she pulled it off her left arm, peeled it from
her breasts, and held it out to the side with her right hand.

She opened her fingers. The bra fluttered to the floor.

Elara slid hands along her hips, hooking the panties with her
thumbs, pulled them down, and kicked the tiny piece of fabric
aside.

Something sparked in his eyes, a dangerous blue fire.

He wanted her naked. Fine. She would be naked for him.

HER STOMACH SLOPED, gently rounded, to the vee between her legs, dusted with white curls. Her breasts were full and heavy, and he wanted to crush her to him and brush his fingers over her nipples. In his mind he lunged from the chair, grabbed her, and dragged her to the bed.

His erection hurt.

The Ice Harpy stood naked in front of him. The Queen of the Castle.

It was a contest now. He didn't think he had another fight in him tonight, but she goaded him, and he would not lose.

She smirked at him.

Hugh opened his mouth. "Crawl to me."

He waited for her to grab her clothes, bolt, and slam the door.

A slow witchy smile bent her lips. She laughed softly. Her knees bent, and she went into a crouch, her hair brushing the floor.

An instinctual alarm pricked his spine with icy claws. Whatever was looking at him from the floor was not human. It looked like a human woman, it was shaped like one, but it was something else. Something ancient and cold, a thing of ice and sharp fangs, woven from eldritch magic. It looked at him through Elara's eyes and it laughed.

She blurred and then she was right there, in front of him, crouching, her hands with long elegant fingers resting on his knees. Her hair floated around her, lifted by phantom wind. Alarm jerked his spine straight. She tilted her face up to him. Her voice caressed him, filled with magic. "Hugh…"

He stared at her. Every instinct he had screamed a warning. He had to decide now if he still wanted her if she was that. He didn't even know what that was.

"Hugh…" She raised her head to his. Her whisper was a soft

breath in his ear. "Guess what I want more than anything else in the world right now?"

Magic, no magic, human, not human, who was he to judge? He would punch this ticket here and now.

He *moved*. He hauled her upright, sliding his arm under her thighs, and heaved her up, to sit on his shoulders, her legs over his back. Elara gasped, her legs squeezing him, her hands in his hair. He pushed her closer and took a long, wet taste. The bud of her clit slid under his tongue. Finally.

She jerked as if shocked by a live wire.

He carried her to the bed and dropped her there, on her back. She landed on the blankets, her eyes wild, her legs parted slightly, the dark nipples of her perfect breasts erect. Oh yes. He had everything he ever needed right here.

Hugh pulled off his pants. Her eyes went wide.

He'd seduced women before. He had patience and finesse, but he couldn't find any now. There was nothing slow and delicate about them. He'd wanted her for too long. He would make her beg for him tonight.

He moved over her. She snapped her teeth at him.

"Does that mean stop?" he asked.

"No. If I want you to stop, I will tell you."

"Works for me."

He leaned forward. She kicked his chest. He grabbed her ankle and yanked her toward him, sliding his right leg between hers. She tried to slap him. He batted her arms aside, pinning her wrists to the blanket. She stared at him, furious, her chest rising. She'd never looked hotter. He closed his eyes for a moment to keep from coming then and there.

She growled and tried to push him off her.

She wanted to fight.

The afterburn of the battle simmering under his skin took over and pushed him into overdrive. He felt hot and focused, the way he did before a kill. He pinned her down. She snapped her small white teeth at him again, and he muscled her back and kissed her neck, pinching the skin with his teeth, painting heat and lust down the slender column of her throat.

She moaned, strong and soft under him. He heard desire in the moan. She wanted him.

He let her have her right arm, and she punched him with her fist. He caught her wrist and kissed it, in just the right place, setting the nerves on fire. Elara struggled under him, trying to buck him off. The excitement took the last shreds of restraint he had. He forced her arms together over her head, grabbed them with his left hand, and let his right roam over her breasts. The rough calluses on his thumb snagged on her left nipple. She gasped. He dove down and sucked on the little dark bud.

Elara moaned.

He smelled the jasmine and green apple on her skin and it drove him wild. He ran his tongue over her nipple, winding her up. Her back arched. Her cool thighs squeezed his leg and she tried to grind against him, looking for his cock.

———◆———

HE WAS UNBELIEVABLY STRONG. The feel of his huge body pressed against hers, all coiled power locked in hot muscle was almost too much. She wanted him desperately, she wanted his lips on her, his huge cock inside her. The need to have him pooled inside her, a hot, aching sensation somewhere on the verge of pain and pleasure.

He sucked on her breasts, squeezing them with his fingers, every stroke in just the right place, every touch with just the right pressure, as if he knew her body better than she did. She smelled the faint hint of sage and citrus from the soap and the heady scent of his sweat.

He was moving lower, his tongue painting heat down her body.

No, not yet. He hadn't worked hard enough yet.

His hand slid off her right wrist. She sank her fingers into his hair and pulled. He jerked his face up and locked his lips on hers. His tongue thrust into her mouth, a hint of what was to come. She licked it and when they broke apart, she stared into Hugh's blue eyes.

"Bastard!"

"Harpy."

She slapped him.

He surged over her and flipped her on her stomach. His left hand caught her hair and he pulled her up, until she sat back on her knees, her spine pressed against his chest. His hand caught her ass from below. He squeezed it and pulled her up to her knees. She felt the blunt head of his cock press against her.

"Is this what you want?"

She struggled, caught by her hair, trying to pull free. His hand slid over her stomach. He yanked her closer and dipped his fingers into her. She was so wet and so ready, she nearly came.

He laughed into her ear. She jerked her head back, trying to ram his face with the back of her head, but missed. He grabbed her hips and jerked her onto him. His hard shaft slid inside her, thick and hot. Elara cried out.

"Is that why you came here?" He thrust into her again. The jolt of it sent electric shivers all through her.

"Harder, Hugh," she breathed. "Harder."

He thrust into her, again and again, each slide of his cock sending her closer and closer to the precipice. He let go of her hair. His hand caught her breast, his thumb flicking over her nipple in a rapid rhythm. The pressure built in her.

His thumb slid over her clit. She sucked in a breath against the sudden burst of pleasure.

He thrust deep. She shifted the angle of her hips and felt him rub against the inside of her.

He groaned, a harsh male sound filled with lust. It drove her wild. She was moaning now too.

He kept thrusting, his clever fingers teasing her.

She couldn't catch her breath, caught between his hand and his hard shaft inside her. She was close, so close...

"Hugh," she cried out. "Don't stop. Don't—"

The climax broke over her in a flood of heat and ecstasy. She slumped forward, feeling her body squeeze him in a steady rhythm, and he caught her before she hit the sheets and turned her over on her back. She floated in a fog of pleasure.

He grabbed her hips and pulled her, repositioning her on the bed. She was still floating when he opened her legs and knelt over her left thigh. He pushed her hips to the right, so her right leg wrapped around his waist, and thrust into her sideways. The unexpected pleasure dashed through her, tearing through the happy fog. On instinct, she tried to jerk upright. He pushed her back down and kept thrusting, finding a smooth rhythm.

She couldn't move. She couldn't shift her hips. She was completely at his mercy. He drove into her as if it were the only thing that mattered.

He was looking at her, his eyes a dark, vivid blue. His face turned harsh and slightly predatory, lost to lust. He bared his teeth and she realized the bastard was smiling.

Excitement and lust drowned her. Somewhere deep within, her rational mind acknowledged that watching him look at her made her want him more. It warned that she was surrendering some of her power. She snarled and tried to push away, but he held her down and went faster. His thick blunt shaft filled her with every move of his hips. The pleasure was exquisite.

A second climax began to build inside her.

He bent over her, blue eyes on fire. "Want me to let you go?"

She bit her lower lip, trying to keep from moaning. She knew exactly what this was – him proving that he could make her come without any help from her.

"All you have to do is say stop, Elara. Tell me to stop."

Dear goddess, she didn't want him to stop. "Fuck you," she breathed.

"Lady's choice."

He hauled her upright and suddenly she was sitting on him as he sprawled on the sheets, huge and muscled like some hot dream.

"Fuck me, honey," he dared.

And she did. She rode him, grinding her hips, taking his shaft inside her and letting it out as he kissed her neck and sucked her nipples, his hot hands locked on her ass, his fingers squeezing her and pulling her onto him.

The second orgasm washed over her, and she slumped over him, out of breath, her hair falling over their faces like a curtain hiding them from the rest of the world. The pleasure drained her so completely, she whimpered.

His lips found hers. He kissed her, and it was almost tender. Her head spun. She had to reassert herself, or she would kiss him back, and he would know she surrendered.

She arched her back and turned on him, facing his legs.

"Fun," he growled. His thumb found the sensitive bundle of nerves between her cheeks, just above her anus. She rocked on him, slipping his shaft into her, and slid her hand over its base.

He swore.

She rode him again, her fingers squeezing and pumping him, milking his shaft as she thrust herself onto him. His body tensed under her, the powerful muscles growing tight from strain. She worked him faster, arching her back, pushing against his hand, slipping him in and out. Her magic slid out of her, winding around her in curls of white vapor. She was losing control.

His shaft thickened in her hand.

He swore again.

"Tell me to stop," she told him.

He thrust into her, arching his hips. They built to a frenzied rhythm. The pleasure crested and broke in her. She cried out, her power simmering around her. He shook under her, every muscle taut with strain. She felt magic coursing through him, so powerful and bright, it shocked her. His shaft flexed in her hand. She felt the hot stream of his release inside her and let go, reveling in his pleasure. They stayed like that for a long moment, out of breath and slicked in sweat. He reached for her, pulled her down to him, and wrapped his arms around her, tucking her against his side.

Sex with Hugh d'Ambray. She should've never done it, because now she wanted more. He was the last person she should've given that much power over her. And he was holding her now. Being caged in his arms, stretched out next to him felt too good.

Elara sighed, still breathless. "Done, Preceptor?"

"I don't know," he said, his voice casual. "We still have a couple of hours until sunrise. Let's see what happens."

———+——

ELARA STRETCHED and slid off the bed. Hugh's hand snapped out and locked on her wrist.

"Hands off," she told him.

He leaned to glance out of the window, where gray pre-dawn light brightened the sky. "The sun isn't up yet."

"That's good then, because I'm not leaving yet."

He let her go and she stood. Her weight hit her feet and she swayed.

"Need some crutches?" he asked.

She flipped him off without turning and made the ten-step journey to grab the envelope. Her body felt liquid, her muscles tired and pliant. She was sore. She'd spent four hours in his room and none of it was sleeping, except for the few stretches when she cat-napped. She didn't mean to fall asleep, but there was something irresistibly comforting about him stretched out next to her. She wasn't sure if it was his size, the heat of his body, or simply knowing that if anything tried to enter the room intending to harm them, he would kill it, probably with his bare hands. Maybe all three.

"You want me to take care of that for you?" he asked.

She glanced at him. A faint blue aura coated him.

"No," she said.

He smiled. It was a self-satisfied smile of a man pleased with himself. She rolled her eyes and collapsed on the sheets next to him, the envelope in her hands.

"Tell me about Aberdine," she said.

"It was blood and fire," he said. "Stay out of my dreams for a while, Elara."

"Fire?"

"It's an army, as we thought. The officers are marked with gold. They spit fire. High heat. One of them caught Richard Sams with it. He died almost instantly."

She heard it in his voice. He'd tried to save Richard and failed.

"They don't run," he said. "They don't beg for their lives. They fight until they die and when you try to restrain them, they burn from inside out."

She drew a sharp breath. That kind of magic was beyond what most human magic users could do. "So, an elder being?"

"Yes. There is a benefit to taking out their officers. In normal circumstances, an officer dies and the next in line takes his place. With them, nobody stepped out. Once you cut them off from leadership, they fall out of formation and stand there until someone with a weapon approaches. Then they fight to the death as individuals. Once I took out the head guy, even the remaining officers stopped responding. That's the only way to fracture and break them."

"This makes no sense. How can an army function this way?"

Hugh grimaced. "It makes sense in a twisted way if you suppose something is controlling the top officer."

"Like a possession?"

"Possibly. Even an elder being can't control that many fighters at once. If it controls the commanding officers, and the rest are blindly obeying orders, it directs the entire army."

An elder being. She sighed. "Did Aberdine survive?"

"Most of it. The Dollar General is a husk and a couple of other buildings are not much better. But we put the fires out. The battle cost us three Iron Dogs. Aberdine lost twenty-one people."

He said it matter-of-factly, his voice flat. It ate at him, she realized. Every time he lost someone, it ate at him.

"Do you think they will try again?" she asked.

"They will, but they won't target Aberdine again. We don't know if there was any communication between the invading forces and reserves back where they came from, but it would be unlikely that there wasn't. We have to assume that they know we were waiting for them in Aberdine. We painted a target on our chests with that move. The next strike, if it comes, will be aimed at us."

She'd thought as much. Elara held the envelope out to him.

Hugh grabbed a pillow and pushed it behind his head to prop himself up. She liked the way the biceps rolled on his arms. *Stop it, stop it, stop it...* The pep talk wasn't quite working. She had opened a can of gasoline and set the fumes on fire.

Hugh opened the flap and pulled the paperwork out. She'd reviewed it with Savannah. It laid out exactly what Nez had promised.

His expression went hard.

"Nez came to see me," she told him. "Via a vampire."

"When?" Hugh asked.

"While you were in Aberdine."

"And you're absolutely sure it was Nez?"

"Yes. I've met him before when he tried to negotiate the purchase of the castle. He always speaks as if he is two steps above you on the intelligence ladder."

"He's a stuck-up asshole."

"Yeah, that too."

"Thinking of taking him up on his offer?"

She arched her eyebrows at him. "Why, do you think I should?"

Hugh tapped the file. "Some years ago, Landon Nez and I were clearing the way for Roland in Nebraska. There was a small remote town on the northern edge of the state called Hayville, protected by a Winnebago shaman. Roland wanted the land the town sat on. The shaman's family lived there for generations and once the Shift hit and their powers returned, they'd started laying wards around Hayville to protect their home. During magic, the place was a fortress. The town was well armed, so direct assault during tech was a bad idea. One day Nez showed up and laid siege to the town. Cut off the two roads leading to it and cut the power and phone lines. The state had its hands full with the Curva cult at the time, so nobody caught on for a bit."

The hint of some emotion flickered over his face. She couldn't quite place it. Pain? Regret? Whatever it was, it wasn't pleasant.

"Nez didn't want to bloody his nose against thirty years' worth of wards, so he sat on Hayville for a week and brokered a deal. If they delivered the shaman to him, he would sign a treaty with the town swearing to leave them alone. They brought the shaman to him trussed up like a hog. Nez got the shaman and left."

"And?" Elara asked.

"And the next morning I came through the town and burned it to the ground."

She stared at him.

"There was an investigation," he said. "Federal government came down. Witnesses were questioned. Reports were written about mysterious people in black burning the place down. Nobody mentioned Nez, because they sold their shaman to him, and nobody mentioned me, because they knew once the authorities left, I would be back. The town was a charred ruin and the next spring Roland bought the land for nothing."

"What happened to the shaman?" she asked.

"Nez tortured and murdered him," Hugh said. "Nez is part

313

Navajo. His family never lived with Navajo Nation, but he went there when he was fifteen. He told them he wanted to learn about his heritage. They taught him for a while until they realized he was a navigator. They consider undeath to be unnatural."

It was.

"There are prohibitions against doing evil," Hugh continued. "The Navajo believe that humans are meant to be in harmony and piloting undead disrupts that harmony, bringing about hóchx̨ǫ, chaos and sickness. Nez was given a choice: to abandon necromancy and continue learning or to leave before his sickness could spread. He left. Since that point, he goes after every shaman, medicine person, and hand trembler who crosses his path. He hunts them down and kills them. Doesn't matter what Tribe."

"Why? Is he trying to punish the Nations?"

"Yes and no. Mostly he is proving to himself that he's superior." Hugh grimaced. "Making deals and agreements with Nez is a waste of time. Might as well write a contract with a fork on the water in that moat out there. His word means nothing. His promises mean nothing. If the man's mouth is moving, he is lying."

She stretched next to him. "Are you worried I will sell you out, Preceptor?"

A hungry spark lit up his eyes.

"Did you buy us any time?" Hugh asked.

"Two weeks." She checked his face. "Tell me you have some sort of plan, Hugh."

"We'll have to deploy the barrels," he said. "I would've liked another week to make sure the moat holds water. If it doesn't, we're fucked."

"What's in the barrels?" she asked.

"If you play your cards right, I'll show you."

His voice had a drop of smugness. He thought he had her. She had to leave now, she realized. If she delayed any longer, she wouldn't get out of his bed at all. She would just lay here, luxuriating in the warmth of his body, cozy and safe.

Get up. Get up, get up, get up...

"The sun is up." She slipped out of the bed and swiped her clothes off the floor. "I've upheld my end of the bargain, Preceptor."

"Paid in full," he said.

She stretched, giving him one last good look, yawned, and went out the door naked.

———+——

THE DOOR SLID SHUT.

It hit Hugh like a gut punch – she was gone. For the few blissful hours she was with him, he had forgotten about the death, the blood, and the void. He'd poured his rage and wretched ache into her, and she'd drained him so completely, the only thing that remained was a satiated calm. Happiness, he realized. For the first time in years he felt happy.

She was only a few feet away, walking to her bedroom. The sheets where she'd lain, curled up against him, still held the warmth of her body. He missed her the moment the door closed behind her. His mind conjured up her face, her scent, the way her skin glided against his. The ache rose in him. He wanted her back.

He would get her back. But first, he had to make sure they survived.

Nez was coming. He showed up "in person" to bargain with her, which meant their time was short and when Nez came for them, he would hit them with the full force of the Golden Legion. They weren't ready. They barely had two weeks.

His mind cycled through everything that still needed to be done to make them ready for the assault. Sleep wasn't in the cards. He would sleep when he was dead.

Hugh pushed himself off the bed, took a pitcher of cold tea

from the refrigerator, and drained half of it. He shook himself, sending the magic through his body, fixing small aches, knitting battle cuts closed, realigning, healing, bringing himself back to fighting shape.

He had to make sure Baile stood firm. He had to make certain that when Nez came, his Golden Legion broke on the old castle like a wave on a pier.

15

Night had fallen, bringing with it an autumn chill. Elara pulled the long blue-and-white shawl around her shoulders and leaned on the wall. Fog had crawled in from the lake, twisting and spilling into the clearing before the castle, thick and milky. The darkness leached the color from the woods and behind the curtain of the fog, the mighty trees looked like a mirage, a careless charcoal sketch on the rough canvas of the night.

Next to her, Rook waited, a silent shadow. He'd come and gotten her a few minutes ago.

In the lower bailey, Hugh and his four centurions pulled the barrels out of storage and loaded them onto a horse-drawn cart.

Elara shifted more of her weight onto the stone. Her feet hurt. It had been a long, long day. First, they'd had to finish evacuating the last of Aberdine's defenders. She had sent them back to their town fed and clean, with their wounds tended. As much as she wanted to help, Aberdine would have to fend for itself now.

That done, she had inspected their siege fund. The possibility of an attack was always there, and they had stockpiled rations and water since they took over the castle. Grain, dried fruit, dried meat, cheese, canned goods. Their short-term supplies, cheeses, smoked sausages, and so on, everything that wouldn't keep for too long, looked good. The long-term stockpiles had taken a hit. Several barrels of grain had gotten pantry moths in them somehow, despite being sealed. The entire affected supply went to the livestock. The loss hurt and now they had pantry moths to deal with, which were damn near indestructible. She had to call the witches to fumigate the entire supply house.

At least the water in the cisterns under the castle hadn't turned foul. They still had the well, but Hugh had been right when he told her on that first day that the well would be a target. Knowing there was an extra supply helped.

Hugh spent most of the day running around the castle like a man possessed, checking the siege engines, healing the last of the wounded, surveying the land around the castle. She saw him only in passing. At some point they'd crossed paths in the kitchen, drawn there by the scent of fresh pirogis. She was on her way in, he was on his way out. They nodded at each other and kept going. Sometime after that, Dugas found her to tell her that Hugh asked for a fog tonight and that he wanted it to look natural. She told the druid to do what he could. And now Hugh was here, doing something with the barrels.

Bale heaved the last barrel in place. Stoyan took the horse by the bridle and walked him forward. The three other centurions followed.

She went down the stairs. Hugh was waiting for her in the lower bailey.

"You promised me you would tell me what was in the barrels, Preceptor. Now you're sneaking off with them."

"I told you I'd show you if you played your cards right. You should've tried harder last night, sweetheart. With more enthusiasm."

Oh you jackass. "If you'd impressed me with what you offered, I would've tried harder. But a woman can only do so much with mediocre equipment."

He grinned at her. They strolled through the gates, following the cart.

Stoyan turned the horse left and stopped. Bale and Lamar took the first barrel off and set it on the ground. Bale raised his hands, index and middle fingers crossed. Stoyan knocked on the cart three times, then spat over his left shoulder.

"What the hell are you two doing?" Lamar asked in a low voice.

"For good luck," Bale told him.

Lamar shook his head. Together they tipped the barrel over the water. Lamar broke the seal, unscrewed the lid, and lowered it into the water. The two men gingerly slid the barrel into the moat and let it sink. Nobody moved.

"Now what?" Elara asked.

"Now we find out if we're fucked." Hugh pulled a small metal flask from his pocket, stepped to the edge of the moat over where the barrel had sunk, unscrewed the lid, and poured the dark contents into the water. The dark liquid spread over the surface. Magic slid over Elara like a tepid rotten smear. Vampire blood.

The water lay placid.

Bale waved his crossed fingers around.

The water boiled, as if something large slid underneath it. The red stain vanished.

"Ha!" Bale barked.

"Shhh," the three other centurions hissed at him.

Stoyan pulled on the horse, leading it around the moat.

"What is it?" she asked.

"What will you give me if I tell you?"

"Hugh," she ground out.

"Fine. Some years ago, Roland sent me up to Alaska to talk to Ice Fury. It's the biggest shapeshifter pack in the US. The talks got us nowhere. The Ice Fury shifters are separatists. All they want to do is to run around their woods and be left alone. They spend most of their time in animal form. The way they're going, in a couple of generations they'll forget how to be human. So the talks didn't go as planned, but since I was already in Alaska, I figured why not make a trip of it. We went up North and ended up in Mekoryuk. It's a city on Nunivak island. Nuniwarmiut people have lived there for two thousand years. While I was there, I met an old woman who told me they weren't worried about Roland or his vampires, because they had dirty ice and it would protect them. Long story short, I went and got some of that dirty ice. Cutting it out and dragging it back home was a pain in the ass, but I knew Nez or whoever came after him would be gunning for me sooner or later. Here we are."

The cart stopped, and Felix and Bale took another barrel off. Elara watched as they took off the lid and sank it.

"Yes, but what's in the ice?"

"A bacterial strain," Hugh said. "Nasty bugger, highly aggressive. We had to cut down to permafrost to get it. Harmless to humans as far as I can tell. Loves water. Guess what it likes for dinner?"

"Vampires?"

He nodded. "Any undead is fair game."

"Have you used it before?" she asked.

"We tested it."

"But not in actual battle?"

"No."

"So you don't know if it will work."

"There are no guarantees in life," he said.

"Now isn't the best time to get philosophical, Preceptor."

"Would you rather have an empty reassurance?"

Yes, she thought. She would. It wouldn't do her any good, but right now reassurance would be nice. Sadly, nice wasn't something she could afford at the moment.

"Vampires don't swim," he said. "No air in the lungs. They sink to the bottom, so they will have to wade through. Considering the distance and typical vampire speed under water, they are likely to be under between ten and twenty seconds. In lab trials, that was enough to cause critical damage. The trick is raising the concentration high enough. The higher the concentration, the more effective the bacteria will be. The bacteria will need food to multiply. Our supplies of undead blood are limited."

"We have some blood and bones in storage. We'll add what we can."

"Thank you."

"Do you think it will be long enough?" she asked.

"We will find out," he said.

They followed the cart again. Dread settled on Elara and weighed her down. Two more weeks. Less now, one week and six days. There were other preparations to be made. The preparation for when everything went wrong. The memory of the ice flickered over her mind. She didn't want to do it again. She didn't want to remember what it was like but knowing she might have to gnawed at her.

"What if we sank some concertina wire?" she asked. "It's a long flexible razor wire that comes in coils. Military grade."

"I know what concertina wire is. How much do you have?"

"I don't know. It comes in 50-foot bails," she said. "We have a warehouse of it."

He stared at her.

"We bought it off a derelict prison," she said. "We meant to use it as a wolf deterrent, but wildlife and livestock kept getting caught in it and it was cruel, so we didn't."

He looked to the sky and laughed.

"I don't see what's so funny."

He turned to her. "I'm trying to save us. Had I known we had concertina wire, I would've planned our defenses differently."

She shrugged.

"I can't effectively protect us if you keep relevant information from me," he said.

"You seem to be doing fine," she told him.

"You really are a harpy, you know that?"

"If you want to know if we have something, Preceptor, I suggest you use your words and ask. We do not volunteer information, because we don't trust you. The only way to change that is by demonstrating your intentions and following through."

Hugh shook his head. "I had a crazy thought."

"By all means, do share it."

"What if I'm dead and this is purgatory, and you're my punishment?"

"I doubt it," she told him.

"Why?"

"Because if I'm your punishment, you're mine. The Christian god is the god of forgiveness. He is too kind to do this, even to us."

He laughed again.

The fog parted, and a creature landed next to them, a shaggy, dark meld of human and wolf. The shapeshifter contorted, collapsing into a human shape. A nude woman shook herself, as if trying to fling the last of the fur from her skin. Karen, Elara remembered. One of Hugh's scouts.

"Found them," she said. "Fifteen clicks north at the Rooster ley line point."

High turned to her. "Call your people. We have a strategy to plan."

——+—

ELARA SLUMPED IN THE CHAIR. Her feet still hurt. She nudged her sandals off, let them drop, and curled her toes.

The study was full. Savannah sat in an overstuffed chair to Elara's right, perfectly dressed, her make up unsmudged. The only indication of the late hour was her loose hair that framed her face like a halo. Johanna perched on the table to Elara's left, in her usual spot. Stoyan sat next to Savannah. He'd glanced in Johanna's direction once when he came in and then proceeded to look everywhere else. *Not fooling anyone.* Across from Stoyan, Bale, who had come in a few minutes ago looking hung over, slumped forward in his chair, his head on the table, resting on his crossed arms. Felix, a quiet shadow, leaned against the wall behind Bale. Karen, the female werewolf scout, paced the length of the study, newly dressed.

Across from Elara, at the other end of the table, Hugh studied Baile's map. He looked thoughtful. Hugh could twist his face into any expression he wanted. The man was a chameleon. She had seen him go from terrifying to *aw shucks, I'm just a dumb oaf* in a blink, but the unguarded moments like this, when he forgot to put on a show, and his intelligence shone through, were her favorite.

Favorite. Ugh. She snapped herself back to reality. It was the fatigue. She was so tired, she could barely see straight.

Lamar hurried into the room, Dugas following him. She had a feeling those two plotted together a lot more than anyone realized.

"Bale?" Stoyan asked.

The berserker snored.

"Is he hung over?" Elara asked quietly.

"No. It's the battle warp," Hugh said. "Wears him out."

Johanna leaned forward, trying to read their lips. Elara signed to her, recounting the conversation.

"He's good for a bit, but then he crashes," Lamar added.

Hugh took a carafe from the table, poured a cup of black coffee, walked over to Bale, and put his hand on Bale's shoulder.

The berserker raised his head, blinking his eyes.

Hugh put the coffee in front of him.

Bale nodded, sniffled, and gulped the coffee.

"You all know why you're here," Hugh said. "We have a date with Landon Nez in two weeks. Karen?"

"He is camped at the Rooster ley point," the werewolf said. "There isn't much there except a small village, a couple dozen buildings at most and a supply station."

"Slow down," Elara told her. She had gotten adept at signing over the years, but she was tired and thinking and signing at the same time took all of her concentration.

"Sorry." The werewolf continued slower. "The security is tight, so I couldn't get close. He's shipping vampires in twenty-foot metal freight containers, five per container. I counted twenty-four containers, and more were coming in."

A hundred and twenty vampires. A single vampire was not an issue. Ten vampires would be too much even for her. Ripping their magic out took an effort, and while she was busy with the first five, the rest of them would get by her, scale the walls, get into the castle... If Hugh's water trap didn't work, and even fifty vampires made it over the wall, Baile would become a killing box, even with all of the Iron Dogs in it.

She checked Hugh's face. He didn't seem worried.

"How many people?" Lamar asked.

"Too many," Karen said. "I'd estimate at least three hundred if not more. The place was dead last time we surveilled it and now it's Saturday morning market."

"He is bringing the entire Legion?" Stoyan asked.

"Probably," Hugh said.

"Lots of black and purple," Karen said. "He definitely brought the Cleaning Crew."

"The Cleaning Crew?" Savannah asked.

"The Legion has three components," Lamar explained. "The navigators, which are Masters of the Dead and the journeymen; the undead; and the Cleaning Crew, human shock troops that follow the vampires and kill anything they leave behind."

"How good are they?" Dugas asked.

"Decent," Stoyan said. "Not a problem for us one-on-one."

"It's never one-on-one," Bale said. "It's always one of us and four of them."

"The Cleaning Crew is expendable," Hugh said. "Nez is pragmatic. Undead are expensive, humans are cheap."

"Also," Karen said, "I saw Halliday."

Bale cursed.

"Are you sure?" Lamar asked.

"I'm sure," Karen said. "It was her. Unless you know some other middle-aged dark-haired bitch, who travels with Nez and carries around a pair of Chinese crested dogs."

"You saw the dogs?" Felix asked.

"Saw, smelled, heard. It's Halliday."

Elara looked at Hugh.

"Beastmaster," he said. "Roland likes to use magical animals in his wars. She is his wrangler."

"What kind of magical beasts?" Dugas asked.

"An elephant the size of a cruise ship with three heads and tusks that shoot lightning," Bale volunteered.

"There is no such thing," Savannah told him.

"There is," Stoyan told her. "It's called Erawan. We've seen it."

Johanna knocked on the table.

They looked at her.

"Seriously?"

Stoyan held up his fist, and made a downward motion, imitating a nodding head. He was signing, *"Yes."* He did it in a hesitant fashion, the way those who have just started learning ASL sometimes second-guessed themselves.

Johanna grinned at him.

"You should see the size of its shit," Bale said. "It's a truckload."

"This tells us two things," Hugh said. "One, Nez will come at us during magic. Two, Roland let him pull on his other resources, which means Nez took this to Roland and Roland approved this fight."

"This changes things," Lamar said.

"How so?" Savannah asked.

"Nez was content to ignore us," Hugh said. "Something happened to bump us up to the head of his queue."

She knew exactly what it was. "Aberdine."

Everyone looked at her. Savannah raised her hands and took over the signing.

"You protected Aberdine against a significant magic force," Elara said. "You're a fighting unit again. An army and a threat. He thought he could come and kill all of you at will, but now he can't."

She saw the calculation in Hugh's eyes. He shook his head. "I doubt it. Did Nez ever explain why he wanted the castle?"

"No," Savannah said. "He just offered to buy it again and again."

"Maybe there is something here that he needs?" Stoyan wondered.

"I can't imagine what it would be," Elara said honestly.

"Let's table that for now," Hugh said. "Before we start planning, are there any ways into the castle that I'm not aware off? Hidden passages, secret tunnels?"

Dugas glanced at her. Elara nodded. *Yes, give him the thing.* Hugh was an infuriating sonovabitch and a bastard, but he would protect them to the bitter end. Baile was the only home he knew now.

Dugas reached into his robe and pulled out a folded piece of paper. He unfolded it once, twice, a third time, and spread it on the table. A complex drawing in black ink marked the large piece of paper: a central ring, from which lines spread out like spokes from a wheel. The lines started straight, then curved, lopped and intersected each other, twisting together into a complex maze.

"What am I looking at?" Hugh asked.

"Tunnels," Dugas said helpfully.

Hugh and the centurions peered at the map.

"Is all of this under us?" Hugh asked, pointing at the map.

"Yes." Dugas nodded.

"Fuck me," Hugh said.

Elara almost laughed.

"Why?" Lamar asked, his eyes wide.

"We didn't dig them out," Elara said. "They were already here when we moved in."

Hugh fixed her with a stare. "Were you planning on telling me about the damn tunnels?"

She pretended to ponder it. "Possibly."

"Would you like to tell me now?"

"There are tunnels under the castle, Hugh."

"There it is. Thank you." If sarcasm was liquid, she would be up to her ankles in it.

"You're welcome."

They glared at each other across the table.

Dugas cleared his throat.

"Is there anything else you would like to disclose?" Hugh asked. "Do the gates open when someone says a magic word?"

"Not that I know of," she told him. "Why don't you scream some magic words at the gates for a while and tell me how it turns out?"

Dugas cleared his throat again.

"I heard you the first time," she told him.

"Do any of these actually come up to the surface?" Hugh tapped the map with his finger.

"We don't know," Dugas said.

"We've tried mapping them several times, but we end up turned around," Elara said. "There is only one way from the tunnels into the castle though, and it's through this ring." She traced the outline of the circular tunnel for him.

"This is a huge security risk," Lamar said. "Do you actually use these tunnels for anything?"

"Those who go into the tunnels don't always come back," Johanna told him.

Lamar turned to Elara.

"She said that those who go into the tunnels don't always come back."

"Why?" Hugh asked.

327

Elara sighed. *I wish I knew.*

"We don't know," Savannah said. "Don't worry about it. We can handle the tunnels."

Hugh leaned forward. "Here is how this assault will go. The attack will come in the evening."

"How do you know that?" Elara asked.

"I've prepared to fight Nez for years. He is a cheapskate. Even the youngest vampire he has costs upward of fifty grand to produce. He will attempt to intimidate us into surrendering by fielding a lot of undead at once. He will follow that with a phone call and a show of force designed to convince us to surrender. When that fails, he will rush the castle with his vanguard. He will count on the psychological impact of this force and our awareness that the sun is setting, and soon it will be dark, and we will be defenseless. If the moat does its job, we can repel this assault."

"If?" Savannah raised her eyebrows.

"If," Hugh said. "If the moat doesn't soften them up, it will get ugly. However, it is unlikely he will commit more than fifty vampires. He typically brings between two and three hundred vampires..."

Elara startled. Three hundred vampires. She couldn't even wrap her head around that many undead.

"Yes?" Hugh asked.

"Nothing. Continue."

"And since he knows he will be fighting the Iron Dogs, we can count on the top range of that number. It's highly unlikely he would send more than a quarter of his force. Fifty is a nice round number and Nez likes round numbers."

Hugh tapped the map of Baile. "He will send the mass of undead straight at the front gate. Even if the moat fails, we can take fifty vampires. We will bleed but we can take them. Once that assault fails, Nez will do something loud and theatrical. He might field beasts or pull some mages out of his sleeve. Whatever form this new threat will take, it will be designed to keep our attention focused front and center. Meanwhile, his crews, which will have been digging since before the fight started, will be breaking into the castle tunnels from below. The vampires are fast diggers, and he might bring specialized help to speed things up. While we are trying to hold off whatever it is battering us from the front, the undead will make their way into the castle and massacre us from the rear."

Hugh fixed Savannah with his stare. "So, when you say don't worry about the tunnels, I need you to be very sure."

"I'll take care of it," Elara said.

"Okay," Hugh said.

She opened her mouth to argue and realized he didn't say anything else. "Then that's settled."

"Can we attack Nez directly?" Savannah asked.

"Unlikely," Lamar told her. "For things like these, Nez travels in a convoy of Matadors. A Matador is an 8x8 armored personnel carrier, nine meters long, three meters tall, and almost three meters wide. It has a monocoque V-hull, which means its nose and hull slope to deflect projectiles."

Lamar held his left hand in front of him, palm up, and touched the fingertips of his right hand to it, forming a sideways V.

"It sits a driver and passenger in the front and can transport up to ten personnel in the back. Level four armor, suspended seats, blast mitigation floor, all the works. It can trench at two meters, ford a stream a meter deep, climb steps and steep hills, and it turns on a dime for a vehicle of its size. It runs like a dream during tech, but it chugs along during magic as well. It also can be set up to carry either a 50 cal or a sorcerous ballista, depending on your preference. Nez has a fleet of them."

"We used to have them too," Stoyan said. "The long and short of it, Matadors are unbreachable by anything we have. We could probably drop a rock on it from above and crush it, but we don't have a catapult precise enough to do it."

"We need to do something about the approach from the north-eastern side," Hugh said. "We are missing a siege engine on the corner tower. It requires specialized parts."

"Is it a budget issue?" Elara asked.

"No, it's an availability issue," Hugh said.

"We have it on order in Lexington," Lamar said. "We traded some silver we recovered for it. It won't be ready in time."

"We'll have to compensate with archers," Hugh said.

"We can dig some fortifications there," Stoyan said. "It may slow down the Cleaning Crew, but it won't do anything against vampires."

"We could plant tangle weed," Savannah said.

Good idea. Elara turned to Johanna. *"How much do we have?"*

"Enough," Johanna signed.

"Can this tangle weed hold a vampire?" Bale asked.

"Yes, if there is enough of it," Dugas said.

"Where would you need it planted?" Savannah leaned toward the map.

The rest of the advisors leaned in, and Elara met Hugh's eyes.

Three hundred vampires.

He winked at her.

For some reason the wink took the dread right out of her. She rolled her eyes and leaned forward to take a glance at the map.

———✦———

ELARA STARED at the roster of families. Around her the bailey bustled with life, people going to and fro, trying to squeeze as much as they could out of the fading evening light. They had two days until the deadline, but it was collectively decided that Nez couldn't be trusted farther than they could throw him, so they'd been pulling people into the castle, in stages. Children with care-takers first, then older people, now finally the able-bodied adults. She squeezed the first wave into the left barracks, praising the source of all life that they had renovated the place when the Iron

Dogs joined them. Once the barracks filled, they put the next wave into the utility buildings behind the keep, then into the chapel building, which they had converted into living quarters. Baile was so crowded, it was bursting at the seams.

"Is the chapel completely full?" she asked.

"Almost," Johanna signed.

Elara sighed, studying the roster. "We're going to have to start putting sleeping bags in the keep hallway. On the second floor—"

Johanna touched her arm. Elara looked up. Serenity Helton was walking toward them, oblivious to the people scurrying all around her, a blank look on her face. Elara's heart dropped. She hurried forward and grabbed Serenity's hands. "What is it?"

The seer stared at her unblinking. Her lips moved, but no sound came.

Johanna grabbed Elara's arm. *"Coming! Now!"*

"What?"

"She is saying 'they are coming' over and over!"

The anxiety that clamped Elara over the last few days burst in a scalding rush.

"Hurry," she whispered, sending her voice through the entire castle. **"They're coming. Hurry."**

The people scattered. In the village a bell rang. Hugh came running around the corner.

"Nez is coming," she told him, pointing at Serenity.

He glanced at the seer and spun off, barking orders. Elara climbed the steps to the outer wall and then to the top of the flanking tower. From here, she could see the entire village. People ran, streaming to the castle.

She turned to Johanna. *"Find Magdalene. Take her to the tunnels."*

Johanna took off at a run.

The village emptied as people rushed to Baile.

Come on, she urged in her head. *Come on.*

Iron Dogs poured out of the gate, forming a protective line, shielding the evacuees. On top of the keep and on the towers, the ballistae and catapult teams cranked the massive siege weapons. She heard chanting, almost in unison, as the artillery teams primed the sorcerous bolts.

Shapeshifters burst out of the woods, running at top speed toward the castle – Hugh's scouts coming in.

Seconds crept by, echoing the beating of her heart. *Come on.*

Creatures streamed out of the woods, like an evil river, flowing in rivulets between the trunks to flood the grass. Vampires. Hundreds and hundreds of vampires, smeared with sunblock in green, blue, and red.

The Iron Dogs unsheathed their weapons.

She tried desperately to sort through the people running to the gates. Did they get everyone? Was someone missing? She couldn't tell.

The vampires kept coming and coming, widening in a crescent, blending together into a monstrous mass, terrifying, stinking of magic that shouldn't have existed. Endless.

Hugh was right. If they hadn't had the warning, they might have panicked. Even she, with all of her power, had to fight a shiver. In a couple of hours the sun would set, and the monstrous horde would roll over the castle. Next to her Johanna squeezed her fingers into fists and relaxed them again.

The evacuees slowed to a trickle. Did they get everyone? Anxiety boiled in her. She tried to count the vampires to keep her mind focused. Three, five, eight, ten…

Hugh ran up the stairs and loomed next to her, his expression hard.

"You were right," she told him.

"This day was a long time coming," Hugh told her.

Beth ran up to the tower. "There is a phone call for you."

"Is it Nez?"

"Yes, lady."

"Right on schedule," Hugh said. "See if you can piss him off. He doesn't think clearly when he's angry."

332

"I can do that."

"Oh, I know you can. Have fun, love."

Elara turned and walked down the stairs, forcing herself to move slowly. The longer she took getting to the phone, the more time she bought them. Finally, she reached the front office. Lamar and Dugas waited by the phone.

Elara took the phone. "You're two days early."

"You have been fortifying," Nez said with clinical precision.

"We had an agreement. You broke it. If you can't keep a simple deadline, what guarantee can you offer that you will honor any other agreements?"

"I'm giving you this one last chance to avoid bloodshed. Consider the fate of your people. Consider the children's lives. Once I clear the wall, I cannot guarantee anyone's safety."

"You're not listening to me," she told him. "Go back to where you came from and come back in two days. That was the agreement. You made it with me and I will hold you to it."

Incredulous silence filled the phone. Lamar grinned.

"You will regret this," Nez said.

"No," she told him. "But you will. You're full of it. You want to negotiate with me, but clearly you can't be trusted."

"You actually expect me to withdraw and come back in two days?"

"Yes."

"No."

"Do you even have the authority to negotiate, Landon?"

"I have all the authority."

"It seems to me that you don't. I understand that you negotiated with Hayville in Nebraska and then the town burned to the ground."

Nez's voice came out clipped, each word razor-sharp. "I didn't burn Hayville. Your husband did."

"Precisely. It didn't matter what deals you made, because there is a higher authority above you that actually makes decisions. You are a servant, Landon. A glorified gofer. We are defending our home. You are just carrying out orders."

Dugas clamped his hand over his mouth.

"I'm not even mad at you, Landon. Everyone has a job they have to do. But don't waste my time again trying to negotiate. You have no power to do it."

"I will take your castle," Nez said. His voice sent a chill down her spine. "I will tear it apart brick by brick. Then I will make you watch as I personally cut the throat of every man, woman, and child that survives the assault."

"Do you know why Hugh burned Hayville? Because you couldn't do it. My husband is better than you."

"You're a stupid whore."

"There goes the mask of civility. Roland had only two Warlords, but you are the twenty-third Legatus of the Golden Legion. Do you know why? It's because Hugh is beloved by his soldiers, while you are reviled by the Masters of the Dead. Every man under his command would die for him, while the people who serve you can't wait to stick a knife in your back."

"I'll make sure it takes you weeks to die."

"Hugh is a better general, a better fighter, and a better man. You're second best. You will always be second best. You're replaceable. One day one of your helpers will kill you and take your place, and Roland won't blink an eye, while Hugh is one of a kind. Oh and his dick is bigger than yours."

A disconnect signal cut off the call.

Lamar clapped and bowed.

She dropped the phone back into its place and turned back to the wall. There were too many people between her and the tower for magic, so she hurried on foot, across the bailey, up the stairs, back to the top of the flanking tower, where Hugh waited. The entire clearing before the tree line was filled with undead.

"How did it go?" Hugh asked.

"He's frothing at the mouth."

"That's my girl." He grinned at her.

The last of the stragglers made it through the gates. The Iron Dogs had followed, and the massive drawbridge rose up, blocking the entrance.

A clump of vampires shot out from the main mass of the undead and fell apart, revealing two people tied to crosses, naked from the waist up. The one on the left, a woman, wore the black shreds of an Iron Dog uniform. The one on the right slumped over, his gray curly hair stained with blood.

Oscar.

Oh no.

——❦——

Elara really pissed Nez off.

Usually Nez would have held back the hostages, waiting to see if he could use them as bargaining chips at the right moment, but instead he dragged them out into plain view, blinded by the need to hit back. Whatever she said to him, he wanted to punish her for it.

The lone Iron Dog on the cross glared at the vampires. Irina. She'd been out by the southern edge of the town, scouting to the rear. That meant the digging crew likely grabbed her. Nez would be digging in from the southwest.

Fury boiled inside Hugh. He hated to lose Irina, hated that her life was over, hated that Nez was the one who took it. If only he could get his hands on that bastard. Hugh stared at the woods behind the undead. Nez was out there somewhere, sipping coffee in his Matador.

None of the front scouting team had made it either. He saw the scouts from the East and West teams, but none from the North. That meant none survived.

Next to him Elara had gone completely still. Her eyes narrowed, measuring the distance between her and the old man on the cross. She was thinking of rushing the field. He put his hand on her shoulder, anchoring her in place.

"No."

She ignored him.

"Elara!"

She turned to look at him, and cold shot through him. Her eyes were pure white.

"Too many and too far," he told her.

"I know," she ground out.

Savannah's voice cut through the noise of the bailey behind them. "To the wall! Come to the wall!"

All around them the villagers streamed to the wall, climbing up the stairs. Men, women, parents lifting small children on their shoulders, they lined up as if for a parade, watching the two people on the crosses. Those who didn't fit ran into the keep and filed out onto the curtain wall and balconies. More still waited in the bailey.

"Don't look away," Savannah called out.

"You must witness and remember," Dugas yelled from the other side.

The Departed held still and silent. The hair on the back of Hugh's neck rose. There was something unnatural in the way they stared, passing judgment on the undead below.

The vampire sitting by the older man jumped up. Sickle claws flashed and ripped him from breastbone to waist. Entrails spilled out, hanging from his body in grotesque garlands. The man screamed, a short guttural sound. Elara didn't move a muscle.

No sound came from the wall. They looked on just as she did, bearing silent witness.

"Do not look away," Savannah said into the silence.

"Watch and remember," Dugas echoed.

The old man screamed and screamed.

A second vampire tore the stomach of the Iron Dog, spilling her innards. Irina howled. It was the long ululating howl the Iron

336

Dogs made when they rode in battle. A chorus of howls answered from inside the castle, the Dogs acknowledging their own.

Hugh turned, finding Yvonne on top of the west gate tower. Their stares connected.

The archery commander whipped back. Two crossbow bolts ripped the air, glowing with magic. The first took Oscar in the throat. The second sank into the Iron Dog's chest. The sorcerous bolts buzzed and exploded. Two people next to Yvonne lowered their crossbows. One of them, slight and short, glanced at him, and Hugh recognized Alex Tong.

The wall stayed silent.

"His name is Landon Nez," Elara said, her voice snaking through the crowd.

A chant rose from the villagers.

"Landon Nez."

"Landon Nez."

Emotion poured out of a thousand throats, indignation and anger melded into a furious mix. Even the children chanted. Hugh saw Stoyan on another tower, looking around wild-eyed.

"We are one," Elara whispered next to him. "We are the Departed."

He felt something rise from the collective chant, something vicious and furious and unimaginably ancient.

"Landon Nez."

A shimmer gathered above the crowd as if the air along the wall had suddenly grown hot. The edge of it brushed him. Ghostly howls echoed in his head and broke into a primitive, savage snarl. He jerked back on instinct.

"LANDON NEZ."

The invisible thing tore free of the wall and hurled itself at the tree line. Trees jerked, as if grasped by an invisible hand. Birds shot out of the woods, screeching. Something thudded, metal whined, and a siren blared. He recognized the sound – it belonged to the People's Armored Troop Transports.

Next to him Elara stood, her teeth clenched.

Okay. First things first. He would win this battle and then he would figure out what the hell she was and what he had gotten himself and his people into.

"Did you get him?" he asked.

"No," she said, her expression hard. "But we rattled his cage."

On the field below, vampires became utterly still. Standard protocol as the navigators waited for orders. They only had a few minutes before Nez shook the surprise off.

A charge was coming.

"EVERYONE not in uniform off the wall!" Hugh roared.

The blast of sound took her by surprise and Elara jerked. The villagers scattered, running down the stairs.

"You know where to be!" Elara called out. "To your places!"

In the bailey Savannah and Dugas herded people into the buildings.

Next to Hugh, Sam put his mouth to the horn and blew a high-pitched note. The Iron Dogs took up positions on the wall, fighting against the current of her people.

"Artillery, fire at will," Hugh ordered.

Sam blew a new note, a harsh war call. The ballistae creaked, the strings of the massive bows twanged, and sorcerous bolts shrieked, tearing the air. A couple of undead jerked, suddenly impaled. Most had dodged, but the emerald green bolt heads exploded with magic, throwing dirt, rocks, and gaunt bodies.

The vampire wave gathered in the clearing before the trees crested and surged toward Baile. Fear pierced the back of Elara's neck.

There were more than fifty. There had to be.

One of the Iron Dogs on top of the gate tower spun around. Hanzi covered her face, drawn in blue ink. She twisted, flexible and fluid like water, and came to rest on one foot, all her weight on her bent back leg, her right leg bent in front of her at an angle, toes barely touching the ground. Her right arm stretched to the sky, hand horizontal as if she was trying to press it against the clouds. Her left arm, bent at the elbow, guarded her chest.

The massive catapult on top of the keep whined. A rock the size of a small car streaked over their heads. The undead scattered, making a hole in their ranks. The stone thudded into it.

The woman moved, fast like a whip, snapping into a new pose, and spat a single word.

The stone pulsed with orange and exploded. Rock shrapnel pelted the undead. Some fell, but more were coming, fast, scurrying forward like ugly twisted lizards.

The ballistae spat more bolts. The air smelled of sorcerous smoke, crackling with expended magical energy. It felt as if she were caught in some magical storm made of explosions, screams, and war horns. It called on her to do something, to run, to scream, to kill. She glanced at Hugh. He stood next to her, immovable like a rock, his face almost relaxed.

"Archers, fire at will."

The horn howled.

The first line of vampires jumped into the moat and sank. One by one they dove down, disappearing into the water, while the archers peppered them with bolts and arrows.

She leaned against the parapet to get a better look. Everything rode on this moment.

Nothing. Only placid water.

Hugh leaned forward, his expression impassive.

A hint of dark red floated to the surface from the moat's depths. The water boiled, and the color vanished.

Seconds ticked by, slow and viscous.

One.

Two.

Five.

Ten.

She fought with herself to stand still.

Fifteen.

The water at the inner edge of the moat swirled. A vampire emerged. It dragged itself forward, its movements sluggish, reached with one long muscular arm, hooked its claws into the wall, and pulled itself up. She watched it climb slowly, each stretch an effort. It was almost directly under her now.

Elara backed away.

The undead heaved itself over the wall onto the tower. It landed heavily on the stones. The flesh on its frame sagged, as if it had gone liquid under its hide.

It worked. It actually worked.

The vampire swayed.

Hugh stepped forward, pulling his sword out and striking in a single explosive move. The black blade sliced through the vampire's torso, cleaving it in two. Black, foul smelling fluid gushed on to the wall. The top half of the undead tumbled back into the moat.

Hugh grabbed the bottom half by the leg and hurled it over the wall. A splash followed.

She sidestepped the dark puddle and looked over the wall. All along the moat vampires staggered to the wall, slow and shaking. Some moved faster, others slower.

Blood red sparks shot out of the trees, a meteorite shower in reverse.

Hugh grabbed her hand and jerked her down, covering her with his body. A red missile shrieked through the air, landed in the bailey, and exploded. The walls of Baile shuddered. Red fire splashed on the wall to the left of them and an Iron Dog vanished in the glow with a sharp cry. All around them the magic missiles fell with a high-pitched whine, crashing against the stones of Baile.

Elara wedged herself against the wall, trying to make herself smaller.

Hugh grinned at her. "Fun!"

The man was a maniac. She had married a raving lunatic.

A deep bellow shook the castle, as if some god blew an enormous trumpet.

Hugh raised his head and she squirmed from under him, trying to see.

The trees snapped, parting. Something snaked between the crowns, a long dark thing that swung and coiled. It caught a tree and yanked it out of the ground, turning it sideways. Clumps of soil rained down from the root ball. The tree flew aside and through the gap Elara saw a moving darkness. It leaned left, then right, still hidden by the forest. Five-foot wide trunks snapped like toothpicks and crashed aside, carrying branches with them, giving way to something impossibly large. A blunt head emerged, level with the top of the forest canopy and crowned by a mesh of braided golden ropes, each as thick as her wrist. A brilliant blue jewel embedded in the flesh sat in the middle of the forehead, where the net came to a point. Two more heads joined it and a creature emerged into the open. It had three heads, each flanked by wide ears. Six ivory tusks thrust into the air, each large enough to impale and carry off a truck. Its hide was solid black, as if it swallowed the evening sunlight.

Erawan.

The colossal elephant took a step forward. The armored cabin on its neck rocked. A huge chain was coiled around his legs. The ground shook. Lightning dashed along Erawan's hide, spattering in bursts of electric blue, and in the light of those explosions, Elara saw long white scars crossing the elephant's hide.

Armed people emerged from the woods, ants next to a giant, and trotted toward the castle. Above him, a rain cloud boiled, just large enough to cover the hill. It ended abruptly, and beyond it the sky was the clear beautiful blue of early evening.

"Elara," Hugh called.

She felt Erawan's mind, dark and turbulent like a storm cloud. It called to her.

"Elara!"

She reached out and brushed the edge of the storm with a wisp of her power. Agony exploded in her mind, images bursting one after another: blood on the tusks, bodies under feet, the trumpet screams, flesh and bone collapsing under the immense weight, forehead smashing a house wall and emerging streaked with concrete dust, blood and rain, buildings, shredded and destroyed, people, tossed and trampled, pain, chains, and blood, the stench, the feel, the vivid red of human blood.

"Honey!" Hugh snarled in her ear.

She jerked, breaking the contact, and clamped her hand over her mouth. The horror of it stained her.

Hugh gripped her shoulder, turning her toward him. "That is a big ass distraction. Nez is going to milk it for all it's got. He wouldn't have deployed it, if the digging crew weren't closing in. I need you in the tunnels."

"He's divine."

"What?"

"Erawan. He is divine."

"Yes, I know. Tunnels, Elara."

"You can't kill him."

Hugh patted her shoulder. "Of course, I can. I can and I will."

"No!" she grabbed his hand, desperate. "He's enslaved. He's suffering. You can't kill him."

He stared at her. "Elara, you're killing me. It's a giant fucking elephant, who is going to knock down our walls in about five minutes."

"It's not his fault!"

Hugh squeezed his eyes shut for a long moment.

"Promise me you won't kill him. Promise me, Hugh, and I'll go into the tunnels. Please!"

Hugh opened his eyes, clenched his fist, unclenched it, and said, "Okay."

"Promise me."

"I promise," he ground out. "Now, please go to the tunnels."

She ran down the steps. Behind her, Hugh roared. "Find Dugas! Get me that fucking druid!"

———+⊢———

ELARA HURRIED DOWN THE STAIRS. The winding stone stairway curved, burrowing lower and lower, and finally came to an end in a heavy wood and metal door. It stood wide open. Elara walked through it. A round chamber waited, walls and floor stone. Torches and fey lanterns glowed on the wall, flooding the space with so much light, they put electric bulbs to shame. Four arched doorways punctured the wall at even intervals, leading from the chamber into a circular hallway ringing the chamber in a semicircle.

In the middle of the floor a twelve-year-old blond girl sat cross-legged, holding on to a teddy bear. Johanna stood next to her.

Elara joined them. "Anything?"

"Three." Magdalena raised three fingers. "One here." She pointed directly ahead. "One there." The finger moved slightly to the right. "And one there." Far right.

Above them something thudded. Elara looked up.

What's going on? Johanna signed.

"Elephant," Elara explained and crouched by Magdalena. "How far are they, honey?"

Magdalena hugged her bear, concentrating. "Getting closer. They're fast. Very fast."

Vampires. Had to be. Killing vampires required an effort. It wasn't as easy as ripping out a human soul. She could kill mrogs by simple touch. She would have to concentrate on the

343

undead. Elara took a deep breath. She'd never had to kill them in bulk.

Another thud. A puff of dust broke off the ceiling.

"They broke into a hallway," Magdalena said. "They are still far, but they're coming faster now. There." She pointed to the far right.

Elara looked at Johanna. *"Take her out and bar the door."*

Johanna shook her head. *"No."*

"Yes. We might need your power. If they get through me, you are the last line of defense."

"I don't want to."

"Johanna, nothing about today has anything to do with want. Your power is vital. We will use it as a last resort only." "Go," she said for emphasis.

Quick steps echoed through the stairs behind them. Bale ran into the chamber, carrying his mace. Four Iron Dogs followed him, two men and two women. The best of the berserkers.

"What are you doing here?" Elara asked.

"We are your support," Bale said.

Hugh had sent backup.

"Leave," she said.

"I'm sorry, ma'am, we can't do that. We will obey your orders, but we have to stay," Bale said.

"What do you fear, Bale?" she asked him.

"Nothing," he said.

"You will fear after today," she said.

The berserker gripped his mace. "We have our orders."

"What did he say?" Johanna asked.

"Hugh sent him to guard me."

"They're coming," Magdalena said. "They are close."

"Take her out now," Elara signed to Johanna. *"Bar the door. Do this for me. Please."*

The witch took Magdalena by the hand and led her outside. The door shut, and the heavy metal bar thudded into place.

"Stand against the wall," Elara said. "Do not move. Do not speak."

Bale opened his mouth.

"My husband told you to obey my orders. Obey."

The Iron Dogs flattened themselves against the wall on both sides of the door. Elara straightened. Her magic uncoiled within her.

The first vampire dashed sideways behind the doorway, a grotesque shadow, silent like a ghost.

She pulled the bracelet off her left wrist and dropped it to the floor. The metal sometimes interfered.

More undead crowded into the hallway.

Her fingers paused over her wedding ring. She grasped it, slipped it off, and held it out to Bale. The berserker held his palm out. She dropped the ring into it. "Keep it safe for me."

"Yes, ma'am."

The leading vampire stepped forward. Its maw gaped open and a precise male voice came through. "There is no need for senseless bloodshed. We have the superior numbers."

She knew how she looked to them. A single human woman, dressed in white, not particularly large or imposing. An easy target.

"Turn around." Elara pulled the metal clasp out of her hair and it tumbled to her shoulders. "Leave and your minds will survive."

"Team three," the vampire said. "Engage hostiles."

Elara pulled on her magic and punched the floor with it, drenching the chamber in her power. Tendrils of ethereal smoke curled from the stones, glowing with white. The walls shook. The hem of her white gown melted into the curls of magic, merging with it, as she acknowledged the power that was ancient before humans had named it.

It was part of her. But she would never let herself become part of it.

The first undead lunged at her. She caught it in midleap. It

345

hung there, its throat in her hand, its navigator stunned. Then she opened her mouth and showed it her real teeth, and the human behind the vampire's mind screamed, the echo of his voice pouring out of the undead's throat.

———‡—

THE RED BALL of sorcerous fire splashed over the keep's wall and exploded, sizzling down. Hugh held his hands out, channeling the magic into the second of four blistered bodies lying in front of him. The blue glow bathed the closest Iron Dog. Ken Gamble, taking short desperate breaths, his dark skin blistered and torn.

Third degree burns, posterior neck, upper back, left upper chest, left lower back, and dorsal side of both upper and lower extremities... He sank the magic in, repairing the cooked tissues.

Nez had resumed the bombardment. Erawan's bulk hampered the ballistae set on top of his Matadors somewhat, but they must've fanned out to shoot around him. The elephant was moving at a crawl. Nez was trying to buy time.

Elara would handle it. Bale would help.

Hugh had lost the engine and half of her crew on the north flanking tower. The other half moaned on the ground in front of him.

Another cluster of explosions drowned the gate towers. Hugh craned his neck to check the artillery. Both catapults still survived.

The Iron Dog's breathing evened, as his skin sloughed off, revealing a new healthy layer. Hugh moved on to Iris, who was next down the line. Ken pushed upright.

"Reinforce the gate crews," Hugh told him.

The Iron Dog rolled to his feet, grabbed his sword, and took off for the gate.

Second degree burns, face, neck, upper chest...

His arm "hummed", the magic vibrating through him. Hugh

346

squeezed his fist to get the blood pumping and concentrated on healing.

Another blast. Dugas dashed along the wall and dropped down next to Hugh. "Where do you want it?"

"On the walls, directly across from where he will hit us."

"Some of those are poisonous."

"Doesn't matter."

Dugas nodded and waved his arm. People ran along the wall, carrying sacks and plastic bags.

The ground trembled. Erawan was close.

Iris rolled to her feet. He grabbed the two remaining Iron Dogs by their shoulders, pouring the magic in, healing in twin streams.

A trumpet blast of sound cut through the explosions. They didn't have much time.

———⊷⊷———

ELARA DROPPED the last undead on the floor and stared into the darkness of the doorway directly in front of her. The first two digging crews lay dead on the floor.

Something was coming.

Something different.

"Do not move," she whispered.

The five Iron Dogs stood completely still.

A shadow moved in darkness, darker than the rest. A dry clacking sound slipped through the tunnels.

Elara swayed like a striking cobra, side to side, her magic lying in wait on the floor. It was still strong, still potent, but she was growing tired.

Clack.

Clack, clack.

Closer and closer.

Scrape.

Clack, clack.

Scrape.

Clack.

It stopped.

It waited.

She could wait too. She had all the patience in the world.

The torches flickered. Magic whispered through the chamber. She saw it, a clump of blackness trailing smoke, smothering each torch in turn. The fey lanterns blinked and went dark.

In the dark, it moved.

Elara smiled and laughed softly, magic dripping from her voice. "Do you think I fear darkness? I was born in it."

Her magic shot up the walls. The fey lanterns sparked with pure white light.

A tall dark creature stood in the chamber. It wore a ragged robe, black and tattered, its many layers stained with rot and grease. The stench of carrion polluted the air.

Its hair was long and black. Two twisted horns, coated in old blood, curved from its head, like those of a bison, but rotated to curve upward and pointed forward. Its skin was the brown of a mummified corpse. Someone had carved its face and the scars had healed badly, twisting and slicing through the flesh. Its mouth was a wide lipless gash. A mask of yellow paint traced its eyes. They were dark and opaque, the eyes of a corpse injected with gray ink, except for the irises. Ringed in black, they were a brilliant pale blue, the pupils tiny dots in the ring of near white.

It felt old. The human had long ago died. His body was just a vessel now, for something dark and ancient.

It raised its hand, showing the long threads hanging from its skeletal fingers, each cord supporting human finger bones. It moved its clawed fingers. The bones bumped into each other.

Clack. Clack-clack.

Two beasts trotted out of the darkness, their long claws scraping the floor. They stood on all fours, gaunt like vampires, with every bone sticking out, but where undead were bald, these were covered in dark human body hair. Someone had shaved designs on their hides and traced them with the same yellow paint. Large wolf-like ears protruded from their skulls. Their heads were too long, the jaws protruding too far, as if someone had jammed the skull of a horse into a human head and tried to stretch the skin over it but didn't quite succeed. Lipless, noseless, their nostrils two holes between the two ridges of exposed bone that ran along the center of their skulls, the creatures glared at her with white eyes.

Lessons from long ago surfaced in Elara's memory. She had been warned about these before. Ah, yes. It made sense.

"I know of you," Elara said. "Once you were a shaman. Once you healed the sick and spoke to spirits."

The creature stared at her.

"But then Nez took you. He made you do evil things. Then, when you died, he used your corrupted shell to invite something over, out of the deep darkness. It took your body. You're a skudakumooch. A ghost witch."

The creature didn't move.

"You're a thing of old magic now." Elara bared her teeth. "But this is my castle. There is room for only one ancient monster here. And you've overstayed your welcome."

The twin beasts lunged at her. She lashed the left with her magic, trying to rip its power from it. The yellow symbols flashed with light. Her powers glanced off.

The beast clamped its jaws on her wrist, the other locked onto her forearm. Teeth pierced her skin, drawing blood. Agony shot up her arms, burning.

The beasts pulled her arms apart, anchoring her. Panic struck at Elara, pushing her straight to the hidden part of herself, where the iceberg of her power waited, locked away. All she had to do was reach for it.

No. She gritted her teeth. *No.*

The ghost witch struck at her, trying to claw her throat open with its talons. Elara pulled the magic out of herself and vomited it into the witch's face. The skudakumooch shrieked, reeling back.

She needed her hands, but the beasts were chewing her flesh to pieces.

The skudakumooch lunged again. Elara spat another torrent of power. The skudakumooch recoiled.

Bale bellowed like an enraged rhino and smashed his mace into the skull of the right creature. Bone cracked. Bale hit it again and again, driving the mace into it in a frenzy. The icy fangs opened. The beast spun toward Bale. Elara leaned and jammed her hand into its mouth. Her fingers closed about its putrid tongue and she punched her power down its throat. Her magic found the dark slimy seed that animated it, swallowed it, and cracked it between its teeth.

The beast sagged and collapsed, suddenly boneless. Its body fell apart, pieces of its flesh dropping.

Elara spun and jammed her fingers into the other beast's eyes. They popped under her fingertips. Her magic pierced the beast and it fell apart, dead. The skudakumooch snarled, biting the air with blood-red fangs the size of Elara's fingers. A cloud of darkness poured out of it, filled with ghostly teeth and claws. The smoke wrapped around Elara. Her skin came alive with pain, as if the air had turned into a whirlwind of broken glass. She tore through it and locked her hands onto the ghost witch's throat.

The creature bucked. She felt the thing inside the once-human body writhe. It was old and powerful, but she was stronger, and she choked it, sinking her claws into the flesh, piercing it with her magic, again and again. All the magic she had flowed from the floor onto the flailing skudakumooch. The glowing white tendrils wrapped around the ghost witch, choking it. Elara opened her mouth, knowing her jaws gaped too wide as she tried to engulf the skudakumooch's head in it.

The darkness tore out of the ghost witch's back. The corpse

deflated in Elara's hands like an empty water skin. The darkness shuddered, fangs, teeth, horns spinning within it, and vanished.

The torches and fey lanterns came back on.

Elara's jaw snapped back in place. She dropped the corpse and held out her hand. "My wedding ring, please."

Bale produced the wedding ring and put it in her palm. His fingers shook. Elara slipped the ring on. There.

A deep blast of sound came from above, muffled by the stone, but still clearly recognizable, the scream of Erawan. Elara whirled and ran to the door.

———•——

HUGH STOOD ON THE WALL, presenting a nice clear target. The damn elephant was so big, he blocked the light. Behind Erawan, the Cleaning Crew was trying to drag the trees he had knocked down to ford the moat. *Fine time for Nez to grow a brain.*

Along the wall the Iron Dogs crouched next to bags and crates, Elara's people sandwiched between them.

"Do you think this will work?" Dugas asked next to him.

"She won't let me kill him," Hugh ground out. "This is all I've got."

Erawan took a ponderous step forward. Lightning rolled off his sides. Only a few dozen feet separated him from the moat. The elephant's eyes glared at Hugh, filled with pain and madness. Erawan had seen him and was heading straight for him.

"Get your people out of here," Hugh told Dugas.

"With your permission, I think we better stay. We're better at this sort of thing than you are."

"If this doesn't work, this entire wall is coming down."

Dugas spread his arms. "Life, death. All part of existence."

Erawan took another step. The castle shook. Waves pulsed through the moat.

Don't step in it, Hugh prayed silently. *Don't you fucking step in it.* The concrete would never take that much weight.

Erawan bellowed. Hugh clamped his hands over his ears. The wail of the tortured elephant shook the castle. The wind of it tore at their clothes. The howl died, and Hugh screamed into the silence. "Hold it!"

The Iron Dogs held still.

The colossal elephant took another step, falling just short of the water. Hugh could see nothing now, no forest, no fields, only Erawan's three huge heads and the armored cabin on his neck. Somewhere in there, the Beastmaster rode. Take out the Beastmaster and you take out the beast.

Wait, Halliday. Just wait.

The gem in Erawan's head pulsed with red. The colossal elephant screamed and leaned forward. Suddenly the enraged eyes were only a few yards away. Breath caught in Hugh's throat. Fear dashed through him. He swallowed it and called out, "Now!"

The Iron Dogs and Elara's people opened the bags and crates and hurled the contents in the direction of Erawan. Flowers rained down on the wall of Baile. The humans dropped to their knees, stretching their hands before them. Hugh scooped two handfuls of the blossoms and bowed, hands held out before him.

"Erawan!" Hugh called out. "Mount of Indra, King of All Elephants, He Who Binds Clouds, He Who Reaches to the Underworld and Brings Forth Rain. We bow before you. Please accept our offering."

He braced himself for the lash of the enormous trunk.

Erawan held still.

Hugh held his breath.

The colossal elephant reached over with his central trunk and swept the bags of flowers up, curling his trunk around them gently as if they were priceless treasures.

The jewel sparked with red. Erawan screamed. The force of his voice nearly knocked Hugh off the wall. He grabbed onto the wall and held on to it. Above him blood poured from under the armored cabin, running over Erawan's skull. Tears swelled in the elephant's eyes. But Erawan didn't move.

Hugh straightened. "Let me help you! Lord of the Clouds, let me help!"

Erawan's eyes focused on him. The divine elephant ducked his central head, uncoiling his trunk.

Now or never. Hugh jumped onto the trunk. The earth moved underneath him and then he was running up Erawan's lifted trunk, over his forehead, and to the cabin. Wards pulsed. The bitch had warded the cabin. *Sweetheart, you'll need more than that.*

Hugh sucked in a lungful of air. "**Habbassu!**" *Break.*

The power word shattered the protective spell. The cabin split apart. Halliday jumped out, a sharp stick with a jewel in one hand and a curved sword in another. She spun like a dervish and lashed at him. He batted her blade aside and bashed at her with his sword. She blocked. She was a large woman, but he was stronger, and the impact knocked her back. Hugh drove her back, across the elephant's spine, raining blows on her. Halliday snarled like a cornered animal, slicing in a whirlwind. He thrust between her strikes and felt the slight resistance as the black blade slid home.

Halliday froze, her mouth opened in a terrified, shocked "O". Hugh grasped the rod out of her hand and kicked her off his blade. She crawled away from him. He chased her, step by step, until she reached the edge of Erawan's enormous back. Halliday bared her teeth. "Fuck you, you piece of shit."

He laughed and kicked her in the face. She slid off Erawan and crashed to the ground with a scream. The elephant's back rolled as a colossal hind leg shifted a few yard to the right.

Hugh turned and ran back to the front of the elephant. Down the trunk and back onto the wall. The control rod flowed with red. It was a vicious thing, three feet long with a razor-sharp metal point with a hook on the blade to rip the flesh on its way out of a wound. The point was covered in blood. Magic crackled down its length, sliding from the gem at the top to the metal tip.

He who controlled the rod controlled Erawan. The thought occurred to him almost as if it came from someone else. He looked up and saw the tears in the elephant's eyes.

He wasn't that much of a bastard.

"Mace!" Hugh roared.

One of the Iron Dogs thrust a mace at him. Hugh put the control rod on the parapet and swung. The mace head crushed the jewel. He lifted the control rod up and broke it over his knee.

The huge gem in Erawan's head cracked. Pieces of it tumbled out, crashing to the ground. The elephant raised his trunks and let out a triumphant bellow.

The chains binding his feet snapped.

Next to Hugh Dugas stared, open-mouthed.

Erawan spread his ears. Above him clouds burst with rain. It poured over his body, washing away the dark pigment from its hide. Rivulets of stained rain dripped to the ground, and where they touched the grass, flowers bloomed.

The humans on the wall stared, mute.

Erawan bellowed again, his voice filled with joy. His scars faded, the last of the darkness slid off, and he stood revealed and glowing white.

The elephant waved his trunks, shook his ears, flinging the rain drops, and vanished. Only a patch of bright flowers remained where he had stood.

"It worked," Dugas said. "How did you know to bring flowers?"

"He's worshipped in Thailand with offerings of flowers and garlands. A god will do almost anything to keep his worshippers safe. They're the source of his power and existence."

Dugas smiled, wiping the rain from his face.

Below, the Cleaning Crew halted its advance, confused, the lines in disarray as Nez tried to regroup.

Hugh grinned. "You're my witness," he said to Dugas. "She owes me one."

"Tell her yourself," the druid said.

Hugh turned. Elara was standing on the steps. In his head, she took the three steps that separated them and kissed him. But she stayed where she was and then she smiled, her whole face lighting up. "Thank you."

Worth it.

"Did you see me free the elephant?" he asked.

"I saw."

He noticed blood caked on her arms.

"They will heal. I won too," she said. "I'm afraid Bale might never be the same."

Hugh saw Bale behind her. The berserker looked white as a sheet.

"He's resilient," Hugh said. "He'll get over it."

Magic cracked like a whip across the battlefield. They spun around to face it.

A portal opened in the middle of the field and mrogs poured onto the grass.

16

Elara stared at the armored column. It kept coming and coming, twenty men to a line, more and more, never ending. They split as they stepped out onto the grass, one line moving left, the next right, forming into two rectangles. There had to be over a thousand soldiers on the field now. The rain drenched them, and still they came, line after line. The mrogs wrapped around the two columns like a shifting dark sea, too numerous to count.

She chanced a look at Hugh. He was watching them with a grim look. He glanced at her, and she saw a savage determination in his eyes, the kind a trapped animal got when he knew he was cornered and escape was unlikely.

Maybe they aren't here for us. Maybe they are here for Nez. She knew this slender hope was absurd, but she clung to it anyway.

The next line of soldiers emerged, carrying wooden planks nailed together. Another line. Another. A third one, carrying wooden poles. Parts of a bridge, Elara realized. They were going to try to bridge the moat.

On the other side of the field, the Cleaning Crew fell back, taking a defensive position on the edge of the woods.

A man emerged, riding on a large dark horse and wearing ornate golden armor. Another man in regular armor rode behind him, holding a standard and a horn.

The portal snapped closed.

"There you are," Hugh muttered.

The horn blower blew a sharp note. As one, the warriors in the two columns turned, those in the first to face the castle and the right toward Nez's forces. The mrogs split in half and charged to the walls and to the tree line, screeching and shrieking. The faint hope inside Elara died. The mrog army was here for Baile. They didn't expect another army on the field, but they didn't have capacity to make quick decisions or negotiate, so now they would fight both.

"Artillery!" Hugh called out. "Fire at will."

Sam blew his horn. The sorcerous siege engines spat bolts at the approaching mrogs. Green explosions tore ragged holes at the advancing mass. The mrogs screeched and kept running.

"To the wall!" Hugh roared. "Defend the perimeter!"

The horn blared.

Hugh turned to her. "Get everyone into the keep."

"What?"

"We can't hold the wall. We're buying you time. Get our people into the keep, Elara, into the tunnels."

The first mrogs dashed into the moat, swimming across it.

She called out commands, throwing her voice around the castle.

The first furry arm clutched onto the parapet. A mrog pulled itself up onto the wall and crouched. He got halfway through the first scream before Hugh beheaded him.

———•·——

ELARA DRAGGED a bloody hand across her face. The bailey floor was covered with blood and mrog bodies. On the wall, battle raged. Next to her Savannah was breathing hard. All of her people already made it to the keep. The Iron Dogs were withdrawing from the wall, fighting in small groups. Only one section of the wall still held, the one directly above them.

Another six people in black uniforms came running around the corner. A clump of mrogs chased them.

Savannah spat a curse. Magic snapped out of her like a striking whip. The leading mrog fell, covered in boils. Savannah swayed. *She won't last much longer.*

The Iron Dogs dashed past them.

Elara thrust herself between the witch and the incoming mrogs. They clawed at her and died at her feet, joining the semi-circle of furry bodies.

Savannah stumbled.

More mrogs came over the wall, coming from all directions now.

"Into the keep," Elara snapped at her. "Now!"

"I..."

"Now!"

Savannah retreated into the keep.

A grotesque creature emerged from the left, hulking, with oversized shoulders and tree trunk-thick arms, splattered with blood and bits of human tissue. Bale's unconscious body slumped over her back. It took Elara a moment to register the Iron Dogs around her. Not a monster. Another berserker. The group rambled past her into the keep.

All around her the mrogs were climbing over the wall, squirming and shrieking.

"Hugh!" Elara called.

A body fell off the wall and landed on the stones with a wet splat. She saw the dark hair. Felix. Oh no. She dropped by him. Blood poured out of Felix's head. The scout master struggled to say something.

"Hugh!"

He came running down the stairs, Stoyan and two others following him, covered in blood.

Felix clutched her hand and died.

She saw Hugh's face, and the pain on it tore her apart.

"Come on!" Savannah screamed.

Hugh grabbed her hand, pulled her up and away from the body into the keep. The huge metal doors swung closed.

Elara stared around the room. Mangled and bloody people stared back at her with terrified eyes, some of them were hers, others Hugh's. Ours, she corrected herself. All of them are ours.

Sam came forward, pushing his way through the crowd, leading Bucky, Hugh's helmet under his arm. Others followed with more horses.

What…

She turned to Hugh. "Are you insane?"

"The only way to stop this is to kill the commander," Hugh said.

"We can hold out. We just need to outlast them until the magic wave ends."

"They will be back," he said with a grim finality. "If we wait them out, they'll just return. We have to break them. If we kill the commander now, they will break."

She shook her head.

He kept talking. "If I succeed, do not engage them. They'll stop fighting and stand around until tech returns and takes them out. Until then, mrogs will be your only problem and you can handle mrogs in a narrow space."

"You can't possibly go out there. It's suicide."

The Iron Dogs were mounting.

"They're not expecting a charge. I want you to take everyone else into the tunnels. The mrogs will try to come through the top windows. The metal grates won't hold them off for long. Eventually they will rip through this door, too."

She couldn't go with him. She was their best defense against the mrogs. "No."

"Elara, this is about survival. Either I kill him, or he will kill us."

"No," she told him.

"This is what I do," he said. "This is why you married me."

"Hugh, don't go out there." She grabbed his hands. "Please, don't go."

He leaned forward and kissed her, hot and desperate. She tasted blood.

"Bar all of the doors on the way down," he said. "Slow them down as much as you can."

He took the helmet from Sam and put it on.

He was going out there. There was nothing she could do. The awful realization hit her, robbing her of the ability to speak.

This is what I do. This is why you married me.

Elara found her voice. "Johanna!"

People looked around. An Iron Dog turned around, reached out to tap someone on the shoulder, and stepped aside. Johanna squeezed out of the crowd.

"Please help us," Elara signed.

Johanna bowed her head and walked up to the door. Stoyan gave her a wild look from the back of his horse.

"Her power is a one-off," Elara told Hugh. "When she is done, she is done until she can recover. Stay behind her."

He mounted Bucky. The huge stallion bared his teeth. Hugh raised his sword and drew it over his left wrist. The blood coated the blade and snapped solid. A blood sword. Roland made blood weapons. She never realized Hugh could.

Something scraped the door. Mrog shrieks echoed through the room, muffled by the wood.

Johanna raised her arms to the sides and closed her eyes. Thin wisps of black smoke spiraled from her hands over her arms. Barely five feet tall, slender, blond hair spilling over her back, she stood there, before a huge door. Behind her, Hugh towered on his huge stallion.

Elara's heart squeezed itself into a hard rock.

"Come back to me," she ordered, her voice vicious. "Come back to me, all of you."

Two Iron Dogs unbarred the door, holding both halves of it.

Johanna leaned her head back. The dark smoke wrapped around her whole body now. She opened her eyes and they were solid black and filled with despair. Her hair streamed, moved by a phantom wind.

"Open the door!" Elara ordered.

The door swung open, revealing a mass of mrogs gathered before it.

Johanna shot up into the air two feet off the ground. The smoke splayed out behind her, trailing her like two wings. She opened her mouth and wailed. Every desperate sound, the shriek of a widowed swan, the howl of a dying wolf, the gut-wrenching cry of an orphaned babe, all of it echoed within that wail. The impossibly high-pitched scream tore through the mrogs. They fell aside, dead. The Black Banshee shot through the gap she'd made and the Iron Dogs rode out after her, breaking into a gallop.

The doors slammed shut. More Iron Dogs barred them.

"Into the tunnels," Elara ordered.

————

THE BLACK BANSHEE'S wail severed the drawbridge chains. It crashed down and Hugh rode across it, Bucky's hoofbeats like thunder. The stallion aimed himself at the line of soldiers and charged it like he was born to be a war horse.

The Banshee cut a path through the ranks, precise like a laser. All Hugh had to do was follow it. Regular banshees wailed and drove you mad, but black banshees killed with their screams. Another resource he wished he'd been aware of. When he finished here, he and the Harpy would have to have a long discussion about keeping things back.

The first line of soldiers blocked their path and fell, cut down by the wail.

He was still detached from it, watching it as if it were happening to someone else.

The second, third, and fourth lines followed.

She screamed and screamed.

The fifth and sixth lines collapsed.

The Banshee shot upward and right. Her smoke wings vanished, and she plunged down.

Only four lines between him and the commander.

Bucky tore into the armored soldiers like a battering ram, ripping his way through. Hugh swung his sword, slicing skulls. Blood sword met metal and metal gave way.

A moment and Bucky and he were through, out in the open, the commander on his horse in front of them, charging at full speed.

"Kill the other horse," he ordered.

The stallion screamed and broke into a desperate charge.

The world snapped into a crystal-clear focus. The colors turned vivid, the smells sharp. He saw everything, he was aware of everything, and he knew with one hundred percent certainty that when the two horses collided, the force of it would unseat them both. He knew exactly where they would land.

He stood in the stirrups and pulled his left leg back, riding on the side of the horse.

The two stallions smashed into each other, screaming. A fraction before they collided, he let go, letting the full force of the gallop fling him into the air, giving power to his swing.

Below him, the commander rolled to a crouch and spat fire, but the heated arc of flames was too slow.

Hugh landed sword first. The blood blade cleaved the

commander from skull to breast bone. The two halves of the man smoked.

Hugh turned and ran.

He didn't see the fire, but he heard it, roaring like an animal behind him. He chanced a single look back and saw a tornado of flames coming straight for him. The world became heat and fire. He wrapped his magic around himself, healing blisters as they formed. The concussive force smashed into him, as if Erawan had returned and kicked him with his colossal foot. Magic plowed into him and all went dark.

The light returned in a rush of agony. Hugh blinked at the twin stabs of pain. Broken legs. He must've been thrown by the blast and landed badly. He tried to move his arms and couldn't. The bones and muscles functioned fine, but something was restraining him.

The light darkened as something blurry blocked it.

Hugh blinked until the blurry thing came into focus and stared at the vampire's face.

The undead opened its mouth.

"Well, well," it said in Nez's voice. "Today is not a total loss."

Fuck.

⸻

ELARA STARED AT THE DOOR. Behind her, hundreds of people waited. If the mrogs got through, she would stop them.

So much time had passed. It had to be hours. It felt like hours.

Someone pounded on the door. "Open!" a familiar voice yelled.

Stoyan.

Elara grasped the bar. People moved to help her, and the door was pried open. Stoyan ran in, carrying Johanna, limp like a ragdoll. "Help her!"

Savannah put her ear on Johanna's chest. "She doesn't need

help. She needs time." She jerked her head and Nikolas ran up to take Johanna from Stoyan's arms.

"What's happened?" Dugas asked.

Stoyan stared at him, his eyes wild, his skin smeared with blood and dirt. "Hugh killed the commander. The guy exploded. The mrogs ran away and the soldiers walked off."

"Walked off where?" Savannah demanded.

"Into the woods. We killed some that were left between us and the castle, but the rest of them are either standing around or wandering off into the brush. As long as you don't go near them, they don't attack."

Elara grabbed Stoyan's arm. "Where is Hugh?"

"Nez has him."

Ice rolled over her. "How?"

"He was thrown by the blast," Stoyan said. "The undead got to him before we could."

Thoughts rushed through her, coming too fast. "Is Nez still out there?"

"No, he cleared out as soon as they captured the Preceptor."

She'd been right. This battle was never about the castle. It was about Hugh.

Stoyan bared his teeth. "I need volunteers. We'll get him back."

"You won't," Dugas said. "Nez has only fielded a small part of his force. He still has most of his undead. There isn't enough of you."

"Your job is to protect us," Savannah said. "With the Preceptor gone, whose orders are you supposed to follow?"

Stoyan clenched his fists.

"We follow his spouse," Lamar said from the depths of the room.

"There you go," Savannah said. "We need you here. The Preceptor is a lost cause. You can't get him back."

Lamar walked into the center of the room and bowed his head to Elara.

Stoyan swore.

"We were given specific orders," Lamar said. "He told us that if he died, you inherited command."

"He isn't dead," Stoyan snarled.

Lamar didn't answer.

Stoyan clenched his fists again and bowed his head.

"I will speak for Bale," the female berserker called out. "We obey the spouse. We won't dishonor his last order."

They were hers, Elara realized. She had the castle and the Iron Dogs. She didn't have to share authority anymore. Hugh trusted her to take care of his people.

There was only one solution to this problem. It was staring her straight in the face. Fear gripped her, so strong she could barely breathe. She was stronger, she reminded herself. She was always stronger.

She had to get him back. There was no other way.

Her voice came out cold. "Bring the cows."

A shocked silence fell. The Iron Dogs looked around, bewildered.

"You can't," Savannah recoiled. "For him? You would manifest for him?"

"Hugh was abandoned by everyone in his life." Her words rang out. "His parents, his teacher, his surrogate father. They all threw him away. He trusted us. He sacrificed himself to save us. This is his home. I'm his wife. I will not abandon him. Bring the cows."

———✦——

ELARA STOOD ON THE WALL. The fires had been lit, fighting back the night. On the field, remnants of the mrog force mulled about, confused. Stoyan was right. Most of them eventually walked off into the wilderness. She had no idea how long the magic wave would last, but tech would kill them, she was sure of it. There was too much magic in their bodies to survive the tech.

The moon had risen.

In the bailey, sigils were being drawn with chalk and salt. Dugas presided over it. He was wearing his white robe. On the walls and in the bailey the Departed waited, wearing white. A line of cows stood waiting, each decorated with sigils drawn in white, dedicated to her. Fifteen total. That would do.

"Don't do this," Savannah said, her voice pleading. "You have everything you want. Just let Nez have him. It solves all of our problems."

"No."

"Elara…"

"Do you remember that night?" she asked. She didn't have to specify which night. It was always the first night, the night she was reborn.

"Of course I remember."

"You said then that loyalty was the only thing we had. Before friendship, before love, before wealth, there is loyalty."

Savannah didn't answer.

"I've made up my mind," Elara said. "I have to bring him back."

Savannah opened her arms and wrapped them around her. "You poor child," the witch whispered.

Elara rested her head on Savannah's shoulder, the way she had done when she was little and for a moment she was ten years old again, frightened and alone on that first night.

"You poor sweet girl. You can do this, you hear? You can hold it at bay. Don't surrender to it. Don't let it devour you." Her voice broke. "You're stronger than it. You hear me? You grip it and you make it obey. Don't forget who you are."

"I won't," Elara promised. She believed it. She had no choice. Any doubt and she would lose.

Savannah let her go, looked at her, and brushed the stray hair off Elara's face. There were tears in her eyes. "It's time then."

Elara walked down the stairs to the bailey.

Dugas pulled out a curved knife covered with sigils.

Stoyan and Lamar moved to stand next to her.

"What's going on right now?" Lamar asked quietly.

"I'm going to manifest," she said.

"Why does the druid have a knife?" Lamar asked.

"Because tonight he isn't a druid. Defend the castle while I'm gone. That's your order."

Stoyan opened his mouth, but she walked away from them and stepped into the ring of sigils.

A low chant rose from the Departed, gaining strength. She felt her magic stir in response.

"Go inside," Savannah told the Iron Dogs. "You don't want to be here for this."

Lamar began to protest.

"Go inside," Elara told them. "Please."

The centurions walked away.

A bare-footed child led the first cow to Dugas and walked away. The beast looked at Elara with liquid brown eyes, trusting. Guilt twisted her. She clenched her teeth and reached deep inside herself, into the place where her magic waited behind a locked door.

Dugas chanted, his face turning savage. The curved knife flashed, catching the light of the fires. Bright red blood splashed across his white robe.

Power punched Elara, catapulting her through the door straight into the depths of her magic to the cold presence that waited for her there. Ancient as the stars, powerful beyond measure, too complex for a human to understand, yet single-minded in its ferocity. It waited for her, no longer a frozen iceberg, but a pool of celestial water.

She sank into it, fueled by the magic of the sacrifice. The liquid closed over her head, submerging her, and she let it flood her with its magic...

The universe opened like a flower, its secrets hers for the taking.

HANGING off a torture rack wasn't the funnest thing he had ever done, Hugh decided. Nez's helpers twisted his arms before chaining him and his ligaments whined at him, the pain constant and difficult to ignore.

He hung in Nez's HQ, a room in a large pre-Shift building, presumably somewhere in Rooster Point, although he couldn't be sure. They had dragged him here in the dark. The only thing he remembered clearly was passing the shell of a Matador, dented and ripped as if something with big teeth had taken it in its jaws and bit. The Departed's handiwork. Somehow the cockroach had survived it.

Several metal braziers full of flames lit the room. Most of Rooster Point had been abandoned for so long, nobody bothered to install fey lanterns, and Nez had to resort to an old-school dungeon. Aside from braziers, there wasn't much to it. Supplies thrown here and there, typical jetsam and flotsam of the Legion on the move. Chains, undead collars, crates of equipment, m-scanners designed to record residual magic signatures, were all pushed against the walls.

Nez was leaning against the table, directly across from him, drinking coffee. He hadn't changed much. Still lean, his face phlegmatic and arrogant. After a while all of the Legatus' got that expression. Hugh had seen more than a dozen come and go. Of all of them Steed was the only one he could stomach. His memory brought up Steed in a cage, staring at him with insane eyes, as Hugh fed him bread.

He had regrets. But then he himself was caged now. Turnabout was fair play.

"How does it feel?" Nez asked.

"Well, doctor, it feels sore and tingly."

"You know what I hate about you?" Nez sipped his coffee. "This idiotic bravado. There are things in this life that have to be taken seriously. At first I thought you were trying to hide weakness behind all the quips, but now I know. You're just stupid." He leaned forward. "Has it sunk into your big dumb brutish head yet? I won."

"Nez, what did you win, exactly? I'm not dead. That's a telling fact. Are you allowed to kill me?"

Silence answered.

"I take that as a no," Hugh said. "So, really, what you're allowed is a little bit of time to do whatever you want to me and gloat. And that's it. Then you'll have to deliver me to Roland. Do whatever you're going to do or grow some balls and kill me. Do it, Nez. I fucking dare you."

The rage in Nez's eyes was delicious. If he pushed Nez far enough, he would snap and kill him, which would be the best outcome possible.

"That's a short leash he's got you on," Hugh said.

Nez grabbed a length of pipe off his desk and swung it like a bat. The pipe connected. Bones crunched as his ribs shattered. Nez erupted into a flurry of hits. The pipe landed again and again, each blow a new burst of agony. Finally, he slumped against the desk and let go of the pipe. It clattered to the floor.

Every breath was like sucking fire into his lungs.

"Ow," Hugh said.

Nez stared at him.

Hugh grinned. "Do you feel better, sweetheart? Do you feel like you won yet?"

"My leash is short, but he muzzles you," Nez ground out. "Do you get it yet? Do you know what he does to keep you in line? He cooks you like a piece of fried chicken. He fries your mind until there is nothing but a shell left. So I'm going to tell you now, because later on you won't care. When I'm done and things quiet down, I'll come back here, and I'll kill every living soul in that castle. Every man, every woman, and every child. I'll make your wife watch. She will be the last to go."

The scumbag would do it. Hugh saw it in Nez's eyes. "Good speech," he said. "I'd clap, but I'm all tied up."

Nez bared his teeth.

"I feel like we've had a real breakthrough here, Landon," Hugh said. "This is the most honest conversation we've ever had."

Nez reached for the pipe.

A careful knock interrupted him in mid-move. Nez turned to the doorway. Hugh craned his neck, but it was too far behind him.

"What?" Nez asked.

"I'm sorry, Legatus. There is fog."

"What kind of fog?"

"An unnatural fog. It's coming from the woods."

Nez swore and strode out.

The room fell silent except for the crackling of the fire. He'd have to start over when Nez returned, and he'd been doing so well. Being killed now was his best option. Facing Roland would be the end of the road. He would do anything to keep from walking it.

Magic whispered through the room, familiar and warm.

Fuck me.

Hugh raised his head. Roland lowered the hood of his brown robe. His face was like no other. He had allowed himself to age to about fifty, to look more fatherly for Daniels, and it served him well. He looked like a prophet walking out of the long-forgotten magical cities of ancient Mesopotamia, a living remnant of a different time and different place, when wondrous things were possible and his name had been Nimrod, the Builder of Towers. A scholar, an inventor, a poet, a father god, wise with kind eyes that were all-knowing and slightly chiding. Hugh looked into his eyes and love washed over him. All Hugh ever needed, all he ever wanted or required, was that love. It sheltered and sustained him, it guided him, it took away all pain. It was like seeing the sunrise after a long, dark winter.

The void tore open behind Hugh, scraping at him with its teeth.

Roland crossed the room and looked over Hugh's shoulder at the void. "Well, that's not good."

The sound of his voice, suffused with power and magic, was so familiar it hurt.

"Hello, Hugh," Roland said.

He managed a single word. "Hello."

They looked at each other.

"You survived," Roland said.

"Why are you here?"

"I'm here because I need your help, Hugh." Roland smiled.

"Daniels kicked your ass," Hugh said. The blasphemy of the words should've broken him, but somehow it didn't.

"We've suffered some setbacks," Roland said. "Nothing that can't be remedied."

It hit him then. The battle was never about the castle. It was about him. Nez was ordered to go and get him out of Baile.

"You've proven yourself," Roland said.

You fucking prick. "You watched me at Aberdine."

"I did. It's time to come back," Roland said. "You've been gone for too long."

"It's too late for that," Hugh said.

"Nonsense." Roland glanced at the chains over his right arm. They fell apart and Hugh hung, suspended by one arm.

The immortal wizard reached out to him. "Take my hand, Hugh. Take my hand and everything will be forgiven. Everything will be as it was."

The world shrunk to the limits of the room. If only he reached out and took Roland's hand, all the problems would fall away. The void would vanish, taking away the guilt and the nightmares. Life would be simple again.

"Take my hand," Roland said again. "You're my son in everything but blood."

The word pierced Hugh. He'd waited decades to hear it and here it was, freely given.

Roland had expected him to stay a wreck. As long as he was a drunkard trying to commit a slow suicide, Roland was content to leave him as he was. But once he had pulled himself together, he was useful again. He was a threat.

The realization rocked him. He looked into Roland's eyes and he saw something else, besides wisdom and approval. It hid in the corners of Roland's soul, a quiet wariness, watching him.

Roland was afraid of him.

Hugh grinned. "No."

"Hugh," Roland said, his voice chiding, catapulting Hugh back to when he was a skinny orphan. "Take my hand. You've earned it. It's your destiny."

"No."

Roland stared at him.

"It's not exactly a surprise," Hugh said. The words rolled off his tongue, amazingly easy. "You're a fucking asshole, you know that?"

"I took you off the street. I gave you shelter, education, and power. And this is how you repay me?"

"You forgot the part where you turned me into a happy idiot every time I tried to do something you didn't like."

"That's what raising a child is," Roland said. "Encouraging some aspects of their personality, suppressing the others."

Hugh laughed quietly.

"I made you effective. I freed you from complications that were holding you back. Did I ever force you to do anything, Hugh? Or did you jump on every task I gave you?"

"Explain something to me. Why did you exile me? I did everything you asked."

"I exiled you because you couldn't see the bigger picture." A note of irritation rose in Roland's voice. "I'm beginning to think you still can't."

"That explains nothing."

"Think about it and it will come to you."

The pain in his ribs was unbearable now. Hugh pushed it aside. "Here is the bigger picture for you: there are two of us, Daniels and me. Neither of us wants anything to do with you. You're not batting a thousand. You're 0 for two. You need one of your children to fight the other, because Daniels kicked your ass once and she will do it again. Think about that."

"There are three," Roland said. "Almost three."

"She hasn't given birth yet."

"No, but soon. Soon I will have a grandson."

"And you can't wait to get your hands on that child. Finally, a real son, the one with the right blood. Why the hell do you think anything will be different? Even if you get him from the moment he draws his first breath, he'll still grow up hating you. Yet here you are, so desperate to get your hands on the new toy, that you send your Legion to capture me, teleport here despite the danger, and call me your son. Take a real good look. Look at me hanging here. If I were your son, what sort of father would that make you?"

"So the answer is no?" Roland asked.

"We could stay in here for the next hundred years and it would still be no. You'll never get your hands on Kate's kid. I'll kill you first."

Roland sighed. "You disappoint me, Hugh."

"Get used to it."

Roland stepped closer. Only a foot of space separated them.

"Without me, you'll die and soon. Is that what you really want?"

"We all have to die eventually."

"Alone, abandoned, stripped of your powers. This is the future you want?"

"No powers?"

"None of my blood."

Hugh pulled on the last thread of magic remaining inside him, a tiny sliver that remained despite the power words and all the healing he had done. He drew the fingers of his free hand across his bloody ribs and sank that magic into the crimson liquid. Magic sparked, and the dark blood snapped into a sharp blood-red needle.

"Explain this to me," Hugh said.

Roland shied back.

The needle crumbled into dust.

Someone screamed outside the building, the shriek cut off in mid-note.

"Last chance, Hugh!" Roland reached out to him. "Take my hand."

"Fuck off."

Mist shot through the doorway, glowing with magic, broke, and there it was, pure white and glowing, too monstrous to comprehend, emanating the kind of cold that rode comets and lived between the stars. Roland jerked back, shock on his face. Hugh just stared at it, mute. Every cell in his body was screaming. And then he saw her among the chaos of teeth, mouths, and eyes. She'd come for him.

She turned to Roland and he took a step back, shock draining all of the blood from his face.

She spoke, and cracks split the walls.

"HE IS MINE, WIZARD."

"Have him then." Roland vanished.

The creature of chaos lowered itself to him, and Hugh made his lips stretch into a grin, before his mind split open from sheer terror. His voice came out hoarse. "Hi, honey."

EPILOGUE

Hugh opened his eyes and saw a familiar ceiling. The tech was up. Everything hurt. Daylight streamed into the room through the east window. It was morning.

Lamar's slow measured voice floated to him.

"For this reason the best possible fortress is—not to be hated by the people, because, although you may hold the fortresses, yet they will not save you if the people hate you, for there will never be wanting foreigners to assist a people who have taken arms against you..."

"Why are you reading him this boring shit?" Bale asked.

"Unlike your half-blood prince, this is a classic."

"Half-Blood Prince is a great book."

"Of course it is. What could be better than stories of clueless teenagers sent off to... Bale, what is that?"

"What, this?"

Lamar's voice took on a sharp edge. "Is that a wand?"

"It's a stick."

"Are you pointing a wand at me?"

"Who, me?"

"Bale, if any Latin comes out of your mouth, it better be a litany of the saints, because I will end you."

Hugh made his mouth move. His voice came out hoarse. "Bale's right. It's too early in the day for Machiavelli."

Bale charged the bed and gripped him in a bear hug. Hugh's bones groaned.

The berserker let go, punched the air, shoveled himself halfway out of the window, and bellowed, "He's awake!"

Lamar heaved a long sigh and took his glasses off. "Brace yourself. The parade is coming."

———————

IT STARTED WITH STOYAN, who came running down the hallway. Unfortunately, Cedric beat him by about ten feet. The huge hound jumped on the bed, squealing, whimpering and licking his face. Hugh had barely fought him off when Elara's people flooded the bedroom. Dugas came in at the head of a procession of apprentices and they walked around the bedroom chanting and waving bunches of wet flowers and herbs.

"Congratulations on surviving," Dugas told him.

"Thanks."

Felix's orphaned scouts were next, followed by the stable girl – he still didn't remember her name. She gave him a detailed report on Bucky, who seemed to be depressed and apparently, Hugh needed to get down to the stables as soon as he could.

Then came the Iron Dogs and the villagers. His head was swimming and he had a hard time keeping faces straight. Somewhere in there, Savannah showed up, peered into his eyes, squinted at him, and shrugged. "No worse for wear."

Johanna came in, hugged him, and walked out.

Bakers, archers, smiths, druids, medical staff, bulldozer crew, they came on and on, until he was sure he would pass out from the noise alone. He smiled and made the right noises, while his mind sorted through the fragments of his memories. Nez's camp, Elara carrying him within her body that faded in and out of existence, sliding beyond the three-dimensional reality of their space, the undead and Masters of the Dead dying as they tried to reach for her, the dark trunks of the trees, the icy presence of her magic, spinning out of control in his soul, threatening to devour... He remembered the walls of Baile and then his recollection stopped, sharp as if cut by a knife.

Finally, Lamar had had enough. He and Stoyan kicked everyone out and shut the doors.

"What happened to the remaining mrogs?" Hugh asked.

"Both the mrogs and the soldiers died with the first tech shift," Stoyan reported. "Mrogs died first. The humans lasted almost twenty-four hours, but eventually died as well. Elara's people are dissecting them."

"Nez?"

"Withdrew," Lamar said. "He evacuated the night Elara brought you back. What the hell happened?"

"I saw Roland," Hugh said. "We talked."

The two centurions went silent. He saw alarm on their faces.

"I burned the bridge," he said. "We're on our own."

The relief in their eyes was so clear, it stabbed at him.

"So this is home?" Stoyan asked.

"It is."

"Good." Stoyan smiled. "It's good to have you back, Preceptor."

Hugh nodded. "It's good to be back."

Stoyan walked out, closing the door behind him. It was only Hugh and Lamar now. Hugh beckoned and Lamar moved to the bed, sitting only a few inches away.

"Did you see what she is?" Hugh asked quietly.

"No," Lamar said. "They made us go in before she turned. They sacrificed the cows. I think she might have fed off of them, but I'm not sure."

"I saw her," Hugh said.

"What is she?"

He struggled for the words to describe the ancient power and chaos existing in more dimensions than a human mind could comprehend and couldn't find any.

"I don't know," he said. "Find out, Lamar. If she turns on us, I need to know how I can kill her."

The centurion nodded and left the room.

Hugh sat alone. Elara... The Ice Harpy. The Queen of the Castle. And something else, something that set off every primitive fear that lived deep inside.

His mind juxtaposed that Elara and the woman gasping with pleasure as he thrust into her. She was the scariest thing he had ever seen, but he'd slept with her, and he'd liked it, and he had wanted her to stay. It was good, and he knew it could be better. The Iron Dogs used to play a stupid game by the campfire, Marry, Fuck, Kill. They were already married, and he had no idea which of the other two he needed to pick.

They were married.

Fuck.

He remembered her words. *"They are my people and I love them. They've proved their loyalty beyond anything I had a right to ask. There is no limit to how low I will sink to keep them safe."*

He had thought it was a figure of speech. Now he knew better. He had to make sure his people never became a threat. What would constitute a threat to her? Would he have to stop her from human sacrifice? Where would he draw that line? It might be wiser to take his people out now, before it came to that. He wasn't sure a blood sword would work. A sword he shouldn't have been able to make. How the hell was the blood power still working? Why?

She came for him. She threw caution to the wind, displayed her power, and came to get him away from Nez. She faced Roland for him and would've fought him.

Hugh never expected it. She should've left him to rot, yet she pulled him out of there and somehow dragged him to the castle.

Nobody, in his entire life, would've done it for him, except for his Iron Dogs.

He wished the world would make sense.

The door swung open, and Elara walked into the room. Her hair fell on her shoulders in a long white wave. Her dress, a pale green, the color of young leaves, hugged her, cradling her breasts, tracing her waist, and skimming the curve of her hips.

He looked into her eyes. They were laughing, but behind the humor, he saw something else, a cautious wariness.

He finally noticed she was carrying something wrapped in towels. She set the object on his night table and looked at him.

He looked back at her.

"I hate you," she told him.

Testing the waters. "Hardly a surprise," he told her.

"If you ever pull a demented stunt like that again, I will make your life a living hell."

He bared his teeth at her. "You already do, darling."

He got the message loud and clear. She wanted to pretend that nothing happened. They were back to normal, sniping at each other every chance they got and stopping just short of drawing blood.

"Do you think the mrogs will be back?"

"Unlikely," he said. "They went all out, and we kicked their ass. We offer too little reward for too great an effort. Most likely whoever commands them will move on, but if not, we will be ready."

"Leonard has a theory about the elder being behind it."

The Pictish scholar. Right. "He does?"

"When you're better, I'll send him up. It's a bit out there, but it makes sense in an odd way."

She turned around.

"Where are you going?" he asked.

"To the greenhouses. Our herbs keep dying. We have to figure out why."

"Elara," he called.

She turned around, walked up to the bed, and leaned over him, one knee on the covers. "You're my husband, Hugh. We no longer walk alone. We are each other's shelter in a storm. As long as you want to stay here, you'll have a home. I'll never abandon you."

She leaned forward. Her lips brushed his and she kissed him. He tasted her, fresh and sweet, a hint of honey on her tongue. He got hard.

She let him go and walked away, closing the door behind her, like a phantom, there one moment, gone the next.

He stared at the door, tried to sort out what the hell just happened, and failed.

He didn't want to let her go.

Fuck.

He reached for the towels and pulled them off. A plate waited for him, covered with a glass cover, fogged up from the inside. He took it off. Stacks of warm crepes waited for him, drizzled with caramel and honey.

The Preceptor of the Iron Dogs laughed and reached for his fork.

THE END

DISCOVER MORE BY ILONA ANDREWS

KATE DANIELS SERIES

Magic Bites

Magic Bleeds

Magic Burns

Magic Strikes

Magic Mourns

Magic Bleeds

Magic Dreams

Magic Slays

Gunmetal Magic

Magic Gifts

Magic Rises

Magic Breaks

Magic Steals

Magic Shifts

Magic Stars

Magic Binds

Magic Triumphs

HIDDEN LEGACY SERIES

Burn For Me

White Hot

Wildfire

ABOUT THE AUTHOR

Ilona Andrews is the pseudonym for a husband-and-wife writing team, Gordon and Ilona. They currently reside in Texas with their two children and numerous dogs and cats. The couple are the #1 *New York Times* and *USA Today* bestselling authors of the Kate Daniels and Kate Daniels World novels as well as The Edge and Hidden Legacy series. They also write the Innkeeper Chronicles series, which they post as a free weekly serial. For a complete list of their books, fun extras, and Innkeeper installments, please visit their website at http://www.ilona-andrews.com/.

Lightning Source UK Ltd.
Milton Keynes UK
UKHW021055150819
348023UK00008B/191/P